ANTHROPOLOGICA
INCOGNITA

ANTHROPOLOGICA INCOGNITA

Wild Men, Strange Apes, and Fantastic Races
in Classic Science Fiction and Fantasy

Chad Arment, Editor

COACHWHIP PUBLICATIONS
Landisville, Pennsylvania

Anthropologica Incognita, edited by Chad Arment
Copyright © 2009 Coachwhip Publications

ISBN 1-61646-000-8
ISBN-13 978-1-61646-000-6

Cover: Gorilla © James Pierce

Coachwhipbooks.com

Translation and Sourcing Notes:
 The Depths of Kyamo is based on an early newspaper re-print translation by Elfried de B. Gude, who added the final section to Rosny's original story.
 The Missing Link translation is by Georges T. Dodds, with only minor modifications. Dodds personally provided *Haunt of the Jinkarras* to the editor some years ago, and three other stories (*Two Nights in Southern Mexico, Beyond the Banyans,* and *The Ape-Man*) come from Dodds' online research article at ERBzine.com.

CONTENTS

Story of Tsoqélem

Salish, From Vancouver Island, British Columbia

About sixty years ago there lived at the foot of the mountain near Cowitchin Harbour a strange and fierce man named Tsoqélem. He was taller than the average man by nearly a foot, his face was long and thin and his tread was as soft and stealthy as that of the mountain-lion, and he could run like a deer. He became the terror of the district, waylaying and robbing anyone who crossed his path. His home was a cave in the side of the mountain, in which he always kept a goodly supply of fire-arms and ammunition. From his boyhood he had been a strange being, passing most of his time roaming in the forest or mountains. His eyes were shifty and roving like those of a wild animal. A great Shaman once saw him at Saanich, and said to the people round about him: "That boy has got remarkable eyes." The boy stared at the man, and would have run away but the Shaman caught him, and bade the people get him some trailing blackberry brambles. With these he rubbed the boy's face, saying as he did so, "I hope your eyes will now keep strong." The boy's face was severely lacerated with the thorns of the brambles, but he did not cry, he simply grinned all the time, and when the Shaman let him go with the command: "Run!" he ran off by himself into the forest again.

Tsoqélem now wandering through the forest, heard a noise before him like the growling of a dog over a bone. He crept stealthily forward and presently perceived a hairy forest monster who, with his wife and children, were devouring in dog-like fashion the body of a youth they had seized.

7

The monster held his victim on his knees, and with his long tierce claws tore off the flesh and passed it to his children. He accosted TsoqélEM, bidding him sit down. TsoqélEM sat down and the monster passed him some of the flesh. TsoqélEM ate like the rest. The monster then said to TsoqélEM, "When you fight and when you kill people I shall be with you. Come here to me and lie down. There is something in your eye. That Shaman did a good thing who rubbed your face, but he only half did his work; I will finish it." So saying he took the bill of a humming-bird and thrust it in the corner of the boy's eyes, telling him to look upwards till he could see the stars. From time to time he questioned him, "Can you see the stars yet?" TsoqélEM answered "No" at first, but presently the stars became visible to him through the blood of his eyes, and he cried out: "Yes, I can see them now." "Very good," said the monster, desisting from his task; "from this time you will be able to see as well in the dark as in the light; day and night will be all the same to you." TsoqélEM now went back to his cave home and danced and sang his mystery song: "*etsen utl tɛna stälem qas! a! a! mustemuq yuq qas kwenɛs. utl lumstalt qas! a! a!*" which signified that he had been given human flesh to eat. While he danced he flourished his gun and knife.

From this time onward TsoqélEM went about the country killing and robbing the people. After many years of this life he one day went to the Semaltca people on Kuper Island. It was about spring time, and the people were all assembled together feasting in one of their long-houses. A young woman sat in the doorway holding her digging stick in her hand with which to keep out the dogs. All at once a gun went off and a man fell shot, and then another and TsoqélEM was amongst them brandishing his weapons and killing all within his reach. Everybody made for the door except the young woman who held the digging stick. She sprang upon the bed platform, and as TsoqélEM passed with his back towards her she was suddenly inspired with the thought that she could hold him down with her stick. Seizing her digging stick at both ends, she quickly passed it over his head and held it tightly across his breast and pulled him backwards, shouting as she did for her husband to come and kill him while she thus held him. TsoqélEM struggled hard to break away from her and sought to stab her with his knife, but she held him fast and shouted the more. Her cries brought an old crone to the door, who called out, "Has he got you down?" "No," she replied; "I have got him down. Tell my husband to come quickly and bring the other men with him." The husband presently came, rushing up, followed by the other men. As they entered the house, the woman said, "Don't use your guns, attack him with your axes." This they did, soon disabling him; they then cut off his head and his body rolled and jumped about for a long time. When they cut him open they found that his heart and entrails were very small—much smaller than those of any ordinary man. Thus was TsoqélEM slain by the wit and pluck of a woman.

Two Nights in Southern Mexico

A Fragment from the Journal of an American Traveller

Karl Anton Postl

"A capital place this for our bivouac!" cried I, swinging myself off my mule, and stretching my arms and legs, which were stiffened by a long ride.

It *was* a fairish place, to all appearances—a snug ravine, well shaded by mahogany-trees, the ground covered with the luxuriant vegetation of that tropical region, a little stream bubbling and leaping and dashing down one of the high rocks that flanked the hollow, and rippling away through the tall fern towards the rear of the spot where we had halted, at the distance of a hundred yards from which the ground was low and shelving.

"A capital place this for our bivouac!"

My companion nodded. As to our lazy Mexican *arrieros* and servants, they said nothing, but began making arrangements for passing the night. Curse the fellows! If they had seen us preparing to lie down in a swamp, cheek by jowl with an alligator, I believe they would not have offered a word of remonstrance. Those Mexican half-breeds, half Indian half Spaniard, with sometimes a dash of the Negro, are themselves so little pervious to the dangers and evils of their soil and climate, that they never seem to remember that Yankee flesh and blood may be rather more susceptible; that niguas and musquittoes, and *vomito prieto*, as they call their infernal fever, are no trifles to encounter; without mentioning the snakes, and scorpions, and alligators, and other creatures of the kind, which infest their strange, wild, unnatural, and yet beautiful country.

I had come to Mexico in company with Jonathan Rowley, a youth of Virginian raising, six and twenty years of age, six feet two in his stockings, with the limbs of a Hercules and shoulders like the side of a house. It was towards the close of 1824; and the recent emancipation of Mexico from the Spanish yoke, and its self-formation into a republic, had given it a new and strong interest to us Americans. We had been told much, too, of the beauty of the country—but in this we were at first rather disappointed; and we reached the capital without having seen any thing, except some parts of the province of Vera Cruz, that could justify the extravagant encomiums we had heard bestowed in the States upon the splendid scenery of Mexico. We had not, however, to go far southward from the chief city, before the character of the country altered, and became such as to satisfy our most sanguine expectations. Forests of palms, of oranges, citrons, and bananas, filled the valleys: the marshes and low grounds were crowded with mahogany-trees, and with immense fern plants, in height equal to trees. All nature was on a gigantic scale—the mountains of an enormous height, the face of the country seamed and split by *barrancas* or ravines, hundreds, ay, thousands of feet deep, and filled with the most abundant and varied vegetation. The sky, too, was of the deep glowing blue of the tropics, the sort of blue which seems varnished or clouded with gold. But this ardent climate and teeming soil are not without their disadvantages. Vermin and reptiles of all kinds, and the deadly fever of these latitudes, render the low lands uninhabitable for eight months out of the twelve. At the same time there are large districts which are comparatively free from these plagues—perfect gardens of Eden, of such extreme beauty that the mere act of living and breathing amongst their enchanting scenes, becomes a positive and real enjoyment. The heart seems to leap with delight, and the soul to be elevated, by the contemplation of those regions of fairy-like magnificence.

The most celebrated among these favoured provinces is the valley of Oaxaca, in which two mountainous districts, the Mistecca and Tzapoteca, bear off the palm of beauty. It was through this immense valley, nearly three hundred leagues in length, and surrounded by the highest mountains in Mexico, that we were now journeying. The kind attention of our chargé-d'affaires at the Mexican capital, had procured us every possible facility in travelling through a country, of which the soil was at that time rarely trodden by any but native feet. We had numerous letters to the alcaldes and authorities of the towns and villages which are sparingly sprinkled over the southern provinces of Mexico; we were to have escorts when necessary; every assistance, protection, and facility, were to be afforded us. But as neither the authorities nor his excellency, Uncle Sam's envoy, could make inns and houses where none existed, it followed that we were often obliged to sleep *à la belle étoile*, with the sky for a covering. And a right splendid roof it was to our bedchamber, that tropical sky, with its constellations, all new to us northerns, and every star magnified by the effect of the atmosphere to an incredible size. Mars and Saturn, Venus and Jupiter, had all disappeared; the great and little Bear were still to be seen; in the far distance the ship Argo and the glowing Centaur; and, beautiful above all, the glorious sign of Christianity the colossal Southern Cross, in all its brightness and sublimity, glittering in silvery magnificence out of its setting of dark blue crystal.

We were travelling with a state and a degree of luxury that would have excited the contempt of our backwoodsmen; but in a strange country we thought it best to do as the natives did; and accordingly, instead of mounting our horses and setting forth alone, with our rifles slung over our shoulders, and a few handfuls of parched corn and dried flesh in our hunting pouches, we journeyed Mexican fashion, with a whole string of mules, a *topith* or guide, a couple of *arrieros* or muleteers, a cook, and one or two other attendants. While the latter were slinging our hammocks to the lowermost branches of a tree—for in that part of Mexico it is not very safe to sleep upon the ground, on account of the snakes and vermin—our *cocinero* lit a fire against the rock, and in a very few minutes an iguana which we had shot that day was spitted and roasting before it. It looked strange to see this hideous creature, in shape between a lizard and a dragon, twisting and turning in the light of the fire; and its disgusting appearance might have taken away some people's appetites; but we knew by experience that there is no better eating than a roasted iguana. We made a hearty meal off this one, concluding it with a pull at the rum flask, and then clambered into our hammocks; the Mexicans stretched themselves on the ground with their heads upon the saddles of the mules, and both masters and men were soon asleep.

It was somewhere about midnight when I was awakened by an indescribable sensation of oppression from the surrounding atmosphere. The air seemed to be no longer air, but some poisonous exhalation that had suddenly arisen and enveloped us. From the rear of the ravine in which we lay, billows of dark mephitic mist were rolling forward, surrounding us with their baleful influence. It was the *vomito prieto*, the fever itself, embodied in the shape of a fog. At the same moment, and while I was gasping for breath, a sort of cloud seemed to settle upon me, and a thousand stings, like redhot needles, were run into my hands, face, neck—into every part of my limbs and body that was not triply guarded by clothing. I instinctively stretched forth my hands and closed them, clutching by the action hundreds of enormous musquittoes, whose droning, singing noise how almost deafened me. The air was literally filled by a dense swarm of these insects; and the agony caused by their repeated and venomous stings was indescribable. It was a perfect plague of Egypt.

Rowley, whose hammock was slung some ten yards from mine, soon gave tongue: I heard him kicking and plunging, spluttering and swearing, with a vigour and energy that would have been ludicrous under any other circumstances; but matters were just then too serious for a laugh. With the torture, for such it was, of the musquitto bites, and the effect of the insidious and poisonous vapours that were each moment thickening around me, I was already in a high state of fever, alternately glowing with heat and shivering with cold, my tongue parched, my eyelids throbbing, my brain seemingly on fire.

There was a heavy thump upon the ground. It was Rowley jumping out of his hammock. "Damnation" roared he, "Where are we? On the earth, or under the earth?—We must be—we are—in their Mexican purgatory. We are, or there's no snakes in Virginny. Hallo, arrieros! Pablo! Matteo!"

At that moment a scream—but a scream of such terror and anguish as I never heard before or since—a scream as of women in their hour of agony and extreme peril, sounded within a few paces of us. I sprang out of my hammock; and as I did so, two white and graceful female figures darted or rather flew by me, shrieking—and oh! in what heart-rending tones—for *"Socorro! Socorro! Por Dios*! Help! Help!"* Close upon the heels of the fugitives, bounding and leaping along with enormous strides and springs, came three or four dark objects which resembled nothing earthly. The human form they certainly possessed; but so hideous and horrible, so unnatural and spectre-like was their aspect, that their sudden encounter in that gloomy ravine, and in the almost darkness that surrounded us, might well have shaken the strongest nerves. We stood for a second, Rowley and myself, paralysed with astonishment at these strange appearances; but another piercing scream restored to us our presence of mind. One of the women had either tripped or fallen from fatigue, and she lay a white heap, upon the ground. The drapery of the other was in the clutch of one of the spectres, or devils, or whatever they were, when Rowley, with a cry of horror, rushed forward and struck a furious blow at the monster with his *machetto*. At the same time, and almost without knowing how, I found myself engaged with another of the creatures. But the contest was no equal one. In vain did we stab and strike with our machettos; our antagonists were covered and defended with a hard bristly hide, which our knives, although keen and pointed, had great difficulty in penetrating; and on the other hand we found ourselves clutched in long sinewy arms, terminating in hands and fingers, of which the nails were as sharp and strong as an eagle's talons. I felt these horrible claws strike into my shoulders as the creature seized me, and, drawing me towards him, pressed me as in the hug of a bear; while his hideous half man half brute visage was grinning and snarling at me, and his long keen white teeth were snapping and gnashing within six inches of my face.

"God of heaven! This is horrible! Rowley! Help me!"

But Rowley, in spite of his gigantic strength, was powerless as an infant in the grasp of these terrible opponents. He was within a few paces of me, struggling with two of them, and making super-human efforts to regain possession of his knife, which had dropped or been wrenched from his hand. And all this time, where were our arrieros? Were they attacked likewise? Why didn't they come and help us? All this time!—pshaw! it was no time: it all passed in the space of a few seconds, in the circumference of a few yards, and in the feeble glimmering light of the stars, and of the smouldering embers of our fire, which was at some distance from us.

"Ha! That has told!" A stab, dealt with all the energy of despair, had entered my antagonist's side. But I was like to pay dearly for it. Uttering a deafening yell of pain and fury, the monster clasped me closer to his foul and loathsome body; his sharp claws, dug deeper into my back, seemed to tear up my flesh: the agony was insupportable—my eyes began to swim, and my senses to leave me. Just then—Crack! crack! Two—four—a dozen musket and pistol shots, followed by such a chorus of yellings and howlings and unearthly laughter! The creature that held me seemed startled—relaxed his grasp slightly. At that moment a dark arm was passed before my face, there was a blinding flash, a yell, and I fell to the ground released from the clutch of my opponent. I remember nothing more. Overcome by pain, fatigue, terror, and the noxious vapors of that vile ravine, my senses abandoned me, and I swooned away.

When consciousness returned, I found myself lying upon some blankets, under a sort of arbour of foliage and flowers. It was broad day; the sun shone brightly, the blossoms smelled sweet, the gay-plumaged hummingbirds were darting and shooting about in the sunbeams like so many animated fragments of a prism. A Mexican Indian, standing beside my couch, and whose face was unknown to me, held out a cocoa-nutshell containing some liquid, which I eagerly seized, and drank off the contents. The draught (it was a mixture of citron juice and water) revived me greatly; and raising myself on my elbow, although with much pain and difficulty, I looked around, and beheld a scene of bustle and life which to me was quite unintelligible. Upon the shelving hillside on which I was lying, a sort of encampment was established. A number of mules and horses were wandering about at liberty, or fastened to trees and bushes, and eating the forage that had been collected and laid before them. Some were provided with handsome and commodious saddles, while others had pack-saddles, intended apparently for the conveyance of numerous sacks, cases, and wallets, that were scattered about on the ground. Several muskets and rifles were leaning here and there against the trees; and a dozen or fifteen men were occupied in various ways—some filling up saddle-bags or fastening luggage on the mules, others lying on the ground smoking, one party surrounding a fire at which cooking was going on. At a short distance from my bed was another similarly composed couch, occupied by a man muffled up in blankets, and having his back turned towards me, so that I was unable to obtain a view of his features.

"What is all this? Where am I? Where is Rowley—our guide—where are they all?"

"*Non entiendo,*" answered my brown-visaged Ganymede, shaking his head, and with a good-humoured smile.

"*Adonde estamos?*"

"*In el valle de Chihuatan, in el gran valle de Oaxaca y Guatimala; diez leguas de Tarifa.* In the valley of Chihuatan; ten leagues from Tarifa."

The figure lying on the bed near me now made a movement, and turned round. What could it be? Its face was like a lump of raw flesh streaked and stained with blood. No features were distinguishable.

"Who are you? What are you?" cried I.

"Rowley," it answered: "Rowley I was, at least, if those devils haven't changed me."

"Then changed you they have," cried I, with a wild laugh. "Good God! have they scalped him alive, or what? That is not Rowley."

The Mexican, who had gone to give some drink to the creature claiming to be Rowley, now opened a valise that lay on the ground a short distance off, and took out a small looking-glass, which he brought and held before my face. It was then only that I began to call to mind all that had occurred, and understood how it was that the mask of human flesh lying near me might indeed be Rowley.

He was, if any thing, less altered than myself. My eyes were almost closed; my lips, nose, and whole face swollen to an immense size, and perfectly unrecognisable. I involuntarily recoiled in dismay and disgust at my own appearance. The horrible night passed in the ravine, the foul and suffocating vapours, the furious attack of the musquittoes—the bites of which, and the consequent fever and inflammation, had thus disfigured us—all recurred to our memory. But the women, the fight with the monsters—beasts—Indians— whatever they were, that was still incomprehensible. It was no dream: my back and shoulders were still smarting from the wounds that had been inflicted on them by the claws of those creatures, and I now felt that various parts of my limbs and body were swathed in wet bandages. I was mustering my Spanish to ask the Mexican who still stood by me for an explanation of all this, when I suddenly became aware of a great bustle in the encampment, and saw every body crowding to meet a number of persons who just then emerged from the high fern, and amongst whom I recognized our arrieros and servants. The new-comers were grouped around something which they seemed to be dragging along the ground; several women—for the most part young and graceful creatures, their slender supple forms muffled in the flowing picturesque *reboxos* and *frazadas*—preceded the party, looking back occasionally with an expression of mingled horror and triumph; all with rosaries in their hands, the beads of which ran rapidly through their fingers, while they occasionally kissed the cross, or made the sign on their breasts or in the air.

"*Un Zambo muerto! Un Zambo Muerto!*" shouted they as they drew near.

"*Han matado un Zambo!* They have killed a Zambo!" repeated my attendant in a tone of exultation.

The party came close up to where Rowley and I were lying; the women stood aside, jumping and laughing, and crossing themselves, and crying out "*Un Zambo! Un Zambo Muerto!*" the group opened, and we saw, lying dead upon the ground, one of our horrible antagonists of the preceding night.

"Good God, what is that?" cried Rowley and I, with one breath. "*Un demonio!* a devil!"

"*Perdonen vos, Senores—Un Zambo mono—muy terribles los Zambos.* Terrible monkeys these Zambos."

"Monkeys!" cried I.

"Monkeys!" repeated poor Rowley, raising himself up into a sitting posture by the help of his hands. "Monkeys—apes—by Jove! We've been fighting with monkeys, and it's they who have mauled us in this way. Well, Jonathan Rowley, think of your coming from old Virginny to Mexico to be whipped by a monkey. It's gone goose with *your* character. You can never show your face in the States again. Whipped by an ape!—an ape, with a tail and a hairy—O Lord! Whipped by a monkey!"

And the ludicrousness of the notion overcoming his mortification, and the pain of his wounds and bites, he sank back upon the bed of blankets and banana leaves, laughing as well as his swollen face and sausage-looking lips would allow him.

It was as much as I could do to persuade myself, that the carcass lying before me had never been inhabited by a human soul. It was humiliating to behold the close affinity between this huge ape and our own species. Had it not been for the tail, I could have fancied I saw the dead body of some prairie hunter dressed in skins. It was exactly like a powerful, well-grown man; and even the expression of the face had more of bad human passions than of animal instinct. The feet and thighs were those of a muscular man: the legs rather too curved and calfless, though I have seen Negroes who had scarcely better ones; the tendons of the hands stood out like whipcords; the nails were as long as a tiger's claws. No wonder that we had been overmatched in our struggle with the brutes. No man could have withstood them. The arms of this one were like packets of cordage, all muscle, nerve, and sinew; and the hands were clasped together with such force, that the efforts of eight or ten Mexicans and Indians were insufficient to disunite them.

Whatever remained to be cleared up in our night's adventures was now soon explained. Our guide, through ignorance or thoughtlessness, had allowed us to take up our bivouac within a very unsafe distance of one of the most pestiferous swamps in the whole province. Shortly after we had fallen asleep, a party of Mexican travellers had arrived, and established themselves within a few hundred yards of us, but on a rising ground, where they avoided the mephitic vapours and the musquittoes which had so tortured Rowley and myself. In the night two of the women, having ventured a short distance from the encampment, were surprised by the zambos, or huge man-apes, common in some parts of Southern Mexico; and finding themselves cut off from their friends, had fled they knew not whither, fortunately for them taking the direction of our bivouac. Their screams, our shouts, and the yellings and diabolical laughter of the zambos, had brought the Mexicans to our assistance. The monkeys showed no fight after the first volley; several of then must have been wounded, but only the one now lying before us had remained upon the field.

The Mexicans we had fallen amongst were on the Tzapoteca, principally cochineal gatherers, and kinder-hearted people there could not well be. They seemed to think they never could do enough for us; the women especially, and more particularly the two whom we had endeavoured to rescue from the power of the apes. These latter certainly had cause to be grateful. It made us shudder to think of their fate had they not met with us. It was the delay caused by our attacking the brutes that had given the Mexicans time to come up.

Every attention was shown to us. We were fanned with palm leaves, refreshed with cooling drinks, our wounds carefully dressed and bandaged, our heated, irritated, musquitto- bitten limbs and faces washed with balsam and the juice of herbs: more tender and careful nurses it would be impossible to find. We soon began to feel better, and were able to sit up and look about us; carefully avoiding, however, to look at each other, for we could not get reconciled to the horrible appearance of our swollen, bloody, and disgusting features. From our position on the rising ground, we had a full view over the frightful swamp at the entrance of which all our misfortunes had happened. There it lay, steaming like a great kettle; endless mists rising from it, out of which appeared here and there the crown of some mighty tree towering above the banks of vapour. To the left, cliffs and crags were to be seen which had the appearance of being baseless, and of swimming on the top of the mist. The vultures and carrion-birds circled screaming above the huge caldron, or perched on the tops of the tall palms, which looked like enormous umbrellas, or like the roofs of Chinese summer-houses. Out of the swamp itself proceeded the yellings, snarlings, and growlings of the alligators, bull-frogs, and myriads of unclean beasts that it harboured.

The air was unusually sultry and oppressive: from time to time the rolling of distant thunder was audible. We could hear the Mexicans consulting amongst themselves as to the propriety of continuing their journey, to which our suffering state seemed to be the chief obstacle. From what we could collect of their discourse, they were unwilling to leave us in this dangerous district, and in our helpless condition, with a guide and attendants who were either untrustworthy or totally incompetent to lead us aright. Yet there seemed to be some pressing necessity for continuing the march; and presently some of the older Mexicans, who appeared to have the direction of the caravan, came up to us and enquired how we felt, and if we thought we were able to travel; adding, that from the signs on the earth and in the air, they feared a storm, and that the nearest habitation or shelter was at many leagues' distance. Thanks to the remedies that had been applied, our sufferings were much diminished. We felt weak and hungry, and telling the Mexicans we should be ready to proceed in half an hour, we desired our servants to get us something to eat. But our new friends forestalled them, and brought us a large piece of iguana, with roasted bananas, and cocoa-nutshell cups full of coffee, to all of which Rowley and I applied ourselves with much gusto. Meanwhile our muleteers and the Tzapotecans were busy packing their beasts and making ready for the start.

We had not eaten a dozen mouthfuls when we say a man running down the hill with a branch in each hand. As soon as he appeared, a number of the Mexicans left their occupations and hurried to meet him.

"*Siete horas!*" shouted the man. "Seven hours, and no more!"

"No more than seven hours!" echoed the Tzapotecans, in tones of the wildest terror and alarm. "*La Santissima nos guarde!* It will take more than ten to reach the village."

"What's all that about?" said I with my mouth full, to Rowley.

"Don't know—some of their Indian tricks, I suppose."

"*Que es esto*?" asked I carelessly. "What's the matter?"

"*Que es esto!*" repeated an old Tzapotecan, with long grey hair curling from under his *sombrero*, and a withered but finely marked countenance. "*Las aguas! El ouracan!* In seven hours the deluge and the hurricane!"

"*Vamos, por la Santissima!* For the blessed Virgin's sake let us be gone!" cried a dozen of the Mexicans, pushing two green boughs into our very faces.

"What are those branches?"

"From the tempest-tree—the prophet of the storm," was the reply.

And Tzapotecans and women, arrieros and servants, ran about in the utmost terror and confusion, with cries of "*Vamos, paso redoblado!* Off with us, or we are all lost, man and beast," and saddling, packing, and scrambling on their mules. And before Rowley and I knew where we were, they tore us away from our iguana and coffee, and hoisted and pushed us into our saddles. Such a scene of bustle and desperate hurry I never beheld. The place where the encampment had been was alive with men and women, horses and mules, shouting, shrieking and talking, neighing and kicking; but with all the confusion there was little time lost, and in less than three minutes from the first alarm being given, we were scampering away over stock and stone, in a long, wild, irregular sort of train.

The rapidity and excitement of our ride seemed to have the effect of calming our various sufferings, or of making us forget them; and we soon thought no more of the fever, or of stings or musquitto bites. It was a ride for life or death, and our horses stepped out as if they knew how much depended on their exertions.

In the hurry and confusion we had been mounted on horses instead of our our own mules; and splendid animals they were. I doubt if our Virginians could beat them, and that is saying a great deal. There was no effort or straining in their movements; it seemed mere play to them to surmount the numerous difficulties we encountered on our road. Over mountain and valley, swamp and barranca, always the same steady surefootedness—crawling like cats over the soft places, gliding like snakes up the steep rocky ascents, and stretching out with prodigious energy when the ground was favourable; yet with such easy action that we scarcely felt the motion. We should have sat in the roomy Spanish saddles as comfortably as in arm-chairs, had it not been for the numerous obstacles in our path, which was strewed with fallen trees and masses of rock. We were obliged to be perpetually stooping and bowing our heads to avoid the creeping plants that swung and twined and twisted across the track, intermingled often with huge thorns as long as a man's arm. These latter stuck out from the trees on which they grew like so many brown bayonets; and a man who had run up against one of them, would have been transfixed by it as surely as though it had been of steel. We pushed on, however, in Indian file, following the two guides, who kept at the head of the party, and making our way through places where a wild-cat would have difficulty in passing; through thickets of mangroves, mimosas, and tall fern, and cactuses with their thorny leaves full twenty feet long; the path turning and winding all the while. Now and then a momentary improvement in the nature of the ground enabled us to catch a glimpse of the whole column of march. We were struck by its picturesque appearance, the guides in front acting as pioneers, and looking out on all sides as cautiously and anxiously as though they had been soldiers expecting an ambuscade; the graceful forms of the women bowing and bending over their horses' manes, and often leaving fragments of their mantillas and rebozas on the branches and thorns of the labyrinth through which we were struggling. But it was no time to indulge in contemplation of the picturesque, and of this we were constantly made aware by the anxious vociferations of the Mexicans. "*Vamos! Por Dios, vamos!*" cried they, if the slightest symptom of flagging became visible in the movements of any one of the party; and at the words, our horses, as though gifted with understanding, pushed forward with renewed vigour and alacrity.

On we went—up hill and down, in the depths of the valley and over the soft fetid swamp. That valley of Oaxaca has just as much right to be called a valley as our Alleghanies would have to be called bottoms. In the States we should call it a chain of mountains. Out of it rise at every step hills a good two thousand feet above the level of the valley, and four or five thousand above that of the sea; but these are lost sight of, and become flat ground by the force of comparison; that is, when compared with the gigantic mountains that surround the valley on all sides like a frame. And what a splendid frame they do compose, those colossal mountains, in their rich variety of form and colouring! here shining out like molten gold, there changing to a dark bronze; covered lower down with various shades of green, and with the crimson and purple, and violet and bright yellow, and azure and dazzling white, of the millions of paulinias and convolvoluses and other flowering plants, from amongst which rise the stately palm-trees, full a hundred feet high, their majestic green turbans towering like sultans' heads above the luxuriance of the surrounding flower and vegetable world. Then the mahogany-trees, the chicozapotes, and again in the barrancas the candelabra-like cactuses, and higher up the knotted and majestic live oak. An incessant change of plants, trees, and climate. We had been five hours in the saddle, and had already changed our climate three times; passed from the temperate zone, the *tierra templada*, into the torrid heat of the *tierra muy caliente*. It was in the latter temperature that we found ourselves at the expiration of the above-named time, dripping with perspiration, roasting and stewing in the heat. We were surrounded by a new world of plants and animals. The borax and mangroves and fern were here as lofty as forest-trees, whilst the trees themselves shot up like church steeples. In the thickets around us were numbers of black tigers—we saw dozens of those cowardly sneaking beasts—iguanas full three feet long, squirrels double the size of any we had ever seen, and panthers, and wild pigs, and jackals, and apes and monkeys of every tribe and description, who threatened and grinned and chattered at us from the branches of the trees. But what is that yonder to the right, that stands out so white against the dark blue sky and the bronze-coloured rocks? A town—Quidricovi, d'ye call it?

We had now ridden a good five or six leagues, and begun to think we had escaped the *aguas* or deluge, of which the prospect had so terrified our friends the Tzapotecans. Rowley calculated, as he went puffing and grumbling along, that it wouldn't do any harm to let our beasts draw breath for a minute or two. The scrambling and constant change of pace rendered necessary by the nature of the road, or rather track, that we followed, was certainly dreadfully fatiguing both to man and beast. As for conversation it was out of the question. We had plenty to do to avoid getting our necks broken, or our teeth knocked out, as we struggled along, up and down barrancas, through marshes and thickets, over rocks and fallen trees, and through mimosas and bushes laced and twined together with thorns and creeping plants—all of which would have been beautiful in a picture, but was most infernally unpoetical in reality.

"*Vamos! Por la Santissima Madre, vamos!*" yelled our guides, and the cry was taken up by the Mexicans, in a shrill wild tone that jarred strangely upon our ears, and made the horses start and strain forward. Hurra! on we go, through thorns and bushes, which scratch and flog us, and tear our clothes to rags. We shall be naked if this lasts long. It is a regular race. In front the two guides, stooping, nodding, bowing, crouching down, first to one side, then to the other, like a couple of mandarins or Indian idols—behind them a Tzapotecan in his picturesque capa, then the women, then more Tzapotecans. There is little thought about precedence or ceremony; and Rowley and I, having been in the least hurry to start, find ourselves bringing up the rear of the whole column.

"*Vamos! Por la Santissima! Las aguas, las aguas!*" is again yelled by twenty voices. Hang the fools! Can't they be quiet with their eternal *vamos*? We can have barely two leagues more to go to reach the *rancho*, or village, they were talking of, and appearances are not as yet very alarming. It is getting rather thick to be sure; but that's nothing, only the exhalations from the swamp, for we are again approaching one of those cursed swamps, and can hear the music of the alligators and bullfrogs. There they are, the beauties; a couple of them are taking a peep at us, sticking their elegant heads and long delicate snouts out of the slime and mud. The neighbourhood is none of the best; but luckily the path is firm and good, carefully made, evidently by Indian hands. None but Indians could live and labour and travel habitually, in such a pestilential atmosphere. Thank God! we are out of it at last. Again on firm forest ground, amidst the magnificent monotony of the eternal palms and mahogany-trees. But—see there!

A new and surpassingly beautiful landscape burst suddenly upon our view, seeming to dance in the transparent atmosphere. On either side mountains, those on the left in deep shadow, those on the right standing forth like colossal figures of light, in a beauty and splendour that seemed really supernatural, every tree, every branch shining in its own vivid and glorious colouring. There lay the valley in its tropical luxuriance and beauty, one sheet of bloom and blossom up to the topmost crown of the palm-trees, that shot up, some of them, a hundred and fifty and a hundred and eighty feet high. Thousands and millions of convolvoluses, paulinias, bignonias, dendrobiums, climbing from the fern to the tree trunks, from the trunks to the branches and summits of the trees, and thence again falling gracefully down, and catching and clinging to the mangroves and blocks of granite. It burst upon us like a scene of enchantment, as we emerged from the darkness of the forest into the dazzling light and colouring of that glorious valley.

"*Misericordia, misericordia! Audi nos peccadores! Misericordia, las aquas!*" suddenly screamed and exclaimed the Mexicans in various intonations of terror and despair. We looked around us. What can be the matter? We see nothing. Nothing, except that from just behind those two mountains, which project like mighty promontories into the valley, a cloud is beginning to rise. "What is it? What is wrong?" A dozen voices answered us—

"*Por la Santa Virgen*, for the holy Virgin's sake, on, on! *No hay tiempo para hablar*. We have still two leagues to go, and in one hour comes the flood."

And they recommenced their howling, yelling chorus of "*Misericordia! Audi nos peccadores!*" and "*Santissima Virgen*, and *Todos santos y angeles!*"

"Are the fellows mad?" shouted Rowley, "What if the water does come? It won't swallow you. A ducking more or less is no such great matter. You are not made of sugar or salt. Many's the drenching I've had in the States, and none the worse for it. Yet our rains are no child's play neither."

On looking round us, however, we were involuntarily struck with the sudden change in the appearance of the heavens. The usual golden black blue colour of the sky was gone, and had been replaced by a dull gloomy grey. The quality of the air appeared also to have changed; it was neither very warm nor very cold, but it had lost its lightness and elasticity, and seemed to oppress and weigh us down. Presently we saw the dark cloud rise gradually from behind the hills, completely clearing their summits, and then sweeping along until it hung over the valley, in form and appearance like some monstrous night-moth, resting the tips of its enormous wings on the mountains on either side. To our right we still saw the roofs and walls of Quidricovi, apparently at a very short distance.

"Why not go to Quidricovi?" shouted I to the guides, "we cannot be far off."

"More than five leagues," answered the men, shaking their heads and looking up anxiously at the huge moth, which was still creeping and crawling on, each moment darker and more threatening. It was like some frightful monster, or the fabled Kraken, working itself along by its claws, which were struck deep into the mountain-wall on either side of its line of progress, and casting its hideous shadow over hill and dale, forest and valley, clothing them in gloom and darkness. To our right hand and behind us, the mountains were still of a glowing golden red, lighted up by the sun, but to the left and in our front all was black and dark. With the same glance we beheld the deepest gloom and the brightest day, meeting each other but not mingling. It was a strange and ominous sight.

Ominous enough; and the brute creation seem to feel it so as well as ourselves. The chattering parrots, the hopping, gibbering, quarrelsome apes, all the birds and beasts, scream and cry and flutter and spring about, as though seeking a refuge from some impending danger. Even our horses begin to tremble and groan—refuse to go on, start and snort. The whole animal world is in commotion, as if seized with an overwhelming panic. The forest is teeming with inhabitants. Whence come they, all these living things? On every side is heard the howling and snarling of beasts, the frightened cries and chirpings of birds. The vultures and turkey-buzzards, that a few minutes before were circling high in the air, are now screaming amidst the branches of the mahogany-trees; every creature that has life is running, scampering, flying—apes and tigers, birds and creeping things.

"Vamos, por la Santissima! On! or we are all lost."

And we ride, we rush along—neither masses of rock, nor fallen trees, nor thorns and brambles, check our wild career. Over every thing we go, leaping, scrambling, plunging, riding like desperate men, flying from a danger of which the nature is not clearly defined, but which we feel to be great and imminent. It is a frightful terror-striking foe, that huge night-moth, which comes ever nearer, growing each moment bigger and blacker. Looking behind us, we catch one last glimpse of the red and bloodshot sun, which the next instant disappears behind the edge of the mighty cloud.

Still we push on. Hosts of tigers, and monkeys both large and small, and squirrels and jackals, come close up to us as if seeking shelter, and then finding none, retreat howling into the forest. There is not a breath of air stirring, yet all nature—plants and trees, men and beasts—seem to quiver and tremble with apprehension. Our horses pant and groan as they bound along with dilated nostrils and glaring eyes, trembling in every limb, sweating at every pore, half wild with terror; giving springs and leaps that more resemble those of a hunted tiger than of a horse.

The prayer and exclamations of the terrified Mexicans, continued without intermission, whispered and shrieked and groaned in every variety of intonation. The earthy hue of intense terror was upon every countenance. For some moments a death-like stillness, an unnatural calm, reigned around us: it was as though the elements were holding in their breath, and collecting their energies for some mighty outbreak. Then came a low indistinct moaning sound, that seemed to issue from the bowels of the earth. The warning was significant.

"Halt! stop" shouted we to the guides. "Stop! and let us seek shelter from the storm."

"On! for God's sake, on! or we are lost," was the reply.

Thank Heaven! the path is getting wider—we come to a descent—they are leading us out of the forest. If the storm had come on while we were among the trees, we might be crushed to death by the falling branches. We are close to a barranca.

"*Alerto! Alerto!*" shrieked the Mexicans. "*Madre de Dios! Dios! Dios!*"

And well might they call to God for help in that awful moment. The gigantic night-moth gaped and shot forth tongues of fire—a ghastly white flame, that contrasted strangely and horribly with the dense black cloud from which it issued. There was a peal of thunder that seemed to shake the earth, then a pause during which nothing was heard but the panting of our horses as they dashed across the barranca, and began straining up the steep side of a knoll or hillock. The cloud again opened: for a second every thing was lighted up. Another thunder clap, and then, as though the gates of its prison had been suddenly burst open, the tempest came forth in its might and fury, breaking, crushing, and sweeping away all that opposed it. The trees of the forest staggered and tottered for a moment, as if making an effort to bear up against the storm; but it was in vain: the next instant, with a report like that of ten thousand cannon, whole acres of mighty trees were snapped off, their branches shivered, their roots torn up; it was no longer a forest but a chaos; an ocean of boughs and tree-trunks, that were tossed about like the waves of the sea, or thrown into the air like straws. The atmosphere was darkened with dust, and leaves, and branches.

"God be merciful to us! Rowley! where are ye?—No answer. What is become of them all?"

A second blast more furious than the first. Can the mountains resist it? will they stand? By the Almighty! they do not. The earth trembles; the hillock, on the leeside of which we are, rocks and shakes; and the air grows thick and suffocating—full of dust and saltpetre and sulphur. We are like to choke. All around is dark as night. We can see nothing, hear nothing but the howling of the hurricane, and the thunder and rattle of falling trees and shivered branches.

Suddenly the hurricane ceases, and all is hushed; but so suddenly that the charge is startling and unnatural. No sound is audible save the creaking and moaning of the trees with which the ground is cumbered. It is like a sudden pause in a battle, when the roar of the cannon and clang of charging squadrons cease, and nought is heard but the groaning of the wounded, the agonized sobs and gasps of the dying.

The report of a pistol is heard; then another, a third, hundreds, thousands of them. It is the flood, *las aguas*; the shots are drops of rain; but such drops! each as big as a hen's egg. They strike with the force of enormous hailstones—stunning and blinding us. The next moment there is no distinction of drops, the windows of heaven are opened; it is no longer rain nor flood, but a sea, a cataract, a Niagara. The hillock on which I am standing, undermined by the waters, gives way and crumbles under me; in ten seconds' time I find myself in the barranca, which is converted into a river, off my horse, which is gone I know not whither. The only person I see near me is Rowley, also dismounted and struggling against the stream, which is already up to our waists, and sweeps along with it huge branches and entire trees, that threaten each moment to carry us away with them, or to crush us against the rocks. We avoid these dangers, God knows how, make violent efforts to stem the torrent and gain the side of the barranca; although, even should we succeed, it is so steep that we can scarcely hope to climb it without assistance. And whence is that assistance to come? Of the Mexicans we see or hear nothing. They are doubtless all drowned or dashed to pieces. They were higher up on the hillock than we were, must consequently have been swept down with more force, and were probably carried away by the torrent. Nor can we hope for a better fate. Wearied by our ride, weakened by the fever and sufferings of the preceding night, we are in no condition to strive much longer with the furious elements. For one step that we gain, we lose two. The waters rise; already they are nearly up to our armpits. It is in vain to resist any longer. Our fate is sealed.

"Rowley, all is over—let us die like men. God have mercy on our souls!"

Rowley was a few paces higher up the barranca. He made me
no answer, but looked at me with a calm, cold, and yet somewhat
regretful smile upon his countenance. Then all at once he ceased
the efforts he was making to resist the stream and gain the bank,
folded his arms on his breast and gave a look up and around him
as though to bid farewell to the world he was about to leave. The
current was sweeping him rapidly down towards me, when suddenly a wild hurra burst from his lips, and he recommenced his
struggles against the waters, striving violently to retain a footing
on the slippery, uneven bed of the stream.

"*Tenga! Tenga!*" screamed a dozen voices, that seemed to proceed from spirits of the air; and at the same moment something
whistled about my ears and struck me a smart blow across the face.
With the instinct of a drowning man, I clutched the *lasso* that had
been thrown to me. Rowley was at my elbow and seized it also. It
was immediately drawn tight, and by its aid we gained the bank,
and began ascending the side of the barranca, composed of rugged, declivitous rocks, affording but scanty foot-hold. God grant
the lasso may prove tough! The strain on it is fearful. Rowley is a
good fifteen stone, and I am no feather; and in some parts of our
perilous ascent the rocks are almost as perpendicular and smooth
as a wall of masonry, and we are obliged to cling with our whole
weight to the lasso, which seems to stretch, and crack, and grow
visibly thinner. Nothing but a strip of twisted cow-hide between
us and a frightful agonizing death on the sharp rocks and in the
foaming waters below. But the lasso holds good, and now the chief
peril is past: we get some sort of footing—a point of rock, or a tree-
root to clutch at. Another strain up this rugged slope of granite,
another pull at the lasso; a leap, a last violent effort, and—*Viva!*—
we are seized under the arms, dragged up, held upon our feet for a
moment, and then—we sink exhausted to the ground in the midst
of the Tzapotecans, mules, arrieros, guides, and women, who are
sheltered from the storm in a sort of natural cavern. At the moment at which the hillock had given way under Rowley and myself,
who were a short distance in rear of the party, the Mexicans had
succeeded in attaining firm footing on a broad rocky ledge, a shelf

of the precipice that flanked the barranca. Upon this ledge, which gradually widened into a platform, they found themselves in safety under some projecting crags that sheltered them completely from the tempest. Thence they looked down upon the barranca, where they descried Rowley and myself struggling for our lives in the roaring torrent; and thence, by knotting several lassos together, they were able to give us the opportune aid which had rescued us from our desperate situation. But whether this aid had come soon enough to save our lives was still a question, or at least for some time appeared to be so. The life seemed driven out of our bodies by all we had gone through: we were unable to move a finger, and lay helpless and motionless, with only a glimmering indistinct perception, not amounting to consciousness, of what was going on around us. Fatigue, the fever, the immersion in cold water when reeking with perspiration, the sufferings of all kinds we had endured in the course of the last twenty hours, had completely exhausted and broken us down.

The storm did not last long in its violence, but swept onwards, leaving a broad track of desolation behind it. The Mexicans recommenced their journey, with the exception of four or five who remained with us and our arrieros and servants. The village to which we were proceeding was not above a league off; but even that short distance Rowley and myself were in no condition to accomplish. The kind-hearted Tzapotecans made us swallow cordials, stripped off our drenched and tattered garments, and wrapped us in an abundance of blankets. We fell into a deep sleep, which lasted all that evening and the greater part of the night, and so much refreshed us that about an hour before daybreak we were able to resume our march—at a slow pace, it is true, and suffering grievously in every part of our bruised and wounded limbs and bodies, at each jolt or rough motion of the mules on which we were clinging, rather than sitting.

Our path lay over hill and dale, perpetually rising and falling. We soon got out of the district or zone that had been swept by the preceding day's hurricane, and after nearly an hour's ride, we paused on the crest of a steep descent, at the foot of which, as our

guides informed us, lay the land of promise, the long looked-for
rancho. While the muleteers were seeing to the girths of their
beasts, and giving the due equilibrium to the baggage, before com-
mencing the downward march, Rowley and I sat upon our mules,
wrapped in large Mexican *capas*, gazing at the morning-star as it
sank down and grew gradually paler and fainter. Suddenly the eastern sky began to brighten, and a brilliant beam appeared in the
west, a point of light no bigger than a star—but yet not a star; it
was of a far rosier hue. The next moment a second sparkling spot
appeared, near to the first, which now swelled out into a sort of
fiery tongue, that seemed to lick round the silvery summit of the
snow-clad mountain. As we gazed, five—ten—twenty hill tops were
tinged with the same rose-coloured glow; in another moment they
became like fiery banners spread out against the heavens, while
sparkling tongues and rays of golden light flashed and flamed
round them, springing like meteors from one mountain summit to
another, lighting them up like a succession of beacons. Scarcely
five minutes had elapsed since the distant pinnacles of the mountains had appeared to us as huge phantom-like figures of a silvery
white, dimly marked out upon a dark star-spangled ground; now
the whole immense chain blazed like volcanoes covered with glowing lava, rising out of the darkness that still lingered on their flanks
and bases, visible and wonderful witnesses to the omnipotence of
him who said, "Let there be light, and there was light."

Above, all was broad day, flaming sunlight; below, all black
night. Here and there streams of light burst through clefts and
openings in the mountains, and then ensued an extraordinary kind
of conflict. The shades of darkness seemed to live and move, to
struggle against the bright beams that fell amongst them and broke
their masses, forcing them down the wooded heights, tearing them
asunder and dispersing them like tissues of cobwebs; so that suc-
cessively, and as if by a stroke of enchantment, there appeared,
first the deep indigo blue of the tamarinds and chicozapotes, then
the bright green of the sugar-canes, lower down the darker green
of the nopal-trees, lower still the white and green and gold and
bright yellow of the orange and citron groves, and lowest of all,

the stately fan-palms, and date-palms, and bananas; all glittering with millions of dewdrops, that covered them like a ganze veil embroidered with diamonds and rubies. And still in the very next valley all was utter darkness.

We sat silent and motionless, gazing at this scene of enchantment.

Presently the sun rose higher, and a flood of light illumined the whole valley, which lay some few hundred feet below us—a perfect garden, such as no northern imagination could picture forth; a garden of sugar-canes, cotton, and nopal-trees, intermixed with thickets of pomegranate and strawberry-trees, and groves of orange, fig, and lemon, giants of their kind, shooting up to a far greater height than the oak attains in the States—every tree a perfect hothouse, a pyramid of flowers, covered with bloom and blossom to its topmost spray. All was light, and freshness, and beauty; every object seemed to dance and rejoice in the clear elastic golden atmosphere. It was an earthly paradise, fresh from the hand of its Creator, and at first we could discover no sign of man or his works. Presently, however, we discerned the village lying almost at our feet, the small stone houses overgrown with flowers and embedded in trees; so that scarcely a square foot of roof or wall was to be seen. Even the church was concealed in a garland of orange-trees, and had lianas and star-flowered creepers climbing over and dangling on it, up as high as the slender cross that surmounted its square white tower. As we gazed, the first sign of life appeared in the village. A puff of blue smoke rose curling and spiral from a chimney, and the matin bell rang out its summons to prayer. Our Mexicans fell on their knees and crossed themselves, repeating their Ave-marias. We involuntarily took off our hats, and whispered a thanksgiving to the God who had been with us in the hour of peril, and was now so visible to us in his works.

The Mexicans rose from their knees.

"*Vamos! Senores,*" said one of them, laying his hand on the bridle of my mule. "To the *rancho*, to breakfast."

We rode slowly down into the valley.

Hunting of the Soko

Phil Robinson

Lying on my back one terribly hot day under the great tamarind that shades the temple of Saravan, in Borneo, I began to think naturally of iced drinks, and from them my mind wandered to icebergs, and from icebergs to Polar bears.

Polar bears! At the recollection of these animals I sat bolt upright, for though I had shot over nearly all the world, and accumulated a perfect museum of trophies, I had never till this moment thought of Greenland, nor of Polar bears! Before this I had begun to think I had exhausted Nature. From the false elk of Ceylon to the true one of Canada, the rhinoceros of Assam to the coyote of Patagonia, the panther of Central India to the jaguars of the Amazon, I had seen everything in its own home, and shot it there. And for birds, I had hunted a so-called moa at Little Farm in New Zealand, the bustard in the Mahratta country, dropped geese into nearly every river of America, Europe, and Asia, and flushed almost all the glorious tribe of game birds, from the capercailzie of Norway to the quail of Sicily. My museum, however, wanted yet another skin—the Polar bear! I cannot say the prospect pleased me. I would much rather have sent my compliments to the Polar bear and asked it to come comfortably into some warm climate to be shot; but regretting was useless, so I gave the order of the day—the North Pole.

In London, however, I heard of Stanley's successful search for Livingstone, and then it was that the sense of my utter nothingness came over me. All Africa was unshot! It is true I had once gone from Bombay to Zanzibar, Dr. Kirke helping me on my way, and, thanks to Mackinnon's agents (who were busy prospecting a road into the interior) had bagged my hippopotamus, and enjoyed many a pleasant stalk after the fine antelope of the Bagomoyo plains. But the Dark Continent itself, with its cloud-like herds of hartebest and springbok, its droves of wind-footed gnu, its zebras, ostriches and lions, was still a virgin ground for me. But more than all these— more than ostrich, gnu, or zebra, more than hippopotamus or lion— was that mystery of the primeval forest, the Soko. What was the Soko? Certainly not the gorilla, nor the chimpanzee, nor yet the ourang-outang. Was it a new beast altogether, this man-like thing, that shakes the forest at the sources of the Congo with its awful voice—that desolates the villages of the jungle tribes of Uregga, carries off the women captive, and meets their cannibal lords in fair fight? With Soko on the brain it may be easily imagined that the Polar bear was forgotten, and I lost no time in altering my arrangements to suit my altered plans. My snow-shoes were countermanded and solar helmets laid in: fur gloves and socks were exchanged for leather gaiters and canvas suits.

In a month I was ready, and in another two months had started from Zanzibar with a following of eighteen men. During my voyage I had carefully read the travels of Grant, Speke, Burton, Livingstone, Cameron, Schweinfurth, and Stanley, and in all had been struck by the losses suffered from fatigue on the march. With large expeditions it was of course necessary for most to go on foot, but with my pygmy cortège I could afford to let them ride. Good strong donkeys were cheap at Zanzibar, and I bought a baker's dozen of them, reserving three of the best for myself, and allotting ten among my men, to relieve them either of their burdens or the fatigue of walking, according to any fair arrangements—fair to the donkeys and to themselves—they chose to make among themselves. The result was no sickness, little fatigue, and constant good spirits. My goods consisted of my own personal effects, all on one donkey; my medicine-chest, etc., on another; fifteen men-loads of beads, wire, and cloth, for making friends with the natives and purchasing provisions; and three loads of ammunition. I was lucky in the time of my start, for Mirambo, "the terror of Africa," who had been scouring the centre of the continent for the past year, had just concluded peace with the Arabs, his enemies, and had moreover ordered every one also to keep the peace. The result to me was that each village was as harmless as the next.

Gaily enough, then, we strolled along, enjoying occasionally excellent sport, and wondering as we went where all the horrors and perils of African travel had gone. We had, it is true, our experience of them afterwards; but the ground has now become so stale, that I will pass over the interval of our journey from Zanzibar to Ujiji and thence to the river, and ask you to imagine us setting out for the forests that lie about the sources of the Livingstone in the district of Uregga, the Soko's home.

Nearly every traveller before me had spoken of the Soko, the man-beast of these primeval forests. Livingstone had a large store of legends and anecdotes about them, their intelligent cruelty and their fierce, though frugivorous, habits. Stanley constantly heard them. In one place he saw a Soko's platform in a tree, and in several villages found the skin, the teeth, and the skulls in possession of the people.

Wherever we went I was eager in my inquiries, but day after day slipped by, and still I neither heard the Soko alive nor saw any portion of one dead. But even without encountering the great simia, our journey in these nightshade forests was sufficiently eventful, for great panther-like creatures, very pale-skinned, prowled about in the glimmering shades; and from the trees we sometimes saw hanging pythons of tremendous girth. But the reptile and insect world was chiefly in the ascendant here, and it was against such small persecutors as puff-adders, centipedes, poisonous spiders, and ants, that we had to guard ourselves. Travelling, however, owing to the dense shade, was not the misery that we had found it in the sun-smitten plains of Uturu, or the hideous ocean of scrub-jungle that stretches from Suna to Mgongo-Zembo. The trees, nearly all of three or four species of bombax, mvule, and aldrendon, were of stupendous size and impossible altitude, but growing so close together their crowns were tightly interwoven overhead, and sometimes not a hundred yards in a whole day's march was open to the sky. Moreover, in the hot-house air under this canopy had sprung up with incredible luxuriance every species of tree-fern, rattan and creeping palm known, I should think, to the tropics, and amongst themselves in a stratum, often thirty feet below the upper roof of tree-foliage, had closely intermeshed their fronds and tendrils, so that we marched often in an oven atmosphere, but protected alike from the killing sun and flooding rain by double awnings of impenetrable leafage. The ground itself was bare of vegetation, except where, here and there, monster fungi clustered, like a condemned invoice of umbrellas and parasols, round some fallen giant of the forest, or where, in a screen of blossom, wonderful air-plants filled up great spaces from tree-trunk to tree-trunk.

At intervals we crossed rivulets of crystal water, icy cold, finding their way as best they might from hollow to hollow over the centuries' layers of fallen leaves, and along their courses grew in rich profusion masses of a broad-leafed sedge, that afforded the panther safe covert and easy couch; and sometimes, on approaching one of these rills, we would see a ghostly herd of deer flit away through the twilight shade. And thus it happened that one evening I was lying on my rug half asleep, with the pleasant deep-sea gloom about me and a deathly stillness reigning over this world of trees, and wondering whether that was or was not a monkey perched high up among the palm fronds, when out from the sedges by a runnel there paced before me a panther of unusual size. From his gait I saw that it had a victim in view, and turning my head was horrified to see that it was one of my own men, who was busy about something at the foot of a tree.

I jumped up with a shout, and the panther, startled by the sudden sound, plunged back in three great leaps into the sedges from which it had emerged. All my men jumped to their feet, and one of them, in his terror at the proximity of the beast of prey, turned and fled away into the depth of the forest. I watched his retreating figure as far as the eye could follow it in that light, and laughing at his panic, went over to where my ass was tied, intending to stroll down for a shot at the panther. And while I was idly getting ready, the sound of excited conversation among my men attracted me, and I asked them what was the matter. There was a laugh, and then one of them, the most sensible, English-minded African I ever met, stepped forward.

"We do not know, master," said he, "which of us it was that ran away just now. We are all here."

The full significance of his words did not strike me at first, and I laughed too. "Oh, count yourselves," I said, "and you will soon find out."

"But we have counted, master," replied the man, "and all eighteen are here."

His meaning began to dawn on me. I felt a queer feeling creep over me.

"All here!" I ejaculated. "Muster the men."

And mustered they were—and to my astonishment, and even horror, I found the man was speaking the truth. Every man of my force was in his place.

Then who was the man that had run away, when all the party started up from their sleep? A ghost? I looked round into the deepening gloom. All my men were standing together, looking rather frightened. Around us stretched the eternal forest. A ghost! And then on a sudden the thought flashed across me—I had seen the Soko.

I had seen the Soko! and seeing it had mistaken it for a human being! And while I was still loading my cartridge-belt, Shumari, my gun-boy, had crept up to my side, with my express in one hand and heavy elephant rifle in the other; but on his face there was a strange, concerned expression, and in the tone of his voice an uneasy tremor, with which something in my own feelings sympathized.

"Is the master going to hunt the wild man?" asked the lad.

"The Soko? Yes, I want its skin," I replied.

"But the wild man cried out, 'Ai! ma-ma' ['Oh! mother, mother'] as it ran away, and—"

"Here is the wild man's stick," broke in Mabruki, the Zanzibari; and as he spoke he held out towards me a long staff, seven feet in length. All the blood in my body ran cold at the sight of it. It was a mere length of rattan, without ferule or knot, but at the upper end the bark had been torn down from joint to joint in parallel strips, to give the holder a firmer grip than one could have had on smooth cane, and just below the second joint the stumps of the corresponding shoots on two sides had been left sticking out for the hand to rest on.

How can I describe the throng of hideous thoughts that whirled through my brain on the instant that I recognized these efforts of reason in the animal that I was now going to hunt to the death? But swift as were my thoughts, Mabruki had thought them out before me, and had come to a conclusion. "The mshenshi mtato [pagan ape] had stolen this stick from some village," said he; "see," and he pointed to the smoothed offshoots, "they have stained them with the mvule juice."

The instant relief I felt at this happy solution of the dreadful mystery was expressed by me in a shout of joy; so sudden and so real that, without knowing why, my men shouted too, and with such a will that the monkeys that had been gravely pondering over our preparations for the evening meal were startled out of their self-respect and off their perches, and plunged precipitately into a tangle of lianes. My spirits had returned, and with as light a heart as ever I had, I ambled off in the direction the Soko had taken.

But soon the voices of the camp had died away behind me, and there had grown up between me and it the wall of mist that in this sunless forest region makes every mile as secret from the next as if you were in the highest ether—surely, the most secret of all places—or in the lowest sea. And over the soft, rich vegetable mould the ass's feet went noiseless as an owl's wing upon the air; and, except for the rhythmical jingling of his ass's harness, Shumari's presence might never have been suspected. And then in this cathedral solitude—with cloistered tree-trunks reaching away at every point of view into long vistas closed in gray mist; overhead, hanging like tattered tapestry, great lengths and rags of moss-growths, strange textures of fungus and parasite, hanging plumb down in endless points, all as motionless as possible; without a breath of life stirring about me—bird, beast, or insect—the same horrid thoughts took possession of me again, and I began to recall the gestures of the wild thing which, when I startled the panther, had fled away into the forest depths.

It had stood upright amongst the upright men, and turning to run had stooped, but only so much as a man might do when running with all his speed. In the gait there was a one-sided swing, just as some great man-ape—gorilla or chimpanzee—might have when, as travellers tell us, they help themselves along on the knuckles of the long fore-arm, the body swaying down to the side on which the hand touches the ground at each stride. In one hand was a small branch of some leafy shrub, far I distinctly remembered having seen it as it began to run. The speed must have been great, for it was very soon out of sight; but there was no appearance of rapidity in the movement,—like the wolf's slow-looking gallop, that no horse can overtake, and that soon tires out the fleetest hound. As it began to run it had made a jabbering sound,—an inarticulate expression of simple human fear I had thought it to be; but now, pondering over it, I began to wonder that I could have mistaken that swiftly retreating figure for human.

It is true that I did not want to think of it as human, and perhaps my wishes may have colored my retrospect; at any rate, whatever the process, I found myself, after a while, laughing at myself for having turned sick at heart when the suspicion came across me that perhaps the Soko of the forests of Uregga, the feast-day dish of the jungle tribes, might be a human being. The long, lolloping gait, the jabbering, should alone have dispelled the terror. It is true that my men heard it say, "Oh, ma-ma!" as it started up to run by them. But in half the languages of the world, mama is a synonym for "mother," and it follows, therefore, that it is not a word at all, but simply the phonetic rendering of the first bleating, babbling articulation of babyhood,—an animal noise uttered as articulately by young sheep and young goats as by young men and women. The staff, too, was of the common type in these districts, and had been picked up, no doubt, by the Soko in some twilight prowling round a grain store, or perhaps gained in fair fight from some villager whom it had surprised, solitary and defenceless. And then my thoughts ran on to all I had read or heard of the Soko, of its societies for mutual defence or food-supply, and the comparative amiability of such communities,—of the solitary outlawed Soko, the vindictive, lawless bandit of the trees, who wanders about round the habitations of men, lying in wait for the women and the children, robbing the granaries and orchards, and stealing, for the simple larceny's sake, household chattels, of the use of which it is ignorant. Shumari, a hunter born and bred, was full of Soko lore; the skin, he said, was covered, except on the throat, hands, and feet, with a short, harsh hair of a dark color, and tipped in the older individuals with gray; these also had long growths of hair on the head, their cheeks and lips. It had no tail.

"Standing up," said he, "it is as tall as I am [he was only five feet one inch], and its eyes are together in the front of its face, so that it looks at you straight. It eats sitting up, and when tired leans its back against a tree, putting its hands behind its head. Three men of my village came upon one asleep in this way one day, and so quietly that before it awoke two of them had speared it. It started up and threw back its head to give a loud cry of pain, and then leaning its elbow against the tree, it bent its head down upon its arms, and so died,—leaning against the tree, with one arm supporting the head and the other pressed to its heart. There was a Soko village there, for they saw all their platforms in the trees, and the ground was heaped up in places with snail-shells and fruit-skins. But they did not see any more Sokos... Another day I myself was out hunting with a party, and we found a dead Soko. I had thrown my spear at a tree-cat, and going to pick it up, saw close by a large heap of myombo leaves. I turned some up with my spear, and found a dead Soko underneath... When a Soko catches a man it holds him, and makes faces at him, and jabbers; sometimes it lets him go without doing him any harm, but generally it bites off all his fingers one by one, spitting them out as it bites them off, and his nose and ears and toes as well, and ends up by strangling him with its fingers or beating him to death with a branch. Women and children are never seen again, so I suppose the Sokos eat them. They have no spears or knives, and they do not use anything that men use, except that they walk with sticks, knocking down fruit with them, and that they drink water out of their hands. Their front teeth are very sharp, and at each side is one longer and sharper than the rest."

And so he went on chattering to me as we ambled through the dim shade in a stupid pursuit of an invisible thing. The stupidity of it dawned upon me at last, and I stopped, and without explaining the change to my companion, turned and rode homewards.

The twilight shadows of the day were now deepening into night, and we hurried on. The fireflies began to flicker along the sedge-grown rills and, high up among the leaf coronets of the elais palm, were clustering in a mazy dance. Passing a tangle of lianes, I heard an owl or some night bird hoot gently from the foliage, and as we went along the fowl seemed to keep pace with us, for the ventriloquist sound was always with us, fast though we rode; and first from one side and then from the other we heard the low-voiced complaining following. And the "eeriness" of the company grew upon me. There was no sound of wings or rustling of leaves; but for mile after mile the low hoot, hoot, of the thing that was following, sounded so close at hand that I kept on looking round. Shumari, like all savages—they approach animals very nearly in this—was intensely susceptible to the superstitious and uncanny, and long before the ghostliness of the persistent voice occurred to me, I had noticed that Shumari was keeping as close to me as possible. But at last, whether it was from constantly turning my head over my shoulder to see what was coming after us, or whether I was unconsciously infected by his nervousness, I got as fidgety as he, and, for the sake of human company, opened conversation.

"What bird makes that noise?" I asked.

Shumari did not reply, and I repeated the question.

And then in a voice, so absurd from its assumption of boldness that I laughed outright, he said,—

"No bird, master. It is a muzimu [spirit] that is following us. Let us go quicker."

Here was a position! We had all the evening been hunting nothing, and now we were being hunted by nothing! The memory of

Shumari's voice made me laugh again, and just then catching sight of the twinkling camp fires in the far distance, I laughed at myself too. And, on a sudden, just as my laugh ceased, there came from the rattan brake past which we were riding a sound that was, and yet was not, the echo of my laugh. It sounded something like my laugh, but it was repeated twice, and the creature I rode, ass though it was, turned its head towards the brake. Shumari meanwhile had seen the camp fires, and his terror overpowering discipline, he gave one howl of horror and fled, his ass, seeing the fires too, falling into the humor with all his will, and carrying off his rider at full speed. My ass wanted to follow, but I pulled him up, and to make further trial of the hidden jester, shouted out in Swahili, "Who is there?"

The answer was as sudden as horrifying. For an instant the brake swayed to and fro, and then there came a crashing of branches as of some great beast forcing his way through them, and on a sudden, close behind me, burst out—the Soko!

Shumari had carried off my guns, and, except for the short knife in my belt, I was defenceless. And there before me in the flesh stood the creature I had gone out to hunt, but which for ever so many miles must have been hunting us. I had no leisure for moralizing or even for examination of the creature before me. It seemed about Shumari's height, but was immensely broad at the shoulders, and in one hand it carried a fragment of a bough. Had it been simply man against man, I would have stood my ground—but was it? The dim light prevented my noting any details, and I had no inclination or time to scrutinize the features of the thing that now approached me. I saw the white teeth flashing, heard a deep-chested stuttering, inarticulate with rage, and flinging myself from the ass, which was trembling and rooted to the spot with fear, I ran as I had never run before in the direction of the camp.

The Soko must have stopped to attack the ass, for I heard a scuffle behind me as I started, but very soon the ass came tearing past me, and looking round I saw the Soko in pursuit. The heavy branch fortunately encumbered its progress, but it gained upon me. Close behind me I heard the thing jabbering and panting, and for an instant thought of standing at bay. I was running my hard-est, but it seemed, just as in a nightmare, as if horror had partly paralyzed my limbs, and I were only creeping along. The horror of such pursuit was, I felt, culminating in sickness, and I thought I should swoon and fall. But just then I became aware of approach-ing lights, the camp fires seemed to be running to me. The Soko, however, was fast overtaking me, and I struggled on, but it was of no use, and my feet tripping against the projecting root of an old mvule, I fell on my knees; but, rising again, I staggered against the tree, drew my knife, and waited for the attack. In an instant the Soko was up with me, and, dropping its bough, reached out its arms to seize me. I lunged at it with my knife, but the length of its arms baffled me, for before the point of my knife could find its body, the Soko's hands had grasped my shoulders, and with such astonish-ing force that it seemed as if my arms were being displaced in their sockets. The next moment a third hand seized hold of my, leg below the knee, and I was instantly jerked on to the ground. The fall par-tially stunned me, and then I felt a rough-haired body fall heavily upon me, and, groping their way to my throat, long fingers feeling about me. I struggled with the creature, but against its strength my hands were nerveless. The fingers had now found my throat; I felt the grasp tightening, and gave myself up to death. But on a sudden there was a confusion of voices—a flashing of bright lights before my eyes, and the weight was all at once raised from off me. In another minute I had recovered my consciousness, and found that my men, the gallant Mabruki at their head, had charged to my rescue with burning brands, and arrived only just in time to save my life.

And the Soko?

As I lay there, my faithful followers round me with their brands still flickering, the voice of the Soko came to us, but from which direction it was impossible to say, soft and mysterious as before, the same hoot, hoot, that had puzzled us on our homeward route.

My narrow escape from a horrible though somewhat absurd death was celebrated by my men with extravagant demonstrations of indignation against the Soko that had hunted me, and many respect-ful reproaches for my temerity. For myself, I was more eager than ever to capture or kill the formidable thing that had outwitted and outmatched me; and so having had my arms well rubbed with oil, I gave the order for a general muster next morning for a grand Soko hunt.

Now, close by our camp grew a great tree, from which hung down liane strands of every rope-thickness, and all round its roots had grown op a dense hedge of strong-spined cane. One of my men, sent up the tree to cut us off some of these natural ropes, reported that all round the tree, that is, between its trunk and the cane-hedge, there was a clear space, so that though, looking at it from the outside, it seemed as if the canes grew right up to the tree trunk, looking at it from above, there was seen to be really an open path-way, so to speak, surrounding the tree, broad enough for three men to walk abreast. I had often heard of similar cases of vegetable aver-sions, where, from some secret cause of plant prejudice, two shrubs, though growing together, exercise this mutual repulsion, and never actually combine in growth. Meanwhile, however, the phenomenon was interesting to me for other reasons, for I saw at once what a convenient receptacle this natural well would make for the baggage we had to leave behind.

Leaving our effects therefore inside this brake, which we did by slinging the bales one after the other over an overhanging bough, and so dropping them into the open pathway, and removing from the neighborhood every trace of our recent encampment, we started westward with four days' provisions, ready cooked, on our backs. The method of march was in line, each man about a hundred yards from the next, and every second man on an ass, the riders carrying the usual ivory horns, without which no travellers in the Uregga forests ever move from home, and the notes of which, exactly like the cry of the American wood-marmot, keep the party in line. By this means we covered a mile, and being unencumbered, marched fast, scouring the wood before us at the rate of four miles an hour for three hours.

And what a wild, weird time it was, those three hours, marching with noiseless footfalls, looking constantly right and left and over-head. I could see the line of shadowy figures advancing on either

side, not a sound along the whole line, except when the horns carried down in response to one another their thin, wailing notes, or
when some palm fruit, over-ripe, dropped rustling down through
the canopy of foliage above us. And yet the whole forest was instinct with life. If you set yourself to listen, there came to your
ears, all day and night, a great monotone of sound humming
through the misty shade, the aggregate voices of millions of insect
things that had their being among the foliage or in the daylight
that reigned in the outer world above those green clouds which
made perpetual twilight for us who were passing underneath. Along
the tree-roof streamed also troops of monkeys, and flocks of parrots and other birds; but in their passage overhead, we could not,
through the dense vault of foliage, branch, and blossom, hear their
voices, except as merged in the one great sound that filled all space,
too large almost to be heard at all. In the midst, then, of this vast
murmur of confused nature, we seemed to walk in absolute silence.
The ear had grown so accustomed to it, that a sneeze was heard
with a start, and the occasional knocking together of asses' hoofs
made every head turn suddenly, and every rifle move to the shoulder.

At the end of the three hours' marching we came to a river,—
perhaps that which Stanley, in his "Dark Continent," names the
Asna,—flowing northwest, with a width here of only one hundred
yards,—a deep, slow stream, crystal clear, flowing without a ripple
or a murmur through the perpetual gloaming, between banks of
soft, rich, black leaf-mould. We halted, and, after a rapid meal, re-
formed in line, and marching for two miles easterly up the river,
made a left wheel; and in the same order, and at the same pace as
we had advanced, we continued nearly two hours rather in a north-
erly direction, and then making a left wheel again, started off due
west, crossing the tracks of our morning's march in our fourth mile,
and reaching the Asna again in our tenth mile,—a total march of
nearly thirty-two miles, of which, of course, each man had traversed
only one half on foot. No cooking was allowed, and our collation
was therefore soon despatched, and before I had lighted my pipe
and curled myself up I saw that all the party were snug under their
mosquito nets.

I had noticed, when reading travellers' books, that they always suffered severely from mosquitoes and other insects. I determined that I would not; so, before leaving Zanzibar, served out to every man twenty yards of net. These, in the daytime, were worn round the head as turbans, and at night spread upon sticks, and furnished each man a protection against these Macbeths of the sedge and brake. The men thoroughly understood their value, and before turning in for the night, always carefully examined their nets for stray holes, which they caught together with fibres. But somehow I could not go to sleep for a long while; the pain in my arm where the Soko seized me was very great at times; besides, I felt haunted; and indeed, when I awoke and found it already four o'clock, it did not seem that I had been asleep at all. But the time for sleep was now over, so, awakening the expedition, we ate a silent meal, and noiselessly remounting, were again on the war-trail. On this, the second day, we marched some three miles down the river, northwest, and then taking a half right wheel, started off northeast, passing to the north of our camp at about the eleventh mile. Here the first sign of life we had seen since we started broke the tedium of our ghost-like progress.

Between myself and the next man on the line was running a little stream, fed probably by the dews that here rained down upon us from the mvule-trees. These, more than all others, seem to condense the heated upper air, their leaves being thick in texture, and curiously cool,—for which reason the natives prefer them for butter and oil dishes. Along the stream, as usual, crowded a thick fringe of white-starred sedge. On a sudden there was a swaying of the herbage, and out bounced a splendidly spotted creature of the cat kind. Immediately behind him crept out his mate; and there they stood: the male, his crest and all the hair along the spine erect with anger at our intrusion, his tail swinging and curling with excitement; beside him, and half behind him, the female crouching low on the ground, her ears laid back along the head, and motionless as a carved stone. My ass saw the pair, and instinct warning it that the beautiful beasts were dangerous to it, with that want of judgment and consideration so characteristic of asses, it must needs bray. And such a bray! At every hee it pumped up enough air from its lungs to have contented an organ, and at every haw it vented a shattering blast to which all the slogans of all the clans were mere puling. It brayed its very soul out in the suddenness of the terror. The effect on the leopards was instant and complete. There was just one lightning flash of color,—a yellow streak across the space before me, and plump! the splendid pair soused into a murderous tangle of creeping palms. That they could ever have got out of the awful trap, with its millions of strong spines barbed like fish-hooks and as strong as steel, is probably impossible; but the magnificent promptitude of the suicide, its picturesque completeness, was undeniable.

The ass, however, was by no means soothed by the meteor-like disappearance of the beasts of prey, and the gruesome dronings that, in spite of hard whacks, it indulged in for many minutes, betrayed the depth of its emotions and the cavernous nature of its interior organization. The ass, like the savage, has no perception of the picturesque.

After the morning meal I allowed a three hours' rest, and in knots of twos and threes along the line, the party sat down, talking in subdued tones (for silence was the order of the march), or comfortably snoozing. I slept myself as well as my aching arm would let me. The march resumed, I wheeled the line with its front due west, and after another two hours' rapid advance we found ourselves again at the river, some seven miles farther down its course than the point from which we had started in the morning; and after a hurried meal, I gave the order for home. Striking southeasterly, we crossed in our fifth mile the track of the morning, and in the thirteenth reached our camp. By this means it will be seen we had effectually triangulated a third of a circle of eleven miles radius from our camp—and with absolutely no result. During the next two days I determined to scour, if possible, the remaining semicircle. Meanwhile, we were at the point we had started from, and though it was nearly certain that at any rate one Soko was in the neighborhood, we had fatigued ourselves with nearly seventy miles of marching without finding a trace of it.

As nothing was required from our concealed store, we had only to eat and go to sleep; and so the men, after laughing together for a while over the snug arrangements I had made for the safety of our goods, and pretending to have doubts as to this being the real site of the hidden property of the expedition, were soon asleep in a batch. I went to sleep too; not a sound sleep, for I could not drive from my memory the hideous recollection of that evening, only two days before, when, nearly in the same spot I was lying in the Soko's power. And thinking about it, I got so restless that, under the irresistible impression that some supernatural presence was about me, I unpegged my mosquito net, and getting up, began to pace about. I wore at nights a long Cashmere dressing-gown, in lieu of the tighter canvas coat. I had been leaning against a tree; but feeling that the moisture that trickled down the trunk was soaking my back, I was moving off, when my ears were nearly split by a shout from behind me— "Soko! Soko!" and the next instant I found myself flung violently to the ground, and struggling with— Mabruki! The pain caused by the sudden fall at first made me furious at the mistake that had been made; but the next instant, when the whole absurdity of the position came upon me, I roared with laughter.

The savage is very quickly infected by mirth, and in a minute, as soon as the story got round how Mabruki had jumped upon the master for a Soko, the whole camp was in fits of laughter. Sleep was out of the question with my aching back and aching sides; and so, mixing myself some grog and lighting my pipe, I made Mabruki shampoo my limbs with oil. While he did so he began to talk,—

"Does the master ever see devils?"

"Devils? No."

"Mabruki does, and all the Wanyamwazi of his village do, for his village elders are the keepers of the charm against evil spirits of the whole land of Unyamwazi, and they often see them. I saw a devil to-night."

"Was the devil like a Soko?" I asked, laughing.

"Yes, master," he replied, "like a Soko; but I was always asleep, and never saw it, but whenever it came to me it said, 'I am here,' and then at last I got frightened and got up, and then I saw you, master, and"—

But we were both laughing again, and Mabruki stopped.

It was strange that he, too, should have felt the same uncanny presence that had afflicted me. But under Mabraki's manipulation I soon fell asleep. I awoke with a start. Mabruki had gone. But much the same inexplicable, restless feeling that men say they have felt under ghostly visitations, impelled me to get up, and this time, lighting a pipe to prevent mistakes, I resumed my sauntering, and tired at last of being alone, I awoke my men for the start, although day was not yet breaking half-asleep a meal was soon discussed, and in an hour we were again on the move. Shumari had lagged behind, as usual, and on his coming up I reproved him for being the last.

"I am not the last," he said; "Zaidi, the Wangwana, is not here yet. I saw him climbing up for a liane" (the men got their ropes from these useful plants) "just as I was coming away, and I called out to him that you would be angry."

"Peace!" said Baraka, the man next to me; "is not that Zaidi the Wangwana there, riding on the ass? It was not he. It was that good-for-nothing Tarya. He is always the last to stand up and the first to sit down."

"No doubt, then," said Shumari, "it was Tarya; shame on him. He is no bigger than Zaidi, and has hair like his. Besides, it was in the mist I saw him."

But I had heard enough—the nervousness of the night still afflicted me.

"Sound the halt!" I cried; "call the men together."

In three minutes all were grouped round me—not one was missing! Tarya was far ahead, riding on an ass, and had therefore been one of the first to start.

"Who was the last to leave camp?" I asked, and by the unanimous voice it was agreed to be Shumari himself.

Shumari, then, had seen the Soko! and our storehouse was the Soko's home!

The rest of the men had not heard the preceding conversation, so, putting them in possession of the facts, I gave the order for returning to our camp. We approached. I halted the whole party, and binding up the asses' mouths with cloths, we tied them to a stout liane, and then dividing the party into two, led one myself round to the south side of the camp by a detour, leaving the other about half a mile to the north of it, with orders to rush towards the canebrake and surround it at a hundred yards' distance as soon as they heard my bugle. Passing swiftly round, we were soon in our places, and then, deploying my men on either side so as to cover a semicircle, I sounded the bugle. The response came on the instant, and in a few minutes there was a cordon round the brake at one hundred yards radius, each man about twenty yards or so from the next. But all was silent as the grave. As yet nothing had got through our line, I felt sure; and if therefore Shumari had indeed seen the Soko, the Soko was still within the circle of our guns. A few tufts of young rattan grew between the line and the brake in centre of which were our goods, and unless it was up above us, hidden in the impervious canopy overhead, where was the Soko? A shot was fired into each tuft, and in breathless excitement the circle began to close in upon the brake.

"Let us fire!" cried Mabruki.

"No, no!" I shouted, for the bullets would perhaps have whistled through the lianes amongst ourselves. "Catch the Soko alive if you can."

But first we had to sight the Soko, and this, in an absolutely impenetrable clump of rope-thick creepers, is impossible, except from above. Shumari, as agile as a monkey, was called, and ordered to climb up the tree, the branches of which had served us to sling our goods into the brake, and to see if he could espy the intruder. The lad did not like the job; but with the pluck of his race obeyed, and was soon slung up over the bough, and creeping along it, over-hung the centre of the brake. All faces were upturned towards him as he peered down within the wall of vegetation. For many minutes there was silence, and then came Shumari's voice,—

"No, master, I cannot see the Soko."

"Climb on to the big liane," called out Mabruki. The lad obeyed, and made his way from knot to knot of the swinging strand. One end of it was rooted into the ground at the foot of the tree inside the canebrake, the other, in cable thickness, hanging down loose within the circle. We, watching, saw him look down, and on the instant heard him cry,—

"Ai! ma-ma! the Soko, the Soko!" and while the lad spoke we saw the hanging creeper violently jerked, and then swung to and fro, as if some creature of huge strength had hold of the loose end of it and was trying to shake Shumari from his hold.

"Help! help, master!" cried Shumari. "I am falling;" and then he lost his hold, and fell with a crash down into the brake, and for an instant we held our breath to listen—but all was quiet as death. The next instant, at a dozen different points, axes were at work clearing the lianes. For a few minutes nothing was to be heard but the deep breathing of the straining men and the crashing of the branches; and then on a sudden, at the side farthest from me, came a shout and a shot, a confused rush of frantic animal noises, and the sounds of a fierce struggle.

In an instant I was round the brake, and there lay Shumari, apparently unhurt, and the Soko—dying!

"Untie his hands," I said. This was done, and the wounded thing made an effort to stagger to its feet.

A dozen arms thrust it to the ground again. "Let him rise," I said; "help him to rise;" and Mabruki helped the Soko on to its feet.

Powers above! If this were an ape, what else were half my expedition? The wounded wood-thing passed its right arm round Mabruki's neck, and taking one of his hands, pressed it to its own heart. A deep sob shook its frame, and then it lifted back its head and looked in turn into all the faces round it, with the death-glaze settling fast in its eyes. I came nearer, and took its hand as it hung on Mabruki's shoulder. The muscles, gradually contracting in death, made it seem as if there was a gentle pressure of my palm, and then—the thing died.

Life left it so suddenly that we could not believe that all was over. But the Soko was really dead, and close to where he lay I had him buried.

"Master said he wanted the Soko's skin," said Shumari, in a weak voice, reminding me of my words of a few days before.

"No, no," I said; "bury the wild man quickly. We shall march at once."

Charles De Kay

I

One day the breeze was talking of grand and simple things in the pines that look across the lower bay at Sandy Hook. The great water spaces were a delicious blue, dotted with the white tops of crushed waves; to the left, Coney Island lay mapped out in bleached surfaces, while beyond and seaward, from the purple sleeve formed by the hills of the Navesink, the Hook ran a brown finger eastward. A hawk which nests among the steep inclines of Todt Hill shot out from a neighboring ravine and hung motionless, but never quiet, in the middle distance.

Birds and beasts will make closer approach to a person clothed in dun-colored garments; therefore it was not odd that the hawk should not notice my presence on the pine needles near the crest of the hill. After steering without visible rustle of a feather through the lake of air before me, he stooped all at once, grasped a hedge-sparrow that had been shaking the top of a bush far down the slope, and, rising, bore it to the low branch of a pine not far from my resting-place.

The sun had fallen in a Titanic tragedy of color beyond Prince's Bay. The fierce bird, leisurely occupied in tearing to pieces the little twitterer, was a suitable accompaniment to the bloody drama in the clouds. Watching keenly, I gradually began to picture to myself the sensation of walking unseen to the murderous fowl and suddenly clasping his smooth back with both hands. How startled he would be! But in truth the thought was only a continuation of

53

another that had been floating through my mind while the hawk was wheeling. Unconsciously I had been mumbling to myself from the Nibelungen,—

> "About the tameless dwarf-kin I have heard it said,
> They dwell in hollow mountains; for safety are arrayed
> In what is termed a tarn-kap, of wondrous quality;
> Who hath it on his body preserved is said to be
> From cuttings and from thrustings; of him is none aware
> When he therein is clothed. Both see can he, and hear
> According as he wishes, yet no one him perceives."

The magic cloak, the tarn-kap, I reasoned, with my eyes on the cruel bird, was only a symbol after all, something physical to make real that invisibility which we cannot readily conceive. But suddenly—could my wish have been felt?—the hawk gave a hoarse croak of fright, dropped his prey, and, springing heavily into the air, was gone.

He had not looked at me, he had not seen or heard me, nor could I see, far or near, the slightest cause for his terror. But I heard! Sh-sh-sh—I was aware of a light step in the needles under the tree he had left. Straining my eyes to watch the ground, surely, surely, in a line passing close to my couch, the needles and thin grass were pressed down, as if by a weight applied at even distances! I had remained motionless as a figure of stone, but when a tuft of hepatica, blooming late where the shade was deepest, fell crushed near my hand, I reached out. As luck would have it I was too conscious, too much ashamed at my own folly to act decisively. I did not grasp, I reached out—and touched a living thing.

On such occasions there comes at first the exuberance of joy; then doubt. I had long debated the possibility of invisibles. As far back as I can remember, elfin tales produced an awful wonderment upon my imagination. On long May nights have I not often stolen from the house to watch for elves? A moon after a rain was to my thinking the best for such mysterious beings, when everything was hazy with an imperceptible mist, when the dogwoods

had flooded the landscape with sheets of reflected white, and somebody was drawing one veil after another slowly past a golden shield
in the sky. On such nights, more than once, a boy might have been
seen creeping on tiptoe through the open woods, over the great
clearing, to the hilltop, where, if anywhere, brownies must play.
But none did he espy, nor did the chance-flung cap ever fall upon
his eager, outstretched hands. And if in later years the subject still
fascinated me, it made me feel what the grown man realizes always more clearly, that fables and fairy tales rest on a solid ground-
work of fact. Why, when so many other legends have been verified, should this universal tradition of vanishers and invisibles
prove entirely false?

It occurs to one very soon that animal life does exist of so transparent a texture that to all intents and purposes it is invisible. The
spawn of frogs, the larvæ of certain fresh-water insects, many ma-
rine animals, are of so clear a tissue that they are seen with difficulty. In the tropics a particular inhabitant of smooth seas is as
invisible as a piece of glass, and can be detected only in the love
season by the color which then mingles in its eyes. On reflection a
thousand instances arise of assimilation of animal life to their surroundings, of mimicry of nature with a view to safety. Why, then,
by survival of the most transparent, should not some invisible life
of a high grade hold a secure position on the earth?

Pondering thus, I had been startled not a little by coming now
and again on facts that seemed to bear this out. Strange tracks
through untrodden grass suggested footsteps of the unseen. Flattened spaces of peculiar shape in the standing rye, where human
beings could not have intruded, looked marvellously like human
visitation. Or I lay concealed and watched the crows in a road-side
field. What was it caused them to look up suddenly and flap away
on sooty-fringed wings? No bird, beast, or man came. Then the
rats, scampering about under a dock like so many gaunt Virginia
swine: all at once came a flurry of whisking tails, and they were
off! Yet I had not stirred, nor did anything move on the dock above.
Nevertheless all seemed to realize a common danger, a noise of
some kind,—perhaps a step? Again, you sit like a block while a

snake basks unconscious in the sun, and may watch many hours without event; but sometimes it happens that he raises his head, quivers for an instant his double tongue, and slides off the stump into a bush. At such times put your ear to the earth. Do you not distinguish—or is it all imagination—a sound, a brushing?

It availed me little, then, that I should have considered the subject, or have even gone the length of debating how a man might attain invisibility. Now that I had a tangible proof of the existence of such beings, I was crushed by misgivings. Like many a man before the supposed impossible, I questioned my own sanity. As to the impression, however, the object I had touched or fancied I had touched was at once hard and soft, smooth and rough; I recalled it as each of these in turn, for it was moving, and at the moment of contact bounded away as if at the shock of a galvanic current. To my excited mind the dusky woods were becoming oppressive, and so, like the hawk, but slowly and pondering, I betook myself home.

Who that has walked or run through autumn woods at night has not sometimes looked curiously over his shoulder at the sound of following steps? It always proves to be dry leaves whirled after you in your rapid course; but this evening my gait was slow, and the leaves of last year were hard to find; nor could I account, except on the ground of nervous illusion, for the pattering that followed in my rear. Yet there it was, albeit so gentle that had I not stretched every sense to the utmost I am confident no sound would have penetrated to my consciousness. And it was evident that I was thoroughly imposed upon by it, for when the small, irregular pond was reached, which, with a cypress-scattered hillock, occupies the highest point of the main hill to the westward, I halted a moment and considered. How, thought I, will this unseen attendant cross a piece of water? Throwing off my shoes I waded over a shallow arm of the pond, and sat down to watch. Presently in the twilight two wedges of ruffled water were discerned advancing swiftly across the surface,—just such tracks as serpents make in swimming,—a light touch was heard on the bank, and all was still. But then a sudden disgust, unreasoning and childish, mastered me completely; a wave of doubt greater than before filled me with disdain of my own imbecility, and I hastened through the orchard to my home, and flung myself into an arm-chair near the window.

The place I had selected long ago as a quiet refuge was a low veranda farm-house, hidden away from north winds under the crest of a hill, and crept over by many rods of honey- suckle. Events had so affected me that I considered nothing left in life but an alternation of hard work and of utter retreat from humanity, and had disposed me favorably toward the ancient apple orchard, and the meagre vegetable and flower garden, which alone remained of a former farm. The barns, the plowed lands, and the fences had disappeared. Only a heavy stone wall with flagged top, which protected the garden from the road, reminded one of a former powerful owner. From the veranda no house was visible; the eye had to travel many miles across the flat lower country to the bay before the distant ships recalled a busy world.

Here, beside myself, lived no one save Rachel, a woman whose Indian origin made it impossible to guess her age. Although she claimed for herself the purest descent from an Indian tribe of a headland a hundred miles to the eastward, and although her features were not without strong marks of her claim, yet in strict truth she was so much mixed with African blood that with most persons she would pass for a negress. Rachel had a talent for cooking breakfasts and suppers from little apparent supply; she was taciturn to speechlessness, hence our intercourse was never marred by discord; and while her box was kept supplied with strong tobacco, a slender meal of some kind was never wanting; and it was served in silence.

For two years Rachel and I had lived in this silent, limited partnership. My home was cool and soundless as the grave, a place in which the mind could stretch its shriveled wings, where everything could be done mechanically and without fear of a sudden jar into disagreeable reality. When of an afternoon I stepped from the hurrying world into the first quiet woods on the way to my home, a great door swung to behind me and another life began, in which Rachel's figure and swarthy, heavy-featured face had long ceased to interfere with my meditation.

This night, however, before the meal was served, the kitchen door opened and my housekeeper's inscrutable dull eyes rolled around the walls of the room; then it closed. What had happened? Why on this night had Rachel noticed my arrival? At supper I broke our unspoken compact and addressed her.

"Rachel, what made you look in just now? Has anything happened?"

The woman made no reply, yet there was evidence in her manner that she was groping for an answer. Presently to a second demand she made a reply that startled me:

"Heard two of you."

So, another ear had detected the steps as well as my own! Then the being, whatever it was, must be in the room, possibly at my elbow; or, seated perchance on that chair before me, was regarding me steadfastly! Except for the excitement bred of a new sensation, it was not a pleasant thought; nevertheless, I pulled a second chair to the table and filled a second plate with food; then, with my eyes fixed on the plate, continued the meal. It was all in vain. Nothing further was seen or heard.

This was my first definite encounter with that unseen which I would have called a spirit had I been a spiritualist. But I could not force myself to the gross materialism of calling this invisible existence a spirit, for tangibility was a quality I could not associate with pure spirit, and I had touched it.

Having once followed me, it seemed thenceforth to take up quarters in my house, at least for the evening and morning hours of the day, and strange as it was, I soon learned to regard the presence of a third person as an established fact; indeed, I came to believe that in some instances a faint breathing might be detected. Nevertheless I would not leave anything to the possibilities of imagination, but was always experimenting, with a view to prove still more clearly that there was no illusion possible. To this end a brass and steel rod, fitted between the floor and a projection from the wall, was connected with an indicator which moved in a large are when the slightest touch shook the floor. By this means my ears were reinforced by sight.

I also began systematically to conceal from the unknown guest the fact that I suspected its presence; but at last the point was reached where, to protect my own reason, it must be settled whether it was all a series of illusions or a sober truth.

For by dint of thought a scheme had been perfected, and on a Sunday morning, when as usual Rachel had disappeared, no man has ever known whither; when, according to its custom, the strange visitant had also, to all appearance, withdrawn,—on a Sunday morning I hastened to put my plan in action. On the main floor in the rear of the house was a chamber, into which the sounds had sometimes intruded, which was small, bare, and lighted by one deep window looking directly out on the orchard. This window I had grated strongly with heavy wire on the outside, where the orchard hill rose steeply from the house; and over against the window, in the wall between chamber and dining-room, was a high closet, in which I had stored a strong net, such as fishermen use for their seines. Fastening stout wires to the ceiling from one end of the room to the other, to be used for slides, and rigging several small blocks above the window and near the floor, I stretched the necessary ropes from closet to blocks and back again, laid everything ready for instant use, cleared the room of furniture, and awaited events.

There was no fear of interruption from Rachel, for during the years we had lived together I had never seen her on a Sabbath. Every Monday she was at her post, although laboring under some excitement, which showed itself in mutterings and a certain wild gesture that I had learned to attach no importance to. There was no fear that I should not have the invisible to myself.

Evening came to close a sultry day with growls of distant thunder and sudden flares of light behind Navesink Hills; the bushes drooped languidly; only the tree-toads were clamorous, and their jubilee was a mournful one on every side. I was sitting by the west window with my head on my breast, and, now that the crisis had come, almost apathetic to the presence itself, when its approach took place. It seemed to stop near my chair, as if it regarded me closely. I had been before in singular predicaments, but it seemed to me this was the most trying. I felt that I must look very pale, but with an affectation of indifference I arose, walked across the room and entered the bed-chamber. In a moment I understood that the unseen had likewise passed the sill and had entered the room; then I slammed the door, locked it, and put the key in my pocket.

Everything had been made ready to cope with a material and not a supernatural being; still it was purely a venture, and at no previous time had there seemed so little hope of success. Nevertheless not a moment was lost in hauling out the net and placing it in position across the room so that it hung straight, filling the space between wall and wall, and ceiling and floor. Then I began to draw it down the room by means of the ropes, and on the axis of the chamber, so that its edges passed smoothly along ceiling, walls, and floor. The anxious moment was at hand.

All the running gear had to be worked evenly; at the same time every nerve was strained in order to detect the slightest bulge in the upright net, should it come in contact with a tangible body.

Until three quarters of the room had been sifted nothing occurred. Then I saw the edge against the left-hand wall carefully drawn aside; to spring forward and close the opening was the instinctive work of a second. Terror combining with a fierce delight lent me an extraordinary force; I drew with convulsive power on the ropes. Every moment an invisible hand seemed to lift the net at some point, but each attempt was luckily frustrated. At last the movements ceased, and I drew the net flat against the farther wall. With feverish haste my hand travelled over its entire surface; the net was scanned in profile for the impression of a body, but there was none. The game had either escaped or withdrawn into the deep window-seat.

Now came a moment for breath, and for reflection. Again the cynical cloud of doubt folded me in. Dupe of my own morbid imagination, I should stand convicted of monomania in the eyes of any reasonable being who should see my actions. Then it was best, was it not? to tear the net away; or should I deliberately pursue to the utmost a plan begun? Never before had I so clearly felt a dual existence urging to opposite courses of action, as if the body's instinct commanded an advance, while the mind, assailing the whole proceeding with ridicule, was for giving up the game. But for all that it was a good sign that I began to feel a slight awe at the near possibility of a discovery. For I retreated to the door, unlocked it, and stood irresolute; then returned again to the window, without strength to come to a decision.

But while I pondered, a low, chuckling noise startled me, and Rachel stood by my side, erect and with features full of energy, her dull eyes blazing, and her short straight hair tossed about; in her hand she brandished with exultation a carved rod hung with bright claws and shells, with lappets of fur and hair; and at her and it I gazed with speechless amazement. Had she too gone mad? She took a few steps, as if in a rude dance, and shook the stick, and while her eyes glared into mine she nodded her head to the time.

"Bad spirit!" she muttered. "I have known, I have heard. But this is strong Wabeno."

As she shook the talisman, which clinked and rattled like the toy of a devil, I snatched the medicine stick from her hand and motioned her to the door. Thither she retreated, muttering words of an unknown tongue, and when it closed upon her I flung the stick angrily on the floor. But hope had come, and decision as well, although from a despised quarter; I was resolved to finish the undertaking at all hazards.

The wild flames of the distant storm still lighted everything at intervals with an intensity now greater and now less. When the sheet lightning flashed strong, the square cage formed by the wire outside the window-seat and the fish-net within stood out clear against the northern sky. With dilated pupils I began to examine the inclosed cube of air. During one particularly long and vivid flash,—there, in that corner, was there not a heap, a translucent shape, indistinguishable in quality or form? It was enough. Swiftly as wild beasts when they spring, I raised the net, leaped into the window, and grasped toward the corner where I thought I saw the mass.

II

A thrill runs through the nerves of an entomologist when he puts his hand on a specimen unknown, undescribed. The hunter

trembles when he espies in the thicket the royal hart whose existence has been called a fable. My emotion was all of this, intensi-
fied; nearer, perhaps, to the feeling of the elected mortal who has
discovered a new continent. For I had discovered a new world.

Had I not cause for exultation? I sat on the window-seat in the
alternate light and darkness, with one hand clenched, the other
arm curved in the air; my left held fast a slender wrist, while my
right was cast about a pair of delicate shoulders; the invisible but
tangible figure was crouched away into the smallest space in the
corner of the window.

With awe I now realized that my capture was a woman. The
delicate moulding of the shoulders and hand was proof enough,
but I also felt on my arm a light flood of the silkiest hair. This was
a shock to one who had lived apart from women for several years,
and had good cause to expect nothing but disaster from their influence. For a moment the impulse was strong to release the captive; luckily reason prevailed, and I tightened my grip on the frail
prize, whose frame was shaken with sobs and whose bearing de-
noted the most abject despair. I gave many timid reassurances by
word and hand before the sobs came slower and fear began to loose
its hold. As she raised her head I took occasion to pass my right
hand lightly over her face. Rendered sensitive by strong excitement,
my palm read her features as the blind read the raised print of their
books, and of this at least I was sure: the features were human,
straight, the eyes large; a full chin and a mouth of unspeakable
fineness were divined rather than felt by my flying touch; but I
found no trace of tears.

After this I do not know how long we sat. It seemed peaceful
and homelike, so that I wondered how it was possible so quickly to
forget wonder. A protective warmth toward the creature whose soft
breathing came and went; slower and slower near my face took a
quiet hold on all my senses. At last the gentle head drooped like a
tired child's, the delicate shoulders heaved in a long, peaceful sigh,
and to my amazement the strange captive fell asleep in my arms.

So while she slept I sat motionless and thinking, thinking. Who
was she? whence and of what order of beings? What was her language;

how and how long did she live. Was she really alive in our sense of the word, that is, human with the exception of her transparency? and was her shape like that of ordinary mortals, or did she end in some monstrosity like a mermaid? Such were the questions agitating me when interruption came with a knock at the door. My captive awoke and instinctively started away, at the same time giving a low, articulate cry; but I held her firmly, and called to Rachel to bring me a certain relic of slavery which had been brought from the South. I had profited by the discovery my prisoner's awakening furnished: the invisible, I argued, could articulate, then why should she not understand and speak the language of the people among whom she was found? Accordingly a few rapid questions were put to her, which were unanswered. Then I bethought me of a proof that at any rate she understood my words.

"My dear child, it is mere perverseness in you to refuse an answer. I am sure you understand. You are in my power for good or evil, and if you refuse to speak I must consider you worthy of the following treatment: you shall be made an example to the crowd of the reality of invisible life."

Under cruel treatment of this kind, conjecture became certainty; I felt her shudder at the idea, and she laid her hand appealingly on mine. This was all I wanted; speech was now a mere affair of time.

Rachel entered with the rusty handcuffs and handed them to me as if she were conscious and acquiescent in what I did. Not a feature moved, only her eyes shone with inner excitement, in a way I had seen before, while I clasped one link about the unseen wrist.

"Pardon," I whispered, "I do not know you yet. I cannot trust you."

My daily work ceased. To the few inquiries from the great city Rachel had evasive answers ready; they were soon over, and I was left to experience the fascination of a beautiful woman whom I had never seen nor could hope ever to see. To be sure, in certain lights and under certain angles of reflection an indistinct outline of a not large, slender girl, which told of pure contours, could be made out, but this was like following the glassy bells that pulsate far down in the waves of northern seas, or the endeavor to catch the real surface of a mirror. Moreover, the slim captive herself resented any attempt to gain acquaintance with her through the eyes. But by degrees the reserve which had taken the place of her terror melted away before gentle and respectful management, and from her own lips I learned much concerning her marvelous race, before the love which presently overwhelmed us put an end to the cooler interests of reason. Thus she astonished me by speaking of her race as widely spread through almost every inhabited land. They never work or educate their children; their food, which is chiefly in liquid form, is taken from the stores laid up by human beings, and such education as they get is picked up by continual contact with mortals. While their passions would seem to be calm, their only laws relate to the observance of secrecy as to their presence on the earth. To secure this end they meet at stated periods and renew their solemn vows, keep a watch upon each other, and disperse again to a settled or wandering life, but one always dependent on the labors of other beings. This alone would explain the paramount importance attaching to secrecy. And as it is impossible to keep always all hint of their existence from human beings, the penalties for disclosure in the latest days have increased to far greater severity than was used in simpler ages; Manmat'ha could not be brought to tell me the fate which awaited her should it be discovered that she had revealed the great secret of her nation, and the very quiet with which she gave me to understand how vast was the danger impressed me more than the most violent words.

It must have been the pain that the thought of any harm befalling her produced in me, which opened my eyes to the strength of my passion. The time for questions had passed, and the days were long only that we might love. One day glided after another unheeded, while we strolled about the neighboring woody hills to catch a broad glimpse of the sea from this point, or to examine in that swampy valley the minute wonders of life in plants and insects. At an early stage of our intimacy I had begged to free her wrist from the handcuffs, but she had implored me to continue at least the appearance of slavery, to serve, in case of need, as a partial excuse for violation of her vows. This did not prevent her daily disappearance during the middle hours when the sun was strongest; but these absences only served to give a time for reflection on her beauties and to involve me deeper in the love which now mastered all my thoughts. There was one subject which was long in broaching, but when the necessary courage was summoned, found in Manmat'ha neither objection nor response. She did not comprehend its force. The subject was our marriage.

I had resolved on legal marriage, even if it were necessary to be content with only one witness to the ceremony; that witness could be no one except Rachel. My housekeeper had regarded my preparations and subsequent conduct with a consistent interest and without the least shadow of surprise, and once I remarked that she had caught sight in the twilight of a cup raised without hands; yet no hint fell from her lips to make me feel she was intruding on my affairs. The old blur was in her eyes; the only change in manner was her treatment of me: she regarded me with a kind of awe. And after it had proved abortive to tell her something and not all, because the pleasure of unbosoming myself of so much love was too great to restrain, I found Rachel not only full of faith, but even surpassing me. She looked upon Manmat'ha as a supernatural being, and plainly invested me with reflected holiness. Some sort of worship she thought due to Manmat'ha, whilst I, as high priest and mortal consort, was entitled to a share; and indeed it was with some difficulty that I persuaded her not to show her faith by uncouth rites. It was as if her life had been a preparation for some such affair as this, and found her enthusiastic, but not astonished.

Our favorite resort was the couch of pine needles looking south from the hillside where we first met. The same hawk, to me the most blessed of birds, would often sail as before in the middle distance, or night-hawks would cut their strange curves in the evening sky. Far out beyond, sea-gulls, mere specks of white, would wheel and plunge into the bay, and at our backs the woodcock, shy enough in any other presence, would whir fantastically through the woods. All nature was the same, but I was no longer its solitary admirer, for I held in my arms a gentle framework of delight such as no other man before or since has known. She was finer than the finest silk, smoother than the smoothest glass, as if the rays of light, falling on the amazing texture of her skin, found no inequalities from which to reflect.

One evening we had been drawing in long breaths of that delight of which the woods and the great bowl of landscape before us were so full, and I had been trying to convince Manmat'ha of the importance of the marriage ceremony. "What," I asked with some trouble in my heart, "what will they do to you in case members of your nation discover your position? I do not mean to ask you what you would not tell me before, but what would be their first step?"

"They would imprison me somewhere under a guard," said Manmat'ha. "It would be many months before a tribunal could be collected together, and still longer before I should be judged. What my fate would be then, it is not well to say."

Had I desired, there is little doubt that I could have compelled Manmat'ha to tell me all she knew, for I had found that my will was much the stronger. But what was curiosity compared with the delight of warming her into responsive love? When I now covered her delicious lips with kisses, she returned the pressure, instead of merely suffering me, as at first, with a mild surprise.

"My first love and my last!" I whispered. "They shall not get you from me while I am alive, if they will only give us warning; but if they rob me of you, I shall follow your trace and rescue you, if it be to the bottom of the sea!"

Manmat'ha laughed a pleased laugh. We both started at an echo, a moment after, which seemed to come from the lower hill, below where we sat. There was no echo possible in that direction.

"Manmat'ha!" I whispered, "tell me quickly! Is some one coming?"

She sat apparently unable to speak, but trembling and cold to the touch. I had enough presence of mind to take her up and place her on the other side of the pine, on the ground, and throw my coat carelessly over her. As once before I heard passing steps, but now my more practiced ear caught them distinctly. They came lightly up the steep hill and stopped a moment at a little distance from the tree. With eyes fixed on the ocean I waited in an agony of suspense, assuming the most unconscious air of which I was capable. The steps hesitated only a moment; then they passed lower and lower into the upper wood. For half an hour neither of us moved; at last, taking heart, we stole home.

The event set me thinking. If at any moment we were liable to be discovered and separated, the marriage must take place at once. A consumptive hastens his wedding, a wounded tree is quick to bear, and the night we had experienced taught me how slight was the thread on which my happiness hung; but Manmat'ha was calm with a maidenly content with little, which in my hasty resentment at even a suspicion of opposition to my plan, I was ready to call indifference.

When we entered I could tell by the unfailing sign of Rachel's eye that she was agitated. Later in the evening I heard her chanting in a discordant undertone an ancient formula of her savage ancestors, and therefore it was with some misgivings that I called and informed her that to-night she was to be the sole witness, by touch, if not by sight, of the lawful ceremony of wedlock between Manmat'ha and me. She listened in an awestruck silence, and left the room abruptly. As no calling was of any avail, we were compelled to wait her pleasure, which I did with great impatience; and when at last she did return, it was in a shape grotesque almost beyond recognition. Her face and arms were painted white and red in broad bands of coarse pigments; an old embroidered robe fastened over one shoulder, with a close-fitting skirt of buckskin, formed her whole attire. She had put feathers in her hair, and with flaming eyes shook her favorite talisman, the medicine-stick. At one bound she had returned to her ancient state of savagery.

Finding Manmat'ha regarding her with interest, I did not oppose the further proceedings. It struck me that it was not displeasing to my invisible love to receive divine honors even in this wild rite, so I held my peace. She seemed to receive them as her due.

The moon had risen, and gave light to the room through window and open door; flooded by its rays, Rachel moved slowly across the room, uttering in guttural tones a broken chant whose meaning I might have once interpreted, but could not now. On a different occasion I might not have been an entirely unsympathetic observer of the singular sight, but here passion had overcome curiosity. I was an impatient lover. With my arm about Manmat'ha, and filled with earnest emotions, I could not help a feeling of disgust at the monotonous discord and frantic gestures of the last of a superstitious race.

"This must end, Manmat'ha," I groaned. "I can wait no longer."

As I spoke, the Indian woman grew ungovernable in wild excitement.

"They are on you! They are here!" she screamed.

I felt Manmat'ha stiffen in my arms with deadly terror. Resistless hands dragged us apart and held me absolutely motionless in spite of the deadly agony which filled me, while Manmat'ha's stifled shriek arose from midway across the room.

"Rachel!" I cried. "For God's sake, Rachel, bar the door!"

My cry roused the woman from a stupor; she sprang to the door. I heard the noise of many light feet, the sound of a blow, a heavy fall; then a deep silence came.

Bounding from the spot to which unseen hands up to that moment had pressed me, I sprang from the room and followed into the night. The earth reeled past me in my swift flight, until I suddenly stopped myself to ask where I was going. Where indeed? As well follow the wind. Wild as was the hope that moved me to return, I hurried back again to the house. Rachel alone, clad in her poor Indian finery, the medicine-stick broken by her side, lay stretched out dead in the moonlight.

A Haunt of the Jinkarras
(A Fearsome Story of Central Australia)

Ernest Favenc

In May, 1889, the dead body of a man was found on one of the tributaries of the Finke River, in the extreme North of South Australia. The body, by all appearances, had been lying there for months and was accidentally discovered by some surveyors making a flying survey with camels. Amongst the few effects was a diary containing the following narrative, which although in many places almost illegible and much weather-stained, has been since, with some trouble, deciphered and transcribed by the surveyor in charge of the party, and forwarded to *The Bulletin* for publication.—

Transcribed from the Dead Man's Diary.

March 10, 1888.—Started out this morning with Jackson, who is the only survivor of a party of three who lost their horses on a dry stage when looking for country; he was found and cared for by the blacks, and finally made his way into the telegraph-line, where I picked him up when out with a repairing-party. Since then I got him a job on the station, and in return he has told me about the ruby-field of which we are now in search; thanks to the late thunderstorms we have as yet met with no obstacles to our progress. I have great faith in him as a bushman, but being a man without any education and naturally taciturn, he is not very lively company, and I find myself thrown on to the resource of a diary for amusement.

March 17.—Seven days since we left Charlotte Waters, and we are now approaching the country familiar to Jackson during his

69

sojourn with the natives two years ago. He is confident that we shall gain the gorge in the M'Donnell Ranges to-morrow, early.

March 18.—Amongst the ranges, plenty of water, and Jackson has recognised several peaks in the near neighbourhood of the gorge, where he saw the rubies.

March 19.—Camped in Ruby Gorge, as I have named this pass, for we have come straight to the place and found the rubies without any hindrance at all. I have about twenty magnificent stones and hundreds of small ones; one of the stones in particular is almost living fire, and must be of great value. Jackson has no idea of the value of the find, except that it may be worth a few pounds, with which he will be quite satisfied. As there is good feed and water, and we have plenty of rations, will camp here for a day or two and spell the horses before returning.

March 20.—Been inspecting some caves in the ranges. One of them seems to penetrate a great distance—will go tomorrow with Jackson and take candles and examine it.

March 25.—Had a terrible experience the last four days. Why did I not return at once with the rubies? Now I may never get back. Jackson and I started to explore the cave early in the morning. We found nothing extraordinary about it for some time. As usual there were numbers of bats, and here and there were marks of fire on the rocks, as though the natives had camped in it at times. After some search, Jackson discovered a passage which we followed down a steep incline for a long distance. As we got on we encountered a strong draught of air and had to be very careful of our candles. Suddenly the passage opened and we found ourselves in a low chamber in which we could scarcely stand upright. I looked hastily around, and saw a dark figure like a large monkey suddenly spring from a rock and disappear with what sounded like a splash. "What on earth was that?" I said to Jackson. "A jinkarra," he replied, in his slow, stolid way. "I heard about them from the blacks; they live underground."

"What are they?" I asked.

"I couldn't make out," he replied; "the blacks talked about jinkarras, and made signs that they were underground, so I suppose that was one."

We went over to the place where I had seen the figure and, as the air was now comparatively still and fresh, our candles burnt well and we could see plainly. The splash was no illusion, for an underground stream of some size ran through the chamber, and, on looking closer, in the sand on the floor of the cavern we could see tracks like those of human feet.

We sat down and had something to eat. The water was beautifully fresh and icily cold, and I tried to extract from Jackson all he knew about the jinkarras. It was very little beyond what he had already told me. The natives spoke of them as something, animals or men, he could not make out which, living in the ranges under ground. They used to frighten the children by crying out "jinkarra!" to them at night.

The stream that flowed through the cavern was very sluggish and apparently not deep, as I could see the white sand at a distance under the rays of the candle; it disappeared beneath a rocky arch about two feet above its surface. Strange to say, when near this place I could detect a peculiar smell as of something burning, and this odour appeared to come through the arch. I drew Jackson's attention to it, and proposed wading down the channel of the stream if not too deep, but he suggested going back to camp first and getting more rations, which being very reasonable, I agreed to.

It took us too long returning to camp to think of starting that day, but next morning we got away early and were soon beside the subterranean stream. The water was bitterly cold but not very deep, and we had provided ourselves with stout saplings as poles and had our revolvers and some rations strapped on our shoulders. It was a nasty wade through the chilly water, our heads nearly touching the slimy top of the arch, our candles throwing a faint, flickering gleam on the surface of the stream. Fortunately the bottom was splendid—hard, smooth sand—and, after wading for about twenty minutes, we suddenly emerged into another cavern, but its extent we could not discern at first, for our attention was taken up with other matters.

The air was laden with pungent smoke, the place illuminated with a score of smouldering fires, and tenanted by a crowd of the most hideous beings I ever saw. They espied us in an instant, and flew wildly about, jabbering frantically, until we were nearly deafened. Recovering ourselves, we waded out of the water, and tried to approach some of these creatures; but they hid away in the dark corners, and we could not lay hands on any of them. As well as we could make out in the murky light, they were human beings, but savages of the most degraded type, far below that of the common Australian blackfellow. They had long arms, shaggy heads of hair, small twinkling eyes, and were very low of stature. They kept up a confused jabber, half whistling, half chattering, and were utterly without clothes, paint, or any ornaments. I approached one of their fires, and found it to consist of a kind of peat or turf; some small bones of vermin were lying around, and a rude club or two. While gazing at these things I suddenly heard a piercing shriek, and, looking up, found that Jackson, by a sudden spring, had succeeded in capturing one of these creatures, who was struggling and uttering terrible yells. I went to his assistance, and together we succeeded in holding him still while we examined him by the light of our candles. The others, meanwhile, ceased their clamour and watched us curiously.

Never had I seen so repulsive a wretch as our prisoner. Apparently he was a young man about two or three and twenty, hardly five feet high at the outside, lean, with thin legs and long arms. He was trembling all over, and the perspiration dripped from him. He had scarcely any forehead, and a shaggy mass of hair crowned his head, and grew a long way down his spine. His eyes were small, red and bloodshot; I have often experienced the strong odour emitted by aborigines when heated or excited, but never did I meet with anything so offensive as the rank smell emanating from this being. Suddenly Jackson exclaimed: "Look! look! he's got a tail!" I looked and nearly relaxed my grasp of the brute in surprise. There was no doubt about it, this strange being had about three inches of a monkey-like tail.

"Let's catch another," I said to Jackson after the first emotion of surprise had passed. We looked around after sticking our candles upright in the sand. "There's one in the corner," muttered Jackson

to me, and as soon as I saw the one he meant we released our prisoner and made a simultaneous rush at the cowering form. We were
successful, and when we dragged our captive to the light we found
it to be a woman. Our curiosity was soon satisfied—the tail was the
badge of the whole tribe, and we let our second captive go.

My first impulse was to go and rinse my hands in the stream,
the contact had been so repulsive to me. It was the same with Jackson. I pondered what I should do. I had a great desire to take one
of these singular beings back with me, and I thought with pride of
the reputation I should gain as their discoverer. Then I reflected
that I could always find them again, and it would be better to come
back with a larger party after safely disposing of the rubies and
securing the ground.

"There's no way out of this place," I said to Jackson.

"Think not?" he replied.

"No," I said, "or these things would have cleared out; they must
know every nook and cranny."

"Umph!" he said, as though satisfied; "shall we go back now?"

I was on the point of saying "yes," and had I done so all would
have been well, but, unfortunately, some motive of infernal curiosity prompted me to say— "No! let us have a look round first."
Lighting another candle each, so that we had plenty of light, we
wandered round the cave, which was of considerable extent, the
unclean inhabitants flitting before us with beast-like cries. Presently we had made a half-circuit of the cave and were approaching
the stream, for we could hear a rushing sound as though it plunged
over a fall. This noise grew louder, and now I noticed that all the
natives had disappeared and it struck me that they had retreated
through the passage we had penetrated, which was now unguarded.
Suddenly Jackson, who was ahead, exclaimed that there was a large
opening. As he spoke he turned to enter it; I called out to him to be
careful, but my voice was lost in a cry of alarm as he slipped, stumbled,
and with a shriek of horror disappeared from my view. So sudden
was the shock, and so awful my surroundings, that I sank down utterly unnerved, comprehending but one thing: that I was alone in
this gruesome cavern inhabited by strange, unnatural creations.

After a while I braced myself up, and began to look about. Holding my candle aloft I crawled on my stomach to the spot whence my companion had disappeared. My hand touched a slippery decline; peering cautiously ahead I saw that the rocks sloped abruptly downwards, and were covered with slime, as though under water at times. One step on the treacherous surface and a man's doom was sealed—headlong into the unknown abyss he was bound to go, and this had been the fate of the unhappy Jackson. As I lay trembling on the edge of this fatal chasm, listening for the faintest sound from below, it struck me that the noise of the rushing water was both louder and nearer. I lay and listened. There was no doubt about it—the waters were rising. With a thrill of deadly horror it flashed across me that if the stream rose it would prevent my return, as I could not thread the subterranean passage under water. Rising hastily I hurried back to the upper end of the cavern, following the edge of the water. A glance assured me I was a prisoner—the flood was up to the top of the arch, and the stream much broader than when we entered. The rations and candles we had left carelessly on the sand had disappeared, covered by the rising water. I was alone, with nothing but about a candle and a half between me and darkness and death.

I blew out the candle, threw myself on the sand and tried to think calmly. I brought all my courage to bear on the prospect before me, so as not to let it daunt me. First, the natives had evidently retreated before the water rose too high, their fires were all out, and a dead silence reigned. I had the cavern to myself, which was better than their horrid company. Next, the rising was periodical, and evidently caused the sliminess of the rock, which had robbed me of my only companion. I remembered instances in the interior where lagoons rose and fell at certain times without any visible cause. Then came the thought—for how long would the overflow continue? I had fresh air and plenty of water, and so I could live for days; probably the flood only lasted twelve or twenty-four hours. But a deadly fear seized on me. Could I maintain my reason in this worse than Egyptian darkness—a darkness so thick, definite and palpable as to be indescribable, truly a darkness that could be felt? I had heard of men who could not endure twenty-four hours in a dark cell, but had clamoured to be taken out. Supposing my reason deserted me, and during some delirious interlude the stream rose and fell again!

These thoughts were too agonising. I rose and paced a step or two on the sand. I made a resolution during that short walk. I had matches—fortunately, with a bushman's instinct, I had put a box in my pouch when we started to investigate the cavern. I had a candle and a half, and, thank Heaven! my watch. I would calculate four hours as nearly as possible, and every four hours I would strike a match and enjoy the luxury of a little light. I pursued this plan, and by doing so left that devilish pit with my reason. It was sixty hours before the stream fell, and what I suffered during that time no tongue can tell, no brain imagine.

That awful darkness was at times peopled by forms which, for hideousness, no nightmare could surpass. Invisible, but still present, they surrounded and sought to drive me down the chasm wherein my companion had fallen. The loathsome inhabitants of that cavern came back in fancy and gibbered and whistled around me. I could smell them—feel their sickening touch. If I slept I awoke from, perhaps a pleasant dream to the stern fact that I was alone in darkness in the depth of the earth. When first I found that the water was receding was perhaps the hardest time of all, for my anxiety to leave the chamber tenanted by such phantoms was over-powering. But I resisted. I held to my will until I knew I could safely venture, and then waded slowly and determinedly up the stream; up the sloping passage, through the outer cave, and emerged in the light of day—the blessed, glorious light, with a wild shout of joy.

I must have fainted: when I came to myself I was still at the mouth of the cave, but now it was night, the bright, starlit, lonely, silent night of the Australian desert. I felt no hunger nor fear of the future; one delicious sense of rest and relief thrilled my whole being. I lay there watching the dearly-loved Austral constellations in simple, peaceful ecstasy. And then I slept, slept till the sun aroused me, and I took my way to our deserted camp. A few crows arose and cawed defiantly at me, and the leather straps bore the marks of a dingo's teeth, otherwise the camp was untouched. I lit a fire, cooked a meal, ate, and rested once more. The reaction had set in after the intense strain I had endured, and I felt myself incapable of thinking or purposing anything. This state lasted for four-and-twenty hours—then I awoke to the fact that I had to find the horses, and make my way home alone—for, alas, as I bitterly thought, I was now, through my curiosity, alone, and, worst of all had been the cause of my companion's death. Had I come away when he proposed, he would be alive, and I should have escaped the terrible experience I have endured.

I have written this down while it is fresh in my memory; to-morrow I start to look for the horses. If I reach the telegraph-line safely I will come back and follow up the discovery of this unknown race, the connecting and long-sought-for link; if not, somebody else may find this and follow up the clue. I have plotted out the course from Charlotte Waters here by dead-reckoning.

March 26th.—No sign of the horses. They have evidently made back. I will make up a light pack and follow them. If I do not overtake them I may be able to get on to the line on foot. The stages between the water-holes on our way out were not very long, and I ought to manage it safely.

End of the Diary

Note.—The surveyor, who is well-known in South Australia, adds the following postscript:—

"The unfortunate man was identified as an operator on the overland line. He had been in the service a long time, and was very much liked. The facts about picking up Jackson when out with a repairing party have also been verified. The dead man had obtained six months' leave of absence, and it was supposed he had gone down to Adelaide. The tradition of jinkarras is common among the natives of the McDonnell Range. I have often heard it. No rubies or anything of value were found on the body."

FROM A SIMIAN POINT OF VIEW

H. Knight Horsfield

"Well, what do you think of it?" said Gerald Newton at last.

The object referred to was a skeleton—or rather parts of a skeleton, for many important bones, including the skull, were missing—which was stretched out on a long table. The Rev. Regius Professor of Obsolete Theologies at St. Boniface's, who prided himself upon his knowledge of anatomy, examined the bones again with an obviously professional air.

"A gorilla—I see," he said.

Newton looked at him with a curious expression upon his face. "I wish you were right," he said suddenly, with a warmth which seemed out of keeping with the nature of his subject.

"Why should you doubt it?" said the Professor. "I do not see how, speaking, of course, without mature consideration, it could possibly belong to any other of the anthropoid apes."

Newton remained silent, staring gloomily before him.

"Let us investigate this matter fully," he said at length, "before we offer any opinion. I have already noted down some rough observations upon the structural peculiarities of the specimen. Will you kindly help me to verify them? In the first place," he went on, "I narrow the inquiry, so far as I may do so with perfect safety, by taking it for granted that the skeleton is that of a true anthropoid ape. You would, of course, assent to that?"

The Professor nodded. "Of course," he said, without looking up.

"In the next place, then, we may, of course, pass by the gibbons. Apart from the question of size, the extreme relative length

77

of hand and arm so characteristic of the gibbons (*Hylobates*) is too conspicuous by its absence here" —indicating the skeleton— "to make further inquiry on that head necessary. Now we come to the orang. As you are aware, the length of the entire foot of the orang, as compared with that of the backbone, is strikingly great. In the present case, please observe that, although tremendously strong, the length is not very remarkable. Again, note the hand of our specimen. You see there is no marked discrepancy in the relative lengths of thumb and fingers; the orang, on the contrary, has the absolutely longest hand and the shortest thumb, as compared with the forefingers, of all the anthropoids."

The Rev. Professor reflected for a few moments. "Yes," he said; "the creature is plainly not an orang. There is nothing now for it but the gorilla or chimpanzee."

Newton was leaning against the table with the same grave, almost distressed, look in his face.

"Count the ribs," he said dryly.

The Professor did so. Then, in evident surprise, he looked up suddenly at Newton.

"Why," he exclaimed, "there are only twelve pairs!"

"Exactly," returned the other; "that is precisely my difficulty. Now, I need not inform so eminent a zoologist as yourself that no gorilla or chimpanzee has ever been discovered with less than thirteen. Again, count the wrist-bones. If I mistake not, there are only eight. If the skeleton were that of either a chimpanzee or a gorilla there would be nine."

The Professor remained silent, with an utterly blank expression on his face.

"Well, I must say" —he remarked slowly, after a time— "I'm quite at a loss. It would appear that there is no animal which fulfils the latter condition, with the exception of man."

"Ah!" said Newton, with something like a sigh. "So you are brought to bay at last in that far-away hypothesis. But I can't leave you in peace even there. In the first place, I may inform you that these bones are the remains of an animal which was shot by my friend the Rev. Dr. Frankland, a very worthy missionary, on the densely wooded banks of the Gaboon. And there is a scientific objection to the theory that our Christian friend at the Equator had, upon some sporting tour, mistaken a lively member of his flock for a true simian, and so put a bullet through him and sent his remains here to baffle European inquiry. Fortunately, the bones of the feet of our specimen are perfect. Kindly look at them. You observe there that the hallux is so constructed as to be able to oppose the other toes (much as our thumb can oppose the fingers), instead of being parallel with the other toes, and exclusively adapted for supporting the body on the ground. In short, you observe that the prehensile character of the hallux is fully developed, and renders the foot a distinct and tremendously muscular hand. No; the remains are those of a true anthropoid ape; but they are those of a member of that family which it has been reserved for us for the first time to determine."

Newton paused, and threw himself back in his chair with a gesture of weariness.

"I shall tell you the tale from beginning to end exactly as it occurred," he went on, almost defiantly; "and then, if you see fit to warn my friends that I am a dangerous madman, you may do so."

In order to get a clearer view of the speaker, the Professor took off his spectacles, rubbed them, and carefully replaced them.

Newton continued, without looking up: "You remember Wallace predicted that, although one species of gorilla only had thus far been determined, it was not improbable that other forms might inhabit the interior of the African continent. You may also remember that, in consequence of a letter received from my friend Dr. Frankland, a missionary stationed at Bakelf, on the Gaboon, I went out there some time ago to make certain scientific investigations."

The Professor nodded.

"The letter was briefly to this effect: Frankland had heard, from the natives, of certain animals which were named, indiscriminately, gina, quqheena, and m'wiri (the latter a term, I believe, signifying satyr-man). Still, although he had been stationed some years at Bakelf, he had at the time of writing never seen one. The natives— even the experienced native hunters—contending that this quqheena was a creature entirely distinct from all the known apes. They had, in fact, surrounded it with a halo of superstition. The prevalent belief was that the spirits of their dead ancestors occupied its body, and not even the promise of unlimited 'dash' would induce them to molest it. Their ancestors, they said, were easily moved to wrath, and any interference was immediately followed by death—either of the rash hunter himself or one of his near kindred. Frankland subsequently secured this specimen, and the following is his account of his first meeting with the brute, or, more strictly, of the means by which the skeleton was obtained. He had gone down the river some distance from the station, in order to get an example of some bird which the British Museum people wanted. He was accompanied in the boat by a native servant, a Fantee boy. He states that they were drifting noiselessly along, carefully examining the dense tangle of creepers and llianas which lined the bank, when the tropical stillness was broken by a strange murmuring sound, almost, he described it, as of two persons whispering together. Directly the lad heard the sound he fell upon his knees in the most abject terror, murmuring 'Quqheena,' and praying vigorously—an accomplishment probably learnt at the mission schools. By dint of whispered threats and expostulations he was at last induced so far to overcome his emotion as to seize an overhanging bough, and they thus came to an anchorage. Then Frankland peered carefully into the interstices in the jungle. For some time the matted masses of branches and leaf appeared almost solid; but at last his eye reached a narrow vista in the woody growth which enabled him to take a more extended view. Following this, and still guided by the murmuring sound, he discerned, shining in the darkness of the leafy tunnel, two glittering eyes, the gloom of the forest and the density of the verdure preventing any other portion of the animal from being visible. Knowing the timidity of all the gorilla tribe, Frankland at once raised his rifle and fired. Although unable to see the effect of his shot, he knew that it must have told; but, owing to the impenetrable barrier of jungle at this point, he was unable to effect a landing to recover his quarry. Some days afterwards, his men, approaching from another point of the compass, managed to reach the place, but, unluckily, some carnivorous beast—or more probably the large and destructive ants (drivers) which abound there—had been busily at work, and only these few bones reached Frankland's bungalow."

"Well?" said the Professor.

"Well, I went to Bakelf; I stayed there some months; but I could find no trace of the mysterious ape. Did I tell you that Frankland had a daughter?"

The Professor shook his head.

"After I had been at Bakelf some months I began to regard the whole thing as a myth. I had beaten the ground thoroughly without result. Now listen; every word I tell you is true. One night we were in the mission house, and Miss Frankland—Dorothy—went to the little blindless window. Suddenly, without the least warning, she fell back. 'Come to me,' she cried, in sudden alarm; 'I see *something*.' Frankland ran to her. 'What is it?' he said. 'What has frightened you?' She seemed too terrified to speak, and almost instantly we heard a sound as though some one were trying to open the outer door. It was an old negress who lived at the place, Monqulamba. The woman was evidently wild with superstitious terror. She gasped out at length that she had seen a dark form pressing close to the window, and as it turned she had identified quqheena. My gun-case was in a corner of the room, and in five seconds I had thrown butt, barrels, and fore-end together. The night was not very dark; but I could see nothing of the ape in the little enclosure which answered for a garden. There was a group of trees just outside, in which it might have taken refuge, and I knew that if I could get it out it would give me a clear shot as it crossed the open. So I went in, striking my foot against the trunks as I walked along. No sign of my quarry was forthcoming. So I continued pressing through the leafy tangle, hoping every moment to hear a mighty rush. Suddenly something touched me very gently. Before I could move or cry out mighty arms, or what seemed like mighty arms, passed round my throat."

"But did you see nothing?" said the Professor.

"Nothing whatever. I remember something just touching my cheek; then something passed round my throat; and then—why, if one of the palm-trees had leaped from the earth and coiled itself round my neck, the sense of awful resistless weight could not have been greater.

"When I came to myself I was lying on the grass, in what appeared to be the recesses of the forest. My brow and hair were wet as though they had been bathed. At my side was a rude cup formed from a husk, containing fresh water. It was not yet daylight, and it took me some time to disentangle the objects around me from the nightmare-like forms in my brain. Then I saw something which sent the blood to my heart. Close to me, within three paces, crouched a huge monster—a creature so unearthly in its vast girth and length of limb, that to see it behind the strong bars of a cage would have been an unnerving sight. As I saw it, it might, without moving a yard, have stretched out one great hairy hand and seized me where I lay. Yet it showed no disposition to attack me. I watched it intently; then, for the first time, I noted that it held a bunch of bananas and dates, freshly torn from the palm. Something in the creature's expression interested, perplexed, yet, somehow, failed to alarm me. For the first time the meaning of an old Fantee saying—always dark before—became less obscure: 'He who kills quqheena kills a *soul*.'

"I moved uneasily. 'Are you in pain?' it said gently. I heard the tones clearly, low, cultured, distinct—and the amazing thing was I felt little or no surprise. 'What are you?' I said. (I tried to speak as calmly as I could, but my voice trembled.) 'That is rather an abrupt way of asking for an introduction,' the thing replied. And its tones were so smooth and easy that I felt guilty of an unpardonable rudeness. 'But I brought you herewith the fixed intention of enlightening you,' it added. 'We decided, unanimously, the other night, that it was absurd for the two highest mammalian forms to remain longer strangers.'"

The Professor again wiped his spectacles, in order to obtain a clearer view of the speaker.

"'But tell me, first, what are you?' I exclaimed involuntarily. It smiled slightly. 'Do you want Darwin's definition or our own?' it said. 'However, neither would be unbiased; so we will let that pass.

For the purposes of this interview, let us say that you and I represent the two highest branches of a common family tree. I wish to
be perfectly frank with you,' it continued; 'so I'll come to the point
at once. The history of man is a wheel, constantly revolving, and
in that sense repeating itself. But it is travelling onwards as well.
Curiously enough, our wheel revolves also; but it never advances.
It is this essential difference which I should like to discuss with
you.'

"I consented readily. The hairy paw with which this strange
creature gently accentuated its sentences could have crushed me
like a fly.

"'Immeasurably inferior as you may be, compared with ourselves,' it went on ('I do not wish to appear disrespectful; but I
have a reason for speaking plainly), you possess something, as a
race, which we lack.'

"I moved a little farther from the emphasizing paw. 'Pardon
me,' I said; 'but if this is in the nature of a diplomatic conference,
I must, in behalf of civilized humanity, protest against such pre-
liminary assumption of superiority.'

"The ape appeared much surprised. 'But really, you must see it
for yourself. It seems to me so obvious. To take the first tangible
illustration. If I stretched out my arm, your fragile frame would be
crushed like an egg-shell. I might go on to your submerged tenth;
but I don't wish to press the point.'

"It raised its arm gently as it spoke, and I saw it was not necessary, for the purposes of our argument, to carry the matter farther.

"'We have never failed,' it proceeded, 'to keep in view what I
understand you call your civilization. It interests, yet at the same
time amazes, us. Some of the humbler members of our community
who have visited London and Paris, attached to barrel-organs, and
who have succeeded in returning, find little to admire in your mode
of life. Travellers' tales are proverbially unreliable; but many of
these bear the stamp of truth. For example, in the dim mists of
antiquity, our race addressed themselves to the solution of the
problem of happiness. How to be constantly happy seemed to them
a question of such paramount importance that they refused to deal

with any other until it was satisfactorily settled. It blocked the way, so to speak. Our European travellers tell us that this is still a moot point with you.'

"I admitted it. With that mighty paw waving so near, I felt that it was still a moot point with me. 'But you must find life dull in these solitudes,' I said. The ape seemed puzzled.

"'Dull?' it murmured. 'But—ah!—I see. You are, of course, unable to appreciate the effect of innumerable successions of absolute tranquility. Still, you have your theories of heredity; but, I remember now, you only use them in connection with crime, insanity, and so forth. Dear me, how very curious! I ought not to smile, I know,' it went on, 'because, after all, it is a serious matter for you. Bred on telegraphs, nurtured on express trains and telephones, maturing beneath electric lights, and constantly haunted by a weird desire to discover something still quicker, stronger, and more dazzling, your condition grows sadder every day. To demonstrate this, allow me to suggest a simple experiment. Take any tall-hatted gentleman haphazard from Charing Cross or Lombard Street. Place him here alone for one single week. Surely no hard fate, for the trees and grasses are green and the winds are warm. Whence comes the strange weariness—the shadow like the fear of death—which creeps to his soul? We don't feel it. Ask the birds and butterflies, and they would be simply unable to understand you. Yet the explanation is simplicity itself. When one stands at the corner of the Mansion House, and watches the hurrying crowds, it might be imagined they are merely bent on ordinary business—buying, selling, cornering markets, floating bogus mines, and so on. A busy broker would probably be annoyed if you stopped him at the door of the House, and seriously warned him against following the example of Frankenstein. Yet the monster he is creating is a terrible one. It may be able only to worry and vex him if he has to wait ten minutes for a train; but it would become a really dangerous adversary if it caught him alone in a wood.'

"I pointed out that it is impossible to institute a comparison between a civilized man and a mere animal. I said that the cases were not parallel. The ape smiled again with a blandness which irritated me. 'They are not at all parallel. I hope I may say, without conceit, that they are widely different. For example, we know what we want. Can you honestly say the same? If I climb up that tree for a bunch of bananas, I know that I want them to eat. Will you tell me what your millionaires want more gold for? Not necessarily for their descendants. Mr. Carnegie pointed out quite recently what a bad thing unlimited money is for descendants, and yet they toil up harder trees than any in this forest to obtain it. As you say, the cases are not parallel.'

"'It is difficult,' I said, 'to explain clearly to an ape—I don't use the term disrespectfully—the complex nature of man as compared with the lower and simpler organization of the brute.'

"The ape reflected for a few moments. 'But, pardon me,' it said, 'what has complexity to do with it? Why should not a man—you will acquit me of any desire to use the term offensively—aspire to be upon a level with apes in this respect? If you cannot attain this position unaided, perhaps your British Association might be induced to visit us in order to determine scientifically the exact nature of the bars which stand between *fin-de-siècle* civilization and happiness?'

"'But do I understand you are absolutely contented here?' I said.

"'If by contentment you mean lack of power to picture and desire to attain a higher life, we are not contented. We are perfectly aware there is no state so hopeless as that of having every hope fulfilled. Surely we may be happy without abandoning hope?'

"When a monkey takes up a position of this kind it is difficult to argue with it. I relapsed into silence.

"The ape soon resumed the attack: 'What amazes us so out here,' it went on, 'is that you don't see the simplicity of this problem of life. A child might solve it. In fact, children do solve it, every day. Watch them as they play, before your Board Schools absorb them. They are happy—happy as the bird in the air, as the despised monkey in the tree. Then, stroll on to any great social function, an "at home," or the dance of a society queen. The estimable people whom you see wish to be happy. They surround themselves with costly accessories—flowers and soon—for that object; but the bird in the hedge beats them still. They strain science to its limits; they descend to the most unmeaning trivialities; yet still the child leaves them hopelessly behind. And the ludicrous part of it all is that they can't tell why. If it were not so intensely sad,' the ape continued, 'nothing would amuse me more than to spend a week in London, and note carefully all your frantic attempts at being happy. The amount of wealth, toil, and toilsomely acquired knowledge which you devote to this object is simply astounding to a monkey. Let us take such a tour in imagination. So this fine building is your Stock Exchange? And what is this ingenious little machine that ticks? The record of all the very latest prices. Marvellous! The cleverest monkey in all Africa could never have invented such a remarkable piece of mechanism. One moment; I wish to note the radiant delight on the countenances of the possessors of this last boon of civilization. Thanks; I'm quite ready to go now. Your Houses of Parliament, you say? The concentrated wisdom of the nation. The concentrated wisdom seems rather hot and excited and angry to-night. Let us go away. Ah! a garden-party, given by a dignitary of your Church. Haven of bliss—at last, at last! But does it not strike you that the men look bored and weary, and that the smiles of the ladies relax with curious rapidity when the object smiled upon has passed? Now, do you mind showing me happiness? Ah! I beg your pardon—I see. That dingy little hedge-sparrow, rejoicing from the depths of its heart in the bright green leaves of summer. Another thing strikes us. You always set so much store upon what you call "high principle." Why upon "high principle"? It is obviously a most dangerous weapon in any but an unerring hand. This term "high principle" has led you astray from the beginning. It was this which made you try to teach some of the most beautiful Christian lessons with a thumbscrew. Why not keep to love? That has never led you wrong, from Christ to Father Damien.'

"'But since you despise us so bitterly, why do you seek communion with us?' I asked.

"The ape looked at me with strange, wistful eyes.

"'I cannot tell. Something faintly moving in our hearts calls out to you. Our wheel is turning peacefully; but it is still in the green forest. Yours revolves roughly, and it jars as it goes along. But, standing here, afar off, we see what you cannot see. It is ascending the mountainside; it is getting nearer to the stars.'

"That is all," said Newton, after a pause. "I suppose I was more roughly shaken than I knew, for when Frankland's people found me, they say, I was insensible and alone."

"Dear me," thought the Regius Professor of Obsolete Theologies as he wended his way home; "what a sad thing it will be if poor Newton has really gone wrong in the head."

Dankwarra, the Isle of Fear

Stevens Vail

I was the only white man in Patuca, the chief town of the Honduras Waikas.

Ever since my arrival at the mosquito shore the Waikas had piqued my curiosity by wonderful tales of a mysterious island which stood in the midst of an inland lagoon and which, they said, was peopled by hideous demons who destroyed all who set foot upon their terrible territory.

Years ago, the present Sukia had once ventured into the lagoon in search for rare herbs and reptiles with which to work her spells and incantations. As she neared the island huge monsters, having the shape of men and the eyes of devils, rushed to the water's edge and, waving their long, hairy arms, uttered the most horrible yells, which so terrified the Sukia that she bent to her paddle and never ceased her frenzied strokes until the pit-pan grated on the pebbly beach of the village.

And, as though this were not in itself a potent enough sign of the island being consecrated to Lassa and his attendant evil spirits, a headstrong Waika buckra, in a moment of bravado induced by a too free use of mishia, had gone to Dankwarra to fight Lassa, and from that day to this had never been heard of.

Old Witatala, the chief of the Waikas, swinging in his hammock within the semi-darkness of his bamboo watta, told me all this and more. "No, no, Buckra," he repeated with a solemn shake of his gray, wooly head, "I tink me you s'pose old Witatala crazy; he no take you to Dankwarra, or he no tell you where Dankwarra is.

S'pose you go, den Lassa catch an' eat you shuah—what you say den 'bout old Witatala? No, no—must go, must die. Make me hunt the manatee instead. Dat plenty fun, an' bineby you forget Dankwarra."

Witatala was obdurate, and I was obliged to content myself with the prospect of a hunt after the manatee, or sea cow, that remarkable connecting link between quadrupeds and fishes, which is to tropical waters what the seal is to those of the frozen zone.

At "first sun up" we made our start. Witatala, Quia, his son, myself and a crew of four paddlers.

Eight long hours we paddled up stream until the river took a strange and unfamiliar aspect. Then, steering for the bush-covered bank, the crew with their sharp machetes lopped off a number of leafy branches which were thrown lightly over the pit-pan until it resembled a floating tree.

Casting loose from the bank we floated down the river with the current. One man stood in the stern to steer. Witatala crouched in the bow with harpoon and line, while the rest, keeping their long, keen lances clear of impediments, knelt on the bottom. The utmost silence prevailed, for the manatee is amazingly acute of hearing and at the slightest sound will submerge itself deep below the water's surface.

After an hour of drifting I was beginning to think that perhaps the manatee had found the tender shoots of river grass unpalatable to his taste, when suddenly Witatala launched his harpoon, and at the same instant gave an ear-splitting yell of triumph. The yell was followed by a heavy plunge, and the pit-pan started forward with a sudden jerk which cost me a hard tumble into the bottom of the canoe. Before I had recovered myself the boughs were all thrown overboard and the Waikas stood with their long lances poised for instant use.

The pit-pan tore along at incredible speed, and small wonder, for at the other end of the rope fastened to the boat was an enormous creature whose black body stuck full of harpoons with ropes attached could be seen sliding beneath the water's surface like a long black cloud.

When the manatee rose for air, the remaining harpoons flashed into its black, hippopotamus-like hide. The only effect the spears seemed to have on the maddened creature was to spur it on to fresh exertions, for, darting from one side of the river to the other, he whipped and jerked the frail craft after him as though it had been a switch of willow.

The harpoons had given out, but still the manatee showed no signs of weakening. "The machetes!" cried Witatala. Catching hold of the taunt line, which held us to the sea cow, he gradually drew the pit-pan nearer to it. The men stood with their sword-like machetes poised, waiting for a chance to hurl them, and when the manatee once more arose for air down flashed the machetes. Some of them struck and stuck, but so thick was the monster's hide that a couple turned their points and glanced off into the river.

Still the manatee kept on in its mad zig-zag flight, until suddenly it swerved and made for a thick clump of bushes overhanging the bank. At this new maneuver Witatala uttered a terrified shriek of dismay. "Dankwarra! Dankwarra!" he screamed. "See, the mantee makes for the entrance to the lagoon of Dankwarra!"

The other Waikas sprang to their feet and made an attempt to cast loose the ropes of the bow, but the tension rendered it impossible. In vain they fumbled for their machetes and knives—every bladed instrument had already been hurled at the manatee.

By this time the monster had rushed us into the bush-hidden mouth of a narrow creek, whose density of overhanging foliage seemed to turn day into night. The dismayed Waikas cast anxious glances at the pitchy waters, through which the canoe was plunging, as if to throw themselves in, but the sullen splashes at either bank showed where uneasy crocodiles had left their muddy lairs, and decided them to risk the uncertain evil that lay ahead, rather than the probable death that was close at hand.

On and on we sped until at last a glimmer in the heavy shade ahead bespoke an outlet to the creek.

A few seconds more and we emerged from the narrow passage into a spacious lagoon whose calm surface was unbroken save by a large island which stood in its centre.

Straight for this island tore the frantic manatee, while with every foot of lessened distance between us and the land, the Waikas' eyes seemed to bulge out bigger with terror. When within 60 yards of the island, a grating, tearing sound came from the pit-pan's bow, and with a sudden wrench and crash, the canoe turned over, a total wreck, from a sharp, jagged rock the manatee, in its wild flight, had thrown us against. Fortunately, the shock was so great as to fling us clear of the hidden rock, and, rising from beneath the water, we struck out for the island, our speed not a little accelerated by the fear of sharks and crocodiles.

Reaching the sandy shore o f the island, we crawled up on the beach, but further than this, the Waikas, with chattering teeth, declared they would not go.

But it did not seem so terrible to me, the "Dankwarra, the Isle of Fear," for it was not unlike a hundred lagoon islands I had seen—a heavy tangle of tropical over and undergrowth, encircled by a shining strip of beach. Of its inhabitants, demons or otherwise, not a trace was to be seen.

In response to an exclamation from Witatala, I looked toward the lagoon, and there on its surface, near the beach, I saw floating the dead body of the manatee which, in its moment of victory, had succumbed to death.

The Waikas waded out into the water, splashing as they went to frighten away the sharks and crocodiles, laid hold of the ropes attached to the harpoons, and drew the sea cow up on the beach.

It was certainly a most remarkable animal, if animal it may be called. It weighed, I should say, between 1600 and 1800 pounds. In general characteristics it resembled the seal, but its head was thick and heavy, with something of the appearance of that of a hornless cow. It had two forefeet, or flippers, but instead of hind feet there was a broad, flat tail, which spread out horizontally, like a fan. The skin was dark and corrugated, and the few scattered hairs upon it gave its body a general resemblance to that of a hippo-potamus.

Witatala surveyed the dead creature with anger, but philosophi-cally resolved to make it pay in part for our misfortune by serving as supper. With the aid of a couple of dry sticks a fire was kindled and the manatee was prepared for eating. I did not wonder at the machetes' failure to penetrate its hide, for as the flesh was cut in strips for broiling I measured the skin and found it one inch and a half in thickness and as tough as whalebone. The manatee steaks proved to be tender, well-flavored and altogether delicious and far surpassed venison, to my palate.

After supper I determined to do a little exploring on my own account, in spite of the warnings of Witatala and his men.

An eighth of a mile down the beach I came upon an old cannon half buried in the sand. Scraping away the loose soil, it proved to be, in spite of its heavy crust of mould and rust, an ancient Spanish cannon, closely resembling those the books picture to us as having been used by the daring Spanish free booters in the days of Drake and Kidd. Further along I came upon other relics—an old flint lock, a dagger, several pistols, and a piece of broken chain, all scattered about as though they had been left in some hasty flight.

As I walked back to the Waikas I recalled tales of the famous "Blackbeard," who made his name a terror along the Spanish Main and it seemed probable to me that the now deserted Dankwarra had been in those days a secret stronghold of "Blackbeard" and his piratical band.

Old Witatala evinced but little interest in the story of my discovery, his mind being chiefly exercised over our getting away from Dankwarra with all possible celerity. This he determined to accomplish by means of a raft, which he intended to construct from the clumps of bamboo growing near the island forest.

Night had descended with its tropical suddenness, but this did not deter Witatala from his preparations for making the raft. Despatching Quila and a couple of Waikas for tie-tie vine with which to secure the bamboo together, the rest of us secured the machetes from the unlucky manatee's hide and started for the bamboo clumps.

The Waikas would not carry torches, for that, they said, would show our whereabouts to the wicked Lassa, but that we might not want for light they caught handfuls of fire-flies, pulling off their wings and scattered them among the bamboo trees where they gave radiance enough to perceive clearly the surrounding objects.

At the first stroke of the machetes on the bamboo the hitherto silent island seemed to break out into a pandemonium. I dropped my machete in dismay. Witatala calmed my nerves by telling me that the sounds were made by the suddenly awakened animals and bird life of the island. But what a diabolical uproar it was!

There were unearthly groans and angry snarls and shrieks; at times the noise was blended and became sullen and distant, then so sharp and near they seemed at our very feet. All the water birds and wild fowls roosting in the trees gave a sudden flutter and set up a series of croaks and screams which sent an adjacent troop of howling monkeys into spasms of delight. The crocodiles plunged into the lagoon and the squawks of a troop of startled parrots and all nature seemed filled with savage warring life.

At intervals, the heavy bodies of prowling animals would be heard crashing through the jungle, and at these noises old Witatala would look anxiously around, in momentary dread of having Lassa and his demons swoop down upon him.

But nothing of the kind happened and we were able to retreat in safety with our load of bamboo logs to the beach, where the construction of the raft began with great rapidity. The great red moon was beginning to grow dim in the approaching dawn, however, before our raft was completed. We had thrown ourselves down upon the beach for a brief rest before launching our rude craft, when suddenly Witatala grasped my arm, and in a hoarse whisper bade me look toward the jungle. I did so, and for a minute every drop of blood seemed to stand still in my veins.

There, peering at us from the half-parted bushes, was a huge white face, terrible in its hideous ferocity. Beneath its low, slanting forehead blazed fierce eyes; its nose was broad and flat; and from its great mouth two fangs protruded. The moon lit up this horribly grinning face with sharp distinctness.

The Waikas seemed rooted to the ground with terrified amazement. Suddenly another frightful face appeared beside the first, then another and another.

The spell of silence was broken, and the Waikas began simultaneously their rapid screech of incantation against Lassa and all other evil spirits, at the same time backing toward the lagoon, shoving the raft as they went.

The four faces in the edge of the thicket grinned and frowned, their jaws rapidly opening and shutting.

As the raft slid into the water the bushes parted, and the faces appeared in the open. They were no longer simply "faces." They were huge, towering hairy forms that stood erect, with arms waving high above their heads. And now they came menacingly towards us.

The Waikas—and perhaps I too—gave one cry, and, throwing ourselves on the raft, with a shove we sent it gliding away from the island. At this the monsters waved their arms more frantically, and advancing to the water's edge gave utterance to a succession of yells. We were really out of reach, but the cry made us clutch the raft.

Just then the sun burst from above the woodland, and fully revealed to my astonished eyes the forms of our pursuers. They were not men, not demons, but monkeys—and yet not manly monkeys, but huge gorillas!

The island faded away, and the roars of the gorillas were lost in the distance. Back through the black creek we paddled out into the broad, swiftly flowing waters of the Rio de la Patuca.

I tried to explain the identity of the creatures to Witatala, but he would receive none of it. "No, Buckra," he replied with a shake of his poor old head. "No, Buckra," he repeated, "old Witatala know monkey when he see him—he eat many monkeys, he know him well, he never see monkey so big like dat—talk like dat. Dat big one was Lassa—de rest de family." Of course there was nothing more to be said.

As to the colony of gorillas living on an island in a Central American lagoon, I can offer but one explanation: "Blackbeard," the pirate, may have brought young gorillas with him on some slaving voyage from Africa, and abandoned them with the rest of his effects on this island. The climatic conditions being the same as those of Africa, the gorillas would naturally have thrived and brought up their flourishing progeny.

Whether or not in time they will escape to the mainland remains to be seen. If they do not leave the island, there is little chance of their being heard of again, for the entrance to the lagoon creek is next to invisible, and after our experience, neither gold nor rum would induce a Waika to act as guide to Dankwarra, the Isle of Fear!

The Depths of Kyamo

J.-H. Rosny the Elder

I

It was early nightfall in the little negro village, Ouan-Mahlei, on the border of the vast Kyamo, one of the largest wildernesses of the Dark Continent.

A pale moon shone through the light, floating clouds, and the palms, waving softly in the breeze, cast long, undulating shadows on the silvery grounds. The air was heavy with the perfume of tropical flowers, and the wind, rising and falling, seemed full of a wild mournful music. At intervals, as it died into silence, one could hear the roaring of a lion, answered often by another from a still greater distance, and the cries and growling of smaller animals, less clear, more undefined.

The natives of the village were not yet asleep. Most of them were grouped around a huge fire, where a colossal feast of roasted meats was to be prepared in honor of their guests. A few, however, loitered near the cabin of their chief, gazing with an interest not unmingled with awe on the white strangers.

Two of them, the Austrian Kamstein and French Hamel, were explorers bent on discovery, eager to see and study all that would enable them to describe with exactitude those parts of Africa of which little is as yet known to Europeans.

Alglave, the third European, was less explorer than naturalist. Forty years of age, independent, a bachelor, a man of rare intelligence, his whole life had been devoted to those studies which seek to penetrate the secrets of the gradual evolution of nature, the emanating source from which man has developed into what he is today. He was eagerly questioning one of the natives about the adjoining forest, and the old Negro, delighted to have so attentive an auditor, told him of its wonders and mysteries, which were full of intense and often romantic interest. The length of the Kyamo, he said, was forty days' march and its breadth twenty days'. It was old—almost beyond conception—as old as the world. The natives never ventured to enter it save singly. Even the lions had been driven beyond its borders, and never to human knowledge, even so far as the oldest legends, had it been owned save by the wild men of the forest, giant black gorillas, who had held it imperiously and victoriously through all the ages.

Alglave, interested, thrilled with the rare delight of the savant, asked eagerly: "Have you seen him—the man of the forest?"

"I have seen him, master; I have been in the Kyamo. The man of the forest is not more tall than a white man, but he is far broader and more strong. His chest is wider and more powerful than that of the lion; his arms are invincible. A few of us have dared to penetrate into the forest, but alone and unarmed. If one goes there humble and timid one may meet with no harm, but to provoke the anger of the gorilla means death. The wrath of the man of the forest is merciless, terrible."

"Are they in great numbers?"

"They are in immense numbers, master. The Kyamo contains many hundreds of their villages."

"But they do not live in groups?"

"No; each dwells apart with his wives, but close to the others. Sometimes they join and form tribes, and then they choose a chief as we do."

Alglave, his head resting against the rough wall of the cabin, fell into profound meditation, fraught with alluring dreams.

There, in the depths of the Kyamo, one might find a majestic revelation of the ancient history of primitive man. In this virgin forest dwelled a race of beings that had preserved from darker ages the traces of a former superior estate, the rudiments of organization, a system of defense well regulated and powerful and immense vital energy. There was the analogy of what man had been in the beginning—a race of beings that had failed through some unknown cause to reach that intellectual development which man, the weaker vessel physically, has attained. It was the genesis of mankind—the most terrible and the most grand of epic poems that the human brain can conceive.

The huge fire had grown higher and higher. Now the glow from the leaping flames made even the moon and stars seem dim and pale. The natives clapped their hands and shouted in childish excitement as they danced around it.

From afar the beasts of the plains, silenced a moment by the sudden light, took up once more the chorus of the wilderness—the clamor of the hunt, of fear, of love.

The scent of the tropical blossoms was overpowered by the smell of the burning meats. Huge buffalo and antelopes had been thrown whole into the flames. It was a weird and interesting scene to Hamel and Kamstein. Alglave was deaf and blind to it all. One invincible thought absorbed and controlled him completely. On the morrow he would enter the Kyamo.

II

The forest of the ages, grander, more wild, more darkly mysterious than the forests of the Amazon or the Australian bush. Alglave, who on the repeated assurances of the natives that it was impossible for more than one person at a time to venture into its domain, resolved if possible to penetrate its inmost depths. Astonished at finding the wild luxuriance and disorder of vegetation intersected by distinct, although narrow and rough pathways, he had pushed steadily forward for four hours. The heaviness of the air, the semi-darkness, above all, the intense, almost menacing sense of solitude, weighed upon his spirits. Nowhere had he found that which he so eagerly sought—the great gorilla, the king of the wilderness.

Sometimes, it is true, he thought he perceived behind a screen of leaves a gleaming pair of dark eyes or the movements of a huge black body, but a nearer inspection proved this to be chimerical.

Here and there he saw upon the ground imprints of an anthropoid's feet, and in places the grasses and moss were trodden down, showing the passage of a herd of heavy animals—sights which quickened his pulses and made him feel furtively for the revolvers in his belt. Yet the loneliness, the knowledge of the dangers he might have to face at any moment, had rather added to than diminished his zeal.

He was on the threshold of a great discovery. Why not, he said to himself, instead of observing them from a distance, live among these strange creatures for a time; why not share their life while Hamel and Kamstein pursued their explorations?

A sudden clamor, a noise that seemed almost human, startled him. It was like the surging and growling of an infuriated mob in time of revolution. Fully alive to the danger, Alglave was yet impelled irresistibly onward, moving warily, crouching as much as possible behind the screen of foliage. As he drew nearer the sound grew more distinct, less human. It was now more like the baying and growling of bloodhounds. Sometimes it ceased for an instant, only to resume again louder and more threatening than before. The danger was the more terrible because its quality was unknown.

The ardor of the scientist blind him to all risks, deadened the voice of reason. Patiently, stealthily, he crept forward. Already he could distinguish a moving mass of black forms. His keen eyes sighted the hollow trunk of a huge tree which might serve as a hiding place—could he reach it? Would not the keen scent of the animals detect his presence, even though he succeeded in passing them unseen?

Yet he had a faint hope. In that immense crowd surely the strong odor of the animals themselves would conceal the odor of human flesh, diminished as it was by the garments he wore.

Creeping slowly forward from tree to tree, from bush to bush, crouching close to the earth, he accomplished over half the distance. Some leaves rustled beneath his touch. Instantly several hundred pairs of gleaming eyes were turned menacingly toward him. Was he discovered? Even in this moment of intense suspense he was thrilled with admiration for these superb creatures. Their forms were colossal. Although their height did not exceed that of the average man, their weight must have been nearly three times as great. Their legs were short, but strong as iron; their chests and shoulders Herculean. Their long arms looked capable of strangling a lion or rhinoceros in their grasp.

The gorillas resumed their clamor. They had held the forest too long to be easily startled or disturbed. A few moments more, and Alglave reached the tree in safety. He drew a long breath of relief as he stood upright within the shelter of its hollow trunk. He found, as he had divined, plenty of fissures in the wood, through which he could make his observations. It was with a feeling of triumph and breathless interest that he looked out from the cover of his citadel on a scene which he has since described as the "Council of the Wild Men of the Forest."

III

In a huge open clearing, the ground carpeted with dark green moss, the leaves forming an arched roof of foliage overhead, were assembled from 400 to 500 gorillas, all adult males. There was a certain order both in their groupings and their actions. Now one, now another, would go through a series of irregular gestures, accompanied by low guttural utterances, while the rest followed his every movement with the keenest interest. As each uncouth orator finished his harangue, a perfect babel of hoarse cries, meant evidently to express assent or disapproval, would break forth for a few moments. It was marvelous to watch the agitation, the excitement, the constant play of expression, on those grotesque physiognomies, which were quite as intelligent and human in appearance as those of many African savages.

Alglave did not for a moment doubt that he was witnessing a formal council of these strange beings. What could they be discussing so excitedly? Undoubtedly something of unusual importance. Alas! He could guess nothing. There was no indication save that of direction. An oft-repeated gesture of the huge arms, a constant turning of their heads toward one point, a little southward. How he longed to understand their language! For that it was a lan-

guage the scientist felt convinced. He discerned positively the repetition of certain combinations, a sort of mathematics of the fingers and arms. Could he but have interpreted this primitive sign
language, what a discovery on the origin of speech, what a page it
would contribute to the history of prehistoric ages!

IV

Morning. How beautiful and how boundless the forest looks!
In the river which traverses it hippopotami are floating heavily in
the water, and on the banks lazy, green crocodiles lie basking in
the sunshine. The gorillas are encamped on the north bank of the
stream. They number perhaps 1,000. And among them, closely
guarded, disheartened, and suffering, a white man is held prisoner.
He is naked, for they have torn his garments from him. He is weary,
for his captors allow him but little rest. He is hungry, for he has
eaten nothing for days save a few handfuls of nuts. For the first
day following that terrible moment when he had been discovered
and dragged form his hiding place, Alglave's captors had been more
curious than cruel. But later (had their instinct warned them that
this white creature, whose weakness they despised, was in cunning and intelligence their superior?) their attitude had changed.
They viewed him with ill-concealed suspicion, guarding him more
closely and menacingly. Daily he asked himself if they would not
kill him in the end. Yet the trial which seemed the hardest to bear
was that in their distrust they concealed from him all the most
important actions of their daily life, thus depriving him even of
the consolation of observing their ways and habits, an end for which
he had risked so much. Heartsick and discouraged, he asked himself if his sacrifice was to be wholly vain. He was sinking fast into
a state of hopeless apathy, and had almost resolved to take his own
life rather than await the horrible fate which might be impending,
when on this, the fifth day of his captivity, a faint ray of hope came
to him. During the night the gorillas, with their captive, had journeyed for many miles, arriving in the early dawn at their present
encampment. The scientist, exhausted from want of food and the
long transport, had for the first time fallen into a deep slumber.

It was broad daylight when a great clamor awoke him. To his amazement he found himself alone. The gorillas had been joined by several hundred of another tribe. In the excitement of the meeting even the prisoner was forgotten. The latter was refreshed and invigorated by his long sleep. A large cocoa-nut was lying near him, dropped there, doubtless, by his guard in the excitement. Seizing the fruit, he devoured it with avidity. Never had nectar tasted more delicious.

Realizing that something important was transpiring among the gorillas, Alglave, finding himself unobserved, crept stealthily toward them, noting their every movement. He soon divined something of the situation. Near the center of the river, some 300 yards from the main land, was a long narrow island on which could be distinguished a number of black figures, which responded to the gestures of those on the bank. They were evidently in distress. They looked emaciated and feeble, particularly the females and their little ones. And the secret of the council was explained. Alglave marveled at the almost human organization existing among the gorillas, at the oneness of purpose, the firmness of resolve, the unanimous consolidation of forces to aid their brethren in distress.

But how came a whole tribe of these beings, who detest water, on an island in midstream?

A huge boulder standing almost perpendicular on the island to the main land directly opposite, a freshly torn cavity in the side of the bank, a mass of loose earth and crushed vegetation, told the tale. A bridge of some sort had existed; placed there, not by the gorillas, but through some accident of nature. In the late rising of the waters it had been washed away by the current.

V

What would they attempt to do? Ignorant of every principle of navigation, they were powerless. A great throb of hope came to Alglave. If he—the man—succeeded where they could not, surely here at last was a chance to win their friendship, perhaps their gratitude. He waited. Two long hours passed. The gorillas had labored unceasingly. The tallest tree available, a tree over 200 feet in height, had been torn bodily out of the ground and carried down to the bank. Slowly, awkwardly, with no other aid than the Herculean strength of their huge arms, they raised it to a perpendicular position, then gradually lowered the top over the river. In their ignorance of distance they were trying to make it touch on the opposite side. There was a breathless pause as it reached a horizontal position. Then, simultaneously, they relaxed their hold. There was a crash and tremendous splashing of water. The tree, some fifty feet too short, had sunk to the bottom of the stream. From both banks arose a terrible cry of rage, of fury, of disappointment. It was followed by an awful silence, the silence of utter despair.

Then Alglave arose and walked toward them. He went directly to the central group and stopped before the largest gorilla among them. It was the chief of the tribe that held him prisoner. With a gesture full of confidence, the naturalist pointed alternately to himself, to the place where the tree had fallen, and to the island. It took time and infinite patience to make them understand. At last they seemed to comprehend vaguely that he wished to do something for them. It was curious to note the distrust and anxiety with which he was regarded. He found with little difficulty a pointed stone, and commenced hacking away energetically at the branches of the fallen tree. Soon he had a number of awkward assistants. Noontide came and passed. After hours of hard work he had some fifty branches, which, with several young tree-trunks, would suffice to make a raft. The gorillas had become less hostile, and many had proved themselves intelligent and able apprentices. He had also been given liberal rations of food. The animals aided him zealously in looking for thongs with which to bind the logs together. Nearly two-thirds of the day passed ere the raft was completed. To launch it required infinite precaution. The gorillas pressed around him as he began once more to point eagerly and intellectually toward the island.

VI

Now the greatest difficulty presented itself. How should he induce one of their number to accompany him? For to make the trip alone would be worse than useless. Those on the island would surely not do what their brothers on this side did not dare to venture. At last he pushed the raft into the water, not without the risk of being misunderstood and attacked. He moved it gently to and fro, using a young sapling as a pole, pointing continually from one bank to the other.

At last the chief, he to whom Alglave had at first addressed himself, decided to go with him. It was a resolve full of heroism on the part of the animal, whose natural terror of water was hard to overcome. Slowly, trembling and shivering, like a frightened child, he crept on the raft. There was a hoarse murmur from the others as it moved gently from the shore. Alglave's companion gradually became calmer. His quick, intelligent eyes, closely observing the man's movements, soon comprehended their relation to the movement of the craft. And between the man of the civilized world, and the primitive man, the lord of the forest, there was formed from that moment a bond of trust and sympathy. Henceforth, Alglave would have a friend, perhaps a pupil in his companion.

Their arrival at the island was hailed with delight and astonishment by a crowd of feverishly excited beings.

"Let him explain," thought the naturalist, "he will do the rest." And in effect the gorilla began a series of animated gesticulations, which the others followed with the utmost attention. It seemed as though the agony and suffering they had endured had quickened their intelligence. Soon about a dozen mustered sufficient courage to venture on the return voyage. Alglave placed them carefully on the center of the raft and pushed off cautiously. The water was calm. The raft moved smoothly. In less than a quarter of an hour his timid passengers were landed in safety. Then there arose a wild and mighty tumult, awakening the echoes of the forest. A chorus of mad and savage joy. Alglave was surrounded, caressed by huge hairy hands, almost smothered under demonstrations of affection. All distrust, all hostility had vanished. As strong in their gratitude as in their dislike, they would offer henceforth only blind devotion to the mysterious white stranger, this pale-face son of an unknown race, who had rescued their fellow-creatures from the very jaws of death.

VII

Once more, as at the opening of my tale, it is early nightfall in Africa. The moon is slowly rising like a disk of fire on the border of the horizon. Alglave lies dreaming on the bank of the river. His desire is to be fulfilled at last. He has become the friend, the hero, of the anthropoids. They respect and admire him. Unconsciously, they offer him a sort of savage worship. He can study them without haste and without fear. And the result! Through him may be handed down the early history of the human race, not the story furnished by imagination and conjecture, but the true epic of man—the evolution of man. He will learn the secret of the dark ages, of the infancy of the species, ere one was chosen from among them to be lord of all the living creatures of the earth. The though to him is full of strange, sweet triumph. He loves these children of the ancestral race with their fierce instincts, their savage passions, their determined war against the extinction of their kind. He would aid them in protecting their domain against human invasion, against the conquering march of civilization.

The moon rises higher and higher. A faint breeze stirs among the foliage. The perfume of the tropical flowers is borne to him on the evening air. Tired from the labors of the day, Alglave's weary eyelids close. His head sinks back upon a cushion of moss. And the rustling of the leaves, the silvery murmurs of the river, the weird cries of the animals in the distance, sing to him a slumber-song.

VIII

In December of 1890, a sentinel at the French post of New Metz, in Central Africa, was startled by a strange apparition. A man, tall and emaciated, naked save for a rough tunic of skins, was slowly approaching the camp. On his back was strapped a huge roll of bark, somewhat resembling an ancient papyrus. His skin was tanned to a dark brown, but his features were not those of an African. And his long, tangled hair and beard were of a light golden color. The sentinel gave the challenge. The answer, prompt and clear, came in his own language: "A French citizen, who demands hospitality!" The call of the soldier brought an officer and two men of the guard to the spot, to whom the new-comer said briefly: "I am Alglave, explorer and naturalist. I am exhausted and nearly starving." When he had slept a little and partaken of a meal of fish, fruit, and bread, he related to his hearers a wonderful story. He told of wanderings through unexplored countries, vast forests, and desolate wildernesses, of swamps and fevers, of hair-breadth escapes from savage tribes, from the fury of wild beasts, of dark and terrible hours of famine and suffering. His tongue had a wonderful eloquence, which charmed his hearers. But of the wild men of the forest and their life in the Kyamo he said nothing. He was silent on this one point in Paris, where he was received as a hero by his colleagues. He concealed it even from us, his closest, warmest friends. He would have withheld his knowledge to this day had not the increasing number of expeditions, many attended with such cruel incidents, convinced him that the discovery of the Kyamo was no longer a question of years but of months at most.

Then at last he revealed his secret in the interest of the gorillas themselves, hoping that his preemptory arguments of the necessity of preserving this marvelous race of beings, so nearly human, might decide a great movement among the scientists of the world, which, since haste is a quality unloved and unappreciated among these wild gentlemen, would retard rather than accelerate the invasion of the gorillas' domain. To this end he at last published the work which has thrilled and amazed the entire scientific world— "Studies of the life and habits of the Anthropodists of the Kyamo."

No-Man's-Land

John Buchan

I

THE SHIELING OF FARAWA

It was with a light heart and a pleasing consciousness of holiday that I set out from the inn at Allermuir to tramp my fifteen miles into the unknown. I walked slowly, for I carried my equipment on my back—my basket, fly-books and rods, my plaid of Grant tartan (for I boast myself a kinsman of that house), and my great staff, which had tried ere then the front of the steeper Alps. A small valise with books and some changes of linen clothing had been sent on ahead in the shepherd's own hands. It was yet early April, and before me lay four weeks of freedom—twenty-eight blessed days in which to take fish and smoke the pipe of idleness. The Lent term had pulled me down, a week of modest enjoyment thereafter in town had finished the work; and I drank in the sharp moorish air like a thirsty man who has been forwandered among deserts.

I am a man of varied tastes and a score of interests. As an undergraduate I had been filled with the old mania for the complete life. I distinguished myself in the Schools, rowed in my college eight, and reached the distinction of practising for three weeks in the Trials. I had dabbled in a score of learned activities, and when the time came that I won the inevitable St. Chad's fellowship on my chaotic acquirements, and I found myself compelled to select if I would pursue a scholar's life, I had some toil in finding my vocation. In the end I resolved that the ancient life of the North, of the Celts and the Northmen and the unknown Pictish tribes, held for me the chief fascination. I had acquired a smattering of Gaelic, having been brought up as a boy in Lochaber, and now I set myself to increase my store of languages. I mastered Icelandic, and my first book—a monograph on the probable Celtic elements in the Eddic songs—brought me the praise of scholars and the deputy-professor's chair of Northern Antiquities. So much for Oxford. My vacations had been spent mainly in the North—in Ireland, Scotland, and the Isles, in Scandinavia and Iceland, once even in the far limits of Finland. I was a keen sportsman of a sort, an old-experienced fisher, a fair shot with gun and rifle, and in my hillcraft I might well stand comparison with most men. April has ever seemed to me the finest season of the year even in our cold northern altitudes, and the memory of many bright Aprils had brought me up from the South on the night before to Allerfoot, whence a dogcart had taken me up Glen Aller to the inn at Allermuir; and now the same desire had set me on the heather with my face to the cold brown hills.

You are to picture a sort of plateau, benty and rook-strewn, running ridgewise above a chain of little peaty lochs and a vast tract of inexorable bog. In a mile the ridge ceased in a shoulder of hill, and over this lay the head of another glen, with the same doleful accompaniment of sunless lochs, mosses, and a tortuous water. East and west and north, in every direction save the south, rose walls of gashed and serrated hills. It was a grey day with blinks of sun, and when a ray chanced to fall on one of the great dark faces, lines of light and colour sprang into being which told of mica and granite. I was in high spirits, as on the eve of holiday; I had breakfasted excellently on eggs and salmon steaks; I had no cares to speak of, and my prospects were not uninviting. But in spite of myself the landscape began to take me in thrall and crush me. The silent vanished peoples of the hills seemed to be stirring; dark primeval faces seemed to stare at me from behind boulders and jags of rock. The place was so still, so free from the cheerful clamour of nesting birds, that it seemed a *temenos* sacred to some old-world god. At my feet the lochs lapped ceaselessly; but the waters were so dark that one could not see bottom a foot from the edge. On my right the links of green told of snake-like mires waiting to crush the unwary wanderer. It seemed to me for the moment a land of death, where the tongues of the dead cried aloud for recognition.

My whole morning's walk was full of such fancies. I lit a pipe to cheer me, but the things would not be got rid of. I thought of the Gaels who had held those fastnesses; I thought of the Britons before them, who yielded to their advent. They were all strong peoples in their day, and now they had gone the way of the earth. They had left their mark on the levels of the glens and on the more habitable uplands, both in names and in actual forts, and graves where men might still dig curios. But the hills that black stony amphitheatre before me—it seemed strange that the hills bore no traces of them. And then with some uneasiness I reflected on that older and stranger race who were said to have held the hilltops. The Picts, the Picti—what in the name of goodness were they? They had troubled me in all my studies, a sort of blank wall to put an end to speculation. We knew nothing of them save certain strange names which men called Pictish, the names of those hills in front of me— the Muneraw, the Yirnie, the Calmarton. They were the *corpus vile* for learned experiment; but Heaven alone knew what dark abyss of savagery once yawned in the midst of this desert.

And then I remembered the crazy theories of a pupil of mine at St. Chad's, the son of a small landowner on the Aller, a young gentleman who had spent his substance too freely at Oxford, and was now dreeing his weird in the Backwoods. He had been no scholar; but a certain imagination marked all his doings, and of a Sunday night he would come and talk to me of the North. The Picts were his special subject, and his ideas were mad. "Listen to me," he would say, when I had mixed him toddy and given him one of my cigars; "I believe there are traces—ay, and more than traces— of an old culture lurking in those hills and waiting to be discovered. We never hear of the Picts being driven from the hills. The Britons drove them from the lowlands, the Gaels from Ireland did the same for the Britons; but the hills were left unmolested. We hear of no one going near them except outlaws and tinklers. And in that very place you have the strangest mythology. Take the story

of the Brownie. What is that but the story of a little swart man of
uncommon strength and cleverness, who does good and ill indiscriminately, and then disappears? There are many scholars, as you
yourself confess, who think that the origin of the Brownie was in
some mad belief in the old race of the Picts, which still survived
somewhere in the hills. And do we not hear of the Brownie in authentic records right down to the year 1756? After that, when people
grew more incredulous, it is natural that the belief should have
begun to die out; but I do not see why stray traces should not have
survived till late."

"Do you not see what that means?" I had said in mock gravity.
"Those same hills are, if anything, less known now than they were
a hundred years ago. Why should not your Picts or Brownies be
living to this day?"

"Why not, indeed?" he had rejoined, in all seriousness.

I laughed, and he went to his rooms and returned with a large
leather-bound book. It was lettered, in the rococo style of a young
man's taste, *Glimpses of the Unknown*, and some of the said
glimpses he proceeded to impart to me. It was not pleasant reading; indeed, I had rarely heard anything so well fitted to shatter
sensitive nerves. The early part consisted of folk-tales and folk-
sayings, some of them wholly obscure, some of them with a glint
of meaning, but all of them with some hint of a mystery in the hills.
I heard the Brownie story in countless versions. Now the thing was
a friendly little man, who wore grey breeches and lived on brose;
now he was a twisted being, the sight of which made the ewes mis-
carry in the lambing time. But the second part was the stranger,
for it was made up of actual tales, most of them with date and place
appended. It was a most Bedlamite catalogue of horrors, which, if
true, made the wholesome moors a place instinct with tragedy.
Some told of children carried away from villages, even from towns,
on the verge of the uplands. In almost every case they were girls,
and the strange fact was their utter disappearance. Two little girls
would be coming home from school, would be seen last by a
neighbour just where the road crossed a patch of heath or entered
a wood and then—no human eye ever saw them again. Children's

cries had startled outlying shepherds in the night, and when they had rushed to the door they could hear nothing but the night wind. The instances of such disappearances were not very common—perhaps once in twenty years—but they were confined to this one tract of country, and came in a sort of fixed progression from the middle of last century, when the record began.

But this was only one side of the history. The latter part was all devoted to a chronicle of crimes which had gone unpunished, seeing that no hand had ever been traced. The list was fuller in last century;* in the early years of the present it had dwindled; then came a revival about the 'Fifties; and now again in our own time it had sunk low. At the little cottage of Auchterbrean, on the roadside in Glen Aller, a labourer's wife had been found pierced to the heart. It was thought to be a case of a woman's jealousy, and her neighbour was accused, convicted, and hanged. The woman, to be sure, denied the charge with her last breath; but circumstantial evidence seemed sufficiently strong against her. Yet some people in the glen believed her guiltless. In particular, the carrier who had found the dead woman declared that the way in which her neighbour received the news was a sufficient proof of innocence; and the doctor who was first summoned professed himself unable to tell with what instrument the wound had been given. But this was all before the days of expert evidence, so the woman had been hanged without scruple. Then there had been another story of peculiar horror, telling of the death of an old man at some little lonely shieling called Carrickfey. But at this point I had risen in protest, and made to drive the young idiot from my room.

"It was my grandfather who collected most of them," he said. "He had theories,† but people called him mad, so he was wise

* The narrative of Mr. Graves was written in the year 1898.

† In the light of subsequent events I have jotted down the materials to which I refer. The last authentic record of the Brownie is in the narrative of the shepherd of Clachlands, taken down towards the close of last century by the Reverend Mr. Gillespie, minister of Allerkirk, and included by him in his *Songs and Legends of Glen Aller*. The authorities on the strange carrying

enough to hold his tongue. My father declares the whole thing mania; but I rescued the book, had it bound, and added to the collection. It is a queer hobby; but, as I say, I have theories, and there are more things in heaven and earth—"

But at this he heard a friend's voice in the Quad., and dived out, leaving the banal quotation unfinished.

Strange though it may seem, this madness kept coming back to me as I crossed the last few miles of moor. I was now on a rough tableland, the watershed between two lochs, and beyond and above me rose the stony backs of the hills. The burns fell down in a chaos of granite boulders, and huge slabs of grey stone lay flat and tumbled in the heather. The full waters looked prosperously for my fishing, and I began to forget all fancies in anticipation of sport.

Then suddenly in a hollow of land I came on a ruined cottage. It had been a very small place, but the walls were still half erect, and the little moorland garden was outlined on the turf. A lonely apple tree, twisted and gnarled with winds, stood in the midst.

From higher up on the hill I heard a loud hail, and I knew my excellent friend the shepherd of Farawa, who had come thus far to meet me. He greeted me with the boisterous embarrassment which was his way of prefacing hospitality. A grave reserved man at other times, on such occasions he thought it proper to relapse into hilarity. I fell into step with him, and we set off for his dwelling. But first I had the curiosity to look back to the tumble-down cottage and ask him its name.

(cont.) away of children are to be found in a series of articles in a local paper, the *Allerfoot Advertiser*, September and October 1878, and a curious book published anonymously at Edinburgh in 1848, entitled *The Weathergaw*. The records of the unexplained murders in the same neighbourhood are all contained in Mr. Fordoun's *Theory of Expert Evidence*, and an attack on the book in the *Law Review* for June 1881. The Carrickfey case has a pamphlet to itself—now extremely rare—a copy of which was recently obtained in a bookseller's shop in Dumfries by a well-known antiquary, and presented to the Advocates' Library in Edinburgh.

A queer look came into his eyes. "They ca' the place Carrickfey," he said. "Naebody has daured to bide there this twenty year sin'— but I see ye ken the story." And, as if glad to leave the subject, he hastened to discourse on fishing.

II
Tells of an Evening's Talk

The shepherd was a masterful man; tall, save for the stoop which belongs to all moorland folk, and active as a wild goat. He was not a new importation, nor did he belong to the place; for his people had lived in the remote Borders, and he had come as a boy to this shieling of Farawa. He was unmarried, but an elderly sister lived with him and cooked his meals. He was reputed to be extraordinarily skilful in his trade; I know for a fact that he was in his way a keen sportsman; and his few neighbours gave him credit for a sincere piety. Doubtless this last report was due in part to his silence, for after his first greeting he was wont to relapse into an extreme taciturnity. As we strode across the heather he gave me a short outline of his year's lambing. "Five pair o' twins yestreen, twae this morn; that makes thirty-five yowes that hae lambed since the Sabbath. I'll dae weel if God's willin'." Then, as I looked towards the hilltops whence the thin mist of morn was trailing, he followed my gaze. "See," he said with uplifted crook— "see that sicht. Is that no what is written of in the Bible when it says, 'The mountains do smoke'?" And with this piece of exegesis he finished his talk, and in a little we were at the cottage.

It was a small enough dwelling in truth, and yet large for a moorland house, for it had a garret below the thatch, which was given up to my sole enjoyment. Below was the wide kitchen with box-beds, and next to it the inevitable second room, also with its cupboard sleeping-places. The interior was very clean, and yet I remember to have been struck with the faint musty smell which is inseparable from moorland dwellings. The kitchen pleased me best, for there the great rafters were black with peat reek, and the uncovered stone floor, on which the fire gleamed dully, gave an air of primeval simplicity. But the walls spoiled all, for tawdry things of to-day had penetrated even there. Some grocers' almanacs—years old—hung in places of honour, and an extraordinary lithograph of the Royal Family in its youth. And this between crooks and fishing-rods and old guns, and horns of sheep and deer.

The life for the first day or two was regular and placid. I was up early, breakfasted on porridge (a dish which I detest), and then off to the lochs and streams. At first my sport prospered mightily. With a drake-wing I killed a salmon of seventeen pounds, and the next day had a fine basket of trout from a hill burn. Then for no earthly reason the weather changed. A bitter wind came out of the north-east, bringing showers of snow and stinging hail, and lash-ing the waters into storm. It was now farewell to fly-fishing. For a day or two I tried trolling with the minnow on the lochs, but it was poor sport, for I had no boat, and the edges were soft and mossy. Then in disgust I gave up the attempt, went back to the cottage, lit my biggest pipe, and sat down with a book to await the turn of the weather.

The shepherd was out from morning till night at his work, and when he came in at last, dog-tired, his face would be set and hard, and his eyes heavy with sleep. The strangeness of the man grew upon me. He had a shrewd brain beneath his thatch of hair, for I had tried him once or twice, and found him abundantly intelligent. He had some smattering of an education, like all Scottish peas-ants, and, as I have said, he was deeply religious. I set him down as a fine type of his class, sober, serious, keenly critical, free from the bondage of superstition. But I rarely saw him, and our talk was chiefly in monosyllables—short interjected accounts of the num-ber of lambs dead or alive on the hill. Then he would produce a pencil and note-book, and be immersed in some calculation; and finally he would be revealed sleeping heavily in his chair, till his sister wakened him, and he stumbled off to bed.

So much for the ordinary course of life; but one day—the sec-ond, I think, of the bad weather—the extraordinary happened. The storm had passed in the afternoon into a resolute and blinding snow, and the shepherd, finding it hopeless on the hill, came home about three o'clock. I could make out from his way of entering that he was in a great temper. He kicked his feet savagely against the door-post. Then he swore at his dogs, a thing I had never heard him do before. "Hell!" he cried, "can ye no keep out o' my road, ye bruits?" Then he came sullenly into the kitchen, thawed his numbed hands at the fire, and sat down to his meal.

I made some aimless remark about the weather.

"Death to man and beast," he grunted. "I hae got the sheep doun frae the hill, but the lambs will never thole this. We maun pray that it will no last."

His sister came in with some dish. "Margit," he cried, "three lambs away this morning, and three deid wi' the hole in the throat."

The woman's face visibly paled. "Guid help us, Adam; that hasna happened this three year."

"It has happened noo," he said surlily. "But, by God! if it happens again I'll gang mysel' to the Scarts o' the Muneraw."

"O Adam!" the woman cried shrilly, "haud your tongue. Ye kenna wha hears ye." And with a frightened glance at me she left the room.

I asked no questions, but waited till the shepherd's anger should cool. But the cloud did not pass so lightly. When he had finished his dinner he pulled his chair to the fire and sat staring moodily. He made some sort of apology to me for his conduct. "I'm sore troubled, sir; but I'm vexed ye should see me like this. Maybe things will be better the morn." And then, lighting his short black pipe, he resigned himself to his meditations.

But he could not keep quiet. Some nervous unrest seemed to have possessed the man. He got up with a start and went to the window, where the snow was drifting unsteadily past. As he stared out into the storm I heard him mutter to himself, "Three away, God help me, and three wi' the hole in the throat."

Then he turned round to me abruptly. I was jotting down notes for an article I contemplated in the *Revue Celtique*, so my thoughts were far away from the present. The man recalled me by demanding fiercely, "Do ye believe in God?"

I gave him some sort of answer in the affirmative.

"Then do ye believe in the Devil?" he asked.

The reply must have been less satisfactory, for he came forward and flung himself violently into the chair before me.

"What do ye ken about it?" he cried. "You that bides in a southern toun, what can ye ken o' the God that works in thae hills and the Devil—ay, the manifold devils—that He suffers to bide here? I tell ye, man, that if ye had seen what I have seen ye wad be on your knees at this moment praying to God to pardon your unbelief. There are devils at the back o' every stane and hidin' in every cleuch, and it's by the grace o' God alone that a man is alive upon the earth." His voice had risen high and shrill, and then suddenly he cast a frightened glance towards the window and was silent.

I began to think that the man's wits were unhinged, and the thought did not give me satisfaction. I had no relish for the prospect of being left alone in this moorland dwelling with the cheerful company of a maniac. But his next movements reassured me. He was clearly only dead-tired, for he fell sound asleep in his chair, and by the time his sister brought tea and wakened him, he seemed to have got the better of his excitement.

When the window was shuttered and the lamp lit, I set myself again to the completion of my notes. The shepherd had got out his Bible, and was solemnly reading with one great finger travelling down the lines. He was smoking, and whenever some text came home to him with power he would make pretence to underline it with the end of the stem. Soon I had finished the work I desired, and, my mind being full of my pet hobby, I fell into an inquisitive mood, and began to question the solemn man opposite on the antiquities of the place.

He stared stupidly at me when I asked him concerning monuments or ancient weapons.

"I kenna," said he. "There's a heap o' queer things in the hills."

"This place should be a centre for such relics. You know that the name of the hill behind the house, as far as I can make it out, means the 'Place of the Little Men.' It is a good Gaelic word, though there is some doubt about its exact interpretation. But clearly the Gaelic peoples did not speak of themselves when they gave the name; they must have referred to some older and stranger population."

The shepherd looked at me dully, as not understanding.

"It is partly this fact—besides the fishing, of course—which interests me in this countryside," said I gaily.

Again he cast the same queer frightened glance towards the window. "If ye'll tak the advice of an aulder man," he said slowly, "ye'll let well alane and no meddle wi' uncanny things."

I laughed pleasantly, for at last I had found out my hard-headed host in a piece of childishness. "Why, I thought that you of all men would be free from superstition."

"What do ye call supersteetion?" he asked.

"A belief in old wives' tales," said I, "a trust in the crude supernatural and the patently impossible."

He looked at me beneath his shaggy brows. "How do ye ken what is impossible? Mind ye, sir, ye're no in the toun just now, but in the thick of the wild hills."

"But, hang it all, man," I cried, "you don't mean to say that you believe in that sort of thing? I am prepared for many things up here, but not for the Brownie—though, to be sure, if one could meet him in the flesh, it would be rather pleasant than otherwise, for he was a companionable sort of fellow."

"When a thing pits the fear o' death on a man he aye speaks well of it."

It was true—the Eumenides and the Good Folk over again; and I awoke with interest to the fact that the conversation was getting into strange channels.

The shepherd moved uneasily in his chair. "I am a man that fears God, and has nae time for daft stories; but I havena traivelled the hills for twenty years wi' my een shut. If I say that I could tell ye stories o' faces seen in the mist, and queer things that have knocked against me in the snaw, wad ye believe me? I wager ye wadna. Ye wad say I had been drunk, and yet I am a God-fearing, temperate man." He rose and went to a cupboard, unlocked it, and brought out something in his hand, which he held out to me. I took it with some curiosity, and found that it was a flint arrow-head.

Clearly a flint arrow-head, and yet like none that I had ever seen in any collection. For one thing it was larger, and the barb less clumsily thick. More, the chipping was new, or comparatively so; this thing had not stood the wear of fifteen hundred years among the stones of the hillside. Now there are, I regret to say, institutions which manufacture primitive relics; but it is not hard for a practised eye to see the difference. The chipping has either a regularity and a balance which is unknown in the real thing, or the rudeness has been overdone, and the result is an implement incapable of harming a mortal creature. But this was the real thing if it ever existed; and yet—I was prepared to swear on my reputation that it was not half a century old.

"Where did you get this?" I asked with some excitement.

"I hae a story about that," said the shepherd. "Outside the door there ye can see a muckle flat stane aside the buchts. Ae simmer nicht I was sitting there smoking till the dark, and I wager there was naething on the stane then. But that same nicht I awoke wi' a queer thocht, as if there were folk moving around the hoose—folk that didna mak muckle noise. I mind o' lookin' out o' the windy, and I could hae sworn I saw something black movin' amang the heather and intil the buchts. Now I had maybe threescore o' lambs there that nicht, for I had to tak them many miles off in the early morning. Weel, when I gets up about four o'clock and gangs out, as I am passing the muckle stane I finds this bit errow. 'That's come here in the nicht,' says I, and I wunnered a wee and put it in my pouch. But when I came to my faulds what did I see? Five o' my best hoggs were away, and three mair were lying deid wi' a hole in their throat."

"Who in the world—?" I began.

"Dinna ask," said he. "If I aince sterted to speir about thae maitters, I wadna keep my reason."

"Then that was what happened on the hill this morning?"

"Even sae, and it has happened mair than aince sin' that time. It's the most uncanny slaughter, for sheep-stealing I can understand, but no this pricking o' the puir beasts' wizands. I kenna how they daett either, for it's no wi' a knife or ony common tool."

"Have you never tried to follow the thieves?"

"Have I no?" he asked grimly. "If it had been common sheep stealers I wad hae had them by the heels, though I had followed them a hundred miles. But this is no common. I've tracked them, and it's ill they are to track; but I never got beyond ae place, and that was the Scarts o' the Muneraw that ye've heard me speak o'."

"But who in Heaven's name are the people? Tinklers or poachers or what?"

"Ay," said he drily. "Even so. Tinklers and poachers whae wark wi' stane errows and kill sheep by a hole in their throat. Lord, I kenna what they are, unless the Muckle Deil himsel'."

The conversation had passed beyond my comprehension. In this prosaic hard-headed man I had come on the dead-rock of superstition and blind fear.

"That is only the story of the Brownie over again, and he is an exploded myth," I said, laughing.

"Are ye the man that exploded it?" said the shepherd rudely. "I trow no, neither you nor ony ither. My bonny man, if ye lived a twalmonth in thae hills, ye wad sing safter about exploded myths, as ye call them."

"I tell you what I would do," said I. "If I lost sheep as you lose them, I would go up the Scarts of the Muneraw and never rest till I had settled the question once and for all." I spoke hotly, for I was vexed by the man's childish fear.

"I dare say ye wad," he said slowly. "But then I am no you, and maybe I ken mair o' what is in the Scarts o' the Muneraw. Maybe I ken that whilk, if ye kenned it, wad send ye back to the South Country wi' your hert in your mouth. But, as I say, I am no sae brave as you, for I saw something in the first year o' my herding here which put the terror o' God on me, and makes me a fearfu' man to this day. Ye ken the story o' the gudeman o' Carrickfay?"

I nodded.

"Weel, I was the man that fand him. I had seen the deid afore and I've seen them since. But never have I seen aucht like the look in that man's een. What he saw at his death I may see the morn, so I walk before the Lord in fear."

Then he rose and stretched himself. "It's bedding-time, for I maun be up at three," and with a short good night he left the room.

III

THE SCARTS OF THE MUNERAW

The next morning was fine, for the snow had been intermittent, and had soon melted except in the high corries. True, it was deceptive weather, for the wind had gone to the rainy south-west, and the masses of cloud on that horizon boded ill for the afternoon. But some days' inaction had made me keen for a chance of sport, so I rose with the shepherd and set out for the day.

He asked me where I proposed to begin.

I told him the tarn called the Loch o' the Threshes, which lies over the back of the Muneraw on another watershed. It is on the ground of the Rhynns Forest, and I had fished it of old from the Forest House. I knew the merits of the trout, and I knew its virtues in a south-west wind, so I had resolved to go thus far afield.

The shepherd heard the name in silence. "Your best road will be ower that rig, and syne on to the water o' Caulds. Keep abune the moss till ye come to the place they ca' the Nick o' the Threshes. That will take ye to the very lochside, but it's a lang road and a sair."

The morning was breaking over the bleak hills. Little clouds drifted athwart the corries, and wisps of haze fluttered from the peaks. A great rosy flush lay over one side of the glen, which caught the edge of the sluggish bog pools and turned them to fire. Never before had I seen the mountainland so clear, for far back into the east and west I saw mountain tops set as close as flowers in a border, black crags seamed with silver lines which I knew for mighty waterfalls, and below at my feet the lower slopes fresh with the dewy green of spring. A name stuck in my memory from the last night's talk.

"Where are the Scarts of the Muneraw?" I asked.

The shepherd pointed to the great hill which bears the name, and which lies, a huge mass, above the watershed.

"D'ye see yon corrie at the east that runs straucht up the side? It looks a bit scart, but it's sae deep that it's aye derk at the bottom o't. Weel, at the tap o' the rig it meets anither corrie that runs doun the ither side, and that one they ca' the Scarts. There is a sort o'

burn in it that flows intil the Dule and sae intil the Aller, and, indeed, if ye were gaun there it wad be from Aller Glen that your best
road wad lie. But it's an ill bit, and ye'll be sair guidit if ye try't."

There he left me and went across the glen, while I struck upwards over the ridge. At the top I halted and looked down on the
wide glen of the Caulds, which there is little better than a bog, but
lower down grows into a green pastoral valley. The great Muneraw
still dominated the landscape, and the black scaur on its side
seemed blacker than before. The place fascinated me, for in that
fresh morning air the shepherd's fears seemed monstrous. "Some
day," said I to myself, "I will go and explore the whole of that mighty
hill." Then I descended and struggled over the moss, found the
Nick, and in two hours' time was on the loch's edge.

I have little in the way of good to report of the fishing. For perhaps one hour the trout took well; after that they sulked steadily
for the day. The promise, too, of fine weather had been deceptive.
By midday the rain was falling in that soft soaking fashion which
gives no hope of clearing. The mist was down to the edge of the
water, and I cast my flies into a blind sea of white. It was hopeless
work, and yet from a sort of ill-temper I stuck to it long after my
better judgment had warned me of its folly. At last, about three in
the afternoon, I struck my camp, and prepared myself for a long
and toilsome retreat.

And long and toilsome it was beyond anything I had ever encountered. Had I had a vestige of sense I would have followed the
burn from the loch down to the Forest House. The place was shut
up, but the keeper would gladly have given me shelter for the night.
But foolish pride was too strong in me. I had found my road in
mist before, and could do it again.

Before I got to the top of the hill I had repented my decision;
when I got there I repented it more. For below me was a dizzy chaos
of grey; there was no landmark visible; and before me I knew was
the bog through which the Caulds Water twined. I had crossed it
with some trouble in the morning, but then I had light to pick my
steps. Now I could only stumble on, and in five minutes I might be
in a bog hole, and in five more in a better world.

But there was no help to be got from hesitation, so with a rueful courage I set off. The place was if possible worse than I had feared. Wading up to the knees with nothing before you but a blank wall of mist and the cheerful consciousness that your next step may be your last—such was my state for one weary mile. The stream itself was high, and rose to my armpits, and once and again I only saved myself by a violent leap backwards from a pitiless green slough. But at last it was past, and I was once more on the solid ground of the hillside.

Now, in the thick weather I had crossed the glen much lower down than in the morning, and the result was that the hill on which I stood was one of the giants which, with the Muneraw for centre, guard the watershed. Had I taken the proper way, the Nick o' the Threshes would have led me to the Caulds, and then once over the bog a little ridge was all that stood between me and the glen of Farawa. But instead I had come a wild cross-country road, and was now, though I did not know it, nearly as far from my destination as at the start.

Well for me that I did not know, for I was wet and dispirited, and had I not fancied myself all but home, I should scarcely have had the energy to make this last ascent. But soon I found it was not the little ridge I had expected. I looked at my watch and saw that it was five o'clock. When, after the weariest climb, I lay on a piece of level ground which seemed the top, I was not surprised to find that it was now seven. The darkening must be at hand, and sure enough the mist seemed to be deepening into a greyish black. I began to grow desperate. Here was I on the summit of some infernal mountain, without any certainty where my road lay. I was lost with a vengeance, and at the thought I began to be acutely afraid.

I took what seemed to me the way I had come, and began to descend steeply. Then something made me halt, and the next instant I was lying on my face trying painfully to retrace my steps. For I had found myself slipping, and before I could stop, my feet were dangling over a precipice with Heaven alone knows how many yards of sheer mist between me and the bottom. Then I tried keeping the ridge, and took that to the right, which I thought would bring me nearer home. It was no good trying to think out a direction, for in the fog my brain was running round, and I seemed to stand on a pin-point of space where the laws of the compass had ceased to hold.

It was the roughest sort of walking, now stepping warily over acres of loose stones, now crawling down the face of some battered rock, and now wading in the long dripping heather. The soft rain had begun to fall again, which completed my discomfort. I was now seriously tired, and, like all men who in their day have bent too much over books, I began to feel it in my back. My spine ached, and my breath came in short broken pants. It was a pitiable state of affairs for an honest man who had never encountered much grave discomfort. To ease myself I was compelled to leave my basket behind me, trusting to return and find it, if I should ever reach safety and discover on what pathless hill I had been strayed. My rod I used as a staff, but it was of little use, for my fingers were getting too numb to hold it.

Suddenly from the blankness I heard a sound as of human speech. At first I thought it mere craziness—the cry of a weasel or a hill bird distorted by my ears. But again it came, thick and faint, as through acres of mist, and yet clearly the sound of "articulate-speaking men." In a moment I lost my despair and cried out in answer. This was some forwandered traveller like myself, and between us we could surely find some road to safety. So I yelled back at the pitch of my voice and waited intently.

But the sound ceased, and there was utter silence again. Still I waited, and then from some place much nearer came the same soft mumbling speech. I could make nothing of it. Heard in that drear place it made the nerves tense and the heart timorous. It was the strangest jumble of vowels and consonants I had ever met.

A dozen solutions flashed through my brain. It was some maniac talking Jabberwock to himself. It was some belated traveller whose wits had given out in fear. Perhaps it was only some shepherd who was amusing himself thus, and whiling the way with nonsense. Once again I cried out and waited.

Then suddenly in the hollow trough of mist before me, where things could still be half discerned, there appeared a figure. It was little and squat and dark; naked, apparently, but so rough with hair that it wore the appearance of a skin-covered being. It crossed my line of vision, not staying for a moment, but in its face and eyes there seemed to lurk an elder world of mystery and barbarism, a troll-like life which was too horrible for words.

The shepherd's fear came back on me like a thunderclap. For one awful instant my legs failed me, and I had almost fallen. The next I had turned and ran shrieking up the hill.

If he who may read this narrative has never felt the force of an overmastering terror, then let him thank his Maker and pray that he never may. I am no weak child, but a strong grown man, accredited in general with sound sense and little suspected of hysterics. And yet I went up that brae face with my heart fluttering like a bird and my throat aching with fear. I screamed in short dry gasps; involuntarily, for my mind was beyond any purpose. I felt that beast-like clutch at my throat; those red eyes seemed to be staring at me from the mist; I heard ever behind and before and on all sides the patter of those inhuman feet.

Before I knew I was down, slipping over a rook and falling some dozen feet into a soft marshy hollow. I was conscious of lying still for a second and whimpering like a child. But as I lay there I awoke to the silence of the place. There was no sound of pursuit; perhaps they had lost my track and given up. My courage began to return, and from this it was an easy step to hope. Perhaps after all it had been merely an illusion, for folk do not see clearly in the mist, and I was already done with weariness.

But even as I lay in the green moss and began to hope, the faces of my pursuers grew up through the mist. I stumbled madly to my feet; but I was hemmed in, the rock behind and my enemies before. With a cry I rushed forward, and struck wildly with my rod at the first dark body. It was as if I had struck an animal, and the next second the thing was wrenched from my grasp. But still they came no nearer. I stood trembling there in the centre of those malignant devils, my brain a mere weathercock, and my heart crushed shapeless with horror. At last the end came, for with the vigour of madness I flung myself on the nearest, and we rolled on the ground. Then the monstrous things seemed to close over me, and with a choking cry I passed into unconsciousness.

IV
This Darkness that is Under the Earth

There is an unconsciousness that is not wholly dead, where a man feels numbly and the body lives without the brain. I was beyond speech or thought, and yet I felt the upward or downward motion as the way lay in hill or glen, and I most assuredly knew when the open air was changed for the close underground. I could feel dimly that lights were flared in my face, and that I was laid in some bed on the earth. Then with the stopping of movement the real sleep of weakness seized me, and for long I knew nothing of this mad world.

Morning came over the moors with bird song and the glory of fine weather. The streams were still rolling in spate, but the hill pastures were alight with dawn, and the little seams of snow were glistening like white fire. A ray from the sunrise cleft its path somehow into the abyss, and danced on the wall above my couch. It caught my eye as I wakened, and for long I lay crazily wondering what it meant. My head was splitting with pain, and in my heart was the same fluttering nameless fear. I did not wake to full consciousness; not till the twinkle of sun from the clean bright out-of-doors caught my face did I realize that I lay in a great dark place with a glow of dull firelight in the middle.

In time things rose and moved around me, a few ragged shapes of men, without clothing, shambling with their huge feet and looking towards me with curved beast-like glances. I tried to marshal my thoughts, and slowly, bit by bit, I built up the present. There was no question to my mind of dreaming; the past hours had scored reality upon my brain. Yet I cannot say that fear was my chief feeling. The first crazy terror had subsided, and now I felt mainly a sickened disgust with just a tinge of curiosity. I found that my knife, watch, flask, and money had gone, but they had left me a map of the countryside. It seemed strange to look at the calico, with the name of a London printer stamped on the back, and lines of railway and highroad running through every shire. Decent and comfortable civilization! And here was I a prisoner in this den of nameless folk, and in the midst of a life which history knew not.

Courage is a virtue which grows with reflection and the absence of the immediate peril. I thought myself into some sort of resolution, and lo! when the Folk approached me and bound my feet I was back at once in the most miserable terror. They tied me, all but my hands, with some strong cord, and carried me to the centre, where the fire was glowing. Their soft touch was the acutest torture to my nerves, but I stifled my cries lest some one should lay his hand on my mouth. Had that happened, I am convinced my reason would have failed me.

So there I lay in the shine of the fire, with the circle of unknown things around me. There seemed but three or four, but I took no note of number. They talked huskily among themselves in a tongue which sounded all gutturals. Slowly my fear became less an emotion than a habit, and I had room for the smallest shade of curiosity. I strained my ear to catch a word, but it was a mere chaos of sound. The thing ran and thundered in my brain as I stared dumbly into the vacant air. Then I thought that unless I spoke I should certainly go crazy, for my head was beginning to swim at the strange cooing noise.

I spoke a word or two in my best Gaelic, and they closed round me inquiringly. Then I was sorry I had spoken, for my words had brought them nearer, and I shrank at the thought. But as the faint echoes of my speech hummed in the rock chamber, I was struck by a curious kinship of sound. Mine was sharper, more distinct, and staccato; theirs was blurred, formless, but still with a certain root resemblance.

Then from the back there came an older being, who seemed to have heard my words. He was like some foul grey badger, his red eyes sightless, and his hands trembling on a stump of bog oak.

The others made way for him with such deference as they were capable of, and the thing squatted down by me and spoke.

To my amazement his words were familiar. It was some manner of speech akin to the Gaelic, but broadened, lengthened, coarsened. I remembered an old book tongue, commonly supposed to be an impure dialect once used in Brittany, which I had met in the course of my researches. The words recalled it, and as far as I could remember the thing, I asked him who he was and where the place might be.

He answered me in the same speech—still more broadened, lengthened, coarsened. I lay back with sheer amazement. I had found the key to this unearthly life.

For a little an insatiable curiosity, the ardour of the scholar, prevailed. I forgot the horror of the place, and thought only of the fact that here before me was the greatest find that scholarship had ever made. I was precipitated into the heart of the past. Here must be the fountainhead of all legends, the chrysalis of all beliefs. I actually grew light-hearted. This strange folk around me were now no more shapeless things of terror, but objects of research and experiment. I almost came to think them not unfriendly.

For an hour I enjoyed the highest of earthly pleasures. In that strange conversation I heard—in fragments and suggestions—the history of the craziest survival the world has ever seen. I heard of the struggles with invaders, preserved as it were in a sort of shapeless poetry. There were bitter words against the Gaelic oppressor, bitterer words against the Saxon stranger, and for a moment ancient hatreds flared into life. Then there came the tale of the hill refuge, the morbid hideous existence preserved for centuries amid a changing world. I heard fragments of old religions, primeval names of god and goddess, half-understood by the Folk, but to me the key to a hundred puzzles. Tales which survive to us in broken disjointed riddles were intact here in living form. I lay on my elbow and questioned feverishly. At any moment they might become morose and refuse to speak. Clearly it was my duty to make the most of a brief good fortune.

And then the tale they told me grew more hideous. I heard of the circumstances of the life itself and their daily shifts for existence. It was a murderous chronicle—a history of lust and rapine and unmentionable deeds in the darkness. One thing they had early recognized—that the race could not be maintained within itself; so that ghoulish carrying away of little girls from the lowlands began, which I had heard of but never credited. Shut up in those dismal holes, the girls soon died, and when the new race had grown up the plunder had been repeated. Then there were bestial murders in lonely cottages, done for God knows what purpose. Sometimes the occupant had seen more than was safe, sometimes the deed was the mere exuberance of a lust of slaying. As they gabbled their tales my heart's blood froze, and I lay back in the agonies of fear. If they had used the others thus, what way of escape was open for myself? I had been brought to this place, and not murdered on the spot. Clearly there was torture before death in store for me, and I confess I quailed at the thought.

But none molested me. The elders continued to jabber out their stories, while I lay tense and deaf. Then to my amazement food was brought and placed beside me—almost with respect. Clearly my murder was not a thing of the immediate future. The meal was some form of mutton—perhaps the shepherd's lost ewes—and a little smoking was all the cooking it had got. I strove to eat, but the tasteless morsels choked me. Then they set drink before me in a curious cup, which I seized on eagerly, for my mouth was dry with thirst. The vessel was of gold, rudely formed, but of the pure metal, and a coarse design in circles ran round the middle. This was surprising enough, but a greater wonder awaited me. The liquor was not water, as I had guessed, but a sort of sweet ale, a miracle of flavour. The taste was curious, but somehow familiar; it was like no wine I had ever drunk, and yet I had known that flavour all my life. I sniffed at the brim, and there rose a faint fragrance of thyme and heather honey and the sweet things of the moorland. I almost dropped it in my surprise; for here in this rude place I had stumbled upon that lost delicacy of the North, the heather ale.

For a second I was entranced with my discovery, and then the wonder of the cup claimed my attention. Was it a mere relic of pillage, or had this folk some hidden mine of the precious metal? Gold had once been common in these hills. There were the traces of mines on Cairnsmore; shepherds had found it in the gravel of the Gled Water; and the name of a house at the head of the Clachlands meant the "Home of Gold."

Once more I began my questions, and they answered them willingly. There and then I heard that secret for which many had died in old time, the secret of the heather ale. They told of the gold in the hills, of corries where the sand gleamed and abysses where the rocks were veined. All this they told me, freely, without a scruple. And then, like a clap, came the awful thought that this, too, spelled death. These were secrets which this race aforetime had guarded with their lives; they told them generously to me because there was no fear of betrayal. I should go no more out from this place.

The thought put me into a new sweat of terror—not of death, mind you, but of the unknown horrors which might precede the final suffering. I lay silent, and after binding my hands they began to leave me and go off to other parts of the cave. I dozed in the horrible half-swoon of fear, conscious only of my shaking limbs, and the great dull glow of the fire in the centre. Then I became calmer. After all, they had treated me with tolerable kindness; I had spoken their language, which few of their victims could have done for many a century; it might be that I had found favour in their eyes. For a little I comforted myself with this delusion, till I caught sight of a wooden box in a corner. It was of modern make, one such as grocers use to pack provisions in. It had some address nailed on it, and an aimless curiosity compelled me to creep thither and read it. A torn and weather-stained scrap of paper, with the nails at the corner rusty with age; but something of the address might still be made out. Amid the stains my feverish eyes read, "To Mr. M—, Carrickfey, by Allerfoot Station."

The ruined cottage in the hollow of the waste with the single gnarled apple tree was before me in a twinkling. I remembered the shepherd's shrinking from the place and the name, and his wild eyes when he told me of the thing that had happened there. I seemed to see the old man in his moorland cottage, thinking no evil; the sudden entry of the nameless things; and then the eyes glazed in unspeakable terror. I felt my lips dry and burning. Above me was the vault of rock; in the distance I saw the fire-glow and the shadows of shapes moving around it. My fright was too great for inaction, so I crept from the couch, and silently, stealthily, with tottering steps and bursting heart, I began to reconnoitre.

But I was still bound, my arms tightly, my legs more loosely, but yet firm enough to hinder flight. I could not get my hands at my leg straps, still less could I undo the manacles. I rolled on the floor, seeking some sharp edge of rock, but all had been worn smooth by the use of centuries. Then suddenly an idea came upon me like an inspiration. The sounds from the fire seemed to have ceased, and I could hear them repeated from another and more distant part of the cave. The Folk had left their orgy round the blaze, and at the end of the long tunnel I saw its glow fall unimpeded upon the floor. Once there, I might burn off my fetters and be free to turn my thoughts to escape.

I crawled a little way with much labour. Then suddenly I came abreast an opening in the wall, through which a path went. It was a long straight rock-cutting, and at the end I saw a gleam of pale light. It must be the open air; the way of escape was prepared for me; and with a prayer I made what speed I could towards the fire.

I rolled on the verge, but the fuel was peat, and the warm ashes would not burn the cords. In desperation I went farther, and my clothes began to singe, while my face ached beyond endurance. But yet I got no nearer my object. The strips of hide warped and cracked, but did not burn. Then in a last effort I thrust my wrists bodily into the glow and held them there. In an instant I drew them out with a groan of pain, scarred and sore, but to my joy with the band snapped in one place. Weak as I was, it was now easy to free myself, and then came the untying of my legs. My hands trembled, my eyes were dazed with hurry, and I was longer over the job than need have been. But at length I had loosed my cramped knees and stood on my feet, a free man once more.

I kicked off my boots, and fled noiselessly down the passage to the tunnel mouth. Apparently it was close on evening, for the white light had faded to a pale yellow. But it was daylight, and that was all I sought, and I ran for it as eagerly as ever runner ran to a goal.

I came out on a rock shelf, beneath which a moraine of boulders fell away in a chasm to a dark loch. It was all but night, but I could see the gnarled and fortressed rocks rise in ramparts above, and below the unknown screes and cliffs which make the side of the Muneraw a place only for foxes and the fowls of the air.

The first taste of liberty is an intoxication, and assuredly I was mad when I leaped down among the boulders. Happily at the top of the gully the stones were large and stable, else the noise would certainly have discovered me. Down I went, slipping, praying, my charred wrists aching, and my stockinged feet wet with blood. Soon I was in the jaws of the cleft, and a pale star rose before me. I have always been timid in the face of great rocks, and now, had not an awful terror been dogging my footsteps, no power on earth could have driven me to that descent.

Soon I left the boulders behind, and came to long spouts of little stones, which moved with me till the hillside seemed sinking under my feet. Sometimes I was face downwards, once and again I must have fallen for yards. Had there been a cliff at the foot, I should have gone over it without resistance; but by the providence of God the spout ended in a long curve into the heather of the bog.

When I found my feet once more on soft boggy earth, my strength was renewed within me. A hope of escape sprang up in my heart. For a second I looked back. There was a great line of shingle with the cliffs beyond, and above all the unknown blackness of the cleft. There lay my terror, and I set off running across the bog for dear life. My mind was clear enough to know my road. If I held round the loch in front I should come to a burn which fed the Farawa stream, on whose banks stood the shepherd's cottage. The loch could not be far; once at the Farawa I would have the light of the shieling clear before me.

Suddenly I heard behind me, as if coming from the hillside, the patter of feet. It was the sound which white hares make in the winter-time on a noiseless frosty day as they patter over the snow. I have heard the same soft noise from a herd of deer when they changed their pastures. Strange that so kindly a sound should put the very fear of death in my heart. I ran madly, blindly, yet thinking shrewdly. The loch was before me. Somewhere I had read or heard, I do not know where, that the brutish aboriginal races of the North could not swim. I myself swam powerfully; could I but cross the loch I should save two miles of a desperate country.

There was no time to lose, for the patter was coming nearer, and I was almost at the loch's edge. I tore off my coat and rushed in. The bottom was mossy, and I had to struggle far before I found any depth. Something plashed in the water before me, and then something else a little behind. The thought that I was a mark for unknown missiles made me crazy with fright, and I struck fiercely out for the other shore. A gleam of moonlight was on the water at the burn's exit, and thither I guided myself. I found the thing difficult enough in itself, for my hands ached, and I was numb from my bonds. But my fancy raised a thousand phantoms to vex me. Swimming in that black bog water, pursued by those nameless things, I seemed to be in a world of horror far removed from the kindly world of men. My strength seemed inexhaustible from my terror. Monsters at the bottom of the water seemed to bite at my feet, and the pain of my wrists made me believe that the loch was boiling hot, and that I was in some hellish place of torment.

I came out on a spit of gravel above the burn mouth, and set off down the ravine of the burn. It was a strait place, strewn with rocks; but now and then the hill turf came in stretches, and eased my wounded feet. Soon the fall became more abrupt, and I was slipping down a hillside, with the water on my left making great cascades in the granite. And then I was out in the wider vale where the Farawa water flowed among links of moss.

Far in front, a speck in the blue darkness, shone the light of the cottage. I panted forward, my breath coming in gasps and my back shot with fiery pains. Happily the land was easier for the feet as long as I kept on the skirts of the bog. My ears were sharp as a wild beast's with fear, as I listened for the noise of pursuit. Nothing came but the rustle of the gentlest hill wind and the chatter of the falling streams.

Then suddenly the light began to waver and move athwart the window. I knew what it meant. In a minute or two the household at the cottage would retire to rest, and the lamp would be put out. True, I might find the place in the dark, for there was a moon of sorts and the road was not desperate. But somehow in that hour the lamplight gave a promise of safety which I clung to despairingly.

And then the last straw was added to my misery. Behind me came the pad of feet, the pat-patter, soft, eerie, incredibly swift. I choked with fear, and flung myself forward in a last effort. I give my word it was sheer mechanical shrinking that drove me on. God knows I would have lain down to die in the heather, had the things behind me been a common terror of life.

I ran as man never ran before, leaping hags, scrambling through green well-heads, straining towards the fast-dying light. A quarter of a mile and the patter sounded nearer. Soon I was not two hundred yards off, and the noise seemed almost at my elbow. The light went out, and the black mass of the cottage loomed in the dark.

Then, before I knew, I was at the door, battering it wearily and yelling for help. I heard steps within and a hand on the bolt. Something shot past me with lightning force and buried itself in the wood. The dreadful hands were almost at my throat, when the door was opened and I stumbled in, hearing with a gulp of joy the key turn and the bar fall behind me.

V

The Troubles of a Conscience

My body and senses slept, for I was utterly tired, but my brain all the night was on fire with horrid fancies. Again I was in that accursed cave; I was torturing my hands in the fire; I was slipping barefoot among jagged boulders; and then with bursting heart I was toiling the last mile with the cottage light—now grown to a great fire in the heavens—blazing before me.

It was broad daylight when I awoke, and I thanked God for the comfortable rays of the sun. I had been laid in a box-bed off the inner room, and my first sight was the shepherd sitting with folded arms in a chair regarding me solemnly. I rose and began to dress, feeling my legs and arms still tremble with weariness. The shepherd's sister bound up my scarred wrists and put an ointment on my burns; and, limping like an old man, I went into the kitchen.

I could eat little breakfast, for my throat seemed dry and narrow; but they gave me some whisky-and-milk, which put strength into my body. All the time the brother and sister sat in silence, regarding me with covert glances.

"Ye have been delivered from the jaws o' the Pit," said the man at length. "See that," and he held out to me a thin shaft of flint. "I fand that in the door this morning."

I took it, let it drop, and stared vacantly at the window. My nerves had been too much tried to be roused by any new terror. Out of doors it was fair weather, flying gleams of April sunlight and the soft colours of spring. I felt dazed, isolated, cut off from my easy past and pleasing future, a companion of horrors and the sport of nameless things. Then suddenly my eye fell on my books heaped on the table, and the old distant civilization seemed for the moment inexpressibly dear.

"I must go—at once. And you must come too. You cannot stay here. I tell you it is death. If you knew what I know you would be crying out with fear. How far is it to Allermuir? Eight, fifteen miles; and then ten down Glen Aller to Allerfoot, and then the railway. We must go together while it is daylight, and perhaps we may be untouched. But quick, there is not a moment to lose." And I was on my shaky feet, and bustling among my possessions.

"I'll gang wi' ye to the station," said the shepherd, "for ye're clearly no fit to look after yourself. My sister will bide and keep the house. If naething has touched us this ten year, naething will touch us the day."

"But you cannot stay. You are mad," I began; but he cut me short with the words, "I trust in God."

"In any case let your sister come with us. I dare not think of a woman alone in this place."

"I'll bide," said she. "I'm no feared as lang as I'm indoors and there's steeks on the windies."

So I packed my few belongings as best I could, flung my books into a haversack, and, gripping the shepherd's arm nervously, crossed the threshold. The glen was full of sunlight. There lay the long shining links of the Farawa burn, the rough hills tumbled beyond, and far over all the scarred and distant forehead of the Muneraw. I had always looked on moorland country as the freshest on earth—clean, wholesome, and homely. But now the uplands seemed like a horrible pit. When I looked to the hills my breath choked in my throat, and the feel of soft heather below my feet set my heart trembling.

It was a slow journey to the inn at Allermuir. For one thing, no power on earth would draw me within sight of the shieling of Carrickfey, so we had to cross a shoulder of hill and make our way down a difficult glen, and then over a treacherous moss. The lochs were now gleaming like fretted silver; but to me, in my dreadful knowledge, they seemed more eerie than on that grey day when I came. At last my eyes were cheered by the sight of a meadow and a fence; then we were on a little byroad; and soon the fir-woods and corn-lands of Allercleuch were plain before us.

The shepherd came no farther, but with brief good-bye turned his solemn face hillwards. I hired a trap and a man to drive, and down the ten miles of Glen Aller I struggled to keep my thoughts from the past. I thought of the kindly South Country, of Oxford, of anything comfortable and civilized. My driver pointed out the objects of interest as in duty bound, but his words fell on unheeding ears. At last he said something which roused me indeed to interest—the interest of the man who hears the word he fears most in the world. On the left side of the river there suddenly sprang into view a long gloomy cleft in the hills, with a vista of dark mountains behind, down which a stream of considerable size poured its waters.

"That is the Water o' Dule," said the man in a reverent voice. "A graund water to fish, but dangerous to life, for it's a' linns. Awa at the heid they say there's a terrible wild place called the Scarts o' Muneraw,—that's a shouther o' the muckle hill itsel' that ye see,—but I've never been there, and I never kent ony man that had either."

At the station, which is a mile from the village of Allerfoot, I found I had some hours to wait on my train for the south. I dared not trust myself for one moment alone, so I hung about the goods

shed, talked vacantly to the porters, and when one went to the village for tea I accompanied him, and to his wonder entertained him
at the inn. When I returned I found on the platform a stray bagman
who was that evening going to London.

If there is one class of men in the world for which I have small
inclination it is this; but such was my state that I hailed him as a
brother, and besought his company. I paid the difference for a first-
class fare, and had him in the carriage with me. He must have
thought me an amiable maniac, for I talked in fits and starts, and
when he fell asleep I would wake him up and beseech him to speak
to me. At wayside stations I would pull down the blinds in case of
recognition, for to my unquiet mind the world seemed full of spies
sent by that terrible Folk of the Hills. When the train crossed a
stretch of moor I would lie down on the seat in case of shafts fired
from the heather. And then at last with utter weariness I fell asleep,
and woke screaming about midnight to find myself well down in
the cheerful English midlands, and red blast furnaces blinking by
the railway-side.

In the morning I breakfasted in my rooms at St. Chad's with a
dawning sense of safety. I was in a different and calmer world. The
lawn-like quadrangles, the great trees, the cawing of rooks, and
the homely twitter of sparrows—all seemed decent and settled and
pleasing. Indoors the oak-panelled walls, the shelves of books, the
pictures, the faint fragrance of tobacco, were very different from
the gimcrack adornments and the accursed smell of peat and
heather in that deplorable cottage. It was still vacation time, so
most of my friends were down, but I spent the day hunting out the
few cheerful pedants to whom term and vacation were the same. It
delighted me to hear again their precise talk, to hear them make a
boast of their work, and narrate the childish little incidents of their
life. I yearned for the childish once more; I craved for women's
drawing-rooms, and women's chatter, and everything which makes
life an elegant game. God knows I had had enough of the other
thing for a lifetime!

That night I shut myself in my rooms, barred my windows, drew
my curtains, and made a great destruction. All books or pictures

which recalled to me the moorlands were ruthlessly doomed. Novels, poems, treatises I flung into an old box, for sale to the second-hand bookseller. Some prints and water-colour sketches I tore to pieces with my own hands. I ransacked my fishing-book, and condemned all tackle for moorland waters to the flames. I wrote a letter to my solicitors, bidding them go no further in the purchase of a place in Lorn I had long been thinking of. Then, and not till then, did I feel the bondage of the past a little loosed from my shoulders. I made myself a night-cap of rum punch instead of my usual whisky toddy, that all associations with that dismal land might be forgotten, and to complete the renunciation I returned to cigars and flung my pipe into a drawer.

But when I woke in the morning I found that it is hard to get rid of memories. My feet were still sore and wounded, and when I felt my arms cramped and reflected on the causes, there was that black memory always near to vex me.

In a little term began, and my duties—as deputy professor of Northern Antiquities—were once more clamorous. I can well believe that my hearers found my lectures strange, for instead of dealing with my favourite subjects and matters, which I might modestly say I had made my own, I confined myself to recondite and distant themes, treating even these cursorily and dully. For the truth is, my heart was no more in my subject. I hated—or I thought that I hated—all things Northern with the virulence of utter fear. My reading was confined to science of the most recent kind, to abstruse philosophy. and to foreign classics. Anything which savoured of romance or mystery was abhorrent; I pined for sharp outlines and the tangibility of a high civilization.

All that term I threw myself into the most frivolous life of the place. My Harrow schooldays seemed to have come back to me. I had once been a fair cricketer, so I played again for my college, and made decent scores. I coached an indifferent crew on the river. I fell into the slang of the place, which I had hitherto detested. My former friends looked on me askance, as if some freakish changeling had possessed me. Formerly I had been ready for pedantic discussion, I had been absorbed in my work, men had spoken of me as a rising scholar. Now I fled the very mention of things I had once delighted in. The Professor of Northern Antiquities, a scholar of European reputation, meeting me once in the Parks, embarked on an account of certain novel rings recently found in Scotland, and to his horror found that, when he had got well under way, I had slipped off unnoticed. I heard afterwards that the good old man was found by a friend walking disconsolately with bowed head in the middle of the High Street. Being rescued from among the horses' feet, he could only murmur, "I am thinking of Graves, poor man! And a year ago he was as sane as I am!"

But a man may not long deceive himself. I kept up the illusion valiantly for the term; but I felt instinctively that the fresh school-boy life, which seemed to me the extreme opposite to the ghoulish North, and as such the most desirable of things, was eternally cut off from me. No cunning affectation could ever dispel my real nature or efface the memory of a week. I realized miserably that sooner or later I must fight it out with my conscience. I began to call myself a coward. The chief thoughts of my mind began to centre themselves more and more round that unknown life waiting to be explored among the wilds.

One day I met a friend—an official in the British Museum—who was full of some new theory about primitive habitations. To me it seemed inconceivably absurd; but he was strong in his confidence, and without flaw in his evidence. The man irritated me, and I burned to prove him wrong, but I could think of no argument which was final against his. Then it flashed upon me that my own experience held the disproof; and without more words I left him, hot, angry with myself, and tantalized by the unattainable.

I might relate my *bona-fide* experience, but would men believe me? I must bring proofs, I must complete my researches, so as to make them incapable of disbelief. And there in those deserts was waiting the key. There lay the greatest discovery of the century—nay, of the millennium. There, too, lay the road to wealth such as I had never dreamed of. Could I succeed, I should be famous for ever. I would revolutionize history and anthropology; I would systematize folklore; I would show the world of men the pit whence they were digged and the rock whence they were hewn.

And then began a game of battledore between myself and my conscience.

"You are a coward," said my conscience.

"I am sufficiently brave," I would answer. "I have seen things and yet lived. The terror is more than mortal, and I cannot face it."

"You are a coward," said my conscience.

"I am not bound to go there again. It would be purely for my own aggrandizement if I went, and not for any matter of duty."

"Nevertheless you are a coward," said my conscience.

"In any case the matter can wait."

"You are a coward."

Then came one awful midsummer night, when I lay sleepless and fought the thing out with myself. I knew that the strife was hopeless, that I should have no peace in this world again unless I made the attempt. The dawn was breaking when I came to the final resolution; and when I rose and looked at my face in a mirror, lo! it was white and lined and drawn like a man of sixty.

VI
Summer on the Moors

The next morning I packed a bag with some changes of clothing and a collection of notebooks, and went up to town. The first thing I did was to pay a visit to my solicitors. "I am about to travel," said I, "and I wish to have all things settled in case any accident should happen to me." So I arranged for the disposal of my property in case of death, and added a codicil which puzzled the lawyers. If I did not return within six months, communications were to be entered into with the shepherd at the shieling of Farawa—post-town Allerfoot. If he could produce any papers, they were to be put into the hands of certain friends, published, and the cost charged to my estate. From my solicitors I went to a gunmaker's in Regent Street and bought an ordinary six-chambered revolver, feeling much as a man must feel who proposed to cross the Atlantic in a skiff and purchased a small lifebelt as a precaution.

I took the night express to the North, and, for a marvel, I slept. When I awoke about four we were on the verge of Westmoreland, and stony hills blocked the horizon. At first I hailed the mountain-land gladly; sleep for the moment had caused forgetfulness of my terrors. But soon a turn of the line brought me in full view of a heathery moor, running far to a confusion of distant peaks. I remembered my mission and my fate, and if ever condemned criminal felt a more bitter regret I pity his case. Why should I alone among the millions of this happy isle be singled out as the repository of a ghastly secret, and be cursed by a conscience which would not let it rest?

I came to Allerfoot early in the forenoon, and got a trap to drive me up the valley. It was a lowering grey day, hot and yet sunless. A sort of heat haze cloaked the hills, and every now and then a smurr of rain would meet us on the road, and in a minute be over. I felt wretchedly dispirited; and when at last the white-washed kirk of Allermuir came into sight and the broken-backed bridge of Aller, man's eyes seemed to have looked on no drearier scene since time began.

I ate what meal I could get, for, fears or no, I was voraciously hungry. Then I asked the landlord to find me some man who would show me the road to Farawa. I demanded company, not for protection—for what could two men do against such brutish strength?—but to keep my mind from its own thoughts.

The man looked at me anxiously.

"Are ye acquaint wi' the folks, then?" he asked.

I said I was, that I had often stayed in the cottage.

"Ye ken that they've a name for being queer. The man never comes here forbye once or twice a year, and he has few dealings wi' other herds. He's got an ill name, too, for losing sheep. I dinna like the country ava. Up by yon Muneraw—no that I've ever been there, but I've seen it afar off—is enough to put a man daft for the rest o' his days. What's taking ye thereaways? It's no the time for the fishing?"

I told him that I was a botanist going to explore certain hill crevices for rare ferns. He shook his head, and then after some delay found me an ostler who would accompany me to the cottage.

The man was a shock-headed, long-limbed fellow, with fierce red hair and a humorous eye. He talked sociably about his life, answered my hasty questions with deftness, and beguiled me for the moment out of myself. I passed the melancholy lochs, and came in sight of the great stony hills without the trepidation I had expected. Here at my side was one who found some humour even in those uplands. But one thing I noted which brought back the old uneasiness. He took the road which led us farthest from Carrickfey, and when to try him I proposed the other, he vetoed it with emphasis.

After this his good spirits departed, and he grew distrustful.

"What maks ye a freend o' the herd at Farawa?" he demanded a dozen times.

Finally, I asked him if he knew the man, and had seen him lately.

"I dinna ken him, and I hadna seen him for years till a fortnicht syne, when a' Allermuir saw him. He cam doun one afternoon to the public-hoose, and begood to drink. He had aye been kenned for a terrible godly kind o' a man, so ye may believe folk wondered at this. But when he had stuck to the drink for twae days, and filled himsel' blind-fou half a dozen o' times, he took a fit o' repentance, and raved and blethered about siccan a life as he led in the muirs. There was some said he was speakin' serious, but maist thocht it was juist daftness."

"And what did he speak about?" I asked sharply.

"I canna verra weel tell ye. It was about some kind o' bogle that lived in the Muneraw— that's the shouthers o't ye see yonder—and it seems that the bogle killed his sheep and frichted himsel'. He was aye bletherin', too, about something or somebody ca'd Grave; but oh! the man wasna wise." And my companion shook a contemptuous head.

And then below us in the valley we saw the shieling, with a thin shaft of smoke rising into the rainy grey weather. The man left me, sturdily refusing any fee. "I wantit my legs stretched as weel as you. A walk in the hills is neither here nor there to a stoot man. When will ye be back, sir?"

The question was well-timed. "To-morrow fortnight," I said, "and I want somebody from Allermuir to come out here in the morning and carry some baggage. Will you see to that?"

He said "Ay," and went off, while I scrambled down the hill to the cottage. Nervousness possessed me, and though it was broad daylight and the whole place lay plain before me, I ran pell-mell, and did not stop till I reached the door.

The place was utterly empty. Unmade beds, unwashed dishes, a hearth strewn with the ashes of peat, and dust thick on everything, proclaimed the absence of inmates. I began to be hideously frightened. Had the shepherd, and his sister also, disappeared? Was I left alone, with a dozen lonely miles between me and human dwellings? I could not return alone; better this horrible place than the unknown perils of the out-of-doors. Hastily I barricaded the door, and to the best of my power shuttered the windows; and then with dreary forebodings I sat down to wait on fortune.

In a little I heard a long swinging step outside and the sound of dogs. Joyfully I opened the latch, and there was the shepherd's grim face waiting stolidly on what might appear.

At the sight of me he stepped back. "What in the Lord's name are ye daein' here?" he asked. "Didna ye get enough afore?"

"Come in," I said sharply. "I want to talk."

In he came with those blessed dogs—what a comfort it was to look on their great honest faces! He sat down on the untidy bed and waited.

"I came because I could not stay away. I saw too much to give me any peace elsewhere. I must go back, even though I risk my life for it. The cause of scholarship demands it as well as the cause of humanity."

"Is that a' the news ye hae?" he said. "Weel, I've mair to tell ye. Three weeks syne my sister Margit was lost, and I've never seen her mair."

My jaw fell, and I could only stare at him.

"I cam hame from the hill at nightfa' and she was gone. I lookit for her up hill and doun, but I couldna find her. Syne I think I went daft. I went to the Scarts and huntit them up and doun, but no sign could I see. The Folk can bide quiet enough when they want. Syne I went to Allermuir and drank mysel' blind—me, that's a God-fearing man and a saved soul, but the Lord help me, I didna ken what I was at. That's my news, and day and night I wander thae hills, seekin' for what I canna find."

"But, man, are you mad?" I cried. "Surely there are neighbours to help you. There is a law in the land, and you had only to find the nearest police-office and compel them to assist you."

"What guid can man dae?" he asked. "An army o' sodgers couldna find that hidy-hole. Forby, when I went into Allermuir wi' my story the folk thocht me daft. It was that set me drinking, for—the Lord forgive me!—I wasna my ain maister. I threepit till I was hairse, but the bodies just lauch'd." And he lay back on the bed like a man mortally tired.

Grim though the tidings were, I can only say that my chief feeling was of comfort. Pity for the new tragedy had swallowed up my fear. I had now a purpose, and a purpose, too, not of curiosity but of mercy.

"I go to-morrow morning to the Muneraw. But first I want to give you something to do." And I drew roughly a chart of the place on the back of a letter. "Go into Allermuir to-morrow, and give this paper to the landlord at the inn. The letter will tell him what to do. He is to raise at once all the men he can get, and come to the place on the chart marked with a cross. Tell him life depends on his hurry."

The shepherd nodded. "D'ye ken the Folk are watching for you? They let me pass without trouble, for they've nae use for me, but I see fine they're seeking you. Ye'll no gang half a mile the morn afore they grip ye."

"So much the better," I said. "That will take me quicker to the place I want to be at."

"And I'm to gang to Allermuir the morn," he repeated, with the air of a child conning a lesson. "But what if they'll no believe me?"

"They'll believe the letter."

"Maybe," he said, and relapsed into a doze.

I set myself to put that house in order, to rouse the fire, and prepare some food. It was dismal work; and meantime outside the night darkened and a great wind rose, which howled round the walls and lashed the rain on the windows.

VII

"IN TUAS MANUS, DOMINE!"

I had not gone twenty yards from the cottage door ere I knew I was watched. I had left the shepherd still dozing, in the half-conscious state of a dazed and broken man. All night the wind had wakened me at intervals, and now in the half-light of morn the weather seemed more vicious than ever. The wind cut my ears, the whole firmament was full of the rendings and thunders of the storm. Rain fell in blinding sheets, the heath was a marsh, and it was the most I could do to struggle against the hurricane which stopped my breath. And all the while I knew I was not alone in the desert.

All men know—in imagination or in experience—the sensation of being spied on. The nerves tingle, the skin grows hot and prickly, and there is a queer sinking of the heart. Intensify this common feeling a hundredfold, and you get a tenth part of what I suffered. I am telling a plain tale, and record bare physical facts. My lips stood out from my teeth as I heard, or felt, a rustle in the heather, a scraping among stones. Some subtle magnetic link seemed established between my body and the mysterious world around. I became sick—acutely sick—with the ceaseless apprehension.

My fright became so complete that when I turned a corner of rock, or stepped in deep heather, I seemed to feel a body rub against mine. This continued all the way up the Farawa water, and then up its feeder to the little lonely loch. It kept me from looking forward; but it likewise kept me in such a sweat of fright that I was ready to faint. Then the notion came upon me to test this fancy of mine. If I was tracked thus closely, clearly the trackers would bar my way if I turned back. So I wheeled round and walked a dozen paces down the glen.

Nothing stopped me. I was about to turn again, when something made me take six more paces. At the fourth something rustled in the heather, and my neck was gripped as in a vice. I had already made up my mind on what I would do. I would be perfectly still, I would conquer my fear, and let them do as they pleased with me so long as they took me to their dwelling. But at the touch of the hands my resolutions fled. I struggled and screamed. Then something was clapped on my mouth, speech and strength went from me, and once more I was back in the maudlin childhood of terror.

In the cave it was always a dusky twilight.

I seemed to be lying in the same place, with the same dull glare of firelight far off, and the same close stupefying smell. One of the creatures was standing silently at my side, and I asked him some trivial question. He turned and shambled down the passage, leaving me alone.

Then he returned with another, and they talked their guttural talk to me. I scarcely listened till I remembered that in a sense I was here of my own accord, and on a definite mission. The purport of their speech seemed to be that, now I had returned, I must beware of a second flight. Once I had been spared; a second time I should be killed without mercy.

I assented gladly. The Folk, then, had some use for me. I felt my errand prospering.

Then the old creature which I had seen before crept out of some corner and squatted beside me. He put a claw on my shoulder, a horrible, corrugated, skeleton thing, hairy to the finger-tips and nailless. He grinned, too, with toothless gums, and his hideous old voice was like a file on sandstone.

I asked questions, but he would only grin and jabber, looking now and then furtively over his shoulder towards the fire.

I coaxed and humoured him, till he launched into a narrative of which I could make nothing. It seemed a mere string of names, with certain words repeated at fixed intervals. Then it flashed on me that this might be a religious incantation. I had discovered remnants of a ritual and a mythology among them. It was possible that these were sacred days, and that I had stumbled upon some rude celebration.

I caught a word or two and repeated them. He looked at me curiously. Then I asked him some leading question, and he replied with clearness. My guess was right. The midsummer week was the holy season of the year, when sacrifices were offered to the gods.

The notion of sacrifices disquieted me, and I would fain have asked further. But the creature would speak no more. He hobbled off, and left me alone in the rock chamber to listen to a strange sound which hung ceaselessly about me. It must be the storm without, like a park of artillery rattling among the crags. A storm of storms surely, for the place echoed and hummed, and to my unquiet eye the very rock of the roof seemed to shake.

Apparently my existence was forgotten, for I lay long before any one returned. Then it was merely one who brought food, the same strange meal as before, and left hastily. When I had eaten I rose and stretched myself. My hands and knees still quivered nervously; but I was strong and perfectly well in body. The empty, desolate, tomb-like place was eerie enough to scare any one; but its emptiness was comfort when I thought of its inmates. Then I wandered down the passage towards the fire which was burning in loneliness. Where had the Folk gone? I puzzled over their disappearance.

Suddenly sounds began to break on my ear, coming from some inner chamber at the end of that in which the fire burned. I could scarcely see for the smoke; but I began to make my way towards the noise, feeling along the sides of rock. Then a second gleam of light seemed to rise before me, and I came to an aperture in the wall which gave entrance to another room.

This in turn was full of smoke and glow—a murky orange glow, as if from some strange flame of roots. There were the squat moving figures, running in wild antics round the fire. I crouched in the entrance, terrified and yet curious, till I saw something beyond the blaze which held me dumb. Apart from the others and tied to some stake in the wall was a woman's figure, and the face was the face of the shepherd's sister.

My first impulse was flight. I must get away and think—plan, achieve some desperate way of escape. I sped back to the silent chamber as if the gang were at my heels. It was still empty, and I stood helplessly in the centre, looking at the impassable walls of rock as a wearied beast may look at the walls of its cage. I bethought me of the way I had escaped before and rushed thither, only to find it blocked by a huge contrivance of stone. Yards and yards of solid rock were between me and the upper air, and yet through it all came the crash and whistle of the storm. If I were at my wits' end in this inner darkness, there was also high commotion among the powers of the air in that upper world.

As I stood I heard the soft steps of my tormentors. They seemed to think I was meditating escape, for they flung themselves on me and bore me to the ground. I did not struggle, and when they saw me quiet, they squatted round and began to speak. They told me of the holy season and its sacrifices. At first I could not follow them; then when I caught familiar words I found some clue, and they became intelligible. They spoke of a woman, and I asked, "What woman?" With all frankness they told me of the custom which prevailed—how every twentieth summer a woman was sacrificed to some devilish god, and by the hand of one of the stranger race. I said nothing, but my whitening face must have told them a tale, though I strove hard to keep my composure. I asked if they had found the victims. "She is in this place," they said; "and as for the man, thou art he." And with this they left me.

I had still some hours, so much I gathered from their talk, for the sacrifice was at sunset. Escape was cut off for ever. I have always been something of a fatalist, and at the prospect of the irrevocable end my cheerfulness returned. I had my pistol, for they had taken nothing from me. I took out the little weapon and fingered it lovingly. Hope of the lost, refuge of the vanquished, ease to the coward,—blessed be he who first conceived it!

The time dragged on, the minutes grew to hours, and still I was left solitary. Only the mad violence of the storm broke the quiet. It had increased in fury, for the stones at the mouth of the exit by which I had formerly escaped seemed to rock with some external

pressure, and cutting shafts of wind slipped past and cleft the heat
of the passage. What a sight the ravine outside must be, I thought,
set in the forehead of a great hill, and swept clean by every blast!
Then came a crashing, and the long hollow echo of a fall. The rocks
are splitting, thought I; the road down the corrie will be impassable now and for evermore.

I began to grow weak with the nervousness of the waiting, and
by-and-by I lay down and fell into a sort of doze. When I next knew
consciousness I was being roused by two of the Folk, and bidden
get ready. I stumbled to my feet, felt for the pistol in the hollow of
my sleeve, and prepared to follow.

When we came out into the wider chamber the noise of the
storm was deafening. The roof rang like a shield which has been
struck. I noticed, perturbed as I was, that my guards cast anxious
eyes around them, alarmed, like myself, at the murderous din. Nor
was the world quieter when we entered the last chamber, where
the fire burned and the remnant of the Folk waited. Wind had found
an entrance from somewhere or other, and the flames blew here
and there, and the smoke gyrated in odd circles. At the back, and
apart from the rest, I saw the dazed eyes and the white old drawn
face of the woman.

They led me up beside her to a place where there was a rude
flat stone, hollowed in the centre, and on it a rusty iron knife, which
seemed once to have formed part of a scythe blade. Then I saw the
ceremonial which was marked out for me. It was the very rite which
I had dimly figured as current among a rude people, and even in
that moment of horror I had something of the scholar's satisfaction.

The oldest of the Folk, who seemed to be a sort of priest, came
to my side and mumbled a form of words. His fetid breath sickened me; his dull eyes, glassy like a brute's with age, brought my
knees together. He put the knife in my hands, dragged the terror-
stricken woman forward to the altar, and bade me begin.

I began by sawing her bonds through. When she felt herself
free she would have fled back, but stopped when I bade her. At
that moment there came a noise of rending and crashing as if the

hills were falling, and for one second the eyes of the Folk were averted from the frustrated sacrifice.

Only for a moment. The next they saw what I had done, and with one impulse rushed towards me. Then began the last scene in the play. I sent a bullet through the right eye of the first thing that came on. The second shot went wide; but the third shattered the hand of an elderly ruffian with a club. Never for an instant did they stop, and now they were clutching at me. I pushed the woman behind, and fired three rapid shots in blind panic, and then, clutching the scythe, I struck right and left like a madman.

Suddenly I saw the foreground sink before my eyes. The roof sloped down, and with a sickening hiss a mountain of rock and earth seemed to precipitate itself on the foremost of my assailants. One, nipped in the middle by a rock, caught my eye by his hideous writhings. Two only remained in what was now a little suffocating chamber, with embers from the fire still smoking on the floor.

The woman caught me by the hand and drew me with her, while the two seemed mute with fear. "There's a road at the back," she screamed. "I ken it. I fand it out." And she pulled me up a narrow hole in the rock.

How long we climbed I do not know. We were both fighting for air, with the tightness of throat and chest and the craziness of limb which mean suffocation. I cannot tell when we first came to the surface, but I remember the woman, who seemed to have the strength of extreme terror, pulling me from the edge of a crevasse and laying me on a flat rock. It seemed to be the depth of winter, with sheer-falling rain and a wind that shook the hills.

Then I was once more myself and could look about me. From my feet yawned a sheer abyss, where once had been a hill shoulder. Some great mass of rock on the brow of the mountain had been loosened by the storm, and in its fall had caught the lips of the ravine. For a moment I feared that all had been destroyed.

My feeling—Heaven help me!—was not thankfulness for God's mercy and my escape, but a bitter mad regret. I rushed frantically to the edge, and when I saw only the blackness of darkness I wept weak tears. All the time the storm was tearing at my body, and I had to grip hard by hand and foot to keep my place.

Suddenly on the brink of the ravine I saw a third figure. We two were not the only fugitives. One of the Folk had escaped.

I ran to it, and to my surprise the thing as soon as it saw me rushed to meet me. At first I thought it was with some instinct of self-preservation, but when I saw its eyes I knew the purpose of fight. Clearly one or other should go no more from the place.

We were some ten yards from the brink when I grappled with it. Dimly I heard the woman scream with fright, and saw her scramble across the hillside. Then we were tugging in a death-throe, the hideous smell of the thing in my face, its red eyes burning into mine, and its hoarse voice muttering. Its strength seemed incredible; but I, too, am no weakling. We tugged and strained, its nails biting into my flesh, while I choked its throat unsparingly. Every second I dreaded lest we should plunge together over the ledge, for it was thither my adversary tried to draw me. I caught my heel in a nick of rock, and pulled madly against it.

And then, while I was beginning to glory with the pride of conquest, my hope was dashed in pieces. The thing seemed to break from my arms, and, as if in despair, cast itself headlong into the impenetrable darkness. I stumbled blindly after it, saved myself on the brink, and fell back into a merciful swoon.

VIII

NOTE IN CONCLUSION BY THE EDITOR

At this point the narrative of my unfortunate friend, Mr. Graves of St. Chad's, breaks off abruptly. He wrote it shortly before his death, and was prevented from completing it by the attack of heart failure which carried him off. In accordance with the instructions in his will I have prepared it for publication, and now in much fear and hesitation give it to the world. First, however, I must supplement it by such facts as fall within my knowledge.

The shepherd seems to have gone to Allermuir and by the help of the letter convinced the inhabitants. A body of men was collected under the landlord, and during the afternoon set out for the

hills. But unfortunately the great midsummer storm—the most terrible of recent climatic disturbances—had filled the mosses and
streams, and they found themselves unable to proceed by any direct road. Ultimately late in the evening they arrived at the cottage of Farawa, only to find there a raving woman, the shepherd's
sister, who seemed crazy with brain fever. She told some rambling
story about her escape, but her narrative said nothing of Mr.
Graves. So they treated her with what skill they possessed, and
sheltered for the night in and around the cottage. Next morning
the storm had abated a little, and the woman had recovered something of her wits. From her they learned that Mr. Graves was lying
in a ravine on the side of the Muneraw in imminent danger of his
life. A body of men set out to find him; but so immense was the
landslip, and so dangerous the whole mountain, that it was nearly
evening when they recovered him from the ledge of rock. He was
alive, but unconscious, and on bringing him back to the cottage it
was clear that he was indeed very ill. There he lay for three months,
while the best skill that could be got was procured for him. By dint
of an uncommon toughness of constitution he survived; but it was
an old and feeble man who returned to Oxford in the early winter.

The shepherd and his sister immediately left the countryside, and
were never more heard of, unless they are the pair of unfortunates
who are at present in a Scottish pauper asylum, incapable of remembering even their names. The people who last spoke with them declared that their minds seemed weakened by a great shock, and that it
was hopeless to try to get any connected or rational statement.

The career of my poor friend from that hour was little short of
a tragedy. He awoke from his illness to find the world incredulous; even the country-folk of Allermuir set down the story to the
shepherd's craziness and my friend's credulity. In Oxford his argument was received with polite scorn. An account of his experiences
which he drew up for the *Times* was refused by the editor; and an
article on "Primitive Peoples of the North," embodying what he
believed to be the result of his discoveries, was rejected by every
responsible journal in Europe. At first he bore the treatment
bravely. Reflection convinced him that the colony had not been

destroyed. Proofs were still awaiting his hand, and with courage
and caution he might yet triumph over his enemies. But unfortunately, though the ardour of the scholar burned more fiercely than
ever and all fear seemed to have been purged from his soul, the
last adventure had grievously sapped his bodily strength. In the
spring following his accident he made an effort to reach the spot—
alone, for no one could be persuaded to follow him in what was
regarded as a childish madness. He slept at the now deserted cottage of Farawa, but in the morning found himself unable to continue, and with difficulty struggled back to the shepherd's cottage
at Allercleuch, where he was confined to bed for a fortnight. Then
it became necessary for him to seek health abroad, and it was not
till the following autumn that he attempted the journey again.

He fell sick a second time at the inn of Allermuir, and during
his convalescence had himself carried to a knoll in the inn garden,
whence a glimpse can be obtained of the shoulder of the Muneraw.
There he would sit for hours with his eyes fixed on the horizon,
and at times he would be found weeping with weakness and vexa-
tion. The last attempt was made but two months before his last
illness. On this occasion he got no farther than Carlisle, where he
was taken ill with what proved to be a premonition of death. After
that he shut his lips tightly, as though recognizing the futility of
his hopes. Whether he had been soured by the treatment he received, or whether his brain had already been weakened, he had
become a morose silent man, and for the two years before his death
had few friends and no society. From the obituary notice in the
Times I take the following paragraph, which shows in what light
the world had come to look upon him:—

"At the outset of his career he was regarded as a rising scholar
in one department of archæology, and his Taffert lectures were a
real contribution to an obscure subject. But in after life he was led
into fantastic speculations; and when he found himself unable to
convince his colleagues, he gradually retired into himself, and lived
practically a hermit's life till his death. His career, thus broken
short, is a sad instance of the fascination which the recondite and
the quack can exercise even over men of approved ability."

And now his own narrative is published, and the world can judge as it pleases about the amazing romance. The view which will doubtless find general acceptance is that the whole is a figment of the brain, begotten of some harmless moorland adventure and the company of such religious maniacs as the shepherd and his sister. But some who knew the former sobriety and calmness of my friend's mind may be disposed timorously and with deep hesitation to another verdict. They may accept the narrative, and believe that somewhere in those moorlands he met with a horrible primitive survival, passed through the strangest adventure, and had his fingers on an epoch-making discovery. In this case they will be inclined to sympathize with the loneliness and misunderstanding of his latter days. It is not for me to decide the question. Though a fellow-historian, the Picts are outside my period, and I dare not advance an opinion on a matter with which I am not fully familiar. But I would point out that the means of settling the question are still extant, and I would call upon some young archæologist, with a reputation to make, to seize upon the chance of the century. Most of the expresses for the North stop at Allerfoot; a ten-miles' drive will bring him to Allermuir; and then with a fifteen-miles' walk he is at Farawa and on the threshold of discovery. Let him follow the burn and cross the ridge and ascend the Scarts of the Muneraw, and, if he return at all, it may be with a more charitable judgment of my unfortunate friend.

The Harbour-Master

Robert W. Chambers

I

Because it all seems so improbable—so horribly impossible to me now, sitting here safe and sane in my own library—I hesitate to record an episode which already appears to me less horrible than grotesque. Yet, unless this story is written now, I know I shall never have the courage to tell the truth about the matter—not from fear of ridicule, but because I myself shall soon cease to credit what I now know to be true. Yet scarcely a month has elapsed since I heard the stealthy purring of what I believed to be the shoaling under-tow—scarcely a month ago, with my own eyes, I saw that which, even now, I am beginning to believe never existed. As for the Harbour-Master—and the blow I am now striking at the old order of things— But of that I shall not speak now, or later; I shall try to tell the story simply and truthfully, and let my employers testify as to my probity and the editor of this magazine corroborate them.

On the Feb. 29 of the present year I resigned my position under the Government and left Washington to accept an offer from Professor Farrago—whose name he kindly permits me to use in this article—and on the first day of April I entered upon my new and congenial duties as general superintendent of the water-fowl department connected with the Zoological Gardens now in course of erection at Bronx Park, New York.

For a week I followed the routine, examining the new foundations, studying the architect's plans, following the surveyors through the Bronx thickets, suggesting arrangements for water-courses and pools destined to be included in the enclosures for swans, geese, pelicans, herons, and such of the waders and swimmers as we might expect to acclimate in Bronx Park.

It was, and is, the policy of the trustees and officers of the Zoological Gardens not to employ collectors, nor to send out expeditions in search of specimens. The society decided to depend upon voluntary contributions, and I was always busy, part of the day, in dictating answers to correspondents who wrote offering their services as hunters of big game, collectors of all sorts of fauna, trappers, snarers, and also to those who offered specimens for sale, usually at exorbitant rates.

To the proprietors of five-legged kittens, mangy lynxes, motheaten coyotes, and dancing bears I returned courteous but uncompromising refusals—of course, first submitting all such letters, together with my replies, to Professor Farrago.

One day towards the end of May, however, just as I was leaving Bronx Park to return to town, Professor Lesard, of the reptilian department, called out to me that Professor Farrago wanted to see me a moment; so I put my pipe into my pocket again, and retraced my steps to the temporary, wooden building occupied by Professor Farrago, general superintendent of the Zoological Gardens. The professor, who was sitting at his desk before a pile of letters and replies submitted for approval by me, pushed his glasses down and looked over them at me with a whimsical smile that suggested amusement, impatience, annoyance, and perhaps a faint trace of apology.

"Now, here's a letter," he said, with a deliberate gesture towards a sheet of paper impaled on a file— "a letter that I suppose you remember." He disengaged the sheet of paper and handed it to me.

"Oh yes," I replied, with a shrug; "of course the man is mistaken, or—"

"Or what?" demanded Professor Farrago, tranquilly, wiping his glasses.

"Or a liar," I replied.

After a silence he leaned back in his chair and bade me read the letter to him again, and I did so with a contemptuous tolerance for the writer, who must have been either a very innocent victim or a very stupid swindler. I said as much to Professor Farrago, but, to my surprise, he appeared to waver.

"I suppose," he said, with his near-sighted, embarrassed smile, "that nine hundred and ninety-nine men in a thousand would throw that letter aside and condemn the writer as a liar or a fool?"

"In my opinion," said I, "he's one or the other."

"He isn't—in mine," said the professor, placidly.

"What!" I exclaimed. "Here is a man living all alone on a strip of rock and sand between the wilderness and the sea, who wants you to send somebody to take charge of a bird that doesn't exist!"

"How do you know," asked Professor Farrago, "that the bird in question does not exist?"

"It is generally accepted," I replied, sarcastically, "that the Great Auk has been extinct for years. Therefore I may be pardoned for doubting that our correspondent possesses a pair of them alive."

"Oh, you young fellows!" said the professor, smiling wearily, "you embark on a theory for destinations that don't exist."

He leaned back in his chair, amused eyes searching space for the imagery that made him smile.

"Like swimming squirrels, you navigate with the help of Heaven and a stiff breeze, but you never land where you hope to—do you?"

Rather red in the face, I said: "Don't you believe the Great Auk to be extinct?"

"Audubon saw the Great Auk."

"Who has seen a single specimen since?"

"Nobody—except our correspondent here," he replied, laughing.

I laughed, too, considering the interview at an end, but the professor went on, coolly— "Whatever it is that our correspondent has—and I am daring to believe that it *is* the Great Auk itself—I want you to secure it for the Society."

When my astonishment subsided, my first conscious sentiment was one of pity. Clearly, Professor Farrago was on the verge of dotage—ah! what a loss to the world!

I believe now that Professor Farrago perfectly interpreted my thoughts, but he betrayed neither resentment nor impatience. I drew a chair up beside his desk—there was nothing to do but to obey, and this fool's errand was none of my conceiving.

Together we made out a list of articles necessary for me, and itemized the expenses I might incur, and I set a date for my return, allowing no margin for a successful termination to the expedition.

"Never mind that," said the professor. "What I want you to do is to get those birds here safely. Now, how many men will you take?"

"None," I replied, bluntly; "it's a useless expense, unless there is something to bring back. If there is I'll wire you, you may be sure."

"Very well," said Professor Farrago, good-humoredly, "you shall have all the assistance you may require. Can you leave to-night?"

The old gentleman was certainly prompt. I nodded, half-sulkily, aware of his amusement.

"So," I said, picking up my hat, "I am to start north to find a place called Black Harbour, where there is a man named Halyard who possesses, among other household utensils, two extinct Great Auks—"

We were both laughing by this time. I asked him why on earth he credited the assertion of a man he had never before heard of.

"I suppose," he replied, with the same half-apologetic, half-humorous smile, "it is instinct. I feel, somehow, that this man Halyard *has* got an auk—perhaps two. I can't get away from the idea that we are on the eve of acquiring the rarest of living creatures. It's odd for a scientist to talk as I do; doubtless you're shocked—admit it, now!"

But I was not shocked; on the contrary, I was conscious that the same strange hope that Professor Farrago cherished was beginning, in spite of me, to stir my pulses, too.

"If he has—" I began, then stopped.

The professor and I looked hard at each other in silence.

"Go on," he said, encouragingly.

But I had nothing more to say, for the prospect of beholding with my own eyes a living specimen of the Great Auk produced a series of conflicting emotions within me which rendered speech profanely superfluous.

As I took my leave Professor Farrago came to the door of the temporary, wooden office and handed me the letter written by the man Halyard. I folded it and put it into my pocket, as Halyard might require it for my own identification.

"How much does he want for the pair?" I asked.

"Ten thousand dollars. Don't demur—if the birds are really—"

"I know," I said, hastily, not daring to hope too much.

"One thing more," said Professor Farrago, gravely; "you know, in that last paragraph of his letter, Halyard speaks of something else in the way of specimens—an undiscovered species of amphibious biped—just read that paragraph again, will you?"

I drew the letter from my pocket and read as he directed—

> "When you have seen the two living specimens of the Great Auk, and have satisfied yourself that I tell the truth, you may be wise enough to listen without prejudice to a statement I shall make concerning the existence of the strangest creature ever fashioned. I will merely say, at this time, that the creature referred to is an amphibious biped and inhabits the ocean near this coast. More I cannot say, for I personally have not seen the animal, but I have a witness who has, and there are many who affirm that they have seen the creature. You will naturally say that my statement amounts to nothing; but when your representative arrives, if he be free from prejudice, I expect his reports to you concerning this sea-biped will confirm the solemn statements of a witness I *know* to be unimpeachable.—Yours truly,
>
> "Burton Halyard.
>
> "Black Harbour"

"Well," I said, after a moment's thought, "here goes for the wild-goose chase—"

"Wild auk, you mean," said Professor Farrago, shaking hands with me. "You will start to-night, won't you?"

"Yes, but Heaven knows how I'm ever going to land in this man Halyard's door-yard! Good-bye!"

"About that sea-biped—" began Professor Farrago, shyly.

"Oh, don't!" I said; "I can swallow the auks, feathers and claws, but if this fellow Halyard is hinting he's seen an amphibious creature resembling a man—"

"—Or a woman," said the professor, cautiously.

I retired, disgusted, my faith shaken in the mental vigor of Professor Farrago.

II

The three days' voyage by boat and rail was irksome. I bought my kit at Sainte Croix, on the Central Pacific Railroad, and on June 1st I began the last stage of my journey via the Sainte Isole broadgauge, arriving in the wilderness by daylight. A tedious forced march by blazed trail, freshly spotted on the wrong side, of course, brought me to the northern terminus of the rusty, narrow-gauge lumber railway which runs from the heart of the hushed pine wilderness to the sea.

Already a long train of battered flat-cars, piled with sluiceprops and roughly hewn sleepers, was moving slowly off into the brooding forest gloom, when I came in sight of the track; but I developed a gratifying and unexpected burst of speed, shouting all the while. The train stopped; I swung myself aboard the last car, where a pleasant young fellow was sitting on the rear brake, chewing spruce and reading a letter.

"Come aboard, sir," he said, looking up with a smile; "I guess you're the man in a hurry."

"I'm looking for a man named Halyard," I said, dropping rifle and knapsack on the fresh-cut, fragrant pile of pine. "Are you Halyard?"

"No, I'm Francis Lee, bossing the mica pit at Port-of-Waves," he replied, "but this letter is from Halyard, asking me to look out for a man in a hurry from Bronx Park, New York."

"I'm that man," said I, filling my pipe and offering him a share of the weed of peace, and we sat side by side smoking very amiably, until a signal from the locomotive sent him forward and I was left alone, lounging at ease, head pillowed on both arms, watching the blue sky flying through the branches overhead.

Long before we came in sight of the ocean I smelled it; the fresh, salt aroma stole into my senses, drowsy with the heated odor of pine and hemlock, and I sat up, peering ahead into the dusky sea of pines.

Fresher and fresher came the wind from the sea, in puffs, in mild, sweet breezes, in steady, freshening currents, blowing the feathery crowns of the pines, setting the balsam's blue tufts rocking.

Lee wandered back over the long line of flats, balancing himself nonchalantly as the cars swung around a sharp curve, where water dripped from a newly propped sluice that suddenly emerged from the depths of the forest to run parallel to the railroad track.

"Built it this spring," he said, surveying his handiwork, which seemed to undulate as the cars swept past. "It runs to the cove, or ought to." He stopped abruptly with a thoughtful glance at me.

"So you're going over to Halyard's?" he continued, as though answering a question asked by himself.

I nodded.

"You've never been there, of course?"

"No," I said, "and I'm not likely to go again."

I would have told him why I was going if I had not already begun to feel ashamed of my idiotic errand.

"I guess you're going to look at those birds of his," continued Lee, placidly.

"I guess I am," I said, sulkily, glancing askance to see whether he was smiling.

But he only asked me, quite seriously, whether a Great Auk was really a very rare bird; and I told him that the last one ever seen had been found dead off Labrador in January, 1870. Then I asked him whether these birds of Halyard's were really Great Auks, and he replied, somewhat indifferently, that he supposed they were— at least, nobody had ever before seen such birds near Port-of-Waves.

"There's something else," he said, running a pine-sliver through his pipe-stem— "something that interests us all here more than auks, big or little. I suppose I might as well speak of it, as you are bound to hear about it sooner or later."

He hesitated, and I could see that he was embarrassed, searching for the exact words to convey his meaning.

"If," said I, "you have anything in this region more important to science than the Great Auk, I should be very glad to know about it."

Perhaps there was the faintest tinge of sarcasm in my voice, for he shot a sharp glance at me and then turned slightly. After a moment, however, he put his pipe into his pocket, laid hold of the brake with both hands, vaulted to his perch aloft, and glanced down at me.

"Did you ever hear of the Harbour-Master?" he asked, maliciously.

"Which Harbour-Master?" I inquired.

"You'll know before long," he observed, with a satisfied glance into perspective.

This rather extraordinary observation puzzled me. I waited for him to resume, and, as he did not, I asked him what he meant.

"If I knew," he said, "I'd tell you. But, come to think of it, I'd be a fool to go into details with a scientific man. You'll hear about the Harbour-Master—perhaps you will see the Harbour-Master. In that event I should be glad to converse with you on the subject."

I could not help laughing at his prim and precise manner, and, after a moment, he also laughed, saying—

"It hurts a man's vanity to know he knows a thing that somebody else knows he doesn't know. I'm damned if I say another word about the Harbour-Master until you've been to Halyard's!"

"A Harbour-Master," I persisted, "is an official who superintends the mooring of ships—isn't he?"

But he refused to be tempted into conversation, and we lounged silently on the lumber until a long, thin whistle from the locomotive and a rush of stinging salt-wind brought us to our feet.

Through the trees I could see the bluish-black ocean, stretching out beyond black headlands to meet the clouds; a great wind was roaring among the trees as the train slowly came to a stand-still on the edge of the primeval forest.

Lee jumped to the ground and aided me with my rifle and pack, and then the train began to back away along a curved side-track which, Lee said, led to the mica-pit and company stores.

"Now what will you do?" he asked, pleasantly. "I can give you a good dinner and a decent bed to-night if you like; and I'm sure Mrs. Lee would be very glad to have you stop with us as long as you choose."

I thanked him, but said that I was anxious to reach Halyard's before dark, and he very kindly led me along the cliffs and pointed out the path.

"This man Halyard," he said, "is an invalid. He lives at a cove called Black Harbour, and all his truck goes through to him over the company's road. We receive it here, and send a pack-mule through once a month. I've met him; he's a bad-tempered hypo-chondriac, a cynic at heart, and a man whose word is never doubted. If he says he has a Great Auk, you may be satisfied he has."

My heart was beating with excitement at the prospect; I looked out across the wooded headlands and tangled stretches of dune and hollow, trying to realize what it might mean to me, to Profes-sor Farrago, to the world, if I should lead back to New York a live auk.

"He's a crank," said Lee; "frankly, I don't like him. If you find it unpleasant there, come back to us."

"Does Halyard live alone?" I asked.

"Yes—except for a professional trained nurse—poor thing!"

"A man?"

"No," said Lee, disgustedly.

Presently he gave me a peculiar glance; hesitated, and finally said: "Ask Halyard to tell you about his nurse and—the Harbour-Master. Good-bye—I'm due at the quarry. Come and stay with us whenever you care to; you will find a welcome at Port-of-Waves."

We shook hands and parted on the cliff, he turning back into the forest along the railway, I starting northward, pack slung, rifle over my shoulder. Once I met a group of quarrymen, faces burned brick-red, scarred hands swinging as they walked. And, as I passed them with a nod, turning, I saw that they also had turned to look after me, and I caught a word or two of their conversation, whirled back to me on the sea-wind.

They were speaking of the Harbour-Master.

III

Towards sunset I came out on a sheer granite cliff where the sea-birds were whirling and clamoring, and the great breakers dashed, rolling in double-thundered reverberations on the sun-dyed, crimson sands below the bedded rock.

Across the half-moon of beach towered another cliff, and, behind this, I saw a column of smoke rising in the still air. It certainly came from Halyard's chimney, although the opposite cliff prevented me from seeing the house itself.

I rested a moment to refill my pipe, then resumed rifle and pack, and cautiously started to skirt the cliffs. I had descended half-way towards the beech, and was examining the cliff opposite, when something on the very top of the rock arrested my attention—a man darkly outlined against the sky. The next moment, however, I knew it could not be a man, for the object suddenly glided over the face of the cliff and slid down the sheer, smooth lace like a lizard. Before I could get a square look at it, the thing crawled into the surf—or, at least, it seemed to—but the whole episode occurred so suddenly, so unexpectedly, that I was not sure I had seen anything at all.

However, I was curious enough to climb the cliff on the land side and make my way towards the spot where I imagined I saw the man. Of course, there was nothing there—not a trace of a human being, I mean. Something *had* been there—a sea-otter, possibly; for the remains of a freshly killed fish lay on the rock, eaten to the back-bone and tail.

The next moment, below me, I saw the house, a freshly painted, trim, flimsy structure, modern, and very much out of harmony with the splendid savagery surrounding it. It struck a nasty, cheap note in the noble, gray monotony of headland and sea.

The descent was easy enough. I crossed the crescent beach, hard as pink marble, and found a little trodden path among the rocks, that led to the front porch of the house.

There were two people on the porch—I heard their voices before I saw them—and when I set my foot upon the wooden steps, I saw one of them, a woman, rise from her chair and step hastily towards me.

"Come back!" cried the other, a man with a smooth-shaven, deeply lined face, and a pair of angry, blue eyes; and the woman stepped back quietly, acknowledging my lifted hat with a silent inclination.

The man, who was reclining in an invalid's rolling-chair, clapped both large, pale hands to the wheels and pushed himself out along the porch. He had shawls pinned about him, an untidy, drab-colored hat on his head, and, when he looked down at me, he scowled.

"I know who you are," he said, in his acid voice; "you're one of the Zoological men from Bronx Park. You look like it, anyway."

"It is easy to recognize you from your reputation," I replied, irritated at his discourtesy.

"Really," he replied, with something between a sneer and a laugh, "I'm obliged for your frankness. You're after my Great Auks, are you not?"

"Nothing else would have tempted me into this place," I replied, sincerely.

"Thank Heaven for that," he said. "Sit down a moment; you've interrupted us." Then, turning to the young woman, who wore the neat gown and tiny cap of a professional nurse, he bade her resume what she had been saying. She did so, with deprecating glance at me, which made the old man sneer again.

"It happened so suddenly," she said, in her low voice, "that I had no chance to get back. The boat was drifting in the cove; I sat in the stern, reading, both oars shipped, and the tiller swinging. Then I heard a scratching under the boat, but thought it might be seaweed—and, next moment, came those soft thumpings, like the sound of a big fish rubbing its nose against a float."

Halyard clutched the wheels of his chair and stared at the girl in grim displeasure.

"Didn't you know enough to be frightened?" he demanded.

"No—not then," she said, coloring faintly; "but when, after a few moments, I looked up and saw the Harbour-Master running up and down the beach, I was horribly frightened."

"Really?" said Halyard, sarcastically; "it was about time." Then, turning to me, he rasped out: "And that young lady was obliged to row all the way to Port-of-Waves and call to Lee's quarrymen to take her boat in."

Completely mystified, I looked from Halyard to the girl, not in the least comprehending what all this meant.

"That will do," said Halyard, ungraciously, which curt phrase was apparently the usual dismissal for the nurse.

She rose, and I rose, and she passed me with an inclination, stepping noiselessly into the house.

"I want beef-tea!" bawled Halyard after her; then he gave me an unamiable glance.

"I was a well-bred man," he sneered; "I'm a Harvard graduate, too, but I live as I like, and I do what I like, and I say what I like."

"You certainly are not reticent," I said, disgusted.

"Why should I be?" he rasped; "I pay that young woman for my irritability; it's a bargain between us."

"In your domestic affairs," I said, "there is nothing that interests me. I came to see those auks—"

"You probably believe them to be razor-billed auks," he said, contemptuously. "But they're not; they're Great Auks."

I suggested that he permit me to examine them, and he replied, indifferently, that they were in a pen in his backyard, and that I was free to step around the house when I cared to.

I laid my rifle and pack on the veranda, and hastened off with mixed emotions, among which hope no longer predominated. No man in his senses would keep two such precious prizes in a pen in his backyard, I argued, and I was perfectly prepared to find anything from a puffin to a penguin in that pen.

I shall never forget, as long as I live, my stupor of amazement when I came to the wire-covered enclosure.

Not only were there two Great Auks in the pen, alive, breathing, squatting in bulky majesty on their seaweed bed, but one of them was gravely contemplating two newly hatched chicks, all hill and feet, which nestled sedately at the edge of a puddle of salt-water, where some small fish were swimming.

For a while excitement blinded, nay, deafened me. I tried to realize that I was gazing upon the last individuals of an all but extinct race—the sole survivors of the gigantic auk, which, for thirty years, has been accounted an extinct creature.

I believe that I did not move muscle or limb until the sun had gone down and the crowding darkness blurred my straining eyes and blotted the great, silent, bright-eyed birds from sight.

Even then I could not tear myself away from the enclosure; I listened to the strange, drowsy note of the male bird, the fainter responses of the female, the thin plaints of the chicks, huddling under her breast; I heard their flipper-like, embryotic wings beating sleepily as the birds stretched and yawned their beaks and clacked them, preparing for slumber.

"If you please," came a soft voice from the door, "Mr. Halyard awaits your company to dinner."

IV

I dined well—or, rather, I might have enjoyed my dinner if Mr. Halyard had been eliminated; and the feast consisted exclusively of a joint of beef, the pretty nurse, and myself. She was exceedingly attractive, with a disturbing fashion of lowering her head and raising her dark eyes when spoken to.

As for Halyard, he was unspeakable, bundled up in his snuffy shawls, and making uncouth noises over his gruel. But it is only just to say that his table was worth sitting down to and his wine was sound as a bell. "Yah!" he snapped, "I'm sick of this cursed soup—and I'll trouble you to fill my glass—"

"It is dangerous for you to touch claret," said the pretty nurse.

"I might as well die at dinner as anywhere," he observed.

"Certainly," said I, cheerfully passing the decanter, but he did not appear overpleased with the attention.

"I can't smoke, either," he snarled, hitching the shawls around until he looked like Richard III.

However, he was good enough to shove a box of cigars at me, and I took one and stood up, as the pretty nurse slipped past and vanished into the little parlor beyond.

We sat there for a while without speaking. He picked irritably at the bread-crumbs on the cloth, never glancing in my direction; and I, tired from my long foot-tour, lay back in my chair, silently appreciating one of the best cigars I ever smoked.

"Well," he rasped out at length, "what do you think of my auks—and my veracity?"

I told him that both were unimpeachable.

"Didn't they call me a swindler down there at your Museum?" he demanded.

I admitted that I had heard the term applied. Then I made a clean breast of the matter, telling him that it was I who had doubted; that my chief, Professor Farrago, had sent me against my will, and that I was ready and glad to admit that he, Mr. Halyard, was a benefactor of the human race.

"Bosh!" he said. "What good does a confounded wobbly, bandy-toed bird do to the human race?"

But he was pleased, nevertheless; and presently he asked me, not unamiably, to punish his claret again.

"I'm done for," he said; "good things to eat and drink are no good to me. Some day I'll get mad enough to have a fit, and then—"

He paused to yawn.

"Then," he continued, "that little nurse of mine will drink up my claret and go back to civilization, where people are polite."

Somehow or other, in spite of the fact that Halyard was an old pig, what he said touched me. There was certainly not much left in life for him—as he regarded life.

"I'm going to leave her this house," he said, arranging his shawls. "She doesn't know it. I'm going to leave her my money, too. She doesn't know that. Good Lord! What kind of a woman can she be to stand my bad temper for a few dollars a month!"

"I think," said I, "that it's partly because she's poor, partly because she's sorry for you."

He looked up with a ghastly smile.

"You think she really is sorry?"

Before I could answer he went on: "I'm no mawkish sentimentalist, and I won't allow anybody to be sorry for me; do you hear?"

"Oh, I'm not sorry for you!" I said, hastily, and, for the first time since I had seen him, he laughed heartily, without a sneer.

We both seemed to feel better after that; I drank his wine and smoked his cigars, and he appeared to take a certain grim pleasure in watching me.

"There's no fool like a young fool," he observed, presently.

As I had no doubt he referred to me, I paid him no attention.

After fidgeting with his shawls, he gave me an oblique scowl and asked me my age.

"Twenty-four," I replied.

"Sort of a tadpole, aren't you?" he said.

As I took no offence, he repeated the remark.

"Oh, come," said I, "there's no use in trying to irritate me. I see through you; a row acts like a cocktail on you; but you'll have to stick to gruel in my company."

"I call that impudence!" he rasped out, wrathfully.

"I don't care what you call it," I replied, undisturbed, "I am not going to be worried by you. Anyway," I ended, "it is my opinion that you could be very good company if you chose."

The proposition appeared to take his breath away—at least, he said nothing more; and I finished my cigar in peace and tossed the stump into a saucer.

"Now," said I, "what price do you set upon your birds, Mr. Halyard?"

"Ten thousand dollars," he snapped, with an evil smile.

"You will receive a certified check when the birds are delivered," I said, quietly.

"You don't mean to say you agree to that outrageous bargain?— and I won't take a cent less, either. Good Lord! haven't you any spirit left?" he cried, half rising from his pile of shawls.

His piteous eagerness for a dispute sent me into laughter impossible to control, and he eyed me, mouth open, animosity rising visibly.

Then he seized the wheels of his invalid chair and trundled away, too mad to speak; and I strolled out into the parlor, still laughing.

The pretty nurse was there, sewing under a hanging lamp.

"If I am not indiscreet—" I began.

"Indiscretion is the better part of valor," said she, dropping her head but raising her eyes.

So I sat down with a frivolous smile peculiar to the appreciated.

"Doubtless," said I, "you are hemming a kerchief."

"Doubtless I am not," she said; "this is a night-cap for Mr. Halyard."

A mental vision of Halyard in a night-cap, very mad, nearly set me laughing again.

"Like the King of Yvetot, he wears his crown in bed," I said, flippantly.

"The King of Yvetot might have made that remark," she observed, re-threading her needle.

It is unpleasant to be reproved. How large and red and hot a man's ears feel.

To cool them, I strolled out to the porch; and, after a while, the pretty nurse came out, too, and sat down in a chair not far away. She probably regretted her lost opportunity to be flirted with.

"I have so little company—it is a great relief to see somebody from the world," she said. "If you can be agreeable, I wish you would."

The idea that she had come out to see me was so agreeable that I remained speechless until she said: "Do tell me what people are doing in New York."

So I seated myself on the steps and talked about the portion of the world inhabited by me, while she sat sewing in the dull light that straggled out from the parlor windows.

She had a certain coquetry of her own, using the usual methods with an individuality that was certainly fetching. For instance, when she lost her needle—and, another time, when we both, on hands and knees, hunted for her thimble.

However, directions for these pastimes may be found in contemporary classics.

I was as entertaining as I could be—perhaps not quite as entertaining as a young man usually thinks he is. However, we got on very well together until I asked her tenderly who the Harbour-Master might be, whom they all discussed so mysteriously.

"I do not care to speak about it," she said, with a primness of which I had not suspected her capable.

Of course I could scarcely pursue the subject after that—and, indeed, I did not intend to—so I began to tell her how I fancied I had seen a man on the cliff that afternoon, and how the creature slid over the sheer rock like a snake.

To my amazement, she asked me to kindly discontinue the account of my adventures, in an icy tone, which left no room for protest.

"It was only a sea-otter," I tried to explain, thinking perhaps she did not care for snake stories.

But the explanation did not appear to interest her, and I was mortified to observe that my impression upon her was anything but pleasant.

"She doesn't seem to like me and my stories," thought I, "but she is too young, perhaps, to appreciate them."

So I forgave her—for she was even prettier than I had thought her at first—and I took my leave, saying that Mr. Halyard would doubtless direct me to my room.

Halyard was in his library, cleaning a revolver, when I entered.

"Your room is next to mine, " he said; "pleasant dreams, and kindly refrain from snoring."

"May I venture an absurd hope that you will do the same?" I replied, politely.

That maddened him, so I hastily withdrew.

I had been asleep for at least two hours when a movement by my bedside and a light in my eyes awakened me. I sat bolt upright in bed, blinking at Halyard, who, clad in a dressing-gown and wearing a night-cap, had wheeled himself into my room with one hand, while with the other he solemnly waved a candle over my head.

"I'm so cursed lonely," he said— "come, there's a good fellow— talk to me in your own original, impudent way.''

I objected strenuously, but he looked so worn and thin, so lonely and bad-tempered, so lovelessly grotesque, that I got out of bed and passed a spongeful of cold water over my head.

Then I returned to bed and propped the pillows up for a back-rest, ready to quarrel with him if it might bring some little pleasure into his morbid existence.

"No," he said, amiably, "I'm too worried to quarrel, but I'm much obliged for your kindly offer. I want to tell you something."

"What?" I asked, suspiciously.

"I want to ask you if you ever saw a man with gills like a fish?"

"Gills?" I repeated.

"Yes, gills! Did you?"

"No," I replied, angrily, "and neither did you."

"No, I never did," he said, in a curiously placid voice, "but there's a man with gills like a fish who lives in the ocean out there. Oh, you needn't look that way—nobody ever thinks of doubting my word, and I tell you that there's a man—or a thing that looks like a man—as big as you are, too, all slate-colored, with nasty red gills like a fish; and I've a witness to prove what I say!"

"Who?" I asked, sarcastically.

"The witness? My nurse."

"Oh! She saw a slate-colored man with gills?"

"Yes, she did. So did Francis Lee, superintendent of the Mica Quarry Company at Port-of-Waves. So have a dozen men who work in the quarry. Oh, you needn't laugh, young man. It's an old story here, and anybody can tell you about the Harbour-Master."

"The Harbour-Master!" I exclaimed.

"Yes, that slate-colored thing with gills, that looks like a man— and, by Heaven! *is* a man—that's the Harbour-Master. Ask any quarryman at Port-of-Waves what it is that comes purring around their boats at the wharf and unties painters and changes the mooring of every cat-boat in the cove at night! Ask Francis Lee what it was he saw running and leaping up and down the shoal at sunset last Friday! Ask anybody along the coast what sort of a thing moves about the cliffs like a man and slides over them into the sea like an otter—"

"I saw it do that!" I burst out.

"Oh, did you? Well, *what was it?*"

Something kept me silent, although a dozen explanations flew to my lips.

After a pause, Halyard said: "You saw the Harbour-Master—that's what you saw!"

I looked at him without a word.

"Don't mistake me," he said, pettishly; "I don't think that the Harbour-Master is a spirit or a sprite or a hobgoblin, or any sort of damned rot. Neither do I believe it to be an optical illusion."

"What do you think it is?" I asked.

"I think it's a man; I think it's a branch of the human race—that's what I think. Let me tell you something: the deepest spot in the Atlantic Ocean is a trifle over five miles deep; and I suppose you know that this place lies only about a quarter of a mile off this headland. The British exploring vessel, *Gull*, Captain Marotte, discovered and sounded it, I believe. Anyway, it's there, and it's my belief that the profound depths are inhabited by the remnants of the last race of amphibious human beings!"

This was childish; I did not bother to reply.

"Believe it or not, as you will," he said, angrily; "one thing I know, and that is this: the Harbour-Master has taken to hanging around my cove, and he is attracted by my nurse! I won't have it! I'll blow his fishy gills out of his head if I ever get a shot at him! I don't care whether it's homicide or not—anyway, it's a new kind of murder and it attracts me!"

I gazed at him incredulously, but he was working himself into a passion, and I did not choose to say what I thought.

"Yes, this slate-colored thing with gills goes purring and grinning and spitting about after my nurse—when she walks, when she rows, when she sits on the beach! Gad! It drives me nearly frantic. I won't tolerate it, I tell you!"

"No," said I, "I wouldn't either." And I rolled over in bed convulsed with laughter.

The next moment I heard my door slam. I smothered my mirth and rose to close the window, for the land-wind blew cold from the forest, and a drizzle was sweeping the carpet as far as my bed.

That luminous glare which sometimes lingers after the stars go out, threw a trembling, nebulous radiance over sand and cove. I heard the seething currents under the breakers' softened thunder louder than I ever heard it. Then, as I closed my window, lingering for a last look at the crawling tide, I saw a man standing, ankle-deep, in the surf, all alone there in the night. But—was it a man? For the figure suddenly began running over the beach on all fours like a beetle, waving its limbs like feelers. Before I could throw open the window again it darted into the surf, and, when I leaned out into the chilling drizzle, I saw nothing save the flat ebb crawling on the coast—I heard nothing save the purring of bubbles on seething sands.

V

It took me a week to perfect my arrangements for transporting the Great Auks, by water, to Port-of-Waves, where a lumber schooner was to be sent from Petite-Sainte-Isole, chartered by me for a voyage to New York. I had constructed a cage made of osiers, in which my auks were to squat until they arrived at Bronx Park. My telegrams to Professor Farrago were brief; one merely said "Victory!" Another explained that I wanted no assistance; and a third read: "Schooner *Borogrove* chartered. Arrive New York July 1. Send furniture-van to foot of Bluff Street."

My week as a guest of Mr. Halyard proved interesting. I wrangled with that invalid to his heart's content, I worked all day on my osier-cage, I hunted the thimble in the moonlight with the pretty nurse. We sometimes found it.

As for the thing they called the Harbour-Master, I saw it a dozen times, but always either at night or so far away and so close to the sea that of course no trace of it remained when I reached the spot, rifle in hand.

I had quite made up my mind that the so-called Harbour-Master was a demented darky—wandered from Heaven knows where—

perhaps shipwrecked and gone mad from his sufferings. Still, it was far from pleasant to know that the creature was strongly attracted by the pretty nurse.

She, however, persisted in regarding the harbour-master as a sea-creature; she earnestly affirmed that it had gills, like a fish's gills, that it had a soft, fleshy hole for a mouth, and its eyes were luminous and lidless and fixed.

"Besides," she said, with a shudder, "it's all slate color, like a porpoise, and it looks as wet as a sheet of india-rubber in a dissecting-room."

The day before I was to set sail with my auks in a cat-boat bound for Port-of-Waves, Halyard trundled up to me in his chair and announced his intention of going with me.

"Going where?" I asked.

"To Port-of-Waves and then to New York," he replied, tranquilly.

I was doubtful, and my lack of cordiality hurt his feelings.

"Oh, of course, if you need the sea-voyage," I began.

"I don't; I need you," he said, savagely; "I need the stimulus of our daily quarrel. I never disagreed so pleasantly with anybody in my life; it agrees with me; I am a hundred per cent. better than I was last week."

I was inclined to resent this, but something in the deep-lined face of the invalid softened me. Besides, I had taken a hearty liking to the old pig.

"I don't want any mawkish sentiment about it," he said, observing me closely; "I won't permit anybody to feel sorry for me—do you understand?"

"I'll trouble you to use a different tone in addressing me," I replied, hotly; "I'll feel sorry for you if I choose to!" And our usual quarrel proceeded, to his deep satisfaction.

By six o'clock next evening I had Halyard's luggage stowed away in the cat-boat, and the pretty nurse's effects corded down, with the newly hatched auk-chicks in a hat-box on top. She and I placed the osier-cage aboard, securing it firmly, and then, throwing table-cloths over the auks' heads, we led those simple and dignified birds down the path and across the plank at the little wooden pier. Together we locked up the house, while Halyard stormed at us both and wheeled himself furiously up and down the beach below. At the last moment she forgot her thimble. But we found it, I forget where.

"Come on!" shouted Halyard, waving his shawls furiously; "what the devil are you about up there?"

He received our explanation with a sniff, and we trundled him aboard without further ceremony.

"Don't run me across the plank like a steamer trunk!" he shouted, as I shot him dexterously into the cock-pit.

But the wind was dying away, and I had no time to dispute with him then.

The sun was setting above the pine-clad ridge as our sail flapped and partly filled, and I cast off, and began a long tack, east by south, to avoid the spouting rocks on our starboard bow.

The sea-birds rose in clouds as we swung across the shoal, the black surf-ducks scuttered out to sea, the gulls tossed their sun-tipped wings in the ocean, riding the rollers like bits of froth.

Already we were sailing slowly out across that great hole in the ocean, five miles deep, the most profound sounding ever taken in the Atlantic. The presence of great heights or great depths, seen or unseen, always impresses the human mind—perhaps oppresses it. We were very silent; the sunlight stain on cliff and beach deepened to crimson, then faded into sombre purple bloom that lingered long after the rose-tint died out in the zenith.

Our progress was slow; at times, although the sail filled with the rising land breeze, we scarcely seemed to move at all.

"Of course," said the pretty nurse, "we couldn't be aground in the deepest hole in the Atlantic."

"Scarcely," said Halyard, sarcastically, "unless we're grounded on a whale."

"What's that soft thumping?" I asked. "Have we run afoul of a barrel or log?"

It was almost too dark to see, but I leaned over the rail and swept the water with my hand.

Instantly something smooth glided under it, like the back of a great fish, and I jerked my hand back to the tiller. At the same moment the whole surface of the water seemed to begin to purr, with a sound like the breaking of froth in a champagne-glass.

"What's the matter with you?" asked Halyard, sharply.

"A fish came up under my hand," I said; "a porpoise or something—"

With a low cry, the pretty nurse clasped my arm in both her hands.

"Listen!" she whispered. "It's purring around the boat."

"What the devil's purring?" shouted Halyard. "I won't have anything purring around me!"

At that moment, to my amazement, I saw that the boat had stopped entirely, although the sail was full and the small pennant fluttered from the mast-head. Something, too, was tugging at the rudder, twisting and jerking it until the tiller strained and creaked in my hand. All at once it snapped; the tiller swung useless and the boat whirled around, heeling in the stiffening wind, and drove shoreward.

It was then that I, ducking to escape the boom, caught a glimpse of something ahead—something that a sudden wave seemed to toss on deck and leave there, wet and flapping—a man with round, fixed, fishy eyes, and soft, slaty skin.

But the horror of the thing were the two gills that swelled and relaxed spasmodically, emitting a rasping, purring sound—two gasping, blood-red gills, all fluted and scolloped and distended.

Frozen with amazement and repugnance, I stared at the creature; I felt the hair stirring on my head and the icy sweat on my forehead.

"It's the Harbour-Master!" screamed Halyard.

The Harbour-Master had gathered himself into a wet lump, squatting motionless in the bows under the mast; his lidless eyes were phosphorescent, like the eyes of living codfish. After a while I felt that either fright or disgust was going to strangle me where I sat, but it was only the arms of the pretty nurse clasped around me in a frenzy of terror.

There was not a fire-arm aboard that we could get at. Halyard's hand crept backward where a steel-shod boat-hook lay, and I also made a clutch at it. The next moment I had it in my hand, and staggered forward, but the boat was already tumbling shoreward among the breakers, and the next I knew the Harbour-Master ran at me like a colossal rat, just as the boat rolled over and over through the surf, spilling freight and passengers among the sea-weed-covered rocks.

When I came to myself I was thrashing about knee-deep in a rocky pool, blinded by the water and half suffocated, while under my feet, like a stranded porpoise, the Harbour-Master made the water boil in his efforts to upset me. But his limbs seemed soft and boneless; he had no nails, no teeth, and he bounced and thumped and flapped and splashed like a fish, while I rained blows on him with the boat-hook that sounded like blows on a football. And all the while his gills were blowing out and frothing, and purring, and his lidless eyes looked into mine, until, nauseated and trembling, I dragged myself back to the beach, where already the pretty nurse alternately wrung her hands and her petticoats in ornamental despair.

Beyond the cove, Halyard was bobbing up and down, afloat in his invalid's chair, trying to steer shoreward. He was the maddest man I ever saw.

"Have you killed that rubber-headed thing yet?" he roared.

"I can't kill it," I shouted, breathlessly. "I might as well try to kill a football!"

"Can't you punch a hole in it?" he bawled. "If I can only get at him—"

His words were drowned in a thunderous splashing, a roar of great, broad flippers beating the sea, and I saw the gigantic forms of my two Great Auks, followed by their chicks, blundering past in a shower of spray, driving headlong out into the ocean.

"Oh, Lord!" I said. "I can't stand that," and, for the first time in my life, I fainted peacefully—and appropriately—at the feet of the pretty nurse.

It is within the range of possibility that this story may be doubted. It doesn't matter; nothing can add to the despair of a man who has lost two Great Auks.

As for Halyard, nothing affects him, except his involuntary sea-bath, and that did him so much good that he writes me from the south that he's going on a walking-tour through Switzerland, if I'll join him. I might have joined him if he had not married the pretty nurse. I wonder whether— But, of course, this is no place for specu-lation.

In regard to the Harbour-Master, you may believe it or not, as you choose. But if you hear of any Great Auks being found, kindly throw a table-cloth over their heads and notify the authorities at the new Zoological Gardens in Bronx Park, New York. The reward is ten thousand dollars.

FOUND BY THE MISSING LINK

W. L. Alden

"If we could only find the Missing Link," said the Professor, "there would be an end to all doubt as to the theory of development. My own idea is that some day he will be found."

"Wasn't there an expedition in search of the Missing Link a few years ago?" asked young Horton. "If I remember rightly, the expedition went to Borneo, or some such place, and never returned."

"Precisely so," replied the Professor. "I fancy that the whole affair was mismanaged, for the man at the head of the expedition was certainly not the man for the place."

We were sitting in the smoking room of the Lord Warden hotel at Dover—a company of weather-bound travellers, waiting for the storm to abate sufficiently to permit the Calais steamer to leave the shelter of the breakwater. There were a dozen of us all told, but the Professor, as we called him, without, however, having any real authority for conferring the title upon him, rather monopolised the conversation, which for some time had been devoted to the Darwinian theory. Suddenly an American, who had something of the look of the merchant sailor about him, took his cigar from his mouth and remarked: "Finding the Missing Link is all right. But having the Link find you mightn't be altogether satisfactory."

"I do not quite understand you," said the Professor rather stiffly.

"O! I ain't giving out any conundrums. I said that having the Link find you might not suit you all the way down to the ground. I'm speaking, sir, from experience, for I was once found by that

identical Missing Link that you are so anxious to see, and the experience was a mighty curious one. If you gentlemen want to hear about
it, just sing out, and I'll give you the whole yarn."

Several of us replied that we should be glad to hear the sailor's
story, and without any further delay he launched into it.

About six years ago I was at Singapore, and I don't mind saying that I was on the beach—if you know what that means. I had
shipped as A.B. aboard a big four-masted ship out of Newcastle,
bound to Shanghai, and I got disgusted with the grub, and the way
in which I and the rest of the men were treated. So when we put
into Singapore for water—having met with calms and head winds
that had delayed us on the passage out—I deserted, and kept shady
till the ship had sailed. I found out afterwards that I would have
done better if I had stuck to the ship, for after waiting pretty near
five weeks in Singapore, and not being able to get a ship, I was
kicked out by the boarding-house keeper, and had to sleep in the
open, and live on food that I could beg from the natives.

Well! One day there came to Singapore a scientific chap by the
name of Butler, and my idea is that he was the identical chap that
the Professor was speaking of just now. He was going into the Interior to hunt for a new style of monkey that he called the Missing
Link, and he was anxious to find a white man who would join him.
I needn't say that I was glad to go with him, for it meant food and
the half of a tent and twenty dollars a month to me. I was the only
white man in the expedition besides Butler. We had three Malays
with us, who were to carry our provisions and things and act as a
sort of guard, and the five of us calculated to travel across the peninsula, heading in a North-easterly direction, and coming out on
the opposite coast. The country that we were to go through had
never been visited by a white man, and we supposed that it was
full of tigers, and savages, and such-like things. But Butler was
full of his project of finding the Missing Link. He had heard from
the natives that somewhere in the Interior there was a big monkey, considerably bigger than a man, who was more of a man than
a monkey. The story said that he hadn't any tail to speak of, and

that he was intelligent enough to build huts, and to knock down other animals with a club. Butler said that he was sure that this monkey was sort of half-way between man and beast, and he expected that if he could find him and bring him to Europe, his fortune would be made. I didn't take any stock in the story, and didn't care whether it was true or not. All I wanted was to get a berth where I could earn my living, and it was all the same to me whether I was hunting Missing Links in the jungle, or doing sailor work aboard ship.

We started in good spirits, but I'm free to say that if any man who knew anything about expeditions in the jungle had seen us and expressed his opinion, he would have said that we were a set of—well, everlasting fools! We were armed all right, for every man had a rifle, and Butler had a spare shotgun besides. And we had plenty of ammunition—about enough, as I judged, to supply a small army for a six months' campaign. But in the matter of food we were on short rations from the first. Butler carried very little except a sort of lozenge, made, as he said, out of meat. He calculated that we would find all the game we wanted, and that the lozenges would come in handy when he happened to be out of game. We didn't take any water except about a pint for each man in a water-bottle, and there was only a pint of brandy in the whole expedition, Butler being a teetotaler.

We had bad luck from the very first. We didn't meet with many natives except for the first week, and most of them were reasonably friendly, though we did have to shoot one chap just to discourage the others from looting. The jungle was that thick that you couldn't force your way through it, except with a machete or an axe, and first along we kept to the paths that the natives had made. After a while we came to a part of the country where there were no natives to speak of, and the only paths were the tracks made by the wild animals. They were quite as good as the native paths, but they ran all round the compass, and you might follow one of them for a whole day and find when night came round again that you were nearer your place of departure than you had been in the morning.

We didn't see much game, but we managed to get enough to keep us from starving, though, as a general thing, we were pretty hungry. About the tenth day, as near as I could reckon, one of the Malays was gathered in by a tiger. We shot the beast, but there wasn't enough left of the Malay to be of any use. Three days later the other two bolted in the night, taking their rifles with them. This left Butler and me alone, but he wasn't a bit discouraged. We filled our pockets with cartridges, and left the rest of the outfit behind us. Butler said that, according to his reckoning, we had about reached the part of the country where he expected to find his Link, but he didn't see any signs of him. We marched along pretty steady during the morning and evening, but we had to halt during the middle of the day on account of the heat. Our tobacco gave out after the first week—that is, mine did, for Butler didn't use tobacco—and I suffered more from that than I did from the heat or hunger. We couldn't make a fire, except once in a long while, for we hadn't brought but a few boxes of matches, and we couldn't afford to run through with them. Of course, we had to take watch and watch at night, so as to be ready for any wild beast that might try to investigate us; but with the exception of the tiger that carried off the Malay, hardly any animal came near us. I suppose the jungle was too thick to be a handy place for big game, but it suited the small fellows and the snakes and other vermin. I never saw such a place for snakes of all sizes and colours, but Butler said most of them were harmless. Perhaps they were, but I never put any confidence in a snake, no matter who he is; and it might have been better for Butler if he'd done the same.

I tell you it was lonesome, sitting down in that jungle in the dead of night, with Butler asleep close by, and all sorts of strange rustlings going on among the trees and the underbrush. Overhead I could see the stars stretched along a narrow lane made by the tops of the trees on each side of the wild beast track. I found it lonesome sometimes at sea when I was on the fo'c'sle-head on the look-out, with the rest of the watch snoring under the weather bulwarks, and not a sound stirring except the creaking of a block and the strokes of the bell from aft. But in that jungle you felt as if you was cast away in a boat without another soul. It's queer what noises go on in such a place—noises that are not made by animals, or yet by the wind. I've heard deep breathing close beside me, when there wasn't a breath of air stirring and not an animal within hearing. An animal can't move in a jungle without rustling the leaves or making the twigs crackle, but that heavy breathing would come within a yard of me without the least rustle or crackle. It was as if the earth itself breathed in the night; as if she had been overheated and tired in the day, and then when night came she took long breaths and settled herself to sleep.

We'd been marching through that jungle for more than a fortnight—perhaps three weeks—after leaving Singapore, when Butler was bitten by a snake, and died in less than six hours. He was a brave man, if he wasn't a first-class explorer, and he died as coolly as if he was going to sleep. There was nothing I could do for him, for we hadn't any medicine for snake bites, and if he had been loaded down with it I don't believe it could have saved him. I got him to take some brandy, but he wouldn't take enough to do him any real good. He talked sensibly with me, though he was suffering a lot of pain. He told me to take his compass and steer northeast till I came to the coast, where I would stand a chance of finding a settlement. He left me all his money, which was about three hundred pounds in gold, and urged me to keep my weather eye lifting for the Missing Link, and, if possible, to capture him and take him down to the coast with me. Finally, he made me promise not to bury him—and, considering that I had no undertaking tools except a knife, I don't know as I could have buried him if I had tried. It was his idea that the wild beasts would superintend his funeral, and he said he had as soon be disposed of in that way as in any other. Perhaps he was right. We do take a lot of trouble about what is left of us when we die, and perhaps it's all sentiment instead of sense.

When Butler was gone, I dragged him a little way into the jungle and covered him as well as I could with leaves and twigs. He and I had never been pals, for I was just a sailorman hired to work for him, but when he died and I was left alone in the jungle, I felt as you feel on a bright, breezy day, when the sun suddenly goes under a thick cloud, and the sea turns grey, and the wind begins to moan in the rigging. I knew that I hadn't any chance worth speaking of. I was alone with the thick jungle around me, that seemed to press tight on my throat like a hot Hooghly fog. If the wild beasts didn't gather me in, or savages make a dinner of me, I should probably die of starvation long before I could reach the coast. All that day I tramped along, getting hungry and tired, and not meeting any game that I could shoot; and when night came I lay down, wishing that I was back at Singapore starving among human beings in what you might call a social sort of way.

When I woke up it was daylight, and what at first I thought was an enormous monkey was standing over me on his hind legs with my gun in his hand. I jumped up pretty lively, but he had me by the scruff of the neck by the time I was on my feet. His hand was like a steam engine. I could fairly feel his fingers sinking into the flesh. However, I didn't say anything, or even try to twist myself loose. He had me, and the only thing I could do was to wait and see what would turn up.

We started along the narrow path, I in front and he behind, shoving me along with his grip on my neck. The only part of him I could see were his feet which now and then came into sight when he took a long step. I noticed that they were like hands. They had fingers instead of toes, and a regular thumb in the place where a man's big toe is placed. All of a sudden it came to me that this was Butler's Missing Link. I had often heard him say that the Link would be covered with hair, and would probably have feet something like hands, but in other respects he would be pretty much like a human being. The creature that had captured me answered exactly to this description; I knew he wasn't any sort of monkey—or ape, as I should say, for apes don't walk on their hind legs, and carry guns in one hand and hold a man by the neck with the other. He wasn't a man, for he had the feet of an ape, and he wore fur instead of clothes. Consequently, he must be the Missing Link, and I remember thinking that it was a big joke that I should have started to find him and that he should have found me instead.

In about half an hour, as I should judge, we left the path, and pushing our way through the jungle where the undergrowth was thinner than usual, we came to a little clearing, where there was a hut built of young saplings, driven into the ground, and lashed together at the top with vines. We stopped outside of the hut and the Link sang out in his lingo, and presently there came out of the hut another Link, his wife, as I supposed. The two chattered about me, Mr. Link shewing me and my gun, and they evidently agreeing that I was a valuable specimen. Finally, Mr. Link stood me up against a tree and made me fast to it with a rope of twisted tendrils, and then, picking up a big club, went into the forest.

I needn't say that I was pretty badly scared. Without my gun I was helpless, and there didn't seem to be much chance that I would get hold of it again. I couldn't get my hands free, for Mr. Link had lashed them to the tree with the judgment of an able seaman. I imagined, from his having taken his club with him, that he had gone off in search of game, which looked as if he and his wife didn't consider me to be good eating. You needn't remind me that monkeys don't eat meat. I knew that, and thought of it at the time, but a Missing Link has risen above the monkey species so far that I thought it very probable that he might have learned to eat his cousin man, as well as other sorts of meat.

Mrs. Link sat on the ground about two yards distant from me, looking at me with what I fancied was a rather admiring expression in her eyes. Says I to myself— "You're in a mighty tight place, and your only chance is to make friends with these Links." So I smiled my best smile and said to Mrs. Link— "Glad to make your acquaintance, my dear!" It fetched her the first time. She couldn't smile, for her mouth wasn't built for it, but she chuckled in a way that shewed she was pleased, and then she came over to me and patted me on the cheek. I kept on smiling for all I was worth, and talking to her in a friendly and respectful way. Of course, I knew that she couldn't understand a word I said, but I calculated that she, being a female, would understand that I was paying her compliments, and that I was full of respect for her character. A woman is a woman even when she is a Link, and I didn't make any mistake about this one.

By-and-by Mr. Link came back with a dead rabbit, and the two sat down to breakfast. They evidently didn't know anything about a fire, for they ate the rabbit raw, pulling it to pieces with their hands and teeth. Presently Mrs. Link tossed me over a choice bit, and when I looked reproachfully at her, as if to say, "How on earth do you expect me to eat with my hands tied behind my back!" she said something to her lord, and he then came and cast off the lashing. I didn't lose any time in sitting down close to Mrs. Link, and smiling at them both, while I ate raw rabbit as if it was plum duff. They were a good-tempered couple, and before I had got through with breakfast they had plainly made up their minds that I was an intelligent and harmless animal, and that they'd take me in and make a sort of domestic pet of me.

I don't propose to read off a regular log of every hour I spent with the Links. I was with them close on to four weeks, and they treated me civilly all the time. At night I slept in the hut with them, and they gave me a pile of leaves for a bed that was twice as thick as the beds they used for themselves. Mr. Link wouldn't let me go into the forest either alone or with him, but that was about all the restriction that he put upon me. He was gone on the hunt for game most of the day, and Mrs. Link and I stopped at home, and slept and talked. That the Links had a genuine language I never had the least doubt, though I could never get to understand more than three or four words of it, and those I have forgotten. It sounded to me something like French, though I don't really know much about French, and perhaps the reason why I fancied it sounded like French was that somehow a man always associates French with monkeys. As I said, Mrs. Link and I talked a lot to one another, and it seemed to do her good, though I could never exactly see why.

I did considerable work for the Links first and last. I improved and enlarged their hut until they regarded it as the swellest place ever built. I made forks for them out of big thorns, and I was tempted to shew them my matches, and teach them the use of fire. But I had only a small box of matches left, and I knew that if ever I escaped from the Links, I would need them myself—the worst way. They never discovered them, for they never dreamed that I had pockets. Their idea was that my clothes were permanent, just like their fur, and as I never took them off while I was with them they never suspected that I wasn't born in a blue flannel shirt and ragged trousers. Why, Mrs. Link mistook a hole in the left leg of my trousers for some new kind of sore, and one day she insisted on rubbing it with some patent salve that she got out of a sort of gum tree. They saw very soon that raw meat didn't altogether meet my views, and after that they always brought me nuts, and a sort of wild turnip. Take those Links by and large they treated me the best they knew how, and in my opinion Mr. Link was more of a gentleman than half the men in Singapore, though I'll allow that isn't saying very much.

As for Mrs. Link, I don't deny that she made a dead set at me. Mind, I'm not saying a word against her character, for as far as I know, she was a perfectly respectable Link. All I mean is that she took a great fancy to me, and tried to make me take the same to her, for which nobody could blame her. She used to pick out the best bones and the biggest nuts for me, and she was always bringing me water to drink in a cocoanut shell, and she never got tired of patting me on the head. Mr. Link never shewed the least sign of jealousy. I supposed that he considered the idea that a Link could fall in love with a creature like man was too ridiculous to be thought of for a moment. All the time I kept longing for my gun, which the Links had hid in some place where I couldn't find it. I don't know what they thought of the gun, or why they hid it. Perhaps their idea was that it wasn't respectable for a Link to be seen in the possession of such a thing, just as an Englishman when he goes to Italy thinks that it is preposterous in the Italians to wear cloaks. I'm ashamed to say that the way I got possession of that gun again was by teaching Missus Link the art of kissing. I often made signs that I wanted the gun, and I could see that she understood them, but she would never bring it to me. One day I put my arm around her waist and gave her a kiss. It hit her where she lived, and you never saw a girl at Christmas time, who had been kissed under the mistletoe by her young man, seem more delighted than Mrs. Link seemed.

The next time we were alone she hinted by her manner that she would like to try the lesson over again, but I wouldn't understand her, and kept on making signs about the missing gun. After a while she got up, and went into the jungle, and I began to think that she was pouting, but in a few minutes she came back and handed me the gun.

Then I did give her an honest kiss, and to tell the truth, though she wasn't much more of a beauty than the orang in the Zoo, I felt almost fond of her.

I hid the gun under my bed, a plan which she evidently approved of, and that made me understand that she had run some risk of displeasing the other Link by sneaking the gun. That night, when the two Links were sound asleep, I reached for the gun and slipped out of the hut. I hated to leave them without saying good-bye, but, of course, that wasn't possible. However, I did leave on the side of Mrs. Link's bed a little bit of a looking glass that I had carried in my pocket, and I hope it reconciled her to my loss.

I ran the most of that night, and must have put fifteen miles between myself and the Links by daylight. Then I lay down for a nap, and when I got up, and started on the march again, I caught sight of something blue shewing through the jungle; I had found the sea after all, and by noon I was safe aboard a ship that I had sighted close into shore, and swam to, taking the chances that it was an honest ship and not a pirate.

Now gentlemen, you may not believe this story, but it's the solemn truth! The Missing Link lives somewhere in the north east part of the peninsula, and though I can't exactly say that I found him, I'm dead certain that he found me. I've never told the story before, because I hate to be taken for one of your newspaper reporters, that are always having tremendous adventures that never happened. But if you should see my old rifle, and notice the marks of teeth on the barrel where one of the Links tested it, you'd have to admit that either the marks were made by the teeth of a man who could bite laminated steel, or that they were made by an animal answering to the description of the Missing Link.

IN THE LOWER PASSAGE

Harle Oren Cummins

We were sitting on the deck of the "Empress of India," homeward bound for Southampton. I was returning on a six months' leave from hospital duty in Calcutta, and the Colonel was retiring from his post in the northern provinces, where he had served with credit for over fifteen years. He had resigned suddenly a month before. His resignation had been refused, whereupon he immediately gave up everything to his second in command, and took the next steamer home, for a year's stay, according to the belief of the home government, but with a private resolution never to return.

I knew that he had had some terrible experience in which his dearest friend, Lieutenant Arthur Stebbins, had been killed; but beyond that I was as ignorant as the home government which had refused to sanction his resignation. That night, however, as we sat on deck, and felt the lingering tremor of the giant screw which was driving us back to home and civilization, something prompted the Colonel to confide in me.

"I was not acting in my official capacity when Arthur Stebbins and I went up into the Junga district," the Colonel said in answer to a chance remark of mine, "it was simply and solely to visit the haunted city of Mubapur. You have been in India for two years, and you may have heard some of the strange tales in regard to the place; but as nearly every little out-of-the-way province in India has its peculiar tale of hidden wealth or strange craft, you have probably paid no attention to the stories of Mubapur.

"I had heard the natives, when they thought no one was listening, speak of the lost tribe of Jadacks, which had once lived up among the Ora Mountains. It seems that they were not like other natives, but a white people almost giant in size, and their chief city was Mubapur. But years ago, some say ten, others fifty, and still others a hundred, for these natives have no idea of time, a great plague came upon the white tribe, and it was smitten from the land.

"They believed that the gods had in some way been offended, and that this people were annihilated in punishment. Anyway, we could not get one of our coolie boys within two miles of the place after nightfall; and they told strange stories of immense white creatures which flitted about the place, and of meanings and wailings which could be heard on still nights when the wind was from Mubapur.

"Stebbins and I were on a shooting expedition in the Junga district when he, remembering the wild tales he had heard, proposed that we turn aside, and make the two days' trip to the haunted city. As time was of no particular account just then, I agreed; and after leaving our coolie bearers two miles from the town, for they refused all bribes and ignored all threats to go farther, we entered the deserted and grass-grown streets of Mubapur. It was near dark when we arrived; and we decided to put up for the night in a little temple, the roof of which still defied the action of the wind and rain, and which offered us a comfortable retreat.

"As I was building a fire just outside the entrance preparatory to getting supper, I heard Stebbins call, and hurrying in, found him standing behind the chief altar of the place, and gazing down a steep stairway which apparently led into the bowels of the earth. He put up his hand as I entered, and whispered, 'Listen; do you hear anything?'

"I held my breath listening, and from somewhere down in the damp depths below I heard a strange sound floating upwards. It might have been a chant such as the hill men sing on the eve of battle; or it might have been only the wind soughing through underground passages, but anyway it was weird enough in its effect on both of us, so that we hurried out to the fire and busied ourselves getting supper. It is strange how differently the tales we had heard seemed in that ruined temple with night coming on, from what they had in the bright daylight in the market place at Calcutta.

"We slept very close together that night just inside the entrance to the temple, and all through the watches I fancied I heard that solemn dirge rising and falling in the stillness of the night. Once I awoke to find Stebbins talking softly, and I heard him mutter something about a great white beast; but when I looked at him his eyes were shut, and he was sleeping soundly.

"The next morning after breakfast I asked him the question for which I knew he was waiting,—should we descend the narrow stairway into the passage? He was anxious to make the attempt; and after getting ready some torches and looking carefully to our guns, we started down the slippery stairway.

"The steps ended abruptly, and we found ourselves in a long, narrow passage. What struck me at once as peculiar as we proceeded were some little cavities in the floor at regular intervals, such as might have been made by a person walking continuously, as a prisoner walks in his cell. But the stride was nearly twice that of an ordinary man. After walking about fifty paces we came to another stairway leading to a still lower passage, and just as we were about to descend we heard a noise as of something running swiftly below us. I looked at Stebbins to see if he had seen anything, for he was nearer to the head of the stairway than I; but there was only a white, determined look on his face.

"'Come on, Colonel,' he called, and led the way down the stairs. At the farther end of this passage we came to a square opening into a kind of vault, and we paused for a moment before it. Then, in that stillness of the tomb, sixty feet below the surface of the ground, and just on the other side of the little opening, we heard a low moaning, and I would have sworn it was a man who made the sounds.

"We held our rifles a little closer, and crawled through the aperture, pausing to look about us. We both nearly dropped our guns in our excitement; for, crouched in the farther corner, was a great white, hairy creature, watching us with red, flaming eyes. Then, even before we could recover ourselves, the thing gave a kind of guttural cry of anger, and started toward us. As it rose to its feet, I swear to you I turned sick as a woman. The beast was over eight feet tall, and was covered with a thick growth of hair which was snow white. Its arms were once and a half the length of those of a common man, and its head was set low on its shoulders like that of an ape or a monkey; but the skin beneath the hair was *as white as yours or mine.*

"I heard the Lieutenant's gun go off, but the Thing never stopped. I raised my four-bore and let drive with the left barrel; then, overcome with a nameless fear of that great white beast, I called wildly to Arthur to follow me, and plunged through the opening and ran with all my strength toward the upper passage. It was not until I felt the fresh air on my face that I stopped to take breath, and I was so weak I could scarcely stand. Then, if you can, imagine my horror to find that I was alone. The Lieutenant was nowhere in sight. I called down the passage, and I could hear my voice echoing down the dismal place, but there was no answer.

"Think what you may; but I tell you it took more courage for me to force myself down into that vault again than it would to have walked up the steps to the scaffold. I crept fearfully along the passage, calling weakly every few minutes, and dreading what I should find; but—there was nothing to find."

The Colonel paused, putting his hand over his eyes, and I could see by the moonlight that his face was white and drawn.

"And did you not find him in the lower passage?" I asked, when the silence had become oppressive.

"No, I did not find the Lieutenant," he answered; "but when I came to the little square opening before the vault, there were some bloody little pieces scattered about the floor, and the place was all slippery, but there was no Lieutenant. You know it takes four horses to pull a man apart, and you can judge of the strength of that white beast when I tell you that there was not left of Arthur Stebbins a piece as big as your two hands.

"As I looked at that floor with the ghastly things which covered it, a wild rage took possession of me. I knew that the creature was in the room beyond, for I could hear a crunching as a dog makes with a bone. I rushed through the opening, straight toward the corner where it was crouching. It saw me coming, and leaped to its feet. Again that sickening fear that I had felt before came over me; but I stood my ground and waited till it nearly reached me. Then, with the muzzle of my gun almost against it, I fired both barrels full into its breast.

"I must have fainted or gone off my head after that, for the next thing I knew I was lying in a native's hut on the Durbo road. Zur Khan, the man who owned the bungalow, said that he had found me four days before, wandering about on the plains, stark mad, and had taken me home."

"And the Thing in the passage?" I asked breathlessly. " Did you never go back?"

"Yes; when I had recovered a little, I went back to the Mubapur Temple," answered the Colonel; but he was silent for some minutes before he answered the first part of my question.

"In my report to the Government I said that Lieutenant Arthur Stebbins was torn to pieces in the lower passage of a Mubapur Temple by an immense white *ape,*—but I lied," he added quietly.

Beyond the Banyans

Epes Winthrop Sargent

I

"Death!"

The grizzled African blew into the air a tiny cloud of smoke.

"Death!" he repeated, as his broad palm swept the air, dissipating the wreath of vapor. "That is death."

"Then, since there is naught to fear from death," suggested Tom Loring, "why, this refusal?"

Bomoni smiled pityingly.

"Much there is that is worse than death that lurks in the mountains," he began slowly. "There is mighty Obeah; more mighty than aught anyone will ever know.

"Once one of my tribe sought the secrets that the mountain locks. One year he was gone, and three months more. Then he came—alone and silent—for his life was nigh spent. A little he dabbled of Obeah and of the men-monkeys and of the mighty magic, but this and that we might not put together to make whole speech. He died the second day, glad that death had come, for death is welcome when one would think no more, and too much had this man seen.

"I was but twenty then," added the chief reminiscently, "and that was full forty-years ago, but even now I see his face as it was then. Naught on earth can put such fear into the heart and eyes of strong men."

"And because one man had failed to gain a path forty years ago, you are afraid to let us have bearers?" asked Loring patiently. "Our men were of the coast. Their hearts longed for Boma, and they would not stay on.

"From here it is but a few hundred miles to Nyanza. In three months they will be at home again and rich men. Many cattle may they buy, and with the cattle buy also wives from the best in the tribe."

"Those who go come not back again," persisted Bomoni. "Some there are who have gone but a little way, to come back hurriedly and with tales of horrors. Others have kept on. They came not back, for in the land of the man-monkeys there is death for all. Not for any price will my men go, for what are many herds of cattle to a man who is dead?"

Loring looked from the white-haired Congo, chieftain to the remnants of his little party, the two white men and the coal-black Kassonga. Carlin and Brailey looked as disconsolate as their leader, but Kassonga spat contemptuously into the fire of green wood that mitigated the plague of winged insects.

"The lion roars," he grunted, "but the lion runs. I, too, have heard of the men-monkeys. Even on the coast I have heard, but I am not afraid. The magic, even the magic of the Obeah, is not as the magic of the white man. Is there game in this land of the monkey-men, O chief with the chicken-heart?"

"Much game, man who talks loud to hide the beating of his heart," replied the offended chief.

"Then we four may get through where these ignorant blacks fear to travel," suggested Kassonga, ignoring his own black skin. "Look, Big Boss. It is but a few hundred miles. On the map less than three hundred miles it is to Albert Lake. Before then we shall find bearers. With guns and ammunition and medicines alone we shall travel fast. In two weeks we shall be where there are white people. Shall we try it?"

Loring looked at the others. Brailey nodded his grave assent, and Carlin smiled broadly.

"We might as well be eaten in a lump by the monkey-men as grain by grain by Brailey's bugs," he assented. "We'll be well done on both sides if we stick here. Look here, Tom, the next time you take a trip make it the north pole. Then you can write a book, 'Fried and *Frappé*, or from the Equator to the Pole,' which will be a great seller."

"Kassonga makes a good suggestion," assented Loring. "It is better to push ahead than to remain here. As he says, it is only a few hundred miles, and we can do it in a couple of weeks. If we can reach Albert Edward Nyanza the rest will be simple."

Kassonga nodded proudly toward the chief.

Educated in one of the mission schools in the French Congo, he was an odd mixture of European and Congo ideas. In his heart he was miserably afraid of the Obeah, even though time and again he had been shown that the Obeah-worship was fanaticism. He was proud to be of the party that feared nothing. It raised himself in his own esteem and in the eyes of the natives, and he would have gone willingly enough to certain death to go a hero.

Once before he had guided Thomas Loring, the "Big Boss," whom he worshiped, and though this trip up the Congo had been little to his liking, he had followed blindly even after the other natives of the party had fled from the unnamed terrors which beset the path on every side.

It was partly this talk of the men-monkeys that had determined Loring to push ahead toward the lakes. He did not believe the tales, but he wished to disprove them.

Orphaned in his boyhood, he had spent his lonesome youth with tales of travel, and with the independence of legal maturity he had headed for Africa to realize those youthful dreams.

He was disappointed at first, for along the beaten routes there was no excitement, and civilization had penetrated well inland. With Dick Carlin and William Brailey, classmates of his at college, he had come up the Congo well beyond Stanley Falls, and had struck off up one of the feeders to find himself away from the beaten path, and in the face of a very apparent mystery. Two days before the last of the bearers had fled from the tales they heard, and only Kassonga remained faithful.

Bomoni, the native chief, refused flatly to furnish bearers, though Loring offered extravagant pay, and Loring had caught the fancy of the old man in the last couple of days.

Now, Bomoni was genuinely distressed at the announcement that they would keep on, and his anxious glance traveled about the circle.

Loring was tall and fair, though now his skin was as brown as a berry, and his rudely cut beard faded by the fierce sun.

Brailey, who was already famous as a naturalist, was short and spare, his intensely black hair and eyes suggesting a Spanish rather than his New England ancestry; but Carlin frankly betrayed his Teutonic strain in the clear skin and blue eyes, to say nothing of a tendency toward stoutness that did not, as a rule, hamper the rapidity of his locomotion.

All three were alert and reliant, and Bomoni nodded approvingly, though he scowled when his glance rested on Kassonga, the last of this oddly assorted quartet.

In the mission school Kassonga had been educated with especial care in the hope that he would become a native missionary. He had learned English and French and the Congo dialects at the same time; but, after a brief service as a missionary, he had become a backslider, and he turned his knowledge of the explored Congo to good use as a guide. He was boastful and overbearing to his own people; but he was reliable and faithful, and Loring trusted much to him.

"At least you will rest before you start this trip," pleaded Bomoni. "Two or three days will not matter much, and meanwhile you can gain the strength you may need."

Loring turned to his companions for their opinions. No word was said, but glances spoke, and in a moment he turned to the chief.

"We appreciate your hospitality," he said quietly, "and some day I hope that we may be able to avail ourselves of it, but now we are anxious to get ahead. We have heard of a tribe called Mongoba that lives far to the northeast. Perhaps it is they who you mean. They are not bad fellows, but hairy men and tall."

"You shall hear," declared Bomoni as he called to the guard who stood a little distance away.

The man darted off, and presently others began to arrive at the circle—the men who had seen, or who at least had been in the territory of the monkey-men. They were agreed that the country was held by men little better than ourangs, who ruthlessly slayed all who crossed their path, and each spoke shudderingly of the man who after fifteen months had returned to die, too stricken by his experiences to give a coherent story, and able only to utter raving cries of warning against trespass in the land where terrible things were done.

"It must be a pretty able bunch to shock these natives," Carlin declared, summing up the opinion of the rest. "If we do get through, we'll have an interesting tale to tell. What was that you said about the white Obeah, Bomoni?"

"He spoke only of the great white god, who made strange sacrifice," explained Bomoni.

I wonder if some renegade explorer is mixed up in this," mused Carlin. "The obeah worship is really the voodoo of the Southern States. Perhaps some chap who had a reason for hiding picked out Central Africa long years ago and set up shop as a god.

"Down on the coast they were telling something about a threatened voodoo uprising. Perhaps our white friend is at the bottom of all that. A clever conjurer, for instance, could give some mighty interesting kinks to the voodoo worship."

"If there is a white man at the bottom of this, we'll see presently.

"Let's turn in. We will make an early start in the morning."

The three white men nodded a pleasant "Good night" to the aged chief, and went off toward the hut which he had assigned them, but Kassonga lingered long at the fire, talking with the natives, for there were many things about the journey that he wished to know. He seemed scarcely to have slept at all, when he was awakened by a cry from Loring, and sprang up to make his rapid toilet.

Loring had apportioned the ammunition into three parcels, leaving but one gun and a revolver apiece, and giving the rest to Bomoni. Some salt and hardtack and a few simple medicines completed the outfit, and even the tent was left behind.

Bomoni headed the crowd of grateful natives, who accompanied them as far as the edge of the jungle, and there the last farewells were said, and the four pushed into the tangled undergrowth that surrounded the place.

As they were lost in the brush there came the sound of a monotonous chant, and Loring turned to Kassonga.

"What is that?" he asked curiously.

"Only a good-by song," was the prompt response, and Carlin eyed the native curiously.

He alone of the whites knew what Kassonga knew—that it was the death-song that is chanted over the brave warriors who die in battle. It was evident that Bomoni was sincere in his belief that danger lay ahead.

II

All through the day the party pressed on through the tangle of jungle undergrowth, keeping when possible to the river-bank, but frequently making a short cut that materially aided their progress.

It was well past noon when the first stop was made, for the thick growth of forest formed, an almost impenetrable canopy overhead, and tempered the fierce heat of the equatorial sun.

Kassonga had brought down half a dozen small birds, and Carlin declared some wild yams to be of the edible species, so at the halt they made a meal; and, after a rest and a dip in the stream, they pushed on again, anxious to press forward as rapidly as possible.

To Carlin it seemed as though the murmur of the river over its rocky bed, the sighing of the occasional gust of wind through the trees, the very sound of their footfalls repeated the dreary dirge that had been their farewell; and he, above all of them, was anxious to leave behind the gloomy forest, even though it facilitated their progress.

From the reports of the various survivors of exploring expeditions from Bomoni's tribe it was apparent that, once the jungle was passed, there was a mountain-chain to be scaled, and Kassonga's aim was to reach a point where the passage of the barrier would offer the least impediment to their progress.

No mountains were charted on the maps, but Kassonga put small faith in maps, and hurried the party ahead as rapidly as possible, though at best their progress was slow through the tangled brush. They found none of the native paths, such as exist between towns, and which the feet of countless generations have beaten into permanent ways.

For full five days they traveled without discovering a trace of human habitation, though from all accounts of the natives there were less than fifty miles of neutral territory, and the expedition had averaged fifteen miles a day. It was in the morning of the sixth day that Kassonga turned sharply aside from the path and clambered into a tree, from which he presently descended, bearing a fragment of cloth, rude in texture, but unmistakably of European origin.

"I have said nothing," he explained, "but for two days past we have been followed. We see none, and none we hear, but always they are there. Last night on my watch I could swear that I saw a figure move among the trees, but though with the light I searched through the soft earth, not a trace of footprints could I find. Here, too, there are no footprints but the cloth. It is not the native cloth."

"Our friends, *messieurs* the monkeys?" asked Carlin laughingly.

There was no laughter in Kassonga's face as he nodded assent.

"They do not strike," he murmured uneasily. "Perhaps they delay that they may be saved the trouble of carrying us. They make us prisoners only when we are close to their great town."

"Then there is a great town?" asked Loring.

"Where is the great white Obeah," explained Kassonga. "No man has seen, but—it is the way of Obeah."

"Kind of funny if we should fall into the headquarters of this new obeah movement we heard of on the coast," suggested Brailey. "Professor Smolak, at Boma, assured me that the entire center of Africa would some day rise in revolt against the intrusion of the railroad and civilization."

"You said you wanted excitement," reminded Carlin. "You are liable to have it delivered in wholesale quantities."

"Nothing to it," insisted Loring; "but if they are waiting to get us in the open, it looks as though they would not have long to wait. The open spaces are growing more frequent."

Kassonga nodded. "By evening we should be out of the jungle," he assented. "We camp to-night in the open."

Carlin brightened up at the announcement. The gloom of the jungle was depressing, and he would be glad even for the equatorial heat after the dank, unwholesome coolness of the shade. In his eagerness he pressed forward beside Kassonga, instead of lagging behind to examine the new growths he found.

Kassonga proved a true prophet, for just before the tropical night set in, with but the briefest interval of twilight, they passed the last of the thick growth, and stood on the edge of a vast plain that led to the foot of the uncharted range.

From northeast to southwest, as far as the eye could reach, the range stood like an impenetrable wall, and a little to the north of their position there rose a single peak fully two thousand feet above the rest.

"Here's a chance to chart Central Africa," declared Loring, as he threw down his gun and pack. "From the top of that peak we can make a map of this section that will add whole pages to the geographies."

"I'm more interested in supper," declared Carlin with a yawn, as he threw himself upon the turf. "It will be a terrific climb, Tom, and you won't see much when you get to the top. Take it easy, man. It's a long walk to Albert Edward still. Don't let's get away on any 'Seeing Africa' trips, unless we can get the automobile that goes with it."

Loring laughed at the suggestion, but the firm lips met over the white, even teeth, and Carlin groaned. There was little to interest a botanist on the top of a mountain, and he hated climbing, as all stout men do, but he knew that Loring would go, and that it would be well to acquiesce.

All that night they kept double watch—Brailey and Kassonga, Loring and Carlin. The finding of the cotton cloth so far in the interior, the trackers who left no prints, combined with the stories they had heard at Boma and in the interior, left them restless and uncertain.

It was the time of the full moon, and as they sat back to back they could sweep the horizon. The watchers were far enough away from the sleepers to be able to converse in low tones, and to Carlin, Loring in their watch confided his plans.

"We can't hope to meet force with force," he continued, "but we may be able to learn something and pass it along to the authorities. The best way is to keep on in our rôles of travelers and leave definite investigating alone."

"Including that mountain inquisition?" he asked hopefully, but Carlin laughed.

"That fits our incognito as travelers," he explained. "We'll be on top of that peak day after to-morrow. Come on, old man, it's our turn to sleep." And he led the way to the sleepers to rouse Brailey and Kassonga.

Loring did not quite make good his promise, for the end of the second day found them no farther than the foot of the range whence Mount Loring, as Brailey insisted it should be charted, towered majestically against the evening sky.

Game was plentiful, and there was an abundance of fish in the clear stream that evidently was one of the feeders of the river that led to the Congo. Loring assented to the suggestion that they rest for a day, and even he appreciated the luxury of inaction after their arduous trip, but on the following morning he roused to action, and insisted upon a start even before the sun was up.

It took but a moment to break camp, and presently they were clambering over the rocks, which Brailey, too, who was something of a geologist, declared to be of volcanic origin.

The ascent was a task of far greater difficulty than they had anticipated, and night fell with but two-thirds of the journey made. They had passed beyond the source of the stream which gushed out of the side of the mountain, and Kassonga was sent back to fill the water-bottles, while Carlin set about building a fire from the scanty stock of wood, and Loring and Brailey gathered brush for beds on the hard rock.

"Lucky it's the dry season," grunted Carlin to himself, as he built the tiny fire. "I shouldn't fancy camping out here without a tent in the rain."

"It will be easier going down," suggested Loring, who came up in time to hear the remark. "Brailey and I think we have found a sort of track more to the north. We'll be at the top by noon to-morrow."

"Let's hope so," assented Carlin devoutly, as he glanced at his shoes, torn and cut by contact with the trap-rock. "Next time I travel on a trip like this you'll have to build a funicular."

"Think of what's at the top," reminded Loring, alluding to the probability of their being able to see their goal from the peak.

The speech came back to him the next morning as he gained the crest, to find it the rim of an ancient crater.

"Hurry up, boys," he called back, as he unslung his glasses. "We've climbed over Africa into Louisiana."

The others hurried forward, and presently stood beside their leader on the edge of the long extinct crater.

They looked down into a valley roughly circular in outline, and some twelve miles in diameter, the upper part of which was covered by a dense growth of trees, from which emerged a broad stream, evidently the same which they found gushing out of the side of the mountain, for there was no break in the rocky wall.

The sides of the hill were thickly timbered, but the center formed a level valley, part of which was covered by fields of cotton, while an artificial marsh formed a broad rice-field.

In the center the stream broadened into a lake, and on the shores of this were rows of huts similar to the slave barracks of *ante-bellum* days, while in front stood the "big house," a low, rambling structure that might have been transplanted bodily from some Mississippi bayou.

Kassonga glanced inquiringly at Loring, who nodded, and presently they were descending the steep slope, tearing their way over the loose stones, utterly unconscious of the falls they were sustaining.

It was better when they reached the timber for the fallen leaves provided a surer footing; and a little later they encountered a rude path, apparently an equestrian road, for the beaten earth was marked by hoof-prints, and even as they bent over these the thud of an approaching animal was heard.

The four faced the direction of the sound, with their guns ready for action, but dropped their weapons shamefacedly when round a turn in the road there cantered a girl riding upon a powerful black. She reined her mount in as she came upon the four.

III

"How come you here?" gasped the girl when she had recovered from her first shock of surprise.

Loring's sweeping gesture appeared to take in the entire continent.

"From all over;" he explained. "We came up the Congo by boat, but our bearers would not continue when they heard that we were to cross to the sources of the Nile.

"We could not replace them from the other tribes, for it was told that there was mighty magic in the path. We did not anticipate that the mighty magic would take the guise of an American plantation presided over by a fairy goddess."

"It would have been well if you had shared the terror of the natives," she said seriously. "There is some blight upon the land."

"We are in search of adventure," reminded Loring. "Since there are Europeans so far inland, we would be discourteous indeed did we fail to pay our respects."

"There is but my father and myself. I am Mona Carroll," announced the girl simply.

She did not offer her hand, and Loring had to content himself with a low bow.

"I am Thomas Loring," he introduced, "amateur explorer and seeker after excitement. Mr. Richard Carlin is the botanist of the expedition, and keeps us from eating poisonous plants. Mr. William Brailey is the naturalist. Kassonga is the sole guide, philosopher, and friend left us."

The girl acknowledged with quaint, old-fashioned courtesy the introduction and wheeled her horse.

"If you will follow, I will take you to my father," she invited. "It is many years since he has seen white visitors."

Loring stepped beside the horse and chatted with their hostess, while Brailey and Carlin followed with Kassonga.

"Looks as though Tommy was pretty hard hit between his lungs and his diaphragm," suggested Carlin with a chuckle. "That's where the heart is," he interpreted for the benefit of the serious-minded Brailey.

"One cannot blame him," was the grave response, as Brailey's eyes rested approvingly upon the trim, rounded figure.

Mona Carroll was a type of the Southern girl before the Northern invasion and Northern conquests had spoiled their charm of simplicity.

"She is a very attractive girl," continued Brailey. "Were it not for a little woman in Boston—"

"I know all about her," broke in Carlin with a chuckle. The little woman in Boston was a favorite allusion of Brailey's, but as mythical as John Doe.

Brailey shrugged his shoulders, and Carlin lagged behind. The girl and the man in front seemed to have forgotten their companions. Loring's stride carried him quickly over the ground, but Carlin's shorter legs refused to keep pace, and presently his distant hail halted them for a moment until he caught up.

When Carlin hurried up they set out again, but the jolly acceptance of the jokes about the shortness of his stride gave place to a look of concern as he took his place beside Brailey.

"Drop back a bit and keep your eyes open," he whispered. "No. I won't say why."

Much amazed, Brailey lingered behind under pretense of examining some plants, and his face, too, was grave as he again caught up with Carlin.

"We are being tracked," he said in an undertone. "I saw nothing, but there are some animals or persons paralleling our path. Send Kassonga back."

Carlin whispered instructions to the black, but the Congo shook his head. "I know," he muttered. "I have heard and seen. They are the men-monkeys. The old chief spoke the truth. We are in a land of enchantment."

"So it seems." muttered Carlin.

Yet his eyes were not for the side of the road where the phantom trailers were, but ahead, where Loring seemed engrossed with the queenly girl who bent in her saddle to catch his remarks.

"The sooner we trek on the better," he murmured to himself. "We're liable to stay here for weeks."

His gloomy train of thought was interrupted by their emergence from the forest. It was still a long walk to the house; but with the goal in sight, they all quickened their pace, and even Carlin hurried forward, happy in the thought that he was to sleep in a bed, and forgetting the dark forebodings in the near presence of creature comforts.

A wide veranda ran round the four sides of the house, and on the porch stood a man, who looked as though he might have stepped from between the covers of some romance of *antebellum* days,

He was spare and thin, and the slightly gray hair was worn long enough to touch the rolling collar of his immaculate shirt. The gray suit, with frock coat and wide-brimmed soft hat, the flowing mustache and imperial, were all a part of the picture, and fitted well into the background of the old Southern homestead.

He came forward to swing Mona to the ground as she galloped up in advance of the travelers and was ready to greet each with a hearty hand-clasp, while he patted Kassonga's shoulder with the air of paternalism that marked the attitude of the old-time planter toward his slaves.

"I make you welcome, gentlemen," he said in the soft Southern drawl. "It has been many years since I saw white faces other than those of my own family. I look forward with pleasure to a long visit."

"I am afraid you will find us but birds of passage," demurred Loring. "We are hurrying toward Albert Nyanza and the Nile."

"I am sure that we shall find means to induce you to prolong your visit," declared the colonel with his slow smile. "Meanwhile, I would suggest that, perhaps—"

He motioned with his head toward the wide French windows to the dining room, where white napery and shining glassware looked most inviting to men who had been roughing it for months, He led the way, the others trooping after; and presently he was busy with the preparation of all old-fashioned appetizer.

Carlin's face grew ecstatic as he listened to the tinkle of ice in the glass.

"I didn't know that there was an ice plant this side of Boma," he cried.

"I had it brought up the river by carriers," explained the colonel. "It is a great convenience. I was here when the Congo Company was in its infancy. As a matter of fact, the existence of this place is not known to the Congo Company. I settled here in 1859. I foresaw that the war must come sooner or later, and sold my plantation on the Yazoo at a handsome profit.

"One of my slaves, Unonyi, had been a king in his own country, and it was he who guided us here. It took long years to bring this volcanic crater to the fine state of cultivation in which you find it; but I was young then—but thirty-five—and work was welcome. It enabled me to forget what was happening in my own country.

"I suppose that the march of progress will reach me in the course of time, but I shall be ready for the invasion then.

"To your good healths, sirs—and a long visit."

They drained their glasses, and, as they placed them on the table, an elderly negro entered.

"Andy will take you to your room," announced the colonel. "He will look well to your wants, for he was trained in a good school. I regret that for the night we shall have to put you in a single room. On the morrow others will be opened, but we have no visitors, and were unprepared."

"We are sorry to put you to this trouble," said Loring with grave courtesy. "We are old campaigners, and can be comfortable anywhere. To-morrow we must push on, so do not trouble. We are anxious to get along."

"Not a bit of it," denied the colonel. "You'll remain here for a week—at least. You must humor an old man who has not seen his kind for years—but I must not detain you now. Supper soon will be ready, and Mona will scold if we are late."

He hurried the three from the room with genial haste, but Carlin, despite the ice and the cocktail, was suspicious still. It seemed as though the colonel sought to avoid debate on the length of their stay.

The body-servant led them through a wide hall, up the broad staircase, and into a large room at the extreme end of the hall. He had borrowed liberally from his master's possessions, and presently the three men were enjoying the luxury of sponge-baths and shaves, while Andy, with a stiff brush and a needle, made their khaki suits more presentable.

Presently he slipped from the room for more hot water. Carlin looked up suddenly.

"I say, fellows!" he cried. "How old do you take our courteous host to be?"

"About fifty," hazarded Brailey.

"Nearer fifty-five," corrected Loring.

"Not more than that?" demanded Carlin, and both men shook their heads.

"To the contrary," said Brailey, "I think I am nearer the truth than Tom."

"Yet he was thirty-five when he came here in 1859," mused Carlin. "That makes him eighty-five now. Either he is a gifted liar, or the mighty Obeah himself."

"It simply speaks well for the African climate," suggested Loring. "It's absurd to imagine that the fine old gentleman is a votary of the voodoo cult."

"Yet he comes from the home of voodooism in America," persisted Carlin. "I tell you, Tom, the sooner we get out of here the better."

"Even if there is ice?" asked Loring with a grin. "I'll bet that by the time dinner is over, you'll feel differently about it. There's no magic here, except the magic of hearty welcome."

"You didn't see the escort," began Carlin: but the entrance of Andy put a stop to the talk, and they hurried to complete their limited toilets.

IV

Dinner was a delight to men who for days had lived on what game they could shoot, baked yams, and fruit. The table was as perfectly served as though the resources of a metropolitan market were at the disposal of the host, and the picture was completed and made more perfect by the appearance of Mona Carroll, standing at the head of the table.

She had exchanged her riding-habit for the ample skirts and low-cut bodice of the early sixties. The rounded shoulders and slender neck rose gleamingly from the *décolletage*, the ivory white shading softly to the darker tan of the face. The full skirts set off the slender waist, and she suggested some old painting in which the colors were still fresh and new.

She smiled slightly at the astonishment of the trio, and indicated that Loring was to have the place at her right, while Brailey sat at her left and Carlin was placed at the colonel's left. The well-trained house-servants moved quietly and skilfully about their tasks under the imposing direction of Andy. The travelers were sorry when, all too soon, the cigars and decanters were set forth and Mona rose to leave them.

Loring sprang to hold the door open for her, and her shoulders grew as rosy red as her cheeks at the look of open admiration in his eyes as she passed him. When he returned to the table the blacks had left the room, and Colonel Carroll looked up.

"I was asking Mr. Carlin," he explained, "to be good enough to refrain from discussing the matter of slavery. With the exception of Andy and Unonyi, my people do not know that slavery has been abolished, and they are entirely content as they are.

"To free them would only be to invite disaster. Paying wages might tempt them to look outside for better pay, and the Congo Company is worse than any slavery that ever existed."

"Do none ever seek to escape?" asked Brailey.

"Some few have sought to escape," admitted the colonel. "The result has acted as a deterrent to the others."

"You track them with hounds?" asked Carlin, recalling that he had not heard a dog bark since he had come into the valley.

"We track them—but not with hounds," explained the colonel with slow emphasis.

Carlin stirred uneasily in his seat. Mystery was something abhorrent to his care-free nature, and, in spite of the peaceful comfort of the place, he felt that the valley masked some horrid secret.

He was glad when at last they rose and sought the veranda, Loring already had slipped away, and he and Mona had sought the lake, Carlin and Brailey gave their attention to the colonel, who stretched himself in one of the wicker porch-chairs and gave himself over to reminiscence, The soft Southern drawl became more pronounced, until the fine head dropped gently back against the chair, and he slept.

"Let's slip away and take a walk, too," suggested Brailey. "We can go to the lake and turn the other way, so we will not interrupt Loring. I guess you were right in what you said about his being hard hit. If it wasn't for a little woman in Boston—"

"We'll take that walk—and forget the little woman in Boston," urged Carlin. "Still, it's better to be in love with a woman in Boston than one in Central Africa. That is, if you want to get back to civilization quickly."

Carlin laughingly led the way down the steps, and they turned in the direction of the lake, heading toward the north, where the stream which fed the artificial pond entered from the thick grove of banyan-trees that virtually cut the valley into two unequal sections.

"Let's walk up to the banyans," suggested Carlin. "I don't remember ever having seen a more remarkable growth."

"I wish we could get Kassonga for a guide," said Brailey, "I wonder what has become of him."

"Andy tells me that he is in the servants' quarters," was the careless reply. "What's the trouble?"

"I feel that we are being followed," explained Brailey. "It gives you an uncanny feeling to be tracked."

"I've had an uncanny feeling ever since we got here," retorted Carlin. "I'm getting used to it now, Those men-monkeys are everywhere. You remember what the colonel said about not using hounds to track the slaves. These monkey-police do the work. I wish I could see one of them."

"We probably shall before the visit is over," Brailey assured with gloomy foreboding. "I wish that we were out of this, Dick."

"We'll be ready if it comes," was the cheerful response. "I have an idea that we are going to stay here longer than we expect. The colonel lays great stress on the importance of keeping his retreat concealed from the knowledge of the rest of the world. Is it to be expected that he will turn us loose to blab round about the wonderful place in the heart of Africa with an ice-plant and electric lights, and all that sort of thing?"

"We must win through somehow," declared Brailey. "Tom will lead the way."

"Tom!" Carlin's emphasis was scornful. "Tom is perfectly willing to stay here the rest of his life, and even be assistant Obeah, for the sake of Miss Mona. I don't know that I blame him. We'll have to win through ourselves, Billy. Tom is out of the running, I'm afraid."

As they spoke they drew within the shade of the banyans, and for a moment both were silent. The huge Indian fig trees grew so close together that it was impossible to distinguish between their interlaced trunks. Some of the trees had sent down from fifty to one hundred false trunks, and the effect was that of miles of a single tree.

"I never saw anything like this," cried Carlin. "The banyan is not often seen in Africa; and not even in India have I seen such specimens. Let's push in a ways."

Brailey nodded, though he did not like the aspect of the place. The dense shade had precluded all undergrowth, and only the bare trunks checked the passage of the explorers.

They had not progressed fifty feet before there came a rustling in the branches overhead, and before they could look up, a score of hairy forms had dropped down and closed in around them.

Neither monkey nor human they seemed, but an odd mixture of both; and as they uttered their shrill cries, both Carlin and Brailey turned and fled for the open.

The shock of surprise had unnerved the seasoned hunters, and not until they had reached the edge of the banyan grove did they think of their revolvers.

The blued steel gleamed in the moonlight as they turned to retaliate, but a fresh surprise awaited them.

Where an instant before the woods had been full of the screaming horde, now there was no trace of life.

The dusky aisles were deserted, and only a slight rustling in the tree-tops gave a clue to their disappearance.

White and shaken, they made their way to the house. The colonel had just been roused from his sleep by the arrival of Loring and Mona, and he listened with a quiet smile to the tale that Carlin had to tell.

"The banyan-grove is infested by apes," he said. "I did not know that your walk would take you that way, or I would have warned you. I would suggest that you do not venture near the banyans unless some one of us is with you. We they know and do not molest; but when new slaves are brought in, there is sometimes trouble with them.

"Will you gentlemen have a nightcap?" he added, as his tones lost their seriousness.

There was a murmur of assent, and the three followed their host into the dining-room.

"To a long and pleasant visit," he cried, as he raised his glass and smiled at Loring."

"I thought that we were to press on to-morrow," protested Brailey.

"I think we had better rest up," explained Loring awkwardly. "The colonel suggests that if we wait a couple of weeks, he can let us have bearers to Albert Lake. It will be better to wait and rest up."

Loring spoke with a finality that checked discussion, even after they went to the room which for that night they shared in common.

Of the three he was the only one who slept well that night, for Brailey and Carlin were apprehensive of a danger the more terrible because they did not know what it might he.

Carlin tossed restlessly on the bed which was nearest the window, and had just succeeded in dropping off into a doze, when a shrill cry awoke him, and, springing from the bed, he rushed to the window.

Down by the shore of the lake two forms were running across the turf. One seemed to be a monkey-man, but the other was white, though his hair was long and matted, and the body was partly covered with a hairy growth.

The white man was in the advance, and the other seemed to be his pursuer. As he looked, they sprang into the branches of a shaddock-tree, and Carlin whistled in surprise. It was a good twenty feet to the lower branches, for he had admired that very tree in the journey to the house. To reach the lowest branch required a clean spring of not less than fifteen feet, yet both white and black swung themselves into the tree without an instant pause.

Carlin stepped out on the roof of the porch, the better to follow the race, when from the shadows of the vine-covered wall there sprang out another hairy form that raised him from his feet as though he had been a child and flung him violently into the room.

The shock of his fall roused the others; and while Loring bent to his assistance, Brailey rushed to the window, presently to report that he could see nothing.

"It's a nightmare, and you've been walking in your sleep," declared Loring laughingly.

"If it's a nightmare, the stable is beyond the banyans," declared Carlin. "I tell you, Dick, we're going to suffer a lot from nightmares while we stay here."

V

All three thought it strange that the colonel took no notice of the commotion in their room, but he did not make allusion to it in the morning, nor did he ask how they had slept.

It was Carlin who introduced the subject, describing what he had seen. "I could have sworn that it was a wild white man," he insisted earnestly, but the colonel laughed away the suggestion.

"Probably a gray ape," he declared. "They are very frisky on moonlight nights. I am afraid that I shall have to set a guard. Sometimes they do considerable damage to the flower-beds. What do you gentlemen propose to do this morning?"

"I have suggested to Mr. Loring that he might like a gallop," announced Mona. "There are plenty of horses for all, if you would like to come," she added.

She looked inquiringly at Carlin and Brailey, but Carlin was looking at Loring, and promptly shook his head as he saw the disappointment in his friend's face.

"I think I'll go fishing," he announced. "It won't do to get used to a horse and then have to walk when we start to trek again. How about you, Brailey?"

"I'll go with you," was the prompt reply. "You know you always fall overboard when you get a bite."

"There is plenty of good fishing," interposed the colonel. "I have had the lake stocked, and you will have good sport. I have some good flies in my library."

Loring was gone long before the others were ready to depart for the lake. Carlin insisted that they did not need a man to row, but the colonel, with an allusion to the heat, insisted, and they put off with a burly Congon in the bow at the oars.

Carlin's fishing had been in part an effort to get where he could talk over the events of the night before with the naturalist. He had become thoroughly imbued with the belief that he was in a land of magic, and he feared to speak openly where there was any chance of being overheard.

The presence of the black prevented freedom of speech, and he could only turn his attention to the fishing. The colonel had spoken truly when he declared that they would have good sport, for the lake was filled with gamey fish, and Carlin almost forgot his apprehensions in his appreciation of' the battles royal with five and six pounders as good fighters as the mountain trout.

He had almost decided that his experience was all a chimera, when there was a loud outcry from the far side of the lake.

As they turned, from the very top of one of the highest banyans a figure sprang far out over the lake, and fell into the water with scarcely a splash.

Brailey gasped with astonishment.

"That is no ape. It is a white man," he cried, and Carlin nodded.

"The same that I saw last night," he declared. "Funniest white ape I ever saw. Row over there, boy, and we'll see about it."

As he spoke a dozen darker figures sprang out from the banyans and into the lake, apparently seeking to head off the white swimmer, who was making a course toward the house. At the sight of the blacks, the rower turned and made rapidly for shore, nor did the shouts of the two men have the slightest effect.

His face was ashen with terror, and as he bent to his task, fear lent strength to the powerful arms, and sent the boat along at a pace that rapidly drew them away from the swimmers.

Brailey rose in the boat and slipped off his coat, but Carlin drew him down upon the seat.

"You'd have no chance with those chaps," he declared. "They've almost headed him."

Even as he spoke the blacks had surrounded the white swimmer, who turned and headed again for the banyan grove. As he dashed up the bank, his body gleaming from the water, he sprang upward and vanished among the branches.

Immediately the blacks followed him into the trees, and only the ruffled surface of the lake remained to remind them of the strange sight.

The boy with the fishermen still pulled for the shore, and presently the boat swung against the landing, and Brailey and Carlin stepped ashore, leaving the native to bring the fish and tackle to the house.

Andy hurried out to receive them with cooling drinks. The colonel, he explained, had been called away to look after some trouble with the electric light plant, and would not be back until lunch-time.

The two men were only too glad to sit on the veranda and rest, for the incident of the chase had shaken them both.

They sat close together and chatted in low tones. Brailey sought to argue himself into the belief that it was an albino ape that they had seen, but Carlin would have none of it.

"Either something in his heathenish rites turns men to monkeys," he declared, "or else the colonel is a scientist trying to prove the Darwinian theory by working backward.

"I tell you, Bill, this is the home of enchantment, and that Island of Dr. Moreau; where they grafted halves of different animals, isn't in it with this place. They use human beings here. I'll swear that those beasts were partly human, and Kassonga declares that he heard them speak. It's not right. We ought to be getting away from here."

"It will not be easy," declared Brailey, as he pointed to where Loring and Mona had just emerged from the forest.

Their horses walked slowly side by side, the reins hanging loosely upon their necks, and it was evident that Tom Loring had well employed his time. Carlin slipped off to wash up before they should arrive, and in the upper hall he met Andy, who had just completed the task of changing their rooms. Loring retained the room they had occupied the night before, and Brailey had the room next to him. Carlin's room was across the hall and at the rear of the house, overlooking the servants' quarters and the distant banyans.

As he stood at the window, drying his hands, the colonel emerged from the grove and came toward the house. Carlin, whose eyesight was uncommonly good, started as he caught sight of the face, for it was drawn and haggard, filled with a mute misery that, even at the distance, caused Carlin to cry aloud.

He quickly stepped back from the window, and as quickly completed his toilet, hurrying down-stairs to join the others just as Loring and Mona rode up and the colonel came forward from the dining-room.

Carlin stared incredulously at the placid, smiling face. Not a trace remained of the mortal anguish which showed so clearly but a few minutes before. The colonel was again the ideal Southern gentleman, with never a trace of care; and as he stood chatting with the fishermen, while Mona and Loring made ready for lunch, his voice was light and steady, even when Carlin spoke of the incident of the apes.

"It probably is an albino," he declared, echoing Brailey's thoughts. "I shall have to tell the boys to thin them out, if they keep on. There is a sort of tacit understanding that they are to stick to the banyan-grove. The field-hands are mortally afraid of them. That is why Joe headed straight for shore.

"It is a good thing in one way that the blacks are afraid, for it keeps them this side of the banyans and away from the power-plant. One inquisitive black can do a lot of damage to my generators and dynamos, and it cost many hundred yards of cotton cloth to get that machinery from the coast."

"I could swear that this was a white man," persisted Carlin.

The colonel turned toward his guest.

"I have lived here for nearly fifty years," he said slowly. "Surely you will allow my authority on the fauna of the country."

He turned toward the dining-room as though that put an end to discussion, and a moment later he was chatting as pleasantly as ever.

Carlin was far from satisfied, but there was nothing to be said; and he ate his lunch in moody silence.

Loring, on the other hand, was more than ordinarily gay, and he laughed and chatted continually. His gaiety only served to make Carlin more quiet, for he felt that Loring and Mona had arrived at an understanding which meant that the start for civilization would be further delayed.

He made an excuse to leave the others when the meal was done, and, while Loring and Brailey walked with Mona to the fruit-plantations, Carlin, under pretense of needing a nap, slipped up to his room and tried to figure out the meaning of the mystery.

On the coast he had been told of a supposed plot to make a holy war against Belgian rule, and, by an appeal to all followers of voodooism, upset the white government. He knew that a successful issue was impossible, but the uprising might retard the settlement of the interior, and that was exactly what Colonel Carroll seemed to desire.

It was not illogical to reason that he was preying upon the superstition of the natives to bring about his own ends, but he could not reconcile Mona in the scheme of things. It could not be that she was implicated in such a plot, nor was it reasonable to believe that she could remain in ignorance of the strange rites that must be practised if voodooism prevailed.

As he sat at the open window, giving free rein to his thoughts, he saw a commotion in the banyans.

The fruit-plantations were well to the east of the house and close to the banyan-grove. With a powerful glass, he could see that the men-monkeys were gathering along the edge of the grove, hiding themselves well among the trees, but not so well that the searcher could not locate them.

Fearful that they had designs on his two friends, Carlin hurried to get his gun. The range was too far, but he could at least give an alarm. He had raised the gun to his shoulder and was about to fire, when he dropped the weapon and reached again for his glasses.

Through the trees he could see the white skin of the fugitive of the morning, and now the other apes were closing in upon him.

It was evident that an ambush had been planned, but the ruse was unsuccessful.

Even as he watched, the white fugitive dropped through the banyans to the ground, and was running across the open toward the house.

VI

Carlin sprang out on the roof of the veranda, the better to follow the progress of the uneven race. He still carried his gun with him, and, as he perceived that the blacks were gaining on the white, he raised it to his shoulder.

Before he could fire, Colonel Carroll sprang through another window and threw up the muzzle of the gun, at the same time catching at the trigger and preventing a discharge.

His thumb was caught between the hammer and the shell, and badly torn, but he did not seem to notice the accident in his excitement.

"If you want hunting, I shall be glad to provide it," he said as he returned the gun to Carlin; "but I must insist that you do not fire upon the apes."

"But they have been chasing that albino all last night and all to-day," pleaded Carlin. "You said that you wanted them thinned out."

"In a proper manner," conceded the colonel, "but not with rifles. A shot would bring them all about the house."

There was truth in the speech, and Carlin rather shamefacedly returned to his room, the colonel following. He replaced the gun in its case, and turned to the window to see what progress had been made. More than a hundred black apes had swarmed from the grove, and surrounding the white one had driven him into the banyans again.

"They'll get him before night," declared Carlin, and he could have sworn that the colonel's eyes lighted, at the thought. Together, they descended the stairs, and the colonel led the way to the dining-room.

"Let us have a tiny drop," he suggested smilingly. "Shall we drink to the success of the chase?

His voice was light, but there seemed an undercurrent of eagerness; and Carlin noticed that the rather stiff drink was swallowed at a gulp, though usually the colonel drank little, and that very fastidiously.

The arrival of the others, laden down with fruit and blossoms, prevented further speech, and Carlin turned to the doorway.

"I'd rather drink to Miss Mona," he said gallantly elevating his glass.

Loring looked curiously from Carlin to the colonel, but the grave, unruffled demeanor of the latter dispelled any lurking suspicion that there had been an argument. He turned again to Mona.

Brailey slipped up-stairs to his room, and Carlin went out on the veranda to wait the coming of the others.

He was in no mood for conversation. He could not rid himself of the idea that the fugitive who had engaged his interest was a white man metamorphosed through some cruel process into an ape, and even when Brailey came down, he did not discuss the matter.

Brailey took things lightly, though, as a rule, he was far more serious than Carlin. He was ready to accept the theory of the albino ape; he had even declared that it was natural that the others should pick upon one of their species so plainly marked as apart from the rest; then he had seemed content to let the matter drop.

It was more than Carlin could do, and he was but poor company through dinner. Afterward, he smoked his cigar apart from the rest. He welcomed the early dispersal of the company and quickly sought his room.

He did not sleep well, and finally decided to get up and smoke a cigar.

He lighted the roll of fragrant tobacco, and took a chair by the open window, watching the smoke drift out and become silvered in the moonlight.

To his surprise, he saw his host crossing the lawn and making for the path that led toward the banyans. For an instant he was tempted to follow, but abandoned the idea. Already he had trespassed on the colonel's courtesy, and until he was more certain that evil was being wrought, he would not further tax his host's forbearance.

The cigar was finished, but Carlin continued to sit by the window, enjoying the light breeze that had swung up. He was not conscious of being sleepy, but presently his head fell forward on his chest, and he did not waken until he felt someone cautiously moving past him, and he looked up to see a white apparition standing over him.

There was no question but that it was a white man—a white man sadly brutalized, but none the less a Caucasian, and apparently an American.

The body was covered by a fine growth of hair, while the face and head were a mass of matted locks from which the eyes shone with feverish glance.

As Carlin roused himself, the figure clutched at his throat, and the long, lean fingers closed about his neck with a tenacity that he could not break, struggle as he might.

He could not cry out for aid, and he felt his strength rapidly leaving him.

Then came a patter of feet on the veranda-roof, and a score of black bodies sprang through the window.

There was a short, sharp struggle; and as Carlin collapsed in his chair, he was conscious that the intruder was being hustled through the window, struggling fiercely, but prevented from making any outcry.

By the time Carlin could rise to his feet and stagger to the window, the little party were almost at the edge of the banyan-grove.

With a sudden determination to see the mystery through to the end, Carlin slipped through the window and dropped to the lawn below.

By the time he reached the banyans the little party had disappeared, but he could hear them crashing through the mass of trunks as their captive still fought them, and he followed the sound. For some fifteen minutes he kept the trail, though he noted with dismay that the sounds were growing fainter.

At last they ceased altogether.

There was nothing to be done but to follow on, and Carlin stumbled blindly forward. The impenetrable mass of leaves overhead made it impossible to guide his course by the stars, and, he began to fear that he was traveling in a circle when there was a thud, behind him and two hairy arms encircled his chest.

The struggle was short, and presently Carlin found himself pushed rapidly ahead until he emerged from the grove and at last stood on the other side of the barrier of banyans.

A short distance ahead, there was a long, one-story building, and; from the whirring that came from the end which was lighted, Carlin knew that it was the power-plant operated by the river which fed the lake in the valley.

He was hurried up a flight of steps into an office to one side of the plant, and found himself face to face with Colonel Carroll.

As he entered the place, Carlin, for the first time, had a good look at the monkey police. The man was speaking in his native tongue to Colonel Carroll, and stood within the circle of light cast by the electrolier over the colonel's desk.

At close range Carlin could see the broad African features that from a distance might be mistaken for the face of an ape, but it was the body that was most deceptive.

The man stood at least seven feet, and the lean but powerfully muscled limbs were covered with a thick growth of soft hair, very unlike the wool of the Congo natives. The feet were large, but longer in proportion, than the foot of the native; and both toes and fingers were extraordinarily developed, suggesting claws rather than hands and feet.

A breech-clout of black was the sole garment.

Carlin stood silent while the native spoke, and watched eagerly the face of his host. When the colonel spoke it was slowly and with evident pain.

"I regret, Mr. Carlin, that you have sought to unveil my secret. You suspected from the start that there was a secret. I had hoped that the vigilance of my watchers would prevent you from penetrating the banyan-grove.

"On your first day you were turned back, as you would have been turned back tonight had it not been that the Mongobas were unable to be on guard."

"I followed; because I saw that your so-called albino monkey was a white man," protested Carlin. "A crowd of them caught him in my room, and I could not see a white man mistreated by a crowd of blacks.

"Of course, you had not told me that these monkey-looking men were your own people; but, even at that—the other was a white man, though sadly tortured and distorted by some unholy rite."

"Even in your own country—our country—" reminded the colonel, "the insane are kept under restraint. This poor soul escaped the day of your arrival, and his freedom very seriously complicated the plans I had made for your entertainment.

"It was my desire that you should see only the beautiful side of this valley. It was not to be, and I am afraid, Mr. Carlin, that curiosity will cost you dear."

"You want another victim to torture and make insane?" demanded Carlin, stung to bitterness by the realization that it was curiosity, rather than chivalrous defense of another, which had led him into the quest.

"Not to torture and make insane," repeated the colonel sadly. "If I should let you go back into the world, Mr. Carlin, the unsolved mystery would act ever as a lodestone to bring you back.

"It is easy to account for your absence to your friends. These men-monkey people will serve as an excuse to them. Your party will grieve over your death, but they will go on their way. I am selfish enough to be rather glad that you force me to keep you here. It will be very lonesome when Mona is gone."

"Gone!" echoed Carlin. "Then Loring has—"

"Mr. Loring has claimed her hand," explained the colonel. "I admit that it was with the idea that one of you three might fall in love with her that I gave orders for your safe conduct when word was brought that you were about to traverse the country held by Unonyi, my old slave,

"Had you not scaled the peak you would have been made captive and brought to me.

"It is but seldom that white men have penetrated this region, and mostly they were of the Congo Company and deserved the death that visited them. With you it was different.

"I realized that Mona was being sacrificed to my selfishness. I determined to let her go out into the world—to find the happiness to which she was entitled. They three will go; and, once they are gone, you will have the freedom of the valley, Mr. Carlin."

"But do you think Miss Mona will be happy?" asked Carlin. "You look at it from a narrow point of view, Colonel Carroll. We came here with weird tales of a mighty Obeah who ruled a tribe of monkeys.

"We find instead a fine old Southern gentleman and a very beautiful girl. Loring is in love—very much in love—just now; but in years to come, when the blood cools and the intoxication of love is past, there will be this dread secret between them. Suppose that doubt comes to Loring's mind, even as it had to mine. What explanation can Miss Mona give?"

"Nothing," cried the colonel. "I pray Heaven that she never may know the dread secrets of this place."

"That will not do," said Carlin gravely. "Her ignorance will be thought to be concealment, and doubt and suspicion will arise that will prove fatal to the happiness you plan. There would also rise up the fact of my death to stand between your daughter and complete happiness. It will be difficult to explain my disappearance, colonel."

Colonel Carroll's head bowed over the desk, and for a few moments he was lost in thought. Carlin, ill at ease, glanced curiously about the room; an odd combination of library, laboratory, and office. At last the colonel raised his head.

"I believe that you are right, Mr. Carlin," he said slowly. "I thank you for bringing the matter to my attention. I have lived too far apart from the world to face problems such as this intelligently. It is best that your friends should know. May I have your promise that you will not mention this matter until I speak?"

"My promise and my apology," cried Carlin sincerely. "I am ashamed of my curiosity, colonel."

"It was for the best," was the weary reply. "Sam will see you safely to the house. Good night, Mr. Carlin."

VII

Carlin woke in the morning with a heavy head. In his dreams he had conjured all sorts of visions, fantastic explanations of the mystery beyond the banyans. He was just in time for breakfast, and found the others in high good humor.

The colonel had not yet come downstairs, and Mona apologized for his absence, saying that he had returned from the power-station very late and wanted to sleep late.

"But he sends word that this fore-noon he will take us out to his power plant and show us round."

"And is that the reason for this smiling gathering?" asked Carlin.

"That's another story," announced Loring with a laugh. "Mona has promised that when we start for Albert Edward Nyanza she will come with us, and the first missionary we meet up with is going to make her Mrs. Loring."

Carlin added his congratulations with a heavy heart. There was a presage of misfortune that weighed heavily upon him, and which he could not shake off.

A bit of toast and a cup of coffee sufficed him, and he was smoking on the veranda when the others came out with Colonel Carroll.

The colonel greeted Carlin with no trace of embarrassment; evidently he wished the meeting of the night before to remain a secret between them.

"We are going out to my power-plant to show modernism in the midst of barbarism," he explained. "Are you ready to come with us, or will you finish your cigar?"

Carlin's answer was to throw away his cigar and put on his pith helmet. The colonel kissed Mona with unwonted tenderness and stepped briskly toward the path that led through the banyans. There was no path visible; but he threaded his way through the myriad trunks with a certainty that showed his familiarity and in half an hour they had passed the grove.

In the light of day the power-station did not look as mysterious as it had to Carlin the night before.

It was a long, low structure of sun-burned brick, with a roof of burned tiles. To the right was Colonel Carroll's office, and behind this a separate building with barred windows; strongly suggestive of a jail.

The colonel led the way into his office and motioned them to take seats, and himself took the chair at the head of the table.

"Mr. Loring does me the honor to ask my daughter's hand in marriage," he began abruptly. "I will admit that I anticipated some such result from your visit, else you would have shared the fate of many blacks and some few whites who have invaded Unonyi's territory.

"A conversation I had last night with Mr. Carlin leads me to the belief that before I give Mr. Loring his answer it would be well to explain certain mysteries."

"I don't care about mysteries," began Loring, but the colonel checked him.

"Mr. Carlin makes it plain that perhaps this question may rise later. When you leave here you leave this place forever, and what is said must be said now.

"Perhaps you have heard of Dr. Charles Montgomery Carroll?"

He looked inquiringly about the table, but saw no gleam of recognition—and he sighed.

"He was my father," explained the colonel, "and in the early forties he was an authority on nervous complaints. So runs the world. He is long forgotten. Attention is now turned to the man who claims to have weighed the soul, and that other who from a soap-bubble produced the lowest form of animal life.

"My father was the son of a planter, and completed his medical education in Paris. On his return he sent me there to study, and when I, too, came back he admitted me to his experiments.

"He had found that the essence of life is a form of electricity—the soul—the animating spark that vivifies the inert body. He sought to locate and isolate this particular form of the electrical fluid, but he made slow progress.

"He did find that the electrical current restored low vitality, and that this current was more effective if administered through the hand of the operator. The mechanical current seemed to carry with it a portion of the life current of the person.

"Elaborating on this idea, he applied the principle of electroplating, in which, by means of a current of electricity, a portion of a metal attached to one pole of the battery is deposited upon an object attached to the opposite pole.

"He constructed huge batteries, and soon he had succeeded in making the weakly strong. We owned hundreds of slaves, and subjects were ready to hand; but my father foresaw the war that was presently to result in the freeing of the blacks, and we knew that soon our experiments would have to come to a close for want of subjects.

"One of my boys—Tom he was called—aided me in my experiments and knew of our anxieties, and it was at his suggestion that we sold our plantation and announced that we would not only manumit our slaves, but return them to Africa.

"I had just married Mona Gourdain, one of the belles of New Orleans, and she brought with her a considerable fortune, which, added to our own, enabled us to charter a steamer and land near the Congo.

"Here Tom resumed his native title of Unonyi, and under his direction we came to this extinct crater, the existence of which he knew.

"With the aid of some cheap magical tricks, he not only regained the supremacy over the king who had replaced him in his tribe, but he became a sort of voodoo demigod; and his word was law, not alone in his own tribe, but in the near-by tribes whose kings acknowledged him as their superior.

"With his assistance we soon converted the crater into the semblance of our old plantation. The growth of banyans formed a natural barrier between the placid plantation life and the scene of our experiments.

"There was a natural water-power that permitted the manufacture of cotton cloth and other things the natives prized; and; best of all, Unonyi kept us supplied with material for our experiments— huge giants from the tribe of the Mongoba to the north of our country.

"These Mongobas were little better than orangs in intelligence, but their splendid physiques enabled them to stand the strain of experimenting, and we made a regular practise of supplying our slaves with fresh vital fluid from the Mongobas.

"I think that first day you found it difficult to reconcile my appearance with my age, for I have regularly kept up the doses of life-fluid. Mona wonders at my eternal youth, but—you will presently understand why I feared to give her treatment.

"My father, some twenty years ago, installed a new and larger electric plant, which not only gave power to the looms, but which enabled us to make experiments on a larger scale. Oddly enough, he had not regularly tried the transfusion of the life-fluid himself, but now failing health made it necessary to regain his strength.

"There was one Mongoba, a splendid specimen of brute strength, who had just been brought in by Unonyi's people. He was fully eight feet tall, quite the tallest I have ever seen.

"My father decided to use him for the experiment, and with infinite trouble we placed him in the tank; but not until I had numbed his senses with chloroform.

"The life-plater, as we called it, was a huge tank of glass filled with a saline solution. At either end were chairs somewhat similar to those I believe are now used in electrocutions in New York State, but these were immersed in the bath.

"My father took his place at the opposite end, and was strapped in, that perfect contact with the electrodes might be assured, and I turned on a mild current.

"The shock revived the Mongoba, and it was well that the straps were stout, else he would have burst his bonds and I would have had to shoot him.

"Almost from the first application I could see the change in my father. His sunken cheeks grew full, his eye was brighter, and at his urge I increased the strength of the current.

"The Mongoba writhed and strained at his straps, uttering wild cries of fear, until at last we had to gag him; no easy task, for the man clearly was insane from terror. He was growing weaker every moment, but so tremendous was his vitality that he still had the strength of three men.

"I suggested that we stop the experiment for the day, but my father was drunken with the new sense of strength, and insisted that the experiment proceed. Much against my will, I let it continue for a while; but the Mongoba was growing so weak that I turned to shut off the power.

"To my horror, the rheostat-switch stuck; and while I frantically struggled with the accursed thing, Unonyi uttered a cry of fear, and I turned in time to see the Mongoba's head fall upon his breast. The application of the current too long continued had drained his vitality to the very last drop. The man was dead.

"Hurriedly I released the straps that held my father in his seat and raised him from the tank. He assisted me in adjusting the rheostat, and was describing his sensations, when suddenly he sprang upon me without warning and bore me to the ground.

"The shock of the fall stunned me, and when I revived Unonyi was bending over me, and a score of blacks were holding down my father, who fought like a wild animal for his freedom.

"I spoke to him, but gained no recognition; and when at last he raised his eyes, I saw in them the fierce maniacal glare of the Mongoba. In that last instant the soul had followed the spirit.

"My father's body was tenanted by a dual personality—his own and that of the insane Mongoba.

"Now one, now the other, was in the ascendant; and when the change would come, no man might know."

VIII

There was a moment of silence, broken only by the rhythmical hum of the machinery.

Colonel Carlin's story had been simply told, but it had gained tremendous pathos through the expression of the care-worn face.

Now he sat back in his chair, his bent form slightly quivering with emotion, and the fine eyes looking fixedly at the opposite wall.

Loring half rose, as though to offer comfort, then sank uncertainly back in his seat. He realized the futility of words in the face of such a tragedy.

Presently the colonel roused himself to continue the explanation.

"That was about eighteen years ago," he went on, "just after Mona was born. The shock was too much for my wife, and she lived but a year and a half, refusing the administration of life-electricity even through my own body.

"Mona never has known the horrors that exist here. She knows that I am conducting a series of experiments of a scientific nature, and she knows that some great mystery is hidden behind the banyans, but she never has sought to penetrate my secret, and she little guesses that her grandfather still lives.

"I have kept the dual entity alive by the use of the life-fluid, and all these years I have vainly sought some method of undoing the damage I have done.

"I have created other double-souled personalities, and I have cast out one of these entities by means of the current, but herein lies the great difficulty. Alternately, the two personalities are in the ascendant, and it is this personality which leaves the body.

"The periods of change are sudden, and occur without regularity. At almost the instant of demission it might be that the change would occur, and, instead of throwing out the soul of the Mongoba, my father's soul would pass, and leave his body entirely to the tenancy of the insane Mongoba.

"Sometimes far into the night I have wrestled with the problem, but not a hair-line of progress have I made, and the discovery that I was about to give to the world eighteen years ago has been withheld until I can restore my father.

"I fear that the end draws near. The soul of the black is the stronger, and, more and more maintains possession of the body. Perhaps there will come a time when my father will be completely subjected by the black.

"In other words, when he will 'die,' though his body will continue to be tenanted by the Mongoba.

"I want Mona to go out into the world. If I should die, Unonyi would take her to the coast; but when word was brought that three white men, not Congo Company officers, were about to make for Albert Lake, I issued orders that they be brought here, as I have explained to Mr. Carlin, in the hope that one of you might come to love her and carry her away.

"The very morning of your arrival the Mongoba broke from restraint and escaped into the banyans. What Mr. Carlin has called my monkey-police are picked men from Unonyi's tribe, who, by means of repeated administrations of life-electricity from the Mongobas, have gained tremendous strength and agility. They can leap incredible distances into the air or across space, and the interlaced network of banyans is their thoroughfare.

"The Mongoba with the craft of the insane eluded capture, though at times his retaking was imminent. Twice, I believe, Mr. Carlin and Mr. Brailey saw the chase and sought to interfere, and a third time—last night—the Mongoba reached the house and very nearly strangled Mr. Carlin before he was caught by my men. Mr. Carlin followed, and was in turn captured by my police, who patrol the banyans constantly."

"You never said anything about it, Dick," cried Loring.

"I had promised not to," explained Carlin. "The colonel wished to tell you the whole story first."

"Shortly after his capture my father's spirit gained the ascendancy," continued the colonel, "and it was an easy matter to place him under restraint again. Mr. Carlin convinced me that before I gave my consent to Mona's marriage it would be best to reveal the secrets of the banyans, that there might rise no misunderstandings at a time when explanations could not be obtained. You are still willing to take her, Mr. Loring?"

"More than ever," was the fervent response. "It is a splendid sacrifice you are making, colonel; but let us hope that presently success will attend your efforts."

Colonel Carroll shook his head in negation.

"I have a feeling that the end is near, but not a happy ending," he said wearily. "Now that Mona is provided for, I feel more at ease."

His hand clasped Loring's, and the others turned away: for a moment no word was spoken; then the colonel again broke the silence.

"Perhaps you would like to see the life-plater, as I call it," he suggested.

They gave silent assent, and the colonel led the way to the small building they had noticed. A door gave into a room about twenty feet square. On the opposite side was another door, this one heavily barred.

"For my subjects," explained the colonel. "I differentiate between my patients and my subjects. With the latter, I find that the dual personality almost always is accompanied by some manifestations of insanity. Under proper restraint, and with plenty of Unonyi's men to help, there is small danger of a mishap."

Beside the door was a huge rheostat for reducing the current from the dynamos to any desired strength, and the colonel patted the glistening brass lovingly.

"With this I can get full current or merely a vibration," he explained. "Some of the devices are my father's inventions, others I have made; but the base is the regulation switchboard and rheostat. The wires lead to the tank by means of conduits in the floor."

He turned to the tank, which stood in the center of the room. Within concrete walls was set a tub of glass several inches thick, three feet across, and about eight feet long.

At either end was a heavy chair, provided with thick straps of hippopotamus hide, and insulated wires, running over the top of the tank, led to copper bosses set into the back and seat.

"It is exactly like the electroplating apparatus," explained the colonel, "but with a human anode and a human being to be plated. Perhaps, you would like to see it work."

The three men made a gesture of dissent, but the colonel was leaning over the tank adjusting the wire. He did not see the distaste with which the suggestion was received, but chatted on, explaining the method of connecting the wires. He was holding both sets of wires in his hand when Loring gave a cry.

Unseen by any one; the Mongoba had entered the chamber, and as Loring cried out he threw the master switch that sent the current, into the board. The resistances were all thrown off, and the full current entered the colonel's body. For a moment it grew horridly stiff, then fell limply over the edge of the tank.

Carlin, who was the nearest, rushed to the switchboard to throw off the current, but before he could do so there was another cry of horror from Brailey and Loring. As he turned, Carlin saw that the Mongoba, too, lay on the floor beside the tank.

"It was the most terrible thing I ever saw," declared Loring when speech came to them again.

"You could see the change from the Mongoba to Dr. Carroll's personality, and, unthinking of the danger, he rushed to the aid of his son. He, too, received the full current just before you had time to throw it off, Dick."

"Perhaps it is better so," said Brailey softly. "I don't believe that the colonel ever would have succeeded in restoring his father; and think what it would have meant to live here alone with the blacks and this poor wreck. It is much better so."

"It will be hard to break it to Miss Mona," said Carlin. "You'll have to do that, Tom. Just tell her that there was a short circuit, and that he was showing us the machinery. You do that, while Brailey and I rout out the blacks and send a runner for this Unonyi. Do you know where Mrs. Carroll is buried?"

"In that clump of shaddock by the lake," replied Carlin. "Mona took me to it yesterday."

"We'll have the grave dug there and bury the colonel before she knows," suggested Brailey. "Then we'll read the burial service over the two graves. Miss Mona need never know it is a double service."

"That will be the best way," assented Carlin. "The less Mona is told, the better. I'll go and prepare her for her father's death."

Reverently he covered the still, cold face with his handkerchief, and Brailey used his to cover the face of the elder Carroll; then, while Loring went through the banyans to bear the tidings, Carlin and Brailey made arrangements for the care of the bodies and dispatched a runner for Unonyi. Late that evening the chief arrived; and Carlin arranged with him for bearers to the Nile sources.

Later yet, they stood round the open grave in the shaddock-grove, and Loring read the burial service over the two men who had found death in seeking the source of life.

As the earth began to fall upon the coffin and the natives took up the long, wailing death-chant; Mona caught Loring's arm, and gently he led her to the house where Unonyi's wife waited to minister to her.

The three men spent the night going through the colonel's papers, destroying all that had bearing upon the discovery and packing for carriage those few documents that would be of use to the girl.

"I suppose that you will move in when we are gone," suggested Loring to Unonyi.

The chief shivered slightly.

"Perhaps, when the spirits of the dead have passed beyond," he said. "I shall come but for a little while, for the night draws fast for me. Those who live by magic go quickly when the magic stops. One hundred and ten years I have lived. It is well that I go.

"Miss Mona will leave to-morrow, and when she has gone, the House of Life, and all that is beyond the banyans, will be destroyed. Those for whom there is no hope also will I destroy. The others may depart into their own country. It is not well, sirs, to take liberties with life and death."

"And Kassonga?" asked Carlin. "The colonel said that he was being cared for."

"He sought to escape that first night," explained Unonyi. "My people found him."

Carlin shook his head sadly. He had grown fond of the black; but it would never have done to let him return to the coast. He moved to the window and stepped out on the piazza.

The sun was rising above the rim of the crater, turning the dew-drops to diamonds with its slanting rays.

Unonyi stepped out beside him.

"A fair scene," he said softly. "The poor old colonel would have had an earthly paradise here. All through the years when we worked to make it like his own beloved plantation, he planned that he should live here forever.

"To the eye it was a paradise, but for seventeen weary years hell lurked beyond the banyans.

"It is well that it is ended."

And Carlin, glancing in the direction of the little grove where at last the scientist lay at rest, reverently echoed:

"Amen!"

Back There in the Grass

Gouverneur Morris

It was spring in the South Seas when, for the first time, I went ashore at Batengo, which is the Polynesian village, and the only one on the big grass island of the same name. There is a cable station just up the beach from the village, and a good-natured young chap named Graves had charge of it. He was an upstanding, clean-cut fellow, as the fact that he had been among the islands for three years without falling into any of their ways proved. The interior of the corrugated iron house in which he lived, for instance, was bachelor from A to Z. And if that wasn't a sufficient alibi, my pointer dog, Don, who dislikes anything Polynesian or Melanesian, took to him at once. And they established a romping friendship.

He gave us lunch on the porch, and because he had not seen a white man for two months, or a liver-and-white dog for two years, he told us the entire story of his young life, with reminiscences of early childhood and plans for the future thrown in. The future was very simple. There was a girl coming out to him from the States by the next steamer but one; the captain of that steamer would join them together in holy wedlock, and after that the Lord would provide.

"My dear fellow," he said, "you think I'm asking her to share a very lonely sort of life, but if you could imagine all the—the affection and gentleness, and thoughtfulness that I've got stored up to pour out at her feet for the rest of our lives, you wouldn't be a bit afraid for her happiness. If a man spends his whole time and imagination thinking up ways to make a girl happy and occupied, he can think up a whole lot. ... I'd like ever so much to show her to you."

He led the way to his bedroom, and stood in silent rapture before a large photograph that leaned against the wall over his dressing-table. She didn't look to me like the sort of girl a cable agent would happen to marry. She looked like a swell—the real thing—beautiful and simple and unaffected.

"Yes," he said, "isn't she?"

I hadn't spoken a word. Now I said: "It's easy to see why you aren't lonely with that wonderful girl to look at. Is she really coming out by the next steamer but one? It's hard to believe because she's so much too good to be true."

"Yes," he said, "isn't she?"

"The usual cable agent," I said, "keeps from going mad by having a dog or a cat or some pet or other to talk to. But I can understand a photograph like this being all-sufficient to any man—even if he had never seen the original. Allow me to shake hands with you." Then I got him away from the girl, because my time was short and I wanted to find out about some things that were important to *me*.

"You haven't asked me my business in these parts," I said, "but I'll tell you. I'm collecting grasses for the Bronx Botanical Garden."

"Then, by Jove!" said Graves, "you have certainly come to the right place. There used to be a tree on this island, but the last man who saw it died in 1789—Grass! The place is all grass: there are fifty kinds right around my house here."

"I've noticed only eighteen," I said, "but that isn't the point. The point is: when do the Batengo Island grasses begin to go to seed?" And I smiled.

"You think you've got me stumped, don't you?" he said. "That a mere cable agent wouldn't notice such things. Well, that grass there," and he pointed— "beach nut we call it—is the first to ripen seed, and, as far as I know, it does it just six weeks from now."

"Are you just making things up to impress me?"

"No, sir, I am not. I know to the minute. You see, I'm a victim of hay-fever."

"In that case," I said, " expect me back about the time your nose begins to run."

"Really?" And his whole face lighted up. "I'm delighted. Only six weeks. Why, then, if you'll stay round for only five or six weeks *more* you'll be here for the wedding."

"I'll make it if I possibly can," I said. "I want to see if that girl's really true."

"Anything I can do to help you while you're gone? I've got loads of spare time "

"If you knew anything about grasses—"

"I don't. But I'll blow back into the interior and look around. I've been meaning to right along, just for fun. But I can never get any of *them* to go with me."

"The natives?"

"Yes. Poor lot. They're committing race suicide as fast as they can. There are more wooden gods than people in Batengo village, and the superstition's so thick you could cut it with a knife. All the manly virtues have perished. ... Aloiu!"

The boy who did Graves's chores for him came lazily out of the house.

"Aloiu," said Graves, "just run back into the island to the top of that hill—see?—that one over there—and fetch a handful of grass for this gentleman. He'll give you five dollars for it." Aloiu grinned sheepishly and shook his head.

"Fifty dollars?"

Aloiu shook his head with even more firmness, and I whistled. Fifty dollars would have made him the Rockefeller-Carnegie-Morgan of those parts.

"All right, coward," said Graves cheerfully. "Run away and play with the other children. ... Now, isn't that curious? Neither love, money, nor insult will drag one of them a mile from the beach. They say that if you go 'back there in the grass' something awful will happen to you."

"As what?" I asked.

"The last man to try it," said Graves, "in the memory of the oldest inhabitant was a woman. When they found her she was all black and swollen—at least that's what they say. Something had bitten her just above the ankle."

"Nonsense," I said, "there are no snakes in the whole Batengo group."

"They didn't say it was a snake," said Graves. "They said the marks of the bite were like those that would be made by the teeth of a very little—child."

Graves rose and stretched himself.

"What's the use of arguing with people that tell yarns like that! All the same, if you're bent on making expeditions back into the grass, you'll make 'em alone, unless the cable breaks and I'm free to make 'em with you."

Five weeks later I was once more coasting along the wavering hills of Batengo Island, with a sharp eye out for a first sight of the cable station and Graves. Five weeks with no company but Kanakas and a pointer dog makes one white man pretty keen for the society of another. Furthermore, at our one meeting I had taken a great shine to Graves and to the charming young lady who was to brave a life in the South Seas for his sake. If I was eager to get ashore, Don was more so.

I had a shot-gun across my knees with which to salute the cable station, and the sight of that weapon, coupled with toothsome memories of a recent big hunt down on Forked Peak, had set the dog quivering from stem to stern, to crouching, wagging his tail till it disappeared, and beating sudden tattoos upon the deck with his forepaws. And when at last we rounded on the cable station and I let off both barrels, he began to bark and race about the schooner like a thing possessed. The salute brought Graves out of his house. He stood on the porch waving a handkerchief, and I called to him through a megaphone; hoped that he was well, said how glad I was to see him, and asked him to meet me in Batengo village. Even at that distance I detected a something irresolute in his manner; and a few minutes later when he had fetched a hat out of the house, locked the door, and headed toward the village, he looked more like a soldier marching to battle than a man walking half a mile to greet a friend.

"That's funny," I said to Don. "He's coming to meet us in spite of the fact that he'd much rather not. Oh, well!"

I left the schooner while she was still under way, and reached the beach before Graves came up. There were too many strange brown men to suit Don, and he kept very close to my legs. When Graves arrived the natives fell away from him as if he had been a leper. He wore a sort of sickly smile, and when he spoke the dog stiffened his legs and growled menacingly.

"Don!" I exclaimed sternly, and the dog cowered, but the spines along his back bristled and he kept a menacing eye upon Graves. The man's face looked drawn and rather angry. The frank boyishness was clean out of it. He had been strained by something or other to the breaking-point—so much was evident.

"My dear fellow," I said, "what the devil is the matter?"

Graves looked to right and left, and the islanders shrank still farther away from him.

"You can see for yourself," he said curtly. "I'm taboo." And then, with a little break in his voice: "Even your dog feels it. Don, good boy! Come here, sir!" Don growled quietly.

"You see!"

"Don," I said sharply, "this man is my friend and yours. Pat him, Graves."

Graves reached forward and patted Don's head and talked to him soothingly. But although Don did not growl or menace, he shivered under the caress and was unhappy.

"So you're taboo!" I said cheerfully. "That's the result of anything, from stringing pink and yellow shells on the same string to murdering your uncle's grandmother-in-law. Which have *you* done?"

"I've been back there in the grass," he said, "and because—because nothing happened to me I'm taboo."

"Is that all?"

"As far as they know—yes."

"Well!" said I, "my business will take me back there for days at a time, so I'll be taboo, too. Then there'll be two of us. Did you find any curious grasses for me?"

"I don't know about grasses," he said, "but I found something very curious that I want to show you and ask your advice about. Are you going to share my house?"

"I think I'll keep head-quarters on the schooner," I said, "but if you'll put me up now and then for a meal or for the night—"

"I'll put you up for lunch right now," he said, "if you'll come. I'm my own cook and bottle-washer since the taboo, but I must say the change isn't for the worse so far as food goes."

He was looking and speaking more cheerfully.

"May I bring Don?"

He hesitated.

"Why—yes—of course."

"If you'd rather not?"

"No, bring him. I want to make friends again if I can."

So we started for Graves's house, Don very close at my heels.

"Graves," I said, "surely a taboo by a lot of fool islanders hasn't upset you. There's something on your mind. Bad news?"

"Oh, no," he said. "She's coming. It's other things. I'll tell you by and by—everything. Don't mind me. I'm all right. Listen to the wind in the grass. That sound day and night is enough to put a man off his feed."

"You say you found something very curious back there in the grass?"

"I found, among other things, a stone monolith. It's fallen down, but it's almost as big as the Flatiron Building in New York. It's ancient as days—all carved—it's a sort of woman, I think. But we'll go back one day and have a look at it. Then, of course, I saw all the different kinds of grasses in the world—they'd interest you more—but I'm such a punk botanist that I gave up trying to tell 'em apart. I like the flowers best—there's millions of 'em—down among the grass. ... I tell you, old man, this island is the greatest curiosity-shop in the whole world."

He unlocked the door of his house and stood aside for me to go in first.

"Shut up, Don!" The dog growled savagely, but I banged him with my open hand across the snout, and he quieted down and followed into the house, all tense and watchful.

On the shelf where Graves kept his books, with its legs hanging over, was what I took to be an idol of some light brownish wood—say sandalwood, with a touch of pink. But it was the most lifelike and astounding piece of carving I ever saw in the islands or out of them.

It was about a foot high, and represented a Polynesian woman in the prime of life, say, fifteen or sixteen years old, only the features were finer and cleaner carved. It was a nude, in an attitude of easy repose—the legs hanging, the toes dangling—the hands resting, palms downward, on the blotter, the trunk relaxed. The eyes, which were a kind of steely blue, seemed to have been made, depth upon depth, of some wonderful translucent enamel, and to make his work still more realistic the artist had planted the statuette's eyebrows, eyelashes, and scalp with real hair, very soft and silky, brown on the head and black for the lashes and eyebrows. The thing was so lifelike that it frightened me. And when Don began to growl like distant thunder I didn't blame him. But I leaned over and caught him by the collar, because it was evident that he wanted to get at that statuette and destroy it.

When I looked up the statuette's eyes had moved. They were turned downward upon the dog, with cool curiosity and indifference. A kind of shudder went through me. And then, lo and behold, the statuette's tiny brown breasts rose and fell slowly, and a long breath came out of its nostrils.

I backed violently into Graves, dragging Don with me and half-choking him.

"My God Almighty!" I said. "It's alive!"

"Isn't she!" said he. "I caught her back there in the grass—the little minx. And when I heard your signal I put her up there to keep her out of mischief. It's too high for her to jump—and she's very sore about it."

"You found her in the grass," I said. "For God's sake!—are there more of them?"

"Thick as quail," said he, "but it's hard to get a sight of 'em. But *you* were overcome by curiosity, weren't you, old girl? You came out to have a look at the big white giant and he caught you with his thumb and forefinger by the scruff of the neck—so you couldn't bite him—and here you are."

The womankin's lips parted and I saw a flash of white teeth. She looked up into Graves's face and the steely eyes softened. It was evident that she was very fond of him.

"Rum sort of a pet," said Graves. "What?"

"Rum?" I said. "It's horrible—it isn't decent—it—it ought to be taboo. Don's got it sized up right. He—he wants to kill it."

"Please don't keep calling her It," said Graves. "She wouldn't like it—if she understood." Then he whispered words that were Greek to me, and the womankin laughed aloud. Her laugh was sweet and tinkly, like the upper notes of a spinet.

"You can speak her language?"

"A few words—Tog ma Lao?"

"Na!"

"Aba Ton sug ato."

"Nan Tane dom ud lon anea!"

It sounded like that—only all whispered and very soft. It sounded a little like the wind in the grass.

"She says she isn't afraid of the dog," said Graves, "and that he'd better let her alone."

"I almost hope he won't," said I. "Come outside. I don't like her. I think I've got a touch of the horrors."

Graves remained behind a moment to lift the womankin down from the shelf, and when he rejoined me I had made up my mind to talk to him like a father.

"Graves," I said, "although that creature in there is only a foot high, it isn't a pig or a monkey, it's a woman, and you're guilty of what's considered a pretty ugly crime at home—abduction. You've stolen this woman away from kith and kin, and the least you can do is to carry her back where you found her and turn her loose. Let me ask you one thing—what would Miss Chester think?"

"Oh, that doesn't worry me," said Graves. "But I *am* worried—worried sick. It's early—shall we talk now, or wait till after lunch?"

"Now," I said.

"Well," said he, "you left me pretty well enthused on the subject of botany—so I went back there twice to look up grasses for you. The second time I went I got to a deep sort of valley where the grass is waist-high—that, by the way, is where the big monolith is—and that place was alive with things that were frightened and ran. I could see the directions they took by the way the grass tops acted. There were lots of loose stones about and I began to throw 'em to see if I could knock one of the things over. Suddenly all at once I saw a pair of bright little eyes peering out of a bunch of grass—I let fly at them, and something gave a sort of moan and thrashed about in the grass—and then lay still. I went to look, and found that I'd stunned—*her*. She came to and tried to bite me, but I had her by the scruff of the neck and she couldn't. Further, she was sick with being hit in the chest with the stone, and first thing I knew she keeled over in the palm of my hand in a dead faint. I couldn't find any water or anything—and I didn't want her to die—so I brought her home. She was sick for a week—and I took care of her—as I would a sick pup—and she began to get well and want to play and romp and poke into everything. She'd get the lower drawer of my desk open and hide in it—or crawl into a rubber boot and play house. And she got to be right good company—same as any pet does—a cat or a dog—or a monkey—and naturally, she being so small, I couldn't think of her as anything but a sort of little beast that I'd caught and tamed. ... You see how it all happened, don't you? Might have happened to anybody."

"Why, yes," I said. "If she didn't give a man the horrors right at the start—I can understand making a sort of pet of her—but, man, there's only one thing to do. Be persuaded. Take her back where you found her, and turn her loose."

"Well and good," said Graves. "I tried that, and next morning I found her at my door, sobbing—horrible, dry sobs—no tears. ... You've said one thing that's full of sense: she isn't a pig—or a monkey—she's a woman."

"You don't mean to say," said I, "that that mite of a thing is in love with you?"

"I don't know what else you'd call it."

"Graves," I said, "Miss Chester arrives by the next steamer. In the meanwhile something has got to be done."

"What?" said he hopelessly.

"I don't know," I said. "Let me think."

The dog Don laid his head heavily on my knee, as if he wished to offer a solution of the difficulty.

A week before Miss Chester's steamer was due the situation had not changed. Graves's pet was as much a fixture of Graves's house as the front door. And a man was never confronted with a more serious problem. Twice he carried her back into the grass and deserted her, and each time she returned and was found sobbing—horrible, dry sobs—on the porch. And a number of times we took her, or Graves did, in the pocket of his jacket, upon systematic searches for her people. Doubtless she could have helped us to find them, but she wouldn't. She was very sullen on these expeditions and frightened. When Graves tried to put her down she would cling to him, and it took real force to pry her loose.

In the open she could run like a rat; and in open country it would have been impossible to desert her; she would have followed at Graves's heels as fast as he could move them. But forcing through the thick grass tired her after a few hundred yards, and she would gradually drop farther and farther behind—sobbing. There was a pathetic side to it.

She hated me; and made no bones about it; but there was an armed truce between us. She feared my influence over Graves, and I feared her—well, just as some people fear rats or snakes. Things utterly out of the normal always do worry me, and Bo, which was the name Graves had learned for her, was, so far as I know, unique in human experience. In appearance she was like an unusually good-looking island girl observed through the wrong end of an opera-glass, but in habit and action she was different. She would catch flies and little grasshoppers and eat them all alive and kicking, and if you teased her more than she liked her ears would flatten the way a cat's do, and she would hiss like a snapping-turtle, and show her teeth.

But one got accustomed to her. Even poor Don learned that it was not his duty to punish her with one bound and a snap. But he would never let her touch him, believing that in her case discretion was the better part of valor. If she approached him he withdrew, always with dignity, but equally with determination. He knew in his heart that something about her was horribly wrong and against nature. I knew it, too, and I think Graves began to suspect it.

Well, a day came when Graves, who had been up since dawn, saw the smoke of a steamer along the horizon, and began to fire off his revolver so that I, too, might wake and participate in his joy. I made tea and went ashore.

"It's *her* steamer," he said.

"Yes," said I, "and we've got to decide something."

"About Bo?"

"Suppose I take her off your hands—for a week or so—till you and Miss Chester have settled down and put your house in order. Then Miss Chester—Mrs. Graves, that is—can decide what is to be done. I admit that I'd rather wash my hands of the business—but I'm the only white man available, and I propose to stand by my race. Don't say a word to Bo—just bring her out to the schooner and leave her."

In the upshot Graves accepted my offer, and while Bo, fairly bristling with excitement and curiosity, was exploring the farther corners of my cabin, we slipped out and locked the door on her. The minute she knew what had happened she began to tear around and raise Cain. It sounded a little like a cat having a fit. Graves was white and unhappy.

"Let's get away quick," he said; "I feel like a skunk."

But Miss Chester was everything that her photograph said about her, and more too, so that the trick he had played Bo was very soon a negligible weight on Graves's mind.

If the wedding was quick and business-like, it was also jolly and romantic. The oldest passenger gave the bride away. All the crew came aft and sang "The Voice That Breathed O'er E-den That Earliest Wedding-Day"—to the tune called "Blairgowrie." They had worked it up in secret for a surprise. And the bride's dove-brown eyes got a little teary. I was best man. The captain read the service, and choked occasionally. As for Graves—I had never thought him handsome—well, with his brown face and white linen suit, he made me think, and I'm sure I don't know why, of St.

Michael—that time he overcame Lucifer. The captain blew us to breakfast, with champagne and a cake, and then the happy pair went ashore in a boat full of the bride's trousseau, and the crew manned the bulwarks and gave three cheers, and then something like twenty-seven more, and last thing of all the brass cannon was fired, and the little square flags that spell G-o-o-d L-u-c-k were run up on the signal halyards.

As for me, I went back to my schooner feeling blue and lonely. I knew little about women and less about love. It didn't seem quite fair. For once I hated my profession—seed-gatherer to a body of scientific gentlemen whom I had never seen. Well, there's nothing so good for the blues as putting things in order.

I cleaned my rifle and revolver. I wrote up my notebook. I developed some plates; I studied a brand-new book on South Sea grasses that had been sent out to me, and I found some mistakes. I went ashore with Don, and had a long walk on the beach—in the opposite direction from Graves's house, of course—and I sent Don into the water after sticks, and he seemed to enjoy it, and so I stripped and went in with him. Then I dried in the sun, and had a match with my hands to see which could find the tiniest shell. Toward dusk we returned to the schooner and had dinner, and after that I went into my cabin to see how Bo was getting on. She flew at me like a cat, and if I hadn't jerked my foot back she must have bitten me. As it was, her teeth tore a piece out of my trousers. I'm afraid I kicked her.

Anyway, I heard her land with a crash in a far corner. I struck a match and lighted candles—they are cooler than lamps—very warily—one eye on Bo. She had retreated under a chair and looked out—very sullen and angry. I sat down and began to talk to her. "It's no use," I said, "you're trying to bite and scratch, because you're only as big as a minute. So come out here and make friends. I don't like you and you don't like me; but we're going to be thrown together for quite some time, so we'd better make the best of it. You come out here and behave pretty and I'll give you a bit of gingersnap."

The last word was intelligible to her, and she came a little way out from under the chair. I had a bit of gingersnap in my pocket, left over from treating Don, and I tossed it on the floor midway between us. She darted forward and ate it with quick bites.

Well, then, she looked up, and her eyes asked—just as plain as day: "Why are things thus? Why have I come to live with you? I don't like you. I want to go back to Graves." I couldn't explain very well, and just shook my head and then went on trying to make friends—it was no use. She hated me, and after a time I got bored. I threw a pillow on the floor for her to sleep on, and left her. Well, the minute the door was shut and locked she began to sob. You could hear her for quite a distance, and I couldn't stand it. So I went back—and talked to her as nicely and soothingly as I could. But she wouldn't even look at me—just lay face down—heaving and sobbing.

Now I don't like little creatures that snap—so when I picked her up it was by the scruff of the neck. She had to face me then, and I saw that in spite of all the sobbing her eyes were perfectly dry. That struck me as curious. I examined them through a pocket magnifying-glass, and discovered that they had no tear-ducts. Of course she couldn't cry. Perhaps I squeezed the back of her neck harder than I meant to—anyway, her lips began to draw back and her teeth to show.

It was exactly at that second that I recalled the legend Graves had told me about the island woman being found dead, and all black and swollen, back there in the grass, with teeth marks on her that looked as if they had been made by a very little child.

I forced Bo's mouth wide open and looked in. Then I reached for a candle and held it steadily between her face and mine. She struggled furiously so that I had to put down the candle and catch her legs together in my free hand. But I had seen enough. I felt wet and cold all over. For if the swollen glands at the base of the deeply grooved canines meant anything, that which I held between my hands was not a woman—but a snake.

I put her in a wooden box that had contained soap and nailed slats over the top. And, personally, I was quite willing to put scrap-iron in the box with her and fling it overboard. But I did not feel quite justified without consulting Graves. As an extra precaution in case of accidents, I overhauled my medicine-chest and made up a little package for the breast pocket—a lancet, a rubber bandage, and a pill-box full of permanganate crystals. I had still much collecting to do, "back there in the grass," and I did not propose to step on any of Bo's cousins or her sisters or her aunts—without having some of the elementary first-aids to the snake-bitten handy. It was a lovely starry night, and I determined to sleep on deck. Before turning in I went to have a look at Bo. Having nailed her in a box securely, as I thought, I must have left my cabin door ajar. Anyhow she was gone. She must have braced her back against one side of the box, her feet against the other, and burst it open. I had most certainly underestimated her strength and resources.

The crew, warned of peril, searched the whole schooner over, slowly and methodically, lighted by lanterns. We could not find her. Well, swimming comes natural to snakes.

I went ashore as quickly as I could get a boat manned and rowed. I took Don on a leash, a shot-gun loaded, and both pockets of my jacket full of cartridges. We ran swiftly along the beach, Don and I, and then turned into the grass to make a short cut for Graves's house.

All of a sudden Don began to tremble with eagerness and nuzzle and sniff among the roots of the grass. He was "making game."

"Good Don," I said, "good boy—hunt her up! Find her!"

The moon had risen. I saw two figures standing in the porch of Graves's house. I was about to call to them and warn Graves that Bo was loose and dangerous—when a scream—shrill and frightful—rang in my ears. I saw Graves turn to his bride and catch her in his arms.

When I came up she had collected her senses and was behaving splendidly. While Graves fetched a lantern and water she sat down on the porch, her back against the house, and undid her garter, so that I could pull the stocking off her bitten foot. Her instep, into which Bo's venomous teeth had sunk, was already swollen and discolored. I slashed the teeth-marks this way and that with my lancet. And Mrs. Graves kept saying: "All right—all right—don't mind me—do what's best."

Don's leash had wedged between two of the porch planks, and all the time we were working over Mrs. Graves he whined and struggled to get loose.

"Graves," I said, when we had done what we could, "if your wife begins to seem faint, give her brandy—just a very little—at a time—and—I think we were in time—and for God's sake don't ever let her know *why* she was bitten—or by *what*—"

Then I turned and freed Don and took off his leash. The moonlight was now very white and brilliant. In the sandy path that led from Graves's porch I saw the print of feet—shaped just like human feet—less than an inch long. I made Don smell them, and said: "Hunt close, boy! Hunt close!"

Thus hunting, we moved slowly through the grass toward the interior of the island. The scent grew hotter—suddenly Don began to move more stiffly—as if he had the rheumatism—his eyes straight ahead saw something that I could not see—the tip of his tail vibrated furiously—he sank lower and lower—his legs worked more and more stiffly—his head was thrust forward to the full stretch of his neck toward a thick clump of grass. In the act of taking a wary step he came to a dead halt—his right forepaw just clear of the ground. The tip of his tail stopped vibrating. The tail itself stood straight out behind him and became rigid like a bar of iron. I never saw a stancher point.

"Steady, boy!"

I pushed forward the safety of my shot-gun and stood at attention.

"How is she?"

"Seems to be pulling through. I heard you fire both barrels. What luck?"

The Ape-Man

Arthur James Ogilvy

Preface

This little sketch, though the locality is laid in the furthest depths of the great Amazon forest, is not meant, as in most boys' books, to be a record of thrilling adventures, but of what the "Missing Link," that is the creature about half way between the highest ape and the lowest savage, might have been, if brought into contact with a highly-civilised man cast away, almost unarmed, and both thrown mutually dependent, to a great extent, on each other. It is, in short, an evolutionary study quite as much as a story.

Evolution is an irregular process. It does not necessarily mean progress in our sense of the word but adaptation to environment, so it may go up, down, or merely sideways, simply different. In the gorilla environment has developed size, muscle and ferocity rather than intelligence, resulting in a dangerous wild beast. In our "Ape Man" it has been checked. Other surrounding races of the same sort have progressed faster than he has and, coming into collision with him, have by their superior weapons, intelligence, and other advantages, killed or hunted him out till accident pressed the few remnants of his race into the locality where I found him: a sort of animal paradise, where, with a warm climate, an ample sufficiency of the kinds of food to which he has been accustomed, freed (so far) from his demi-human foes and little beset by any others, he found himself in pretty fair accord with his environments and so was not forced into any higher phase; and there, reduced to a single family at last, with no prospect of further increase, he was doomed to speedy extinction like the iguanadons and mastodons of past ages; and I, on my return home, would be able to show not a vestige of proof of my ever having met him; not a flint weapon, not a broken potsherd; and if I could it would be no proof of my adventures. People would say these were mere relics of some savage human tribe. So the less I said the better. I will put my adventures into this little book and leave it at that, to be believed or disbelieved as might be.

I

Some years ago, before the great Rubber Boom had set in, I was commissioned by one of the first Rubber Companies, which had already been communicating with the Brazilian Government, to proceed to Para and in compliance with arrangements, secure certain options; then to take the first steamer to Manoa, complete my preparations, secure a boat, engage the necessary attendants, lay in stores, and start exploring up one of the tributaries south of the great stream into the vast unexplored regions of the great Amazon basin, seeking rubber trees.

I was, while in Para, to make myself well acquainted with the appearance of the various species of rubber trees, with their habits and habitats (so far as known), to lay in at once the chief requisites for my journey—such things as I might not be able to get at Manoa—and learn as much as possible of the lingua-geral, which was much more spoken in those regions than correct Portuguese, and trust to getting the usual food supplies and minor requirements at an Indian settlement higher up the river.

Behold me, then, arrived at Manoa, provided with the most suitable kind of boat for my explorations, carefully securing every kind of article that, with the best advice, seemed absolutely necessary and nothing that was not necessary, for my boat space was limited.

I had secured three assistants—Pedro, a half-caste Portuguese, with a not very prepossessing countenance, but fairly recommended, and two Indian river men, well up in forest lore and well used to the wilds.

I had taken care to learn what tributaries seemed to have been most explored, what sort of people had done the exploring and how far they had gone.

There had been little to tempt the merchants or the company promoters into those wild regions, and the naturalists had kept mainly to the neighborhood of the chief rivers. Moreover, the further back one got into the rising ground up the tributaries, the more the rapids that would be encountered, and that would check the exploration. Altogether there seemed a vast, practically unexplored region, promising to the rubber hunter.

So on a certain day our little party of four set forth from Manoa, keeping well in shore to avoid the full current of the stream, but well enough out to avoid the frequent caving in of the banks, for one such fall on our little craft would have obliterated us all.

We went somewhere about a hundred miles and then turned up one of the large affluents that seemed by all accounts to have been not much explored. There was a favorable breeze that helped us along, a slow current that did little to check us, and we got along finely. But the river was immensely broad and we could only inspect one bank, so I crossed over, selecting the left bank, and I carefully scrutinised the kind of country (and especially the vegetation) through my binoculars. So far there was no appearance of the rubber tree.

There is no twilight in these regions, but as it was bright starlight, I thought I might as well push on by night as well as by day, so long as there seemed no marked change in the country or the vegetation; but if the night was dark or the country seemed to require daylight scrutiny, we moored to a tree and camped for the night, when, of course, we had our fishing lines out and generally caught some fish, which helped to eke out our provisions. Still, our provision supply was necessarily limited, as our boat was small; and presently my crew began to suggest that it was getting time to return. However, as we should have the stream in our favor all the way back and I had done practically no exploring yet, I decided that we should go on for at least one day more. My crew acquiesced silently but rather sulkily, and we went on after one more night's rest. And soon on the next day we came to a fork in the stream, and I at once noticed a difference in the color of the two streams—that from the East was discolored, that from the West was clear and was also slower. This indicated that the Eastern stream came from rising ground, and it meant rapids not far off. That from the West had clearly come a long distance through flat country, so I chose that stream. It was a much narrower stream, too, than the other, though still a good big river, but yet narrow enough for me to be able to scrutinise both banks fairly well through my binoculars; and before noon I distinctly made out a rubber tree, and not long after another and then another. We pulled in at once to the shore.

My men were now openly grumbling and muttering that it was high time to turn back instead of actually beginning my exploration. But to turn back now just as the goal was in sight was out of the question.

We tied up, and leaving the crew to take care of the boats and catch some fish if possible, I started off after a night's rest to explore the country. The ground was fairly open and easy travelling for a short distance and I was travelling light for I had to go far in a short time. It was my last chance and would take a whole day. I took a light axe stuck in my belt behind, my sheath knife, pocket knife, my pocket compass, a few fishing lines and a small coil of brass wire, some cakes of chocolate, for all these were light to carry and none but the light axe at all heavy, and I cut a strong supple cane to carry in my hand, for experience has long shown me that this is the most effective weapon against venomous snakes (the most dangerous enemy I was likely to meet). But before starting I sat down for a minute, looked over what I was taking and considered had I got everything really necessary, for this was the first time I was venturing into the wilds really alone, and there was no knowing what might happen before I got back. A falling bough, a twist of the ankle, a snake, any accident might happen, and my men would have no suspicion of it till darkness fell and I had not appeared.

Discarding everything that I did not absolutely need, I thought of my purse, which I certainly should not need. I opened it and glanced at the contents—a little gold, some silver, some notes, and all in a rather heavy purse. I rolled these in a coat and tossed it into a corner, telling Pedro, who was standing by, to look after all these things. Then at the last minute I thought it would be really better in every way to take one of the Indian lads with me. I might want him. I might have something heavy to bring back, and there was always the possibility of a disabling accident in a lonely wilderness, and it would be safer at any rate to have someone either to assist me or to hurry off for help. So I gathered my goods together while Assi, my Indian boy, exchanged a few parting words with his companions and then we were off.

But we had not been gone half an hour when Assi tripped over a liana and was down with a twisted ankle, helpless. What was to be done? I could not possibly leave my work at the last moment undone. I took off my kerchief and hurriedly helped Assi to twist it round the injured ankle, telling him to hobble back if he could or wait for my return to help him. Then off I went.

But the travelling grew rapidly worse, the undergrowth increased—here and there the jungle was almost impenetrable and the rubber trees, never plentiful, became still scarcer; also the day was passing and I had to get back with, perhaps, a wounded boy to help. So, very reluctantly, I turned back. I had, of course, blazed my trail as I went, wherever it seemed necessary, so had no difficulty in judging my way back.

When I got to the spot where I had left Assi he was gone, but had left his billy can behind him. I was glad to see this for it showed he could get along somehow, so I should not be much delayed with him. I got back the whole way without overtaking him, but when I reached the river he was not visible and the boat was gone! I was perplexed, but as yet only perplexed. The tie had not snapped. It had been regularly untied. The boat must have been released purposely. Why? I shouted but no answer came. I ran along the bank but though I could see down the stream a long way, there was no appearance of the boat. I began to feel uneasy. However, I set a few lines and sat down to make the best of things till some explanation appeared. But I sat on and on until far into the night, getting more and more anxious, till at last very late I fell asleep.

When I awoke in the morning I was still alone. Then it began to dawn upon me that I was deliberately abandoned, foully left to die alone in that desolate wilderness, where probably no white man had ever been and where no man of any sort was likely to come again for many years.

Little incidents cropped up to confirm my suspicions—the mutinous disposition of the men, their anxiety to start home at once, their fears that I, finding rubber, would want to stay on longer. Above all I remembered that Pedro had seen my money supply and where I had left it, that there was gold in it and notes; he did not know how much and probably exaggerated the amount. There were also all my goods to divide amongst them, and how easy it would be to account for my disappearance!—a snake bite, an alligator, anyone of a hundred accidents, all quite likely to happen.

Then, again, I was a stranger. There was no one specially interested in me to push enquiry about me. It was all simple—so very simple, and I had absolutely nothing left but what I stood up in. My gun, binoculars, provisions, everything gone except the few simple tools I had taken with me. My situation was desperate.

Well, I must get away from here into some better surroundings. But as I looked about to see if there was anything left of my possessions that might be of any use to me, my eye was caught by a flutter of white on a tree. It proved to be a scrap of paper with the single word "Adios" scrawled across it, and pinned by a thorn into the bark. Whether it was meant as the parting derisive taunt of an enemy or the half-remorseful warning of a traitor removing all doubts as to my position, and setting the plain facts before me, I could not tell. But strange to say, instead of throwing me into despair, it cleared my brain and strengthened my nerve, for I am a man of action more than of sentiment, and to find myself in a corner sharpens my wits and braces my energies.

The first clear fact was that I had to face the situation somehow and get out of this place. How was I to live meanwhile? Game I knew to be scarce in these dense forests; it was the flora, not the fauna, that was luxuriant. What few animals there were would be up the trees like the monkeys, off on the wing like the birds, into the water like the tapirs and capybara, or into the dense thickets like other game, on the first hint of danger; and I had no gun to shoot with or hunting weapon of any kind.

The most numerous and most active creatures were the birds and monkeys; the ant bear was rare; the puma was, like the lion elsewhere, a beast of the plains or the open woods and hills, not of the thick forest; his place was taken by the jaguar, whose colour and spots, corresponding with the dappled play of lights and shades through the foliage, make him inconspicuous. At any rate he rarely attacked man, unless he found him asleep or disabled. The python, too, rarely attacked man, and the alligator kept to the water; so that I had little to fear from wild beasts. Venomous snakes were the chief danger, and there was no very great danger from them so long as I did not travel noiselessly and so come upon them un-awares, for a snake will always rather get out of your way than fight you if he can. Besides, a good stout flexible cane is the safest weapon to deal with them. You cannot hit flat with a bludgeon but a flexible cane accommodates itself to the blow, and a snake's back is easily broken. As to water that was always available. Clothing of any sort was hardly wanted in the tropics, and as to shelter at night I must coil myself in a thicket or the fork of a tree and take my chance.

My only hope of not living miserably like a beast and gradually sinking to the level of a beast, lay in the hope of my finding some tribe of Indians and trusting myself to their hospitality and help, and being passed on from one tribe to another towards civilisation. True, they might kill me instead, but then I should only die suddenly and I believe painlessly from a poisoned dart from an ambushed blowpipe, or fall in open battle honorably and there be an end of it.

It takes some time to state all these cogitations, but it took much less time to think them; they all passed through my brain in a rapid, wordless flash almost, and I finished them out on the way as I started on my return track along yesterday's march.

As I said, the scrub grew speedily thicker as I proceeded, till it became impossible to force my way through, but some reeds and rushes, with fewer bushes, appeared to the left, so I made that way;

the bushes grew thinner and the reeds longer as I went, till I found I was getting into a swamp. Presently there was a rustle in the reeds ahead. I poked my cane forward and a snake wriggled out; a few swift blows with my cane disabled him and I then cut off his head, and went on with my next meal provided. I kept as near as possible to the dividing line, so far as there was any, between the scrub and the swamp.

The tangled forest was now quite impenetrable, and I saw by the great sweep of thickening reeds that a vast swamp lay out there. At one place the swamp and the jungle ran thickly close up together, and I paused a minute to recover my breath before pushing through between them.

Then I heard the sound of a breaking branch. There was no wind to account for it, and it sounded like a gradual tear, as if some animal was doing it. I pushed quietly through and found that just beyond the soil changed and the vegetation with it. The scrub thinned out rapidly, the ground sloped up, the trees grew fewer and shorter, and again I heard that breaking, tearing sound. Working towards it as well as I could locate it, I saw I was nearing an opening in the woods; and then a form appeared. Quietly I crept up, and peering from behind a bush could make out clearly what it was.

II

I saw before me an ape-like, man-like creature, standing about five and a half feet high, or nearly; like an ape it was naked and hairy, but like a man it stood and moved upright; its hair was thinner than any ape's and grew thicker over the head and round the face, like beard and whiskers, and above all it used a tool. It had the branch of a tree, roughly trimmed, upside down, with a fork on the end; and with this forked stick it alternately beat the branches of a tall shrub to shake off the nuts, or pulled the boughs down to gather them. I made a note at once of those nuts as eatable.

The creatures arms seemed longer than a man's and its legs shorter, and it stood less upright than a man; moreover, the upright attitude did not seem altogether its natural attitude. I had the idea that if it was suddenly startled by danger, it would drop on all fours and so scamper quadrupedally to its natural refuge, the tree. But what struck me most of all was the shape of its foot; the anthropoid ape's big toe is really an opposable, grasping thumb, never a true big toe, in alignment with its other toes making a true walking foot. It must have taken long ages in evolution for the ape's hind hand (so to speak) to completely change its character to the pedestrian foot; so that, if this was the "missing link," as I suspected it to be, it had travelled a long way from the true ape towards the human being. For its hind hand was more than half way towards the human foot, showing that it was fast losing (in a geological sense) its arboreal habits; for a creature with a true foot could have nothing like the necessary arboreal agility. This creature's hind thumb (so to speak) had half shifted its position and character; it was making towards the toe, but still had enough grasping power to make him much more nimble than a man among the branches. All these points and more I carefully noted as I kept quiet, for I wanted to know as much as possible about this singular being from whom I hoped to learn so much as to making a living, before I showed myself.

The two chief points I had noticed and which gave me most hope were that his facial angle was much more human than an ape's, indicating more intelligence, and that he habitually used a tool—the hooked stick. So I moved cautiously forward. The slight sound of my movement caught his ear immediately, and he turned swiftly. I stopped at once, and with a smiling face and courteous words waved my hands in friendly greeting. He (I will no longer call him It) regarded me with astonishment. I was so apparently harmless and anxious to be friendly that it never occurred to him either to assume an attitude of defence or to run away. I was so like him in some respects, yet so different in details.

As he evidently knew nothing about clothes, my clothes, of course, appeared to him to be part of my natural body—curious excrescences. I did not offer to approach nearer, but continued to make friendly gestures, which he received suspiciously. After a minute or two, I took a step nearer, whereupon he raised his stick threateningly. It was not much of a weapon, so that did not trouble me. I took one step more, appealingly, when he struck at me. I made another quick step, snatched the stick out of his hand and gave him a sharp cut across the arm with it, then threw it aside and renewed my conciliatory gestures. This showed him two things—that I was quite able to take care of myself and would stand no nonsense, but also that I really wanted to be friends with him. He looked offended and inclined to be spiteful, but did nothing, only croaked; whereupon another figure, the female, rather smaller, with longer hair on her head and no whiskers, stepped out of the bushes hesitatingly and took her place behind him; and almost simultaneously two other beings, a boy and a girl (if I may call them so) stole out and stood behind them both. I saluted them all, smilingly, but received no response.

Then an idea occurred to me. I took out one of my papers of chocolate from my bosom (the only receptacle I had, as I had no coat), and I showed them the gaudy paper covering. This astonished them greatly, as I appeared to have produced it from my inside. Then I thought that though it was part of my very slender store of provisions, I could not use it for a better purpose; so I tore off a corner, broke off a small piece of the contents, showed it to them and then ate it. I then broke off a rather larger piece, showed it to them and threw it towards the children, who seemed about 12 and 10 years of age respectively, the boy eldest. The girl, with the natural curiosity of her sex, moved first, picked up the chocolate, smelt it, put her tongue to it, tasted it and finally ate it; liked it, and looked as if some more would be agreeable. I gave her another piece, then thought I had given them about enough of me for one lesson; so turned quietly aside and began gathering the nuts, taking apparently no further notice of them, but watching them carefully from the corner of my eye.

Left to themselves, they seemed not to know what to do. There seemed no reason either to attack me or to run away, so after staring at me a little longer, they began to disperse and resume their occupations. I seemed solely occupied with the nuts while they moved away, and I wandered about apparently aimlessly, but always managing to keep sufficiently near them to note everything they did. Luckily they had not eaten their fill yet, so food was their chief object, and this seemed, so far as I saw, to be much what the monkeys fed on—chiefly vegetables, nuts, fruit, tender shoots, but also small animal food—snakes and lizards and such like, grubs and insects—all of which they ate raw, which was not promising as a forecast of what my diet would have to be.

I noticed carefully not only what they ate, but where they looked for it and how they got it. I had not had nearly enough to eat myself by this time, though they seemed soon satisfied, and I had yet my snake that I had killed and that would have to be cooked before I could eat it. But I did not want to light a fire till dark, as the blaze would be more striking in the dark, and I was curious to see how they would take it.

But as sunset approached the whole party had gradually worked round to an open space, on the edge of which stood one great tree, with pretty open forest all round, where the ape people seemed to settle down finally. Seeing this, I began to gather up some sticks, the ape people regarding me curiously not understanding my purpose. Turning my back to them I produced my match box and struck a light, and in a few seconds had a bright little blaze; then I laid on more sticks.

Intense amazement was produced. Evidently they had never seen fire. What was this strange appearance that danced and sparkled and seemed alive? They drew a little nearer, anxiously watching. After some minutes, when there was a good bed of hot coals, I raked them out, coiled up my snake, laid it in the glowing coals and covered it up with them; then sat down while it cooked. After a little I made another and larger fire against a log and then went to collect more wood for it. By the time I thought my snake was about done I pulled it out and commenced my evening meal, for I was very hungry by this time.

The ape people were now gathered about my second fire, exhibiting intense curiosity while I watched them. It may seem strange that a people so nearly human should never have seen or ever heard of fire, as surely a stroke of lightning, or fermentation of decaying matter, must in the long years have started forest fires. But when we remember that this was humid Brazil, a country of everlasting green growth, where lightning storms were rare, and that this was a race without speech and therefore without traditions, or even knowledge of what might have happened even in the preceding generation, it will be intelligible enough.

Presently one of them touched the flame with his finger, and started back with a cry. Not only was this strange appearance alive and jumping about, but it was vicious, too. It bit! So there was fear as well as astonishment in their faces, and they retreated a pace or two, especially as it gave out heat all round as well as light. But I sauntered up and gave the fire a careless kick. Evidently I, at any rate, was not afraid of it. Anyhow, they continued to sit round this new, strange, interesting phenomenon, till the fire died down.

The night thickened and they sauntered up to the great tree, ascended it, and disappeared among the branches.

While food-hunting or sitting by the fire they had often made little guttural noises that might be construed as remarks; but these never elicited anything like a connected reply, and they had often called each other's attention by gestures that brought out corresponding actions. But there was never anything like real language, real conversation.

However, I knew too little about them as yet to draw any sound conclusions about them; but time and patience would, no doubt, reveal plenty more. For the present I merely renewed the sinking fire, collected some more fuel for the night (for I was determined never to let that fire go out once it was lighted, matches being so precious), and then I. lay down behind the log, trusting to the fire to scare away any prowling wild beasts and sure that the sunrise, with its sudden blaze of light, would wake me up in the morning as soon as the ape people. So I went pretty comfortably to sleep. I woke once or twice in the night and mended the fire. So ended my first day with my new companions.

As I expected, sunrise woke all up together, and I was attending to the fire when the ape people descended from their roost. They came at once to the fire, glancing inquisitively at me, but soon sauntered off into the woods to seek their daily food, dispersing in a fresh direction to-day, for I soon found that they never took the same route two days running.

I had the remains of my snake for a snatch breakfast then sauntered after my companions, taking with me all my few worldly goods, my axe and my fish-hooks in their leather pouch, my roll of brass wire, etc., for I had no place in which to leave them, and might want them at any moment. Within half an hour we came to a broad stream, about twenty yards wide, clear and shallow so that one could see clearly that there were no alligators or gymnoti or other foes about, and waded across in water, not up to our waist in the deepest part. Here I stripped and had a good, much needed bath; then digging a worm or two out of the moist bank baited and set two of my lines and moved off. The cracking of branches and other sounds soon told me of the direction in which the others had gone. I gathered some nuts, the same sort as yesterday, and picked some berries. These were not very nice; wild fruits seldom are. It takes generations of careful selection and cultivation to produce our fine dessert fruits; still all were eatable, some few really good, and I supposed would help to nourish me as they did the ape people. But I touched no kind of native fruits till I had seen the others or the birds or monkeys eat them, for fear of poison.

Coming up with the rest, I found the two old people trying to get some grubs out of the cracks in an old, rotting log. Here was my first chance to-day to show my value. Peering about I found a sound hard branch, and cutting it into short lengths made and roughly sharpened three good wooden wedges; then with the back of my axe I drove one of them into the crack, widening it; then pushing another wedge beyond it, I widened the crack further, and so on, bursting open the log and revealing a whole colony of grubs. A greedy shout brought the whole family up to the feast and they began gorging themselves. I supposed I should have, sometime or other, to come down to a live grub diet, but I was in no hurry to begin it unnecessarily, so I left, the whole prize to the rest of them.

A little further on I noticed a decaying log of no great size, so turning round I ought out a stout sapling, and cutting it down and trimming it, converted it into a handspike with which I rolled the log over, revealing various insects, which the family pounced upon and which I left to them.

Here, then, I had found for them two new tools, the wedges and the handspike, and had shown them how to use them. Clearly, I was a great discoverer, almost a magician, and therein showed that they appreciated the fact.

Later, I found the girl using a stick to grub up a yam-like root, which she pounced on. She did not offer me any of it. Indeed, I soon found that she never offered me anything, it was not her nature; she was a mean, selfish, capricious little thing, and I never became fond of her. But I looked about and soon found more of the same roots, dug them up with a piece of wood, put some away in the breast of my shirt and gave the others to the party.

What with these roots, the nuts I had gathered and perhaps a fish on my lines, I thought I should have enough for a meal, such as it was; so I left the others and turned back. I had no fears of their deserting me. I was becoming too valuable an ally and no trouble or danger to them.

I found on my lines one fish, as I had hoped, so coiling my lines up I went "home," rounded up my fire, then raked out the ashes, and burying the yams, the fish and the nuts all together waited till they were cooked, more or less, and had my breakfast.

I was no smoker, luckily for me, as I had no tobacco or substitute of any kind, so after a short rest I thought I would explore the big tree during its occupants' absence, and see what sort of a roost they had. I was nothing like so nimble among the branches as my friends, but I got up all right and soon found the parent nest, so to speak, where the father and mother roosted. It was a, rough nest of branches, lined with grass, in a big fork about 30 feet up, the sticks projecting well over the sides, making it pretty safe from the jaguar, for they were, no doubt, light sleepers and would soon hear him if he started climbing up the trees, and looking out to meet him, one on each side, could smash his paws with their clubs, or poke him in the eyes with a long sharp stick, before he could reach them. One such attempt, if he made it, would be enough for the jaguar; he would not try to storm the nest again.

The two younger apes had been in similar but more roughly-constructed nests a little higher up.

There were no other trees within reach by which an enemy could come round and get at them from above; the barrier of the parents would have to be passed before the offspring could be reached, so they were quite safe.

Having found out all about the parental domicile I came down, and my work for the rest of the day was clear. I wanted a bag, or portable receptacle, to carry my goods about in and put in any provisions or other valuables I might collect.

Near the stream I spoke of, was a bed of large rushes like New Zealand flax, about five feet long and, perhaps, four inches broad. I had only to cut a good bundle of these, split them up, cut out the gummy interior and plait the material into baskets; I did so. It gave me light and interesting occupation for the whole afternoon, and before nightfall I had two good baskets or bags ready made, and materials ready for two more. By nightfall the family had returned and we "went to bed" as usual. But never did I lose sight of the fire. This I carefully attended to, and whenever firewood easy of reach was becoming scarce I shifted my fireplace and couch, for it was much easier to carry the fireplace to the wood than the wood to the fireplace. But I must train some of the others, if possible, to share this duty with me.

III

Now that my first pressing wants had been fairly met. Now that I had learned pretty well what things were eatable, where to look for them and how to get them; now that I had got thoroughly in touch with my family and regarded as one of themselves; now that I had provided most of the chief aids to the ape life, such as the wedges, handspike, baskets, etc., and had leisure to turn to secondary needs, my first desire was a house or hut.

I had deeply disliked spending my nights on the bare ground behind a log and beside a fire, and was quite determined not to sleep up a tree in a sort of bird's nest, and knowing that the rains would come some day and were probably not far off. I wanted a roof over my head and walls around me, and as I knew well how to make a bark hut, this should not be difficult.

I had only to mark out the tops, bottom and sides of the sheets wanted from a big tree, loosen the sheets from the tree, spread them flat on the ground with weights on them to dry flat, and there was everything wanted but the skeleton of the hut. For this some upright poles let into the ground for the supports, poles for wall plates and rafters, with stout canes across for battens and then fix the slabs of bark up, tied securely with pliable bark or thongs, and a moveable sheet of bark for the door. There was no window needed, for I only wanted my shelter at night, in the dark, or perhaps on a rainy day; and I would leave a triangular open space at the top of each gable, which would not only give about all the light I wanted but also, through the current of air passing along from one opening to other, carry off most of the smoke if I wanted a fire. The hut would also serve as storehouse for my roots, nuts, baskets and miscellaneous small stores.

So, with Joe to help me, I set to work at my house in all my hours of spare time. I had fixed a good site, near the parental tree on one side, near the water on another, and pretty clear of all danger of falling trees or heavy boughs.

But I had to make it perfectly clear to the family that this hut which I had built was mine and there was no admittance for them, for Joe was in intense delight when he saw the result of my work and all the family wanted to come in. I had to make this quite clear to Dad by very peremptory strong measures, but the rule was inflexibly established, for not only would these semi-brute companions be an intolerable nuisance in a hundred ways and occupy most valuable space, but like all such primitive beings they had parasites, which alone would be fatal to their admission.

But as for Joe it was different; he would really be some sort of companion, besides being of much real use. But I should first have to cut off all his hair, sweep and scrub his head twice daily with a broom (having no toothcomb) until he was perfectly free from all nits, and as to having his head shaved he did not see why, in spite of my explanatory gestures, and was dead against it. But I made him understand that unless he submitted to this there was an inexorable fiat of no admittance to him. So he finally consented. But I also had to make him understand that he was not only to get perfectly clean but to keep clean, and would have to bathe in the river every day or nearly. So behold us two finally settled in our house. It took two or three weeks to do it, but it was done.

Assured of a pretty comfortable and safe dwelling my conditions were enormously improved, and that, of course, was always my first aim; but my second was always to improve those of my family, and I was constantly considering how I could do that.

I had noticed, of course, that where one species of animals branched off into new and improved conditions it was always through some modification of their structure or habits, one leading to the other. Flight, for instance, covering so wide an area began with the flying fish, whose chief aim in life (next to getting in food which was all around it in the water) was to escape from pursuing foes, and a quick, long leap out of the water was their most immediate needs. Those fish then that had the longest, strongest pectoral fins could make the longest leaps, and natural selection would preserve those that had that advantage, always selecting the longest and strongest fins, and so improving the breed in that respect. But that advantage was strictly limited in degree. The thing required was a powerful leap, or flight, that would take it out of reach of the enemy. It would never give the power of sustained flight, because the fish was essentially and emphatically a fish not a bird; its habitat, its food, its breathing apparatus were and must always be in the water, and to soar into the air would but make it the easy prey of the sea birds. Later on the pterodactyl, however it originated, was not a fish, but essentially a bird, flying mainly over the land, not the water.

Now, there was nothing in the structure or habits of the ape to suggest any improvement in its construction by any degree of flight. So improvement in that direction was barred. Then there was the storage of food, dependent mainly on habit not structure; and the first appearance of it was the squirrel that stored up nuts, and that suggested nothing further, for the squirrel's nest was a hole in a tree, and that provided shelter and storage room incidentally.

Then came the bee, also in a hollow tree; but the food it stored was honey, a liquid, and that needed a receptacle, viz., comb, to contain the honey. We do not see how the power to make comb originated, but we do see that a cup, or receptacle of some sort, was the next need. There are many as yet unfilled gaps in the process of evolution, but we are in slow process of filling them in one by one. Then there is the ant, and the ants, some of them, have a whole system of city architecture in their hill; rooms for the eggs, for the larvæ, for the pupæ, for the adults, with galleries and passages between.

There seemed no opening for my family in development of flight, nor for storage of food, for in this region of perpetual spring there was no threat of scarcity at any time. But in one direction there was a clear opening; in their roosts. If I could suggest to them a way of securing a dwelling on the ground, that would save them the trouble of climbing a tree every night, that would give them a perfect shelter from the torrential rains and a wall around them against foes; that would be an improvement indeed ... in short a bark hut like mine.

But this would require things that they had not as yet, viz., a sharp tool to mark out and divide the bark slabs on the tree (they could then easily separate and remove the slabs); then sense enough to lay the bark slabs flat, the rest would be easy; they would be like children with a pack of cards, they could build a house almost spontaneously.

But as there was no tool except my axe, which I would not trust in their hands, and as they certainly would not mark the slabs off decently, I resolved to help them if they were willing to learn, and when they saw how comfortable my house was, they really seemed as if they would like to learn; so I collected them all together and calling their attention to the careful way in which I made the cuts, I marked out the slabs. Then I set them to loosen the bark, an operation which would require care and which they would have to learn if they meant to have a hut.

They were careless and clumsy about it, as I expected, and damaged the sheets considerably; still they got them off somehow.

Then, all working together, we laid them flat, weighted them down
and left them to dry. A week or two later we set the dried sheets
up. I made no attempt to build such an elaborate hut as mine. We
set the sheets up like an A, leant other slabs up, back and front,
and that was good enough for them. If they wanted it larger and
better they would know how to do it, if they had any sense at all. If
they had not, they could never have a house at all. Then it was a
shelter at any rate, and the three curled into it and seemed pleased.

IV

So the days passed. You may think it was deadly monotonous.
No! Nearly everyone's life is monotonous; the bank clerk's, the shop
assistant's, the housewife's, the sailor's, and in peace time, at any
rate, even the soldier's; there was more variety in our lives than
many of these.

Half of every day at least was spent in the mere search for necessary food, poor food at that; but most toilers' life is that. And
nearly every day we took a different route, and no two routes alike.
The soils, the scenery, the plants and animals, even the food was
always more or less different. And we found other useful things
different besides food, and to me, at any rate, who knew something of the different hidden natures and resources of the plants,
suggestive of great possibilities to those who knew how to develop
and use them. There were rubber trees, vanilla bushes, splendid
timbers, essences, and products of all sorts; but they needed the
chemist, the manufacturer, the skilful mechanic to put these resources to use; and the products, even if we could secure them,
would not be of interest or use to the ape men.

And every now and then there was a bit of a thrill, an adventure.

For instance, one day, when Joe and I were a little distance
apart from the rest (he clung to my companionship more and more
and followed me about like a dog) Joe suddenly stopped, and looking eagerly in a particular direction and pointing, said *nay*, which
was the nearest approach to words that he could make to "snake,"
which he had picked up from me. I looked intently but could see

no snake; but he only repeated more insistently *nay*, pointed more eagerly, and even approached a step or two, fearfully. Then suddenly I saw what he meant, one of what I took to be a liana hanging from a bough seemed to make a slight movement, and I saw it was a monstrous anaconda, a great boa constrictor, hanging over the path motionless and await for prey. Instantly I saw what to do, for possibilities of this kind had several times occurred to me and I had reckoned on what to do. Seizing Joe by the arms and pressing down I said, "wait and watch," and hurried back "home," which was not far off. Joe did not understand what I said, but he saw clearly enough what I wanted and stayed watching. Arrived at home I seized a long pole, one of the things we had been using, and which I had left at home in case it should be wanted again, and collecting a quantity of dried grass and dead leaves I tied these in and out with a bit of my brass wire round the end of the pole and hurried back, calling urgently to the family to hasten and help.

Arrived, where I left Joe on the watch, I saw the boa hanging as before, apparently lifeless, but I knew it was not.

Approaching as closely as we dared, I struck a match and lighted the mop end, which blazed up instantly. I thrust the pole end blazing into the monster's face. Like a flash it flew back to the overhanging bough, but I met it there. Wherever the brute moved the blaze was thrust into its face; it dropped to the ground writhing. Shouting to the family, who had assembled, to help with their sticks, they, and I with my blazing torch, attacked the brute. It turned with gaping jaws upon me but the blaze was instantly thrust into them and it turned back writhing, abandoning all attempts to fight and only trying to wriggle away. But blows were raining upon it; its back was broken in a dozen places and it was now only a squirming mass, utterly helpless. I cropped off its head, and seizing the dead but still muscular writhing brute by the tail we dragged it home, the whole family dancing a sort of war dance as they went.

Arrived at home I would not allow them to mutilate the carcass, but first disembowelled it, then took off the skin, cutting it into long strips about three inches wide, twisting these strips like a horse-hide rope, then I fastened one end of each by a peg driven into the green bark of the tree and twined them round and round the trees to dry into ropes. I then carefully dissected out the long strong sinews and stretched and fastened them out too, leaving the flesh, a good two or three days food supply, for the general use. The family began to gorge upon the meat, raw as it was, while I proceeded to cook my supply in the ashes as usual. All this was excitement enough for one day.

We were quite a happy family together, or at any rate a united one, and both sides were profiting by the union; they by their long forest experience, sharp eyes and arboreal agility, finding me food supplies which I should never have found for myself and without which I should have died, and I, with my superior intelligence and my few but most effective tools, giving them untold help in their life.

The study of their lives and the teachings of them afforded me unending interest and I found I was actually doing them permanent good, opening their eyes to endless possibilities and actually developing their intelligence all round. For I had soon discovered that every creature with any sort of intelligence at all had much more intelligence in posse than in esse; that is, that one new idea starts another, that a fresh hint once fairly taken in expands, and that just as a dog soon learns how to herd sheep, and not only learns but loves it, and as an elephant knows how to stack timber and do many sagacious things, so these ape men with their even superior intelligence, low as it was, could learn much, if taught, and profit by the learning, though the dog and the elephant might not be actually any the better from their own point of view, by what they learned.

All evolution is progressive. We are all moving somewhere, up towards improvement or down to destruction like the Jurassian reptiles. Often there seems a pause, occasionally a long one as with the scorpion, which has remained much the same from remote ages.

There are times when a creature has reached such a stage of adaptation to an unchanging environment that nothing occurs to stimulate further change, no alteration in its foes, its food supplies, or its surroundings; and there remains only the competition of its own species to keep it up to the mark.

Imaginary accounts of the ape man, of the missing link almost always represent him as a compound of the ape and the tiger, an increasingly intelligent but always ferocious being, and often, no doubt, that would be a correct description, but not always. It would depend upon his environment.

For ages these people found themselves in a warm, luxuriant tropical forest, requiring no clothes and little shelter, but from the rains. With a food supply of a sort, easily obtained and varying of course with the seasons, but always more or less sufficient, entailing sometimes short commons but never anything like a Siberian winter or an Australian drought, when all live animals had either migrated or were in winter slumber or had perished, and all the vegetation was either dormant or dried up, and where they would be face to face with starvation but for a previously collected and stored up food supply, they were pretty well adapted to their surroundings.

If we look across the visible field of evolution to where signs of the lost link should appear, if anywhere; that is, where the most highly developed, man-like creatures exist amongst the anthropoid apes, the process of evolution seems to have been more along the lines that led to my ape family. For there are only three known species of anthropoid apes... the gorilla, the orang-outang, and the chimpanzee. And the only trace of the tiger-like disposition is with the gorilla, who has little of the man about him but the shape. In all other respects he has developed only into a more powerful and savage brute than into a man. His environment has made him so. He has only the leopard for a possible antagonist, but the leopard though smaller than the jaguar is much more fierce and aggressive. But there is always man, the African savage, to contend with, and to meet his strength, courage and ferocity are needed. Otherwise, intelligence is not greatly needed. His food is all about him, such as he needs, and he is monarch of the woods.

The orang-outang is a powerful and dangerous beast to tackle, but be never seeks to meddle with anyone so long as the other one does not meddle with him. He is apparently not much more intelligent than the gorilla.

The most intelligent of all is the chimpanzee, and he has been taught to dress himself, eat with a knife and fork, and behave himself a good deal like a man in many ways: but though ready to defend himself if attacked, as almost every animal must be, there seems to be no natural ferocity about him, and I believe it would not require very much teaching to develop him very rapidly; he is almost in the condition in which I found my "family." He can be affectionate, too, like Joe.

Another example. One day we had come back to our rendezvous early, had had good luck and were in good humor. I was plaiting some leaves to make a kilt, for my clothes were worn all to rags, when the mood seized me and I began to sing. I had a good voice, though I had not used it for long. It was a rollicking air, with well marked time, and I warmed into it. Glancing up after the second verse, I suddenly noticed that the whole family were up and were regarding me intently. I jumped up and began capering a wild, impromptu sort of hornpipe. Instantly the whole family were up and capering about me in grotesque imitation. I broke into wild laughter but capered on, more wildly than ever. So for over twenty minutes we all waltzed round in wild excitement till I fell exhausted, and all dropped to earth simultaneously. Now these folk had evidently never heard music in their time, yet they had kept perfect time throughout. I remembered an old colonist had told me that in early days he had been travelling with a party of whites, accompanied by some Tasmanian blacks, when they had struck up a song. The blacks had listened attentively till the close of the first verse; then all had struck up the same air, without the words, with perfect accuracy, yet they, too, had never heard music. Here then, as with my apes, was one faculty, time at any rate, absolutely latent, yet started into life at the first note. Often since then my family, in their afternoon rest, had said to me, *Ting, ting* (Sing, sing), and I had acquiesced, when in the mood, to their great delight.

V

But with abundant food, hardly any dangerous enemies, and every opportunity apparently to improve, why had my ape people not improved? This puzzled me at first till the explanation, or at any rate an explanation, occurred to account for it; of which later on. Under these favorable, but non-stimulating, surroundings, our ape people gradually grew into an indolent, easy-going, harmless community, such as I had found them.

But, in the course of evolution, they were in a specially transitional stage in one respect. They had clearly emerged from the purely brute stage and yet were not thoroughly into the human. For example, take fire. Accounts say that when an anthropomorphous ape comes across a traveller's abandoned, but still alight, fire, if the weather be at all cold it will sit by it and warm itself. But it never occurs to it that it is the fuel that feeds the fire; it never occurs to it to round up the embers or put more wood on; it simply sits by until the fire dies down and then it goes on. But our ape people, when the surprise and awe of this living, bright, warmth affording yet biting phenomenon had subsided, very quickly learned that it was the fuel that fed it, and that it had to be fed if it was to be kept up. They did not know the trick of the matches, for I had never let them actually see me strike the light. They had only seen the fire break out, apparently at my command. And they had soon learned that chips of sticks, logs, woody material of some sort was the only fuel that they knew of that would feed it. So they fed it up, if at the moment they wanted it, but not otherwise. They would never think of putting on a big supply so that it would still be alight when they came back. Still less could they realise the necessity of keeping the fire always alight, of never letting it go out; for, as I said, they knew nothing about the matches.

My little store of matches was so absolutely precious, so irreplaceable, that I treasured everyone of them. I had to use a fresh one every now and then, but never if I could help it. And Joe was the only one that could ever be trusted to see to the fire, and even then he had to be reminded of it and told to go and see to it. I had in the night, or at any time, to point in the direction of the fire and say "Fie," which was the nearest approach he could make to the word fire.

It was much the same with the wedges. They quickly saw how it was that the wedges split up the log, but they would never think of taking the wedges on to the next log, unless the next log was close by. Nor would they put them carefully by when done with, to be found again at once when next wanted. Everything, if used, was used for immediate needs only, and then dropped. And so it is with nearly all the brute creation, even when artificially trained.

It has always been a mystery to me how the birds began to make nests; for a nest is made not only for the future but for an unknown use. The bird, especially, at any rate, the young bird, making its first nest does not—cannot—know why it is making it. It cannot know that it is to hold future eggs; it cannot know that there are any eggs coming, nor that the eggs will hatch into chicks, nor that the chicks will have to be mothered and fed; and that the solitary caged bird that will never have a mate, and will need no nest, makes a nest all the same if it has the chance, and can find the materials; but it makes it all the same, apparently from blind instinct.

We had constantly, off and on, seen monkeys and birds up above and around us in the high trees, and they would be welcome food; but how to get at them? The birds flew off, and the monkeys scrambled out of reach at our approach. But occasionally they had to come down lower. For the fruit trees, as distinguished from the nut trees, were generally of no great height, so the fruit-eating creatures had, to get the fruit, to come within reach of the throwing stick with which the ape people were pretty expert, so the fruit-eaters got knocked over now and then. But they were generally pretty wide awake and were off at our approach. How could we get at them better?

I had thought, of course, of the bow and arrow, and there was good suitable timber that, like the yew, would make good bows, and there were long, strong reeds that, sharpened, would make good arrows, but where to find cords fine enough and strong enough for bow strings, and how fix on the feathers properly to the arrows, without which the arrows would not fly straight, and where to find points to the arrows that would penetrate any but the softest hides, with barbs, without which the arrows, when in, could be pulled out by the monkeys, or would drop or work out, and the wounded animals would crawl into a fork or hang by their hands or tails when dead, without falling?

Above all, bows and arrows were no use unless you could shoot straight, and to learn to do that effectively would take long practice, that is, the ape people would have to train themselves by long practice to do something in the future; which I knew they would never do. And for myself, it seemed hardly worth the long trial and the repeated failures of experiment to learn to do a thing that I alone could profit by; I, who had so much to do as it was; not only, like the rest, in feeding myself, in making, collecting, and storing secondary requisites, and, above all, in teaching and developing the others. So I abandoned that idea.

Then there was the sling, that was much easier to make; a bit of hide for the pouch to hold the missile and some twisted strips of hide for the strings. But then, again, in this alluvial forest land there were no stones to sling nor any substitute, that I could think of; and, again, sling stones would only strike, not stick in. Above all, slinging, like archery, would have to be learned by long practice, and they would never practice. So I gave that up too.

Then there was the trap, but what bait could I use for the trap, when good bait, fruit, etc., was all round? I could think of no contrivance.

But one chance did come. One day Joe pointed out to me a well-worn track; following it up, I saw in a muddy spot the imprint of a foot and recognised it as that of a tapir. Now a tapir is a good big beast, the biggest, probably, in the Brazilian forest, and it would mean a pretty big food supply so long as it kept fresh, and the ape people were not over particular on that score. Could I manage to get this beast somehow?

Presently I thought of a dead fall. I knew the tapir generally follows one particular track to and from the river, and that he is a pig-headed brute; if he finds an obstacle in his track, he will suppose it has fallen across naturally and will charge against it to remove it by the dead force of his blow.

I followed the course of his track for some distance till I came to a heavy, stout young tree; I cleared away some of the scrub so that the tree would fall full and clear of any substantial impediment, and then I felled it so that it would fall straight and full across the track. When it fell, just as I had calculated to make it fall, it would break the beast's back. My next step was to raise the butt and prop it up with a stick resting on a chip, so that it would not get forced into the ground by the falling weight but slip off easily with a slight push. The next thing was to raise the butt to get the support under it. And now was the difficulty; I could not do this all by myself. I should have to get help, and how to make the ape people understand and do what I wanted?

I got the stick and the chip for it to rest on all right, but then I had to make Joe understand that he was to set the stick all right under the butt when I lifted it. But I found I could not lift the butt all by myself; I should have to get the family to help me, and then to make Joe understand how to slip the support under the butt when the butt was raised; and twice Joe fixed it too much on one side and the whole thing came down and had to be done all over again.

When a power ceases to be necessary it begins to shrivel up and eventually to disappear. So the cave fish has lost its eyes, the condor its scent, the ostrich its power of flight, and the immature swimming young of the whelk has fastened itself as a stationary shellfish fast to a rock.

The more varied and variable a creature's members are the more does their power of expression by gesture increase. The dog's tail is a simple enough feature, but even that has several expressions. It stands straight up when it means to fight, it wags to express pleasure, it tucks it between its hind legs to express fear. But the ape's flexible hands and fingers give a power of expression in pointing, grasping, clenching, and numberless ways as to give a whole unspoken dictionary.

For all that, I felt terribly the need of spoken language between myself and the family, especially with Joe. Even in such a simple matter as fixing the dead fall for the tapir, I had the greatest difficulty in getting them to understand what I wanted them to do to lift the heavy log up, to fix the support underneath, and to fix it so nicely that it would hold the log up effectively till it was pushed aside and thus let the whole weight fall at once. Twice he let the whole affair fall, through not balancing the weight properly on the support.

I have said that the ape people had no spoken language. This, as a practical statement, is true, but in mathematical exactness it is untrue. Dogs, for instance, may be said to exchange ideas by vocal sounds, but there seems no good reason to assume that this impart of ideas is deliberately intentional. The dog utters several sounds that convey distinct ideas; there is the growl of defiance, the bark of welcome, the hunting bay, the whine of distress; and the rest of the pack have learned by experience to know what these several sounds indicated. But does the dog that utter these sounds *intend* to indicate them? Is it not rather that the sound is merely the instinctive outburst of its own feelings, just as the varying expressions on a man's face indicate his feelings, and other people have found out what they indicate. Indeed, so far, as a man's facial movements indicate his feelings, they come quite involuntarily, and often indicates what he wishes to conceal. And when he tries to make his face express something quite different from what he feels, he rarely deceives a skilled observer. It requires a natural gift, as well as long practice, to become a good actor. And the dog rarely tries to "act," though I have known occasional cases.

The dog's apparent "talk" then is not intentional talk at all, but merely the instinctive response to internal mental stimuli. But our apes uttered sounds more clearly, deliberately intended to convey particular ideas.

The "words" were very few, I suppose hardly over thirty altogether. And they were meant to convey those ideas only which there was urgent necessity to convey, such as *food* (the opportunity or desire to eat), *water* (the opportunity or desire to drink), *help* (I am in a difficulty), *hurt* (I am injured or sick and cannot help myself), *haste* (hurry up), and so on. They were almost always simple substitutions or words that could be conveyed by a substitution. And they were always as short as possible, as the apes' vocal chords could not express more than about half the sounds in our alphabet; they could not distinguish between b and p, f and v, s and z, or any two sounds that were nearly alike, and they could not run several consonants together without vowels between them. By no possibility could they pronounce anything faintly approaching one word— "strength." Indeed most human language cannot pronounce particular sounds common in the other language. A Chinaman cannot pronounce R, a Japanese L, an Arab P, few but the English th, and so on.

A county magistrate told me he had a Chinaman come to him with a complaint but could not understand what the Chinaman had to complain of, because the complaint was that someone had "jumped his ground" (his gold claim), and the nearest approach the Chinaman could make to the word *ground* was *kowlong*.

So you will see that the difficulties of speech to our apes were pretty great. Moreover, their lives were so simple, their wants so few, their gestures so expressive, that really spoken words were hardly needed. Indeed, the few words they had were hardly required. Food or hunger were easily expressed by gestures, so was water or thirst. A cry would call for help whatever the cause was. So what was surprising was not that their language was so brief but that they had any at all. For Nature never supplies a fresh gift except to absolute necessity. Once a species has got so well adapted to its environment as to be able to hold its own fairly well, it remains stationary until some fresh danger threatens, some food supply falls short, or some great change of environment occurs that threatens extinction unless some modification of the species' powers begins to fit it to the new conditions.

One of the first new words I wanted them to learn was *come*, meaning to come to me, or go from me, or proceed in any direction as I might point. Another was *all together*, meaning that they were to exert all their strength at the same moment; and in a particular way (as to secure a balance) which was much more difficult. But every word had to be a simple monosyllable, or next thing to it, with vowels between the consonants, and almost always with accompanying gesture.

I had named the father, mother, brother, and sister—Dad, Mum, Joe, and Sue, and they quickly learned their names and looked up when addressed, as a dog will; and as a dog quickly learns some other commands, as fetch, carry, guard, so did they, though they rather responded to the words than actually used them.

Such communications were not of very much use with Dad, because, though not really old (he was, I suppose, barely fifty), yet, from his simple, monotonous life he had become so set in his ways, habits, and simple ideas that he was hard to change. Moreover, he did not like to be told to do things.

Mum was better; she was really glad to learn new things, as far as she could, and liked to please. She had also wifely sympathies, and even seemed inclined to be motherly. For even when I had run a splinter into my arm she seemed to show some anxiety on seeing the blood flow, came up and examined the wound, and tried to help to bind it up with a rag torn from my shirt; though she did it rather clumsily, still she really helped, or tried to.

As for Sue, she was, as I have said, of little use. She was capricious, selfish, and apt to be sullen.

But Joe was quite different. He had regularly attached himself to me like a dog, was devoted to my wishes, and would earnestly do, or try to do, anything I wanted.

VI

The territory in which my family lived, and out of which they never wandered, indeed could not wander, afforded really quite an abundant and varied living. There were nuts, fruits, seeds and roots, amongst which the best flavored and most nutritious were the manioc, Brazil nut, banana, swamp rice; also there was a bay, mostly shallow, with sand banks edged with reeds. In the sand banks they often got turtles eggs; standing on a projecting log they could spear the fish that occasionally rose to the surface or passed by in the shallows; indeed the jaguar, with merely its claws to fish with, lived a good deal on fish, though he had other animals to prey upon; while my people had at any rate three tools, the digging stick, the throwing stick, and the spear (a strong sharpened reed) humble, but pretty effective implements. Lying hidden in the reeds, too, they could now and then knock over a wading bird and sometimes find their nests, with eggs; while there were capybaras (about the size of a pig), and sometimes, though rarely, larger game.

But the scarcity of these did not matter, for in the hot Brazilian climate one does not hanker for solid meat, though they occasionally partook of it when it came in, but more for an occasional change of diet than from a general preference for that kind of food.

So they were in general thoroughly well supplied, except in the rainy season when the waters were up, the rain pouring, and the getting about was difficult. They had not discovered the famous South American poison, the curari, with which the Indian tips his blowpipe arrows, and without which the blowpipe would be of little use, so they had not come to the blowpipe.

I had pretty often heard the roar of the jaguar and had seen his tracks, but never actually met the beast himself; which was scarcely to be wondered at as he is a nocturnal animal and we were never about at nights. Indeed; even in Africa, one may live for years in a lion country without ever seeing a lion, though one may hear them at night all about.

Our territory was not only well supplied with necessaries but was extensive enough for all purposes. It covered, excluding the impenetrable thickets and impassable swamps, an area of about eight miles long and four or so broad, quite big enough to wander about in and find varieties. And our people, too, had no fanciful prejudices, as we have, to limit their diet. We cannot, or, at any rate, do not, accept the Frenchman's horseflesh, the German's raw brawn, the Scotchman's haggis, the insides of all animals and the meadow plants of various kinds with which the foreigner will make a decent salad. I myself have tried to get over my prejudices, knowing them to be mere prejudices, against various kinds of food. I have tasted snake, kangaroo rat, platypus and shark, but though I felt there was really nothing objectionable in the flavor, still my stomach rose against the food, and I would never, or, at any rate, did never, attempt to make a meal off them though; no doubt, if driven by hunger, I could do so, and quite likely get to enjoy them. But our people had no prejudices of any sort, they ate and enjoyed whatever was eatable without indulging in any fancies about it; so they not only ate but enjoyed their grubs, just as much as we enjoy our bread and vegetables. And I was slowly, very slowly, getting to be something like them in this respect.

So we all lived together and got on together, mutually helpful; I acquiring from them gradually their forest lore, their knowledge of what was good for them and where to find it, and they profiting largely by my few but superior tools and my much greater intelligence. Besides, I was actually adding, or in the way of adding, to their total stock of supplies. For I seldom missed the chance of collecting useful seeds or shifting young, suitable plants to fairly open sites, cutting away the surrounding creepers and weeds, and generally looking after them when I passed, to see that they were thriving. In times to come they would find, if they survived, many more useful plants growing about and within their reach than there were originally.

When I had got to know their territory and its resources, I used to speculate whence they came and their probable destiny. And I guessed that they were the last remnants of a race that had been superseded by more progressive varieties of the same species; that other families of the original "missing link" having got better tools and weapons, and developing slightly higher intelligence, had driven out these inferior specimens, just as the Romans, the Saxons, and the Normans had driven out the original Britons into barren Cornwall and mountainous Wales, and these, hunted out, had wandered somehow into this territory, which proved to be well able to maintain them but not stimulating enough to further develop them, and into which the more progressive "missing links" could hardly follow them, and, at any rate, were not driven or were tempted to try. For I remembered through what obstacles I myself had come to get here, and by what lucky chance I had managed to get through. I remembered the tangled thicket that had turned me aside this way and that, the cane-brake between which and the great swamp on one side and the thicket on the other I had just managed to squeeze; and remembering, too, how, after I had explored the territory and realised its boundaries, how it was bounded by the thickets here, by the swamp there, by the deep river on another side, and by a rising barren plain on the south, where there was no apparent life but a few small lizards, and here and there a few very small flying birds, where there was nothing to live upon, and nothing to attract, I could see that none were likely to follow, and settled finally on this too easy tract there had been nothing to stimulate further development; no wild beasts worth mentioning to contend with, no human or semi-human foes to resist, no dangers of any sort to meet, no difficulty in procuring food, there was nothing else to stimulate further progress.

So they had not only risen no higher, but had possibly even sunk lower. As the cave fish has lost its eyesight in the dark, as the condor has lost its scent up in the air, where no scents could reach it, and as the primitive swimming whelk has fastened itself to a rock and sunk into a mere stationary shell fish when it found that the sea would bring it its food without its having to take the trouble to seek for it. So these ape people had, perhaps, sunk into what they were, a safe, comfortable, easy-going, deteriorating race. Anyhow, they had originated somewhere. Why not here? And while the surrounding tribes had progressed they had not.

They had actually ceased to be a "missing link," for they had joined on to nothing. They, like the giant saurians and such like of ancient days, that had not developed into anything but had simply died out, through lack of food, too sudden change of environment, or most likely of all, been quietly crowded out of existence by smaller, apparently inferior but more generally fit creatures, as the rabbit in Australia has crowded, and eventually would certainly have crowded out the sheep but for man's incessant war against it.

In short, these were a dying, not a developing, race. So their numbers had died down till only a single family was left (for in all the territory I saw no trace of any others of them). Perhaps they originated there, I did not know; but there they were, the last of their race. They would die off one by one till the last survivor remained, and he, if no special accident happened to him, would gradually age, become feeble, less able to find sustenance, become too weak to climb his tree, and finally lie down to die. He would not suffer much, for he had no keen sensibility, and he would have no superstitions to haunt him as to his future and no regrets as to his past. He would simply flicker out, like a candle. And when, or if, in long later years other people should wander into his territory they would find no trace of him, no flint knives, no pottery, no ruins, no bones even. For bones always rapidly and mysteriously disappear, except in the rare cases when the creatures die in a cave or their remains get washed into a silt bed, get covered up and gradually fossilised. Even of the so recently lost Tasmanian race not a bone has ever been discovered, though they inhabited only some parts, well-known parts, of the island, and we know pretty well how and whereabouts the last of them died.

VII

The first need daily of each of my family was to get its "daily bread," but that did not take more than half the day at the outside on the average. Now and then, as at the height of the rains when everything was sodden and getting about unpleasant, this daily bread became hard to get and all were reduced to short commons, but these times did not often last very long or press too hardly; they never threatened existence, only comfort. Were it otherwise the recurrent pressure would either have driven them to the habit, and finally to the instinct (which is only a confirmed and trans- mitted habit) of laying by supplies like the squirrels and ants.

And so it is with nearly all the lower animals. There are a few, like the white ants and the caterpillars, whose whole life seems to be a continued process of converting woody fibre into ant or fruit into caterpillar. But barring these mere masticating machines, all the lower orders of Creation have more than half their lives avail- able for play, for lounging, or for poking about. With man it is, or should be, even more so. With his superior intelligence, tools, and productive power he should in general be able to get his "daily bread" even quicker, and so have even more spare time for play— or for self-improvement. But man in the early days generally had wild beasts or human foes to guard against, which required arms, acquired skill in their use, fortifications and so on; and on top of all his very intelligence led him into superstitions. For directly he began to inquire into why such and such disasters, sickness, accidents, death occurred, the only explanation then available seemed to be the malicious action of beings with wills like himself, but invisible, which he called spirits, or incorporated in certain objects which he called fetishes, hence certain practices arose to propitiate these spirits or fetishes, and hence gradually arose the whole superstructure of idolatry. Benevolent beings of this sort he rarely worshipped, as these being well intentioned already, needed no propitiation. Later on, good spirits, whose aid might be invoked, were added to the superstition.

But my people had no idea of any supernatural beings, good or bad, or of any life, past or future, only of their present animal existence. So they had no religion? No; nor morals. They had not got into the higher plane where these things come in. By which they missed pleasures on one side, pains on the other.

My people had generally half the day available for enjoyment. On one such occasion I was lying half asleep in the warm air under the shady trees when I heard a crack, followed by lamentation. I rushed to the spot indicated, arriving last, and found the family assembled, Mum weeping bitterly over the motionless body of Sue lying in her arms, Joe crying silently, he hardly knew why, except that something had gone wrong somehow, and Dad standing by in gloomy silence.

I saw at once by the way Sue's head hung that she was dead, that her neck was broken and that death was instantaneous. It seems that she and her mother had been up in a tree exploring for arboreal treasures when Sue saw a young bird, out of the nest but not yet able to fly, and she had pursued it up the branch and then caught sight of the nest, further up still, with something alive in it. Eagerly following up, too eagerly, she had gone too far up, and the branch she was on breaking she had fallen some fifty feet, alighting on her shoulders.

Now, as we know, I had no particular personal affection for Sue, still we had not been strangers. She had often come to me calling my attention to this thing, asking for that thing, and dumbly soliciting my help in many ways, and I had always readily given it when I could. We had all, too, been members of the same family in a way, so I felt a touch of regret for her loss as well as of sympathy with the family. So I stood by silently till Mum's cries died away and she laid the body down. Then I waited a few minutes to see what they would all do; how dispose of the body.

What had they done on previous occasions of death? Where were the remains of their predecessors? They could not have buried them for they had no tools, would not have thought of it, and there were no graves. They could not have burnt them for they had no fire; could not have hoisted them on Towers of Silence for the vultures, like the Parsees, nor stick them in a tree like some savages, for there were no such remains, as I could see. If they left them on the ground, the worms, the growing jungle, and the rotting vegetation would soon obliterate all signs. At any rate, what did the local apes do with their dead bodies? Probably they did the same; left them where they fell.

At any rate, I knew what I was going to do. Mum, when her sobs had died down, laid the corpse on the ground. After a short interval I patted Mum gently on the head, stroked her sympathetically a time or two, then picked up the body and strode towards the densest part of the thicket where they never went, for I knew of a tall tree that had forked and shot up in two stems. At this junction the stem had cracked and the rain had got in and the timber had rotted downwards. I laid her down, then climbed into the tree, dug out the rotten wood as far down as I could with a stick, then signed for the body to be handed to me. They obeyed in silence; then I tucked the body feet downwards into the opening, doubling up the lower limbs so that it rested there up to the waist; then I stuck a bough on each side lest by any chance it might topple over and fall out. Then, as some sort of a ceremony seemed desirable, I made the sign of the cross over it, descended and walked slowly home, leaving the rest of the family gazing at the tree.

There might be poignant regret amongst her relatives for a short time but it would soon pass. Their sensibilities were dull, their memories short, they had no traditions. Joe could not know what death meant, for his predecessors had passed away, probably

before be was born or in his infancy, and he would remember nothing about it. All he would know was that his sister had gone—somewhere—and he would see her no more. For the old couples' real
grief, if there was any, would subside, memory grow dull, and all
would go on much the same as before, except that there would be
one less of them. She, who of the family died soonest would probably last the longest, so far as her remains were concerned, because these would remain protected in the tree. For the rest, what
would become of them when they died? Who knows! That night we
all retired to our dwellings and slept, I suppose, as usual.

VIII

And now time was getting on; the rainy season was—must be—
approaching, and the great object I had always in view must he
seen to. For it was quite impossible that I, an educated man, should
stay on forever in this savage, semi-brute state of existence. I must
break away somehow, if I died in the attempt. I did not see how I
could possibly make my way for these hundreds of miles, across
rivers swarming with alligators, through dense thickets and cane-
brakes, over pestilential swamps full of venomous snakes, without
food, without a boat, without tools, on the mere chance of possibly
meeting some low savages who might charitably help me on, but
would be more likely to kill me.

Still, I must make a try somehow, and take my chance, all the
odds being against me.

As I had no boat, no tools, or materials to make one and no
skill in boat building, the only resource was a raft to float down
stream. But as the weight of myself and such goods and stores as I
could collect would certainly sink the top of the raft below water
level, and as I could not think of attempting a long journey, of perhaps months, constantly immersed in water, my raft would have
to be in double or triple tiers high.

I had to plan out my project in every minute detail before I
began to work on it. First I should want at least six, probably more,
foundation logs of light specific gravity, the heaviest on the outside. I should have to fill in with other logs, as large as I could

manage to deal with, and fill up the gaps between these. The logs would have to be twelve to twenty feet long, making a raft eight to ten feet wide, and all the logs firmly lashed together with flexible bark or wide thongs. Also poles laid across; then, if necessary, a double layer of them, all also firmly lashed to each other and to the logs above and below them, then a thick layer of strong reeds for a floor, a bamboo mast, a sail of plaited flax leaves and a roof over me to keep off the rain. This would have to be of light poles set up in a triangle and thatched with palm leaves; also a paddle, or two in case one should break or got lost; not that I hoped to paddle my way on (the raft would have simply to drift with the stream), but I must have some control over the drift, to keep myself far enough from the banks to prevent getting stranded, and get near enough to the bank to prevent getting lost in the great open stream, which, once I reached the great river, would be miles wide, possibly quite out of sight of land on either side. Yet the more I got out into the strength of the current the faster I would go. So I had much to consider and arrange for. Then there was the food supply. There was nothing of this kind that I could think of to take that would keep for any time except nuts and roots, and I would have to eat these raw for there was no taking a supply of fuel, and to land occasionally to gat it would be extremely difficult and dangerous with my unmanageable raft and clumsy paddle, in short it would not be worth attempting. Moreover, I could not hope to catch fish as I went along, for I had only four hooks left, with short lines attached (as I had trusted when I started to attach the necessary lengths as I went on), and these hooks were only of a certain size and might easily be too small, or more likely too large, for the fish I met, and they might easily be broken off by reeds or floating timber, or get snapped off by larger fish or by turtles. Still I would set them and have them trailing on the chance, not expecting much from them.

Well, this was about all I could think of. There was much to do and little time to do it in, and there were signs that the rains were not very far off.

So I had to work feverishly, Joe helping me, and both of us making the utmost use of every spare moment and every scrap of daylight. Indeed we worked harder than our strength permitted, properly speaking, so that before we were ready to start I was half worn out.

And with all our haste and all our carefulness we made mistakes, and had accidents and delays. We had found a huge dead tree near our shipping place, uprooted by some great tempest long ago but still perfectly sound. The butt, even if divided into lengths, would have been far too heavy for us to shift; but we had marked it off into lengths and burnt it into those lengths, starting two fires, and every now and then seeing to them and keeping them going, while we worked all about collecting our other requirements and lighter timbers.

Burning a tree into lengths is easy enough when you know how. The fires, at their regular intervals, are lighted and kept going. It takes a day or two to get well into the wood, but once the timber is well warmed through and the fire has evidently began to get a hold of it, the rest is easy. You have but to throw a big bough across it, rounding up the ends as they fall apart, and the work goes on merrily. But when we had with much labor, chiefly Joe and I, got the parts burnt through, we found that with all our efforts we could not move the biggest logs an inch, so all that part of the work was lost. One good log, when we had got it into the water, drifted off before we could get it properly moored so that was lost too. Other accidents had occurred, and the rains had began before we were ready; so we had to work in the rain, which was not very hard as yet, and the fires wanted more constant and careful attendance, and we were getting pretty well worn out. And all the time what troubled me was what was to become of Joe when I left. The others would not much matter. They were too steeped in the life of the woods, too absolutely ignorant of the great outside world, too stolid, incautious and indifferent to suffer anything worse than a faint regret and a dim loss of my assistance when I left. But Joe was as devoted to me as a faithful dog, and his whole life was merely as my assistant in my wonderful doings. Yet, if I took him with me and we both survived the long, mysterious and dangerous journey, what was to become of him at the end? No one among the

Brazilians would care to be bothered with the maintenance of this strange, only half human being with undeveloped intelligence and no spoken language. So I could not abandon him at Para. And to take him on with me home would be no better. For I was not a rich man, I had to earn my living, and who would employ me with this creature attached to me? And out of the forest, tied to a lodging, with no employment, it seemed hopeless. So, deeply as I regretted it, I had to leave him behind, and had to let him understand before I left that it had to be, though he would never understand why.

At last the time came when all was ready. There was no use trying to make the family understand matters, no use for special adieus, and even Joe would not fully understand that I was actually going to pass away from them for ever. So the stores being all shipped, a careful look round to see that I was leaving nothing behind, and with a parting pat on the head and all affectionate and not too doleful smile to Joe, I pushed off.

Well, my tale is well nigh told, and the less I speak of that last dreadful journey, the better. Floating down with the stream it took me over two days to reach the tributary in which I had been deserted, but far from the actual spot. It took me over a week drifting on, day and night, down the tributary till I got into the broad Amazon, a sea of water with not even the dim line of the opposite bank visible. And all the time here was I, on a small raft, with insufficient, diminishing and unpalatable stores, naked but for my kilt of leaves, with almost incessant and increasing rain, alone and half despairing, and what with the insufficient food, the rain, the exposure, the loneliness and low spirits, I felt myself growing daily weaker, my senses becoming dulled and my wits going. I became unconscious. The next thing I knew was that I was in a canoe with two Indians and a half-breed.

I learned, but not until long after, that this was a small party of forest Indians who, though they rarely had any intercourse with the whites, yet knew enough about them to visit them once a year or so with what marketable stores, skins, and so on, they could collect to buy the few European goods, arrow tips, axes, knives and so on that had become indispensable to them. These, noticing a strange craft far out on the wide waters, apparently untenanted, yet with an unmistakable human made hut upon it, had, impelled by curiosity, made for it and found me lying unconscious and with almost exhausted stores, stretched under the now leaking, imperfect shelter. To leave me so at all would have been to leave me to certain death, which even these savages did not like to do, and as I was an apparently civilised white man it might pay them and would cost them little to take me on to the nearest settlement, where they might receive a decent reward for their care and trouble. So they did so, delivering me to the chief Portuguese resident, who, guessing who I was and remembering the circumstances under which I had been there before, gave the Indians a reward that satisfied them, and after taking care of me for a week or so and partly recovering me, passed me on with a bill for my expenses. And so in due time I reached Para, where the Rubber Company's agent at once took full charge of me, and on the first opportunity shipped me back to England.

The Rubber Company, recognising at once that I was their accredited agent and had a clear call on them for all my expenses, and for all I had suffered, especially as I had actually discovered the rubber country I had been sent to find, met their obligations well and paid me off.

I absolutely refused to go out again to the scene of my discoveries and adventures, but gave them a sufficiently clear account of the route and the locality so that they could carry the enterprise on if they chose. But they did not choose. The place was too far off, the communications too difficult, the rubber trees hardly numerous enough for further prospecting, so they closed the deal.

THE MISSING LINK

A MYSTERIOUS ENCOUNTER ON THE ISLAND OF BORNEO

MARCEL ROLAND

From the village where they had set up the centre of their explorations, they had left with the rising sun and had already been walking for three hours. The part of Borneo through which they made their way was mountainous, and divided by deep, dark valleys. Rocky peaks alternated with nigh-impenetrable jungles. Accompanied by a native guide and carrying their plant presses, the two naturalists had just climbed half-way up a precipitous outcropping. After stopping in the shade of one of the rare trees growing on this gravelly slope, they went on their way. Suddenly, they found themselves in a natural hollow, carved out of the rock.

"A cave!" cried out Mounier.

"No, a tunnel!" answered the other.

On saying these words, the second European, Steiner, pushed aside a curtain of dried lianas which half covered the opening. A narrow circle of pale daylight appeared at the other end. It was indeed a passageway which extended at both ends into open air.

"Let's go in!" Mounier offered resolutely. "I'll go first!"

They silently made their way down the passage, their rifle at the ready, followed by the native, whose supple tread barely brought a crackle from the granitic debris strewn across the floor. They could walk upright, but sometimes the ceiling would abruptly drop or bristle with sharp spikes, forcing them to bend over. Large bats, hanging upside-down from the roof, their serenity disturbed, took wing with cries that spun through the oppressive air. They finally reached the end of the straight passageway

Steiner, who had taken the lead, lifted a sort of blind made of twigs hanging together, but suddenly stepped back.

"Just in time," he grumbled, "I was going to take quite a tumble."

Indeed, the ground dropped off abruptly in front of the cave floor, sloping down sharply, almost perpendicularly to heaps of boulders. The three companions stopped and took in the scene which presented itself to them. They saw an extremely deep, funnel-shaped cirque, at the bottom of which, amongst fearful shadows, one could hear the roar of an invisible torrent. The edges of this deep granite basin were lost at a dizzying height, far above their heads, and the light from the sky, falling on the chaotic assemblage of irregularly-shaped boulders, contrasted areas of light with black pits.

The corridor from which the explorers were emerging, continued on the other side of the cirque, but to reach it one had to follow an extremely narrow platform, created by a freak of Nature, which ran all along the wall.

"It's dangerous!" pointed out Steiner: "but if we want to know what this underground passage leads to, there's no hesitating!"

"Let's go! ... You don't suffer from vertigo, do you, Sikoula?" said Mounier.

The native smiled. Vertigo, pah! he was well acquainted with peaks, experienced in the most awkward of balancing acts!

They continued their perilous hike. Here and there the suspended walkway widened and the piles of boulders beneath made any possible fall much shorter.

But Steiner burst out happily. There, mere meters away, he had made out, upon a crag, a bunch of pale mauve flowers.

"*Velamina Sigillata*!" he cried out triumphantly, his face glowing with happiness... "Finally! I knew I would succeed in finding it!"

This *Velamina Sigillata*, an extremely rare plant, a genuine jewel of Botany, of which only one living example existed in cultivation and which he had searched for in vain for years! He had come to Borneo with the hope of perhaps finding, in the midst of its abundant vegetation, the coveted specimen, which he counted upon to cement his professional reputation. This expectation had not been disappointed! On the edge of the walkway, his eyes asparkle, he contemplated the object of his dreams.

He extended a finger

"There, Sikoula... Ten dollars for you if you bring me back that plant with its roots!"

In a flash, the native had slipped down a granite rib to a spot a few feet below the walkway, and began to leap from boulder to boulder to where the *Velamina* opened it mauve corollas.

Suddenly, there was a stifled cry and his arms flailed out: he had lost his footing. The Europeans, who had been following him, saw him waver and drop, head first, over the precipice. But at the very moment he was to disappear, from behind a rocky outcropping emerged a huge, muscular black arm, bearing a crooked hand. This hand grabbed the man as he fell, and held him still, suspended over the abyss like a gesticulating puppet. Slowly, something fearful, a gigantic, hideous creature, was revealed before the explorers' eyes.

They had enough time to make him out clearly, to notice his body's long fawn-coloured hair, his spindly legs, bending under the weight of the torso, the head's flattened skull, the sunken brow, the prominent cheeks and forward-jutting jaws that made up its features. Buried beneath the beetling brow, gleamed furtive yellow eyes. Still holding Sikoula at arm's length, the marvelous creature had turned towards the strangers and was looking them over. They too looked him over, frozen in fear and amazement. This was no orang, for it was much bigger, better proportioned and missing the pair of lateral cranial protrusions characteristic of the Asian anthropoid. There was, all told, over his features a singular, indefinable expression, less bestial than human. The features of this creature would not allow it being assigned to any species of ape. The two naturalists, accustomed to all forms of the simian race, of which the island had supplied them numerous examples, had no doubt whatsoever of this. What they were seeing was a new, unknown life-form.

Struck by a sudden thought, Mounier leaned over and whispered: "Steiner! Could it be the... the ape-man? ... You know of course, the pithecanthrope, the missing rung in the ecological ladder between the gorilla and us! There are claims it is not extinct. Travelers have met it in certain old-growth forests. I myself didn't believe it, however..."

But already, his partner, driven by his haste to save the native had shouldered his rifle. Before his partner could stop him he had shot at the monster without further thought.

It jerked, threw down its stick and put its free hand to its chest, over its heart. With its other arm it still held Sikoula, suspended motionless over the abyss. It had but to open its fingers and the poor wretch would have been splattered over the bottom. At this thought the two explorers shuddered. Furious at his own thoughtlessness, Steiner muttered: "What an idiot I am!"

But, rather than perpetrate the act of vengeance they feared, to their amazement the creature put the native softly down on a boulder from which he could easily regain the platform. Then in a look which give away its suffering it seemed to say: "Go back to your own kind, go... You are safe now!"

And while a still trembling Sikoula returns to his companions, the mysterious creature, leans tottering against a boulder. His hairy hand presses against the thorax from which a red stream flows. It moans, and turning its head several times towards the men, towards those who have just struck him unto death, he moves off towards the underground passage. Helping himself up by way of great masses of stone, he climbs the fairly steep slope leading to it. Having reached the tunnel's entrance, he calls feebly. The travelers immediately see a long-haired female and her agile children emerge and busy themselves around him... One last look back and the creature disappears."

"I feel like I've committed murder," Steiner admitted.

Perplexed, almost anguished, they turned back. A few days later they returned to this spot with a large escort. The tunnel, the cirque, the neighbouring areas were searched, but no trace was found of the family of anthropoids.

Had they come face to face with a human ancestor, which remained the matter of legends, or had they simply encountered an orang-outang of superior instincts? None was ever able to solve this enigma.

Facts Concerning the Late Arthur Jermyn and His Family

H. P. Lovecraft

I

Life is a hideous thing, and from the background behind what we know of it peer daemoniacal hints of truth which make it sometimes a thousandfold more hideous. Science, already oppressive with its shocking revelations, will perhaps be the ultimate exterminator of our human species—if separate species we be—for its reserve of unguessed horrors could never be borne by mortal brains if loosed upon the world. If we knew what we are, we should do as Sir Arthur Jermyn did; and Arthur Jermyn soaked himself in oil and set fire to his clothing one night. No one placed the charred fragments in an urn or set a memorial to him who had been; for certain papers and a certain boxed object were found which made men wish to forget. Some who knew him do not admit that he ever existed.

Arthur Jermyn went out on the moor and burned himself after seeing the boxed object which had come from Africa. It was this object, and not his peculiar personal appearance, which made him end his life. Many would have disliked to live if possessed of the peculiar features of Arthur Jermyn, but he had been a poet and scholar and had not minded. Learning was in his blood, for his great-grandfather, Sir Robert Jermyn, Bt., had been an anthropologist of note, whilst his great-great-great-grandfather, Sir Wade Jermyn, was one of the earliest explorers of the Congo region, and had written eruditely of its tribes, animals, and supposed antiquities. Indeed, old Sir Wade had possessed an intellectual zeal amounting almost to a mania; his bizarre conjectures on a prehistoric white Congolese civilisation earning him much ridicule when his book, Observation on the Several Parts of Africa, was published. In 1765 this fearless explorer had been placed in a madhouse at Huntingdon.

Madness was in all the Jermyns, and people were glad there were not many of them. The line put forth no branches, and Arthur was the last of it. If he had not been, one can not say what he would have done when the object came. The Jermyns never seemed to look quite right—something was amiss, though Arthur was the worst, and the old family portraits in Jermyn House showed fine faces enough before Sir Wade's time. Certainly, the madness began with Sir Wade, whose wild stories of Africa were at once the delight and terror of his few friends. It showed in his collection of trophies and specimens, which were not such as a normal man would accumulate and preserve, and appeared strikingly in the Oriental seclusion in which he kept his wife. The latter, he had said, was the daughter of a Portuguese trader whom he had met in Africa; and did not like English ways. She, with an infant son born in Africa, had accompanied him back from the second and longest of his trips, and had gone with him on the third and last, never returning. No one had ever seen her closely, not even the servants; for her disposition had been violent and singular. During her brief stay at Jermyn House she occupied a remote wing, and was waited on by her husband alone. Sir Wade was, indeed, most peculiar in his solicitude for his family; for when he returned to Africa he would permit no one to care for his young son save a loathsome black woman from Guinea. Upon coming back, after the death of Lady Jermyn, he himself assumed complete care of the boy.

But it was the talk of Sir Wade, especially when in his cups, which chiefly led his friends to deem him mad. In a rational age like the eighteenth century it was unwise for a man of learning to talk about wild sights and strange scenes under a Congo moon; of the gigantic walls and pillars of a forgotten city, crumbling and vine-grown, and of damp, silent, stone steps leading interminably down into the darkness of abysmal treasure-vaults and inconceivable catacombs. Especially was it unwise to rave of the living things that might haunt such a place; of creatures half of the jungle and half of the impiously aged city—fabulous creatures which even a Pliny might describe with scepticism; things that might have sprung up after the great apes had overrun the dying city with the walls and the pillars, the vaults and the weird carvings. Yet after he came home for the last time Sir Wade would speak of such matters with a shudderingly uncanny zest, mostly after his third glass at the Knight's Head; boasting of what he had found in the jungle and of how he had dwelt among terrible ruins known only to him. And finally he had spoken of the living things in such a manner that he was taken to the madhouse. He had shown little regret when shut into the barred room at Huntingdon, for his mind moved curiously. Ever since his son had commenced to grow out of infancy, he had liked his home less and less, till at last he had seemed to dread it. The Knight's Head had been his headquarters, and when he was confined he expressed some vague gratitude as if for protection. Three years later he died.

Wade Jermyn's son Philip was a highly peculiar person. Despite a strong physical resemblance to his father, his appearance and conduct were in many particulars so coarse that he was universally shunned. Though he did not inherit the madness which was feared by some, he was densely stupid and given to brief periods of uncontrollable violence. In frame he was small, but intensely powerful, and was of incredible agility. Twelve years after succeeding to his title he married the daughter of his gamekeeper, a person said to be of gypsy extraction, but before his son was born joined the navy as a common sailor, completing the general disgust which his habits and misalliance had begun. After the close of the American war he was heard of as sailor on a merchantman in the African trade, having a kind of reputation for feats of strength and climbing, but finally disappearing one night as his ship lay off the Congo coast.

In the son of Sir Philip Jermyn the now accepted family peculiarity took a strange and fatal turn. Tall and fairly handsome, with a sort of weird Eastern grace despite certain slight oddities of proportion, Robert Jermyn began life as a scholar and investigator. It was he who first studied scientifically the vast collection of relics which his mad grandfather had brought from Africa, and who made the family name as celebrated in ethnology as in exploration. In 1815 Sir Robert married a daughter of the seventh Viscount Brightholme and was subsequently blessed with three children, the eldest and youngest of whom were never publicly seen on account of deformities in mind and body. Saddened by these family misfortunes, the scientist sought relief in work, and made two long expeditions in the interior of Africa. In 1849 his second son, Nevil, a singularly repellent person who seemed to combine the surliness of Philip Jermyn with the hauteur of the Brightholmes, ran away with a vulgar dancer, but was pardoned upon his return in the following year. He came back to Jermyn House a widower with an infant son, Alfred, who was one day to be the father of Arthur Jermyn.

Friends said that it was this series of griefs which unhinged the mind of Sir Robert Jermyn, yet it was probably merely a bit of African folklore which caused the disaster. The elderly scholar had been collecting legends of the Onga tribes near the field of his grandfather's and his own explorations, hoping in some way to account for Sir Wade's wild tales of a lost city peopled by strange hybrid creatures. A certain consistency in the strange papers of his ancestor suggested that the madman's imagination might have been stimulated by native myths. On October 19, 1852, the explorer Samuel Seaton called at Jermyn House with a manuscript of notes collected among the Ongas, believing that certain legends of a gray city of white apes ruled by a white god might prove valuable to the ethnologist. In his conversation he probably supplied many additional details; the nature of which will never be known, since a hideous series of tragedies suddenly burst into being. When Sir Robert Jermyn emerged from his library he left behind the strangled corpse of the explorer, and before he could be restrained, had put an end to all three of his children; the two who were never seen, and the son who had run away. Nevil Jermyn died in the successful defence of his own two-year-old son, who had apparently been included in the old man's madly murderous scheme. Sir Robert himself, after repeated attempts at suicide and a stubborn refusal to utter an articulate sound, died of apoplexy in the second year of his confinement.

Sir Alfred Jermyn was a baronet before his fourth birthday, but his tastes never matched his title. At twenty he had joined a band of music-hall performers, and at thirty-six had deserted his wife and child to travel with an itinerant American circus. His end was very revolting. Among the animals in the exhibition with which he travelled was a huge bull gorilla of lighter colour than the average; a surprisingly tractable beast of much popularity with the performers. With this gorilla Alfred Jermyn was singularly fascinated, and on many occasions the two would eye each other for long periods through the intervening bars. Eventually Jermyn asked and obtained permission to train the animal, astonishing audiences and fellow performers alike with his success. One morning in Chicago, as the gorilla and Alfred Jermyn were rehearsing an exceedingly clever boxing match, the former delivered a blow of more than the usual force, hurting both the body and the dignity of the amateur trainer. Of what followed, members of "The Greatest Show On Earth" do not like to speak. They did not expect to hear Sir Alfred Jermyn emit a shrill, inhuman scream, or to see him seize his clumsy antagonist with both hands, dash it to the floor of the cage, and bite fiendishly at its hairy throat. The gorilla was off its guard, but not for long, and before anything could be done by the regular trainer, the body which had belonged to a baronet was past recognition.

II

Arthur Jermyn was the son of Sir Alfred Jermyn and a music-hall singer of unknown origin. When the husband and father deserted his family, the mother took the child to Jermyn House; where there was none left to object to her presence. She was not without notions of what a nobleman's dignity should be, and saw to it that her son received the best education which limited money could provide. The family resources were now sadly slender, and Jermyn House had fallen into woeful disrepair, but young Arthur loved the old edifice and all its contents. He was not like any other

Jermyn who had ever lived, for he was a poet and a dreamer. Some of the neighbouring families who had heard tales of old Sir Wade Jermyn's unseen Portuguese wife declared that her Latin blood must be showing itself; but most persons merely sneered at his sensitiveness to beauty, attributing it to his music-hall mother, who was socially unrecognised. The poetic delicacy of Arthur Jermyn was the more remarkable because of his uncouth personal appearance. Most of the Jermyns had possessed a subtly odd and repellent cast, but Arthur's case was very striking. It is hard to say just what he resembled, but his expression, his facial angle, and the length of his arms gave a thrill of repulsion to those who met him for the first time.

It was the mind and character of Arthur Jermyn which atoned for his aspect. Gifted and learned, he took highest honours at Oxford and seemed likely to redeem the intellectual fame of his family. Though of poetic rather than scientific temperament, he planned to continue the work of his forefathers in African ethnology and antiquities, utilising the truly wonderful though strange collection of Sir Wade. With his fanciful mind he thought often of the prehistoric civilisation in which the mad explorer had so implicitly believed, and would weave tale after tale about the silent jungle city mentioned in the latter's wilder notes and paragraphs. For the nebulous utterances concerning a nameless, unsuspected race of jungle hybrids he had a peculiar feeling of mingled terror and attraction, speculating on the possible basis of such a fancy, and seeking to obtain light among the more recent data gleaned by his great-grandfather and Samuel Seaton amongst the Ongas.

In 1911, after the death of his mother, Sir Arthur Jermyn determined to pursue his investigations to the utmost extent. Selling a portion of his estate to obtain the requisite money, he outfitted an expedition and sailed for the Congo. Arranging with the Belgian authorities for a party of guides, he spent a year in the Onga and Kahn country, finding data beyond the highest of his expectations. Among the Kaliris was an aged chief called Mwanu, who possessed not only a highly retentive memory, but a singular degree of intelligence and interest in old legends. This ancient confirmed every tale which Jermyn had heard, adding his own account of the stone city and the white apes as it had been told to him.

According to Mwanu, the gray city and the hybrid creatures were no more, having been annihilated by the warlike N'bangus many years ago. This tribe, after destroying most of the edifices and killing the live beings, had carried off the stuffed goddess which had been the object of their quest; the white ape-goddess which the strange beings worshipped, and which was held by Congo tradition to be the form of one who had reigned as a princess among these beings. Just what the white apelike creatures could have been, Mwanu had no idea, but he thought they were the builders of the ruined city. Jermyn could form no conjecture, but by close questioning obtained a very picturesque legend of the stuffed goddess.

The ape-princess, it was said, became the consort of a great white god who had come out of the West. For a long time they had reigned over the city together, but when they had a son, all three went away. Later the god and princess had returned, and upon the death of the princess her divine husband had mummified the body and enshrined it in a vast house of stone, where it was worshipped. Then he departed alone. The legend here seemed to present three variants. According to one story, nothing further happened save that the stuffed goddess became a symbol of supremacy for whatever tribe might possess it. It was for this reason that the N'bangus carried it off. A second story told of a god's return and death at the feet of his enshrined wife. A third told of the return of the son, grown to manhood—or apehood or godhood, as the case might be—yet unconscious of his identity. Surely the imaginative blacks had made the most of whatever events might lie behind the extravagant legendry.

Of the reality of the jungle city described by old Sir Wade, Arthur Jermyn had no further doubt; and was hardly astonished when early in 1912 he came upon what was left of it. Its size must have been exaggerated, yet the stones lying about proved that it was no mere Negro village. Unfortunately no carvings could be found, and the small size of the expedition prevented operations toward clearing the one visible passageway that seemed to lead down into the system of vaults which Sir Wade had mentioned. The white apes and the stuffed goddess were discussed with all the native chiefs of the region, but it remained for a European to improve on the data offered by old Mwanu. M. Verhaeren, Belgian agent at a trading-post on the Congo, believed that he could not only locate but obtain the stuffed goddess, of which he had vaguely heard; since the once mighty N'bangus were now the submissive servants of King Albert's government, and with but little persuasion could be induced to part with the gruesome deity they had carried off. When Jermyn sailed for England, therefore, it was with the exultant probability that he would within a few months receive a priceless ethnological relic confirming the wildest of his great-great-great-grandfather's narratives—that is, the wildest which he had ever heard. Countrymen near Jermyn House had perhaps heard wilder tales handed down from ancestors who had listened to Sir Wade around the tables of the Knight's Head.

Arthur Jermyn waited very patiently for the expected box from M. Verhaeren, meanwhile studying with increased diligence the manuscripts left by his mad ancestor. He began to feel closely akin to Sir Wade, and to seek relics of the latter's personal life in England as well as of his African exploits. Oral accounts of the mysterious and secluded wife had been numerous, but no tangible relic of her stay at Jermyn House remained. Jermyn wondered what circumstance had prompted or permitted such an effacement, and decided that the husband's insanity was the prime cause. His great-great-great-grandmother, he recalled, was said to have been the daughter of a Portuguese trader in Africa. No doubt her practical heritage and superficial knowledge of the Dark Continent had caused her to flout Sir Wade's tales of the interior, a thing which such a man would not be likely to forgive. She had died in Africa, perhaps dragged thither by a husband determined to prove what he had told. But as Jermyn indulged in these reflections he could not but smile at their futility, a century and a half after the death of both his strange progenitors.

In June, 1913, a letter arrived from M. Verhaeren, telling of the finding of the stuffed goddess. It was, the Belgian averred, a most extraordinary object; an object quite beyond the power of a layman to classify. Whether it was human or simian only a scientist could determine, and the process of determination would be greatly hampered by its imperfect condition. Time and the Congo climate are not kind to mummies; especially when their preparation is as amateurish as seemed to be the case here. Around the creature's neck had been found a golden chain bearing an empty locket on which were armorial designs; no doubt some hapless traveller's keepsake, taken by the N'bangus and hung upon the goddess as a charm. In commenting on the contour of the mummy's face, M. Verhaeren suggested a whimsical comparison; or rather, expressed a humorous wonder just how it would strike his correspondent, but was too much interested scientifically to waste many words in levity. The stuffed goddess, he wrote, would arrive duly packed about a month after receipt of the letter.

The boxed object was delivered at Jermyn House on the afternoon of August 3, 1913, being conveyed immediately to the large chamber which housed the collection of African specimens as arranged by Sir Robert and Arthur. What ensued can best be gathered from the tales of servants and from things and papers later examined. Of the various tales, that of aged Soames, the family butler, is most ample and coherent. According to this trustworthy man, Sir Arthur Jermyn dismissed everyone from the room before opening the box, though the instant sound of hammer and chisel showed that he did not delay the operation. Nothing was heard for some time; just how long Soames cannot exactly estimate, but it was certainly less than a quarter of an hour later that the horrible scream, undoubtedly in Jermyn's voice, was heard. Immediately afterward Jermyn emerged from the room, rushing frantically toward the front of the house as if pursued by some hideous enemy. The expression on his face, a face ghastly enough in repose, was beyond description. When near the front door he seemed to think of something, and turned back in his flight, finally disappearing down the stairs to the cellar. The servants were utterly dumbfounded, and watched at the head of the stairs, but their master did not return. A smell of oil was all that came up from the regions below. After dark a rattling was heard at the door leading from the cellar into the courtyard; and a stable-boy saw Arthur Jermyn, glistening from head to foot with oil and redolent of that fluid, steal furtively out and vanish on the black moor surrounding the house. Then, in an exaltation of supreme horror, everyone saw the end. A spark appeared on the moor, a flame arose, and a pillar of human fire reached to the heavens. The house of Jermyn no longer existed.

The reason why Arthur Jermyn's charred fragments were not collected and buried lies in what was found afterward, principally the thing in the box. The stuffed goddess was a nauseous sight, withered and eaten away, but it was clearly a mummified white ape of some unknown species, less hairy than any recorded variety, and infinitely nearer mankind—quite shockingly so. Detailed description would be rather unpleasant, but two salient particulars must be told, for they fit in revoltingly with certain notes of Sir Wade Jermyn's African expeditions and with the Congolese legends of the white god and the ape-princess. The two particulars in question are these: the arms on the golden locket about the creature's neck were the Jermyn arms, and the jocose suggestion of M. Verhaeren about certain resemblance as connected with the shrivelled face applied with vivid, ghastly, and unnatural horror to none other than the sensitive Arthur Jermyn, great-great-great-grandson of Sir Wade Jermyn and an unknown wife. Members of the Royal Anthropological Institute burned the thing and threw the locket into a well, and some of them do not admit that Arthur Jermyn ever existed.

SPIRIT ISLAND

Captain Henry Toke Munn

I have told this story to only a few people, and my attempt to get a hearing before the Natural History authorities, both in New York and in London, completely failed, the secretaries treating me in pretty much the same manner. 'Oh yes,' they said indulgently, looking at my card, 'that's all right. We have heard about it, and we'll take the matter up sometime. But don't call again; wait till we write you.' Then they rang, and one of the attendants was told to show me round, if I cared to see the place, and put me on the way to where I was staying. Of course, they thought I was a crank.

I publish the narrative, therefore, rather reluctantly, accepting the fact that it will not be believed, but with a hope that it may inspire some credulous and courageous naturalist, with a taste for adventure, to visit Spirit Island, and return with a live or a dead specimen of what I saw there. If he can do this, his name will go down in history, and the museums—and the circuses—of the world will grovel at his feet for its possession. But he needn't ask me to accompany him.

In 1914 I was sent to the Arctic by my employers (a London firm well known in the mining world) to investigate certain localities for alluvial gold, and others for tin ore. In 1914-15 I wintered at Ponds Inlet, the north-east end of Baffin Land—lat. 72.48° N., long. 76.10° W. I made the investigations according to my instructions, and in August 1915 returned to the depot to await the arrival of my ship. By 15th October no ship had appeared, and I knew I was in for another winter. I had with me a Scottish lad to look after

306

the depot in my absence—for the Eskimo will steal if no white man is about, and we were not short of supplies.

In the event of the non-arrival of my ship, and a second winter being enforced, I had been asked to try to investigate a certain local-ity on the north coast of a large island, known as Prince of Wales Land, about five hundred miles west of my depot. This island lies at the southwest end of Barrow Strait, and between Peel Sound and Franklin Strait to the east and M'Clintock Channel and M'Clure Strait to the west. It can be seen on any Arctic map.

I set out from the depot in February, with seven natives and three dog-sleds, leaving orders for the ship to come for me to Leopold Island in Lancaster Sound if I did not return before the ice broke up. My party were Panne-lou, my head man, who drove my sled with ten dogs; Akko-molee, who had his own sled and team of nine dogs; and Now-yea, who also had his own sled and eleven dogs, four of which were only three-quarter-grown puppies. Each man had his wife, without whom no native will make a prolonged journey, and Akko-molee had the only child in the party, a lad of about eleven years old, named Kyak-jua.

A word as to my natives. Panne-lou was a steady, reliable fel-low, a good seal-hunter and dog-driver. His wife, Sal-pinna, was a disagreeable, cross-grained—and cross-eyed—woman, but capable and a good worker. Akko-molee was taken mainly because he was a native of Admiralty Inlet, two hundred miles west of my depot, and had hunted bear on the North Somerset coast. He was only moderately useful, and very inclined to sulk on any provocation. His boy, Kyak-jua, was a capital little fellow, the life of our party, full of energy, and a great favorite with all of us. I had given him a .22 rifle, and he was constantly getting me ptarmigan and Arctic hares with it when we were on the land. His mother, Anno-rito, was a quiet, pleasant woman, and entirely devoted to her boy.

Now-yea, my third native, was an active merry little man, will-ing and tireless, but irresponsible and very excitable. His number two wife (he had a couple), In-noya, was the best woman, and even-tually proved to be the best man, in the party. I shall have more to say about her later on. Now-yea had left his number one wife and four children, all of whom were hers, at my depot, and I had agreed to provide for them till our return.

The pay, arranged before starting, consisted of tobacco, sugar, tea, and biscuit for the trip—or as long as our supplies lasted and to each man, on our return to the depot, a new rifle, ammunition, a box (twenty-two pounds) of tobacco, a barrel of biscuit, some tea, coffee, and molasses, and a spy-glass, or some equivalent if they already had one; also some oddments, such as cooking-utensils, day-clocks, needles, braid, scented soap, &c., for the women, and ten pounds of tobacco to each one. These were regarded as high wages by the other natives, of whom I could have had my pick, but they were fully earned, and many extras I threw in, as the sequel will show.

My outfit—besides the supplies already mentioned—consisted of twenty pounds of dynamite, some caps and fuse, also one of these new, very small, 'Ubique' batteries, six short drills, and a two and a half pound hammer. We had a rifle per man, and one spare one—all single shot .303 carbines, except mine, which was an ordinary English service magazine-rifle; plenty of ammunition; a complete sailing-gear for each man, and two spare harpoons and lances; a hand-axe for each sled; native lamps for cooking and heating, and cooking-utensils. We had *ogjuke* (bearded seal) skins, for boot-soles later on, and seal-skins and deer-skin legs for cold-weather foot-wear, plenty of dressed deer-skin for stockings and socks, deer-skin blankets and heavy winter-killed hides to sleep on. We all had new deer-skin clothes, and expected to get young seal 'white coats' for wear on the return journey, when the others would be too warm.

My medicines were a flask of brandy, some tabloid drugs and antiseptics, a few bandages, and some surgical needles and thread. My personal luxury was a few dozen of the excellent 'Cambridge' soup-powders. I took a small kayak (skin canoe) as far as Leopold Island for sealing later, if we had to wait there, and also a tent.

One item of my outfit, a small Kodak camera, I was unfortunate enough to smash hopelessly a few days before starting. I shall for ever regret this disaster—for such it proved to be—and the irremediable loss it occasioned me.

This is not a story of Arctic travel, so I will omit the details of the journey. My route lay through Navy Board Inlet, and thence west along Lancaster Sound to Prince Regent Inlet, crossing to Leopold Island, and over the North Somerset Land—which is a flat tableland in from the coast—to Peel Sound and Prince of Wales Land. We had to make about six hundred and twenty-five miles of travelling, though, as I have said, it was only five hundred miles as the crow flies, and, of course, we had to depend on sea and land animals for ourselves and our dogs to live on, and for blubber for light, cooking, and warmth. Such journeys are made every winter by some of the Eskimo, either when visiting other parties or on hunting-trips, and are by no means unusual. The main, indeed the indispensable, thing being to find seals, halts of a day or two are made for the purpose.

Now, I want to emphasize the fact that Prince of Wales Land is by no means what literary people call a *terra incognita*, at least so far as the coast-line is concerned. Parry discovered it a hundred years ago, and Roald Amundsen sailed his famous little ship the Gjoa down Peel Sound and Franklin Strait when he made the North-West Passage.

No natives have been found on North Somerset or on Prince of Wales Land, though hunting-parties visit North Somerset occasionally.

I had not told my destination to the natives beyond North Somerset, and when we arrived at Leopold Island, and I unfolded my plans in the igloo that night, there was great consternation. We should starve; the ice would go out and leave us stranded there; and, lastly—here was the real hitch—it was a 'bad' country.

"Why bad," I asked, "when you say none of you have been there?"

There was a pause before Panne-lou said reluctantly, "It is full of *Torn-ga* [bad spirits]; we are afraid of them."

It took me half the night, talking and cajoling, before I overcame this absurd objection. Finally they consented to go on, but stipulated that we should travel close to the shore at Prince of Wales Land, to which I, of course, willingly agreed.

A small building, once full of stores, stands on Leopold Island. Naturally, it had been completely looted by the natives, but it served excellently to store our kayak and tent in, out of the weather.

I will relate one incident of the journey, as it shows the stuff one member of our party was made of. The day after we left Leopold Island we camped on the tableland of North Somerset, and I decided to stay a day there, and try for some deer, both as a change from seal-meat, of which we were all tired, and also to provide a 'cache,' or store of meat against our return.

I sent the three men off with all the dogs early in the morning; not feeling very well, I remained at the igloo. I had taken my rifle to pieces to clean it, and had all the parts in my lap, when I heard a cry outside, and Sal-pinna said, "Quick! He says a bear." My rifle was, for the moment, useless, so I plunged out of the igloo to get the spare rifle, which was always in In-noya's care in the other igloo. Outside I saw little Kyak-jua, about a hundred yards away, running for his life towards the igloos with a very large bear within fifteen or twenty paces of him. In-noya was out of the igloo, with the rifle, running towards them. I did not think the boy had a chance, for he was directly between the rifle and the bear, and one blow of those formidable paws would have brained him, but suddenly In-noya called sharply, *"Tella-peea-nin; tella-peea-nin"* ("To the right; to the right"). The boy, instantly divining he was in the line of fire, doubled to the right like a hare. A shot rang out, and the bear roared with pain, then turned and savagely bit his hindquarter, which had been hit. The next instant he was charging full tilt at In-noya. She had dropped on one knee to shoot, and, without moving, coolly levelled her rifle again. So close was the bear when she shot, and laid him dead with a bullet in his brain, that as she sprang on one side the impetus of his charge carried him half his length over where she had knelt; the record was written plainly on the snow.

I asked In-noya later why she did not fire sooner. "I had only taken two cartridges, when I ran out of the igloo," she said indifferently, "and I had to make sure of him." It was as fine an exhibition of coolness and steady nerve as I have ever seen.

We reached my objective on 25th March, crossing Peel Sound from North Somerset in one day's travel of about forty-five miles. We kept very close to the Prince of Wales Land shore, and I noticed we always built our igloos now on the land, even if suitable snow was not so handy as on the ice, though we often had to negotiate some rough ground-ice before getting to shore.

A very disastrous mishap occurred the day after we arrived. Seven of our dogs, divided amongst the three teams, ate something poisonous they found along the shore, and died the same night; three more were very bad, but recovered. I cannot imagine what an Eskimo dog could find to poison him in his own country, but this was certainly the cause of death. The natives, of course, blamed the *Torn-ga*, and were greatly disturbed.

By 27th March I had seen all I needed to. The reported tin-vein was a vein of iron pyrite ore. I do not know who started this yarn about tin, but the description and locality of the vein agreed so closely with the data given me that I have always concluded the information was found in one of the private logs of the old Arctic voyagers, perhaps one of Parry's or Ross's crews.

Seals had been very hard to find since we crossed Peel Sound, and our dogs were getting hungry, so, after wasting the 28th looking for seals, which refused to come to the breathing-holes we found, we started the return journey on the 29th, and reached the north-east end of Prince of Wales Land on the 31st, only getting one small seal in that time.

About fifteen miles north of Prince of Wales Land lies a large island, and Panne-lou volunteered the information that the Eskimo name of it was 'Spirit Island'; but he could not, or would not, tell me anything more, the subject being strictly taboo by him, and also by the others.

When we left the next morning early, a south-east breeze was blowing up Peel Sound, and it looked as if it would be a fine day for the crossing. We had made only about half-way over when one of those sudden Arctic storms swept down on us, shutting out all sight of land at once. The natives had a discussion whether to go ahead or return, and decided to push on. Panne-lou complained he was feeling ill, and was on the sled all day. Soon after the storm broke, the wind must suddenly have changed, for by five o'clock no land came in sight, and the storm was increasing in violence every minute. Panne-lou became very ill, so there was no alternative but to camp where we were.

Next morning it was blowing a blizzard, and Panne-lou was delirious and in a high fever. Even if it had been fit weather, it would have killed him to move him.

This part of the Arctic lies north of the Magnetic Pole, and the compass variation is nearly one hundred degrees; it is so sluggish and unreliable that it is quite useless for making a course in thick weather. We did not know, therefore, if we were north or south of our course.

That night—1st April—the first two dogs disappeared. My log says: "At 11 P.M. dogs suddenly started howling; thought it was a bear, but dogs stampeded to igloo door much afraid. Suddenly one gave a queer stifled yap, and about same time door broke and dogs tumbled pell-mell into igloo..." The 'door' is a block of snow set up on the inside of the igloo. Now-yea and In-noya were sleeping in my igloo, to help nurse Panne-lou—for he had to be constantly watched—and as soon as the row started Now-yea, at In-noya's instigation, jumped up, and throwing his *kouletang* (deer-skin jumper) on the floor of the igloo from the snow sleeping-bench, stood on it naked—Eskimo always turn in thus—and held the snow 'door' till it broke in his hands, letting the dogs in.

Meantime I had slipped on my *kouletang* and some deer-skin stockings, and, as soon as the door was clear of dogs, cautiously crawled out with my rifle, expecting to find an unusually bold and hungry bear at our 'store-house,' a small snow-house built against the side of the igloo, containing the meat, blubber, harness, &c., which the dogs might damage or eat. As a rule rifles are kept outside, to prevent the frost coming out of them; but the natives insisted that they must all be taken inside that night.

I saw or heard nothing; it was a very dark night, and the drifting snow was blinding, stinging the eyes like sand. I crawled back, half-frozen, and we put up another snow door. The other igloo, fifteen or twenty yards away, had the same experience, so there must have been two visitors, as we each lost a dog at the same time.

The blizzard lasted three days, and though we built porches for the dogs in front of igloo doors and shut them in, we lost two dogs each night in the same mysterious manner. The 'doors' were always broken inwards, and a dog quickly and neatly snatched away. Obviously no bear was doing this, for his methods would have been more clumsy.

On the third night I made a hole in the igloo over the 'door,' and as soon as the dogs yelped put my rifle through and fired three or four shots into the porch. Next morning Akko-molee's dog was gone, but outside our porch our dog lay dead. His neck was broken and his throat torn out.

By this time the natives were completely demoralised, with the exception of In-noya. Now-yea sat shivering, as if with ague, the whole night, and Sal-pinna was little better. She had trodden on a knife-blade in the igloo, and cut her foot so badly that I had to put seven stitches in it. In Akko-molee's igloo they remained in their blankets all the time, and he would hardly answer me when I called to him.

Meanwhile Panne-lou improved but little, and I kept him alive on a few spoonfuls of brandy-and-water every hour. On the third day the fever had abated, but he was still wandering and semi-conscious.

There was good excuse for the natives. An igloo is not the slightest protection against an attack; an arrow or a lance would go through it like paper. It was a trying job, therefore, to sit inside expecting something—one could not tell what—to happen. For the natives, who believed implicitly it was the *Torn-ga*, it was worse than for me. In-noya, however, never lost her self-control, and she and I fed and watched Panne-lou in turn.

On the morning of the fourth day—3rd April—the storm had blown itself out, but there was a dense fog, and we could not see more than a hundred yards or so. The natives would have harnessed the dogs and left at once, in spite of my urging that it would certainly kill Panne-lou to do so, but until it cleared they did not know which way to go, for till we saw some land, or even the stars to steer by, we were completely lost.

Akko-molee said the fog showed there was open water not far away, and vaguely opined it was a bad sign. A pressure-ridge was behind the igloos; in fact, it was at this we found snow suitable for building. I asked Akko-molee to walk in one direction along it for a short distance with a sealing-dog to try to find a breathing-hole, as we were completely out of feed, and the poor brutes were starving. I would walk down the pressure-ridge in the opposite direction for the same purpose. I arranged we should both return the moment the fog cleared. Now-yea, who was much too shaky to go away alone, was to remain at the igloo on guard.

Akko-molee demurred at first, but finally consented to go, adding, "Only a very little way, though." In-noya looked after Panne-lou, who was now sleeping quietly and in a profuse perspiration. I made some soup for him, gave her a few instructions, then left with my sealing-gear and rifle, leading a dog.

It was nine o'clock in the morning. I walked. along the pressure-ridge for eight or ten minutes, when, to my surprise, I came to open water. The tide ran strongly in Barrow Strait, I knew, and the gale must have opened the ice up. We had, therefore, got far to the north of our course to reach the floe-edge, as the ice fast to the land is called. The water seemed to be of some extent, but the fog made it impossible to see how large it was. As the floe-edge is generally very irregular, deep bights forming in it where the moving pack exercises pressure, it would be very dangerous to move before we saw where we were.

It was a mere chance that we had not driven into the water or on to the moving ice in the blizzard. Seeing a seal in the water a short distance from the pressure-ridge, I let the dog go, as I did not need him, and he ran back to the igloo; I then sat down and waited for the seal to appear. Presently I shot one, but found the tide was running away from the floe, and I lost him, so I waited till it turned, which it did in about three hours. I then shot two seals; though I had to wait another hour before they came in to the floe. By this time a fairly strong tide was running under it.

As I was tying the seals together to drag them back to the ig-loo, I caught through the fog, in the direction of the pressure-ridge, a glimpse of a man walking down to the water's edge. It was only an uncertain impression, for the fog shut him out immediately. I rather wondered why Akko-molee had followed me, but remem-bering I had sent the dog back, supposed that had to do with it.

When I arrived at the pressure-ridge, I saw nothing of Akko-molee, but leading down to the water were large drops of blood, and at the floe-edge lay a little deer-skin mitten; it could only have been Kyak-jua's. The snow was packed as hard as a pavement by the gale, so it was no use to look for tracks on it, but right at the water's edge, where it was softer and wet, was an odd-looking track, rather as if it had been made by some gigantic bird with webbed feet. The claw-marks did not show, as the toes overlapped the edge of the ice.

What did the blood mean? Flow came little Kyak-jua's mitten to be there? I felt sick at heart as I quickly thought it over. A trag-edy had happened, I was sure. I ran back to where I had left the seals, about sixty yards from the water's edge; hastily buried one in the snow to keep it thawed, cutting a hole with my sheath-knife for the purpose; threw the other on my shoulder—they were both small seals—and ran towards the igloo. The tell-tale drops of blood stopped about three hundred yards from the floe-edge.

At the igloo I found Now-yea pacing back and forth before the door, shouting 'spirit-talk,' and nearly crazy; Anno-rito, the boy's mother, inside unconscious; and In-noya gray-faced and crying quietly, but faithfully tending Panne-lou as I had told her. My ar-rival upset her for a moment, however, as she cried out, "I thought you had gone too." I shut up Now-yea by cuffing him, and sent him into the igloo, where he sat and shivered.

In-noya told me the story succinctly. Kyak-jua had left his mother's igloo to come and see In-noya, for they were great friends. Now-yea as inside, warming himself, at the time; by-and-by Anno-rito called out, and In-noya replied the boy was not there. The poor mother rushed out shrieking for the boy, and on entering our ig-loo fell unconscious. In-noya did not dare to leave Panne-lou, who was very restless—Sal-pinna was useless—but she made Now-yea go out and look about. The tears streamed down her face, for she loved the little lad dearly. "It is no good to look," she sobbed; "the *Torn-ga* have taken him." Akko-molee's dog had returned, and In-noya said she feared for poor little Kyak-jua's father. "I am going to fetch Akko-molee," I declared; "he is not far away."

As I left the igloo I realised what had happened. Something had been lying hidden behind the pressure-ridge, and had crept close to the igloo. It had swiftly and silently seized Kyak-jua, and as swiftly and silently departed. The dogs, all asleep inside the porch, had given no alarm, the lad himself not made a sound. What manner of beast was this to do such a daring deed? It explained those drops of blood near the water. I at least, knew where the boy had gone, and a fierce anger surged over me when I thought of his merry face, and the happy smile with which he would bring me a ptarmigan, saying, "For you, *kabloona* [white man]."

I thought of all this as I ran along the pressure-ridge through the fog, when suddenly I nearly fell over Akko-molee's body. He was lying on his face, dead, with a hole in the back of his skull, from which the brain was oosing. He had evidently been sitting at a seal-hole, and his assailant had crept up behind him. His right sleeve was torn open, and the artery under the arm had been ripped up, *but there was no blood on the snow from it.*

I felt sick when I realised what this ghoulish murderer had done; he had sucked the blood from the artery till it was dry. The sealing-spear, harpoon, seal-line, and lance were gone, but the rifle rested against a block of snow where Akko-molee had placed it. I left him lying there on the snow; my business was with the living.

I returned to the igloo, to find Anno-rito had been persuaded by In-noya to turn in under her blanket, which she had done, native fashion, with nothing on. She looked up when I took off my mitts and *kouletang*, and said dully, "Akko-molee is dead. I have seen him. Is it not so?"

Then I did a fool thing, but I was overstrung and rattled. I nodded "Yes," and said, "He is dead." There was a silence while you might have counted ten; then, without any warning, Anno-rito sprang up, dived under the low exit of the igloo, and fled shriek-ing, *"Oo-wonga ky-it; oo-wonga ky-it"* ("I come; I come").

I was into my *kouletang* in a few seconds, grabbed my rifle (without which I would not have gone ten yards), and was after her, but, stripped naked as she was, she could keep her lead. She ran along the pressure-ridge, where I had gone in the morning, and I shouted when I realised a few minutes would take her to the water's edge. I was near enough to see her fling up her arms and spring into the water, and her despairing cry, *"Oo-wonga ky-it,"* was borne faintly back to me through the fog. Unhappy Anno-rito had joined her boy and her man.

It was now about four o'clock, and, live or die, Panne-lou must be moved in the morning. I would have left at once, but it was im-possible to travel in the fog after dark. If it did not lift, I would try a compass course, uncertain as it was, in the morning, or steer by the breeze, if there was one, away from the open water. If the fog lifted, I would steer by the stars that night.

Meantime the dogs might as well be fed, and, with this in my mind, I pulled out the seal I had left in the snow. The fog was for a moment thinner than it had been, and I had just done this when I saw another seal in the water on the far side of the pressure-ridge. Running to the floe edge, I sat down beside an up-ended piece of ice about ten yards from the water to wait for him to come up again. After a few minutes I leaned forward to look along the floe-edge, peering round the piece of ice. About sixty or seventy yard from me, standing on the ice, close to the water and looking intently at the seal lying near the pressure-ridge, I saw a man—or, rather, a two-footed beast in a man's shape.

He was but that moment out of the water, for it was dripping off him, and even as I looked his body began to turn white, as if the drops had been frozen on him in glistening little nodules. His head was thrown back and he was sniffing the air, as if using his scenting-powers. Suddenly he ran—rather clumsily, I thought, but swiftly and with unusually long strides—towards the dead seal. My brain started working again, and I knew I had him; I was between him and the water.

As he stopped and picked up the seal, throwing it over his shoulder very easily, I sprang out from behind the slab of ice, and he saw me. Without a second's hesitation, and before the seal fell from his shoulder on to the ice with a thud, he was running swiftly and silently at me, a short throwing-lance poised in his right hand. I covered him without haste, and pulled the trigger, but the cartridge missed fire. I jerked in another cartridge, and as I threw my rifle to my shoulder his arm shot forward like a piston-stroke, and I dropped quickly on one knee. As I did so, the hood of my *kouletang* was thrown back from my head and—it seemed to me at the same instant—I fired.

I suppose the lance, which had struck my hood, threw my aim off, for the shot went high, and broke my assailant's left shoulder, causing him to drop a second lance he held in his hand. But it did not stop him, and before I could jerk in another cartridge he was on me. Dodging the muzzle of my rifle, he seized my left arm above the elbow with incredible strength, for I felt the nails or claws sink deeply into my flesh through my thick deer-skin clothes. At the same time he pulled me towards him and tried to get at my throat with his teeth. I seized his neck with my free hand, and for some seconds we swayed back and forward thus, the blood from his wound drenching me. Flecks of bloody foam ran down from his mouth, and as we tussled he made a snarling growl, as a dog does when at grips with his foe. This was the only sound I heard from him.

We were unpleasantly near the water, so I bent my energies on working back from it, and was able to make some yards farther in on the ice. I soon found it quite beyond my strength to squeeze his windpipe and choke him, the neck being very strong and thick; and although I had the advantage of at least five inches in height, and am over the average of my size in strength, it was all I could do to hold him off me. Had his other arm been whole, he would have torn my throat out with his claws.

We twisted and turned, struggling desperately, when suddenly he relinquished his grasp of my left arm, I suppose for a hold at my throat. As I felt him do so, I pushed him violently away and sprang back. He came at me again like a wildcat, snarling savagely; but I was readier now, and beating down his outstretched hand with my left fist, I landed him on the point of the jaw with all the weight and strength I could put into an upper-cut. It lifted him clean off his feet, and he fell backwards. As he dazedly and unsteadily recovered his feet again, I snatched up the lance he had dropped—for we had reached the place in our struggle—and rushing on him, drove it with both hands and all my might at his heart. He fell dead at my feet.

For a few minutes I sat down, feeling sick and giddy. I was blood from head to foot, and I saw for the first time some of it was my own, for my arm was bleeding freely enough for it to run down inside my sleeve over my hand. The indescribable horror of the Thing's appearance, the smell of his breath, and the ferocity and courage of his attack, badly wounded as he was, all affected me strongly. More and more I realised that I could have done nothing against him had he been unwounded.

Pulling myself together, I turned the *Torn-ga* over—so I call him, from this date, in my log, and the name will serve. Sticking out under his left shoulder-blade was a harpoon-head, lashed to the point of an ivory lance with sinew. I set my foot on the body and drew the lance out at his back, and, after cleaning it in the snow, examined it. The harpoon-head was Akko-molee's! I knew it instantly, for I had seen him filing it a few days before. I felt better, somehow, when I had seen this, and turned to examine more fully the body of my grim foe.

He was perhaps an inch over five feet in height, and was covered, except the palms of his hands and the soles of his feet, with short, fine seal-hair of a grayish-brown colour. The eyes were enormous, with no eyelashes, very like a seal's, the hips tremendously developed, and the legs disproportionately long; the instep was very broad and flat, and both the toes and the fingers very long, webbed, and ending in thick nails like claws. It struck me he would have been a truly formidable antagonist in the water. The face was hideous; it had a wide receding jaw, with very prominent eyebrows overhanging the huge eyes, a low forehead, and small furry ears. I noticed, too, the teeth were sharp, the dog-teeth much developed, and the front-teeth of the lower jaw noticeably longer than the others. He had died with his lips drawn back in a savage snarl. Jets of very dark blood were flowing from his breast. The limbs and the body had a smooth roundness that could mean only one thing, but to satisfy myself I drew my knife and cut a gash in the thigh. As I expected, there was over an inch of blubber under the skin, exactly as a seal has.

Behind where I had knelt and fired, an ivory lance was sticking deeply in the hard snow. I looked at my hood—the lance had torn the top off it.

Acting on some impulse, I dragged the body to the floe-edge, and shot it into the water. It floated buoyantly, but the strong tide soon swept it out of sight under the ice; and as its blood-smeared, snarling face disappeared, I thought of little Kyak-jua, and felt glad that some, at least, of the account was paid.

Throwing the seal on my shoulder, I returned to the igloo. There was no one now to take counsel with but In-noya, for the other two only sat huddled up and moaning. Calling her outside, I assured her I was not hurt—she was horrified at the mess I was in—and related what I had done, and how I planned to leave the moment the fog permitted.

These Eskimo know more about this mystery than they will tell, because In-noya shook her head, saying, "Many will come to-night and kill us, *kabloona*." She told me she had put my revolver beside her, adding very quietly she wanted it to shoot Panne-lou and herself with if the *Torn-ga* broke into the igloo. "They suck your blood when you are alive," she said calmly. I had not mentioned what I had seen on Akko-molee's body. How did she know this was their ghoulish habit?

I patted the plucky girl on the back, and told her we should come through the night all right as I had a plan. Fortunately, there was a spare *kouletang* in my kit-bag. Before I went inside the igloo I took off my blood-soaked garment and threw it away behind the pressure-ridge, explaining to the others that the blood on my foot-gear and deer-skin outer trousers was from the seal. These garments I took off, and started Sal-pinna thawing and cleaning them. My arm pained me, and was still bleeding. Examining it in the unoccupied igloo, I found five claw-like incisions, which had cut deeply into the flesh. I washed them with antiseptic, and In-noya bound them up.

I then shook up Now-yea, made him come out and feed the two seals—saving a meal for ourselves—to the dogs, and carefully ice the sledrunners and get all the harness ready. The dogs would need five or six hours after feeding, but I hoped that by midnight we should have the stars to steer by, and could make a start.

I thawed ten pounds of dynamite, wrapped it up in several pieces of deer-skin, and as soon as it was dusk laid it the full length of my wires along the pressure-ridge, making a track for the wires, and carefully covering it all over with snow. I brought the wires into the igloo through the wall, and connected them up with the battery. Then, shutting the dogs into the porch, I ran a reel of strong thread I happened to have with me round the igloo and porch about ten paces away, setting up blocks of snow some two and a half feet high, and driving into them bits of stick, to which I fastened the thread. As I was short of sticks, I used one of the two lances I had brought from the scene of the fight; the other I put away in a dun-nage-bag. Midway between each of the blocks, I ran pieces of thread fastened to the thread circling us, and led them into the igloo through paper tubes, to keep them from freezing to the wall. I then pulled them gently taut, and fastened them to small strips of wood, so that when they were struck into the igloo wall they were bent by the pull of the line; there were five of them. In-noya helped me deftly and intelligently, asking no questions, except what I wanted done. When back in the igloo, I insisted on their finishing the seal meal, and we made a brew of strong tea. Panne-lou was now conscious and free from fever, but utterly prostrated.

It was a nerve-racking watch. I am not sure if I would come through another like it. I had seen now what we were waiting for, and if—as In-noya said they would—many came, if indeed only a few attacked us, I knew now we should have no chance at all, penned up inside the igloo. Yet we should be worse off freezing outside in the gray fog and darkness. I had seen their swiftness and savage determination. How many could we account for before the end came?

Suddenly I remembered there would be a young moon up about one o'clock, and I decided to start then and steer by it, if the weather was clear enough to locate it.

The hours dragged on till nearly midnight. Now-yea and Sal-pinna dozed fitfully, and awoke shivering. Panne-lou slept; In-noya sat beside him, gray-faced and self-possessed, occasionally trim-ming the native lamp, but with my revolver ever ready at her hand. We whispered once or twice, and listened, straining our ears for some sound outside, till every minute seemed an hour, watching the little bent sticks, and waiting.

I kept my hand on the battery-handle, and my rifle across my knees. Suddenly a stick straightened with a faint click, and I nod-ded to In-noya, who touched the other two natives. I lifted the handle and pressed it down smartly. The roar of the explosion tore the silence of the night. The ice shook, threatening to demolish the igloo, and snow fell down on us inside. The dogs yelped with fear once or twice; then came silence. Presently an inarticulate, eerie, wailing cry rang out, distinct and very high-pitched; then silence once more, and we listened, listened. And then I knew how it is men go mad with the strain of waiting for some unseen danger to strike them.

At one o'clock we had some more tea, and I crept outside to see the weather. The fog was thinning fast, and I could see the young moon faintly, low down towards the open water. I knew it rose in the north-east, and gave the word to hitch up the dogs and start. It seemed certain I was giving Panne-lou his death-sentence, but there was probably a more terrible death for him, and all of us, if we delayed. Now-yea worked feverishly; the dogs were divided between two sleds; Panne-lou was rolled like a mummy in deer-skin blankets and lashed on; and we started.

With a match I hastily examined the snow outside the circle of thread, where I had purposely scraped it soft, and could see that only one track had been made. The lance to which the thread had been fastened was gone. The last thing I took out of the igloo was a deer-skin parcel containing the rest of the dynamite, thawed and ready for the fuse and cap, and the six drill-steels and the hammer-head. I put the dynamite between Panne-lou's blankets to keep it thawed. The fuse was marked in half-minutes. Panne-lou knew everything we were doing, and whispered to me, "The land, *kabloona*; get the land. *Torn-ga* will not come there."

Now-yea drove one sled with Sal-pinna on it. She walked with great pain, the cut on her foot being a deep one. Till daylight I led with the other sled, which In-noya drove. Now-yea had nine and I had eight dogs, but three on my sled were very weak from the poison they had eaten a few days before, and four of Now-yea's were puppies. In-noya handled the mixed team of dogs with wonderful skill.

By three o'clock it was light, and at half-past four the blessed sun rose, dispersing the last of the fog—never did I welcome him more—and there to the south-east of us was the bold coast-line of North Somerset, some twenty-five miles or so away. Behind us lay the north-east end of Spirit Island, and near it, extending far to the eastward, a curtain of mist rose in the still, cold air from the floe-edge, a dark patch of water-sky behind it denoting a large hole of water. Our igloos were not visible, but they must have been very close to the north-eastern end of Spirit Island.

With the bright morning sun shining in our faces; our hearts rose to cheerfulness, and the horrors of a few hours before seemed like some bad dream, till I thought of merry little Kyak-jua, and how I had left his father lying out there on the ice. That was no dream, but a grim reality.

I told Now-yea to take the lead, warning him I would shoot him if he did not stick to his sled, but tried to run away. In-noya also shouted out the message to him, and added on her own account, "And you know the *kabloona* does not often miss." We walked and trotted alongside the sleds, not sparing the whip. In-noya handled it and its twenty-seven-foot lash as skilfully as any native I have ever seen.

Soon after sunrise we came to rather rough ice, which, though not bad enough to delay us seriously, quickly took the ice-shoeing off the runners of the sleds, so that they pulled heavily. The walking was hard and good, and by skilful handling the sleds were steered clear of any large rough hummocks; but this all helped to retard our progress.

By half-past six we were apparently fifteen or sixteen miles from the land and making a good five miles an hour, but some of our dogs were flagging, and presently one lay down, and had to be taken out of the team. Soon after this two of Now-yea's puppies were turned loose, but they followed on, and eventually made the land, unlike our dog, who did not rise again.

At seven o'clock I climbed a piece of ice and had a look back with the telescope. I speedily made out a number of black dots coming in an irregular line along our track; they were about five or six miles away. I ran after the sled and told In-noya quietly—it was no use frightening the others yet. She only glanced at the revolver lying in its case under the lashing, and applied herself to the sled and team. She was the bravest person (man or woman) I have ever met. We halted for two or three minutes to clear the traces, and while this was being done I took the dynamite parcel out, rolled it and the drill-steels and hammer-head into one parcel with deer-skin, and adjusted the cap and fuse, slipping it all under the lashing, ready instantly to be taken out.

As we drew nearer the land I saw the cliffs ran sheerly down to the ice, and thought for a minute or two we were going to be trapped, for the only man who had known the coast was dead—Akko-molee. After a while, however, I picked up a little bay with my telescope, perhaps three-quarters of a mile wide and rather deeper, from the head of which the land sloped steeply back, so I ran forward and pointed out to Now-yea where to steer for. He seemed to have his nerves under better control now, for he answered "All right" quite cheerfully. Perhaps he thought he could make a race for it, and reach the land alone, if the pinch came, though I may be doing him an injustice. The fact that the natives had dared to come to this region at all, knowing what they did, lent some colour to their reiterated assertion that we should be safe on the land. My reason rebelled, nevertheless, at the seeming absurdity of the idea. If our pursuers could travel on the snow of the ice, of course they could do the same on the land. Yet, somehow, among them the natives had imbued me with a quite unreasonable but firm faith in our salvation could we win *terra firma*.

At half-past eight the *Torn-ga* were about a mile away, and coming up on us fast. They were spread in an irregular line extending across our track,: but I was glad to see a number of them were straggling badly. The pace was telling on them, for we must have had a long start. There seemed to be at least a hundred of them.

Presently we came to a small pressure-ridge, and as soon as we had passed it I took the time very carefully; to when the first of our pursuers appeared on our side, it was exactly six and a half minutes. I cut the fuse and lighted it, and laid the smoking parcel down on the ice, running on with my watch in my hand. Ten seconds or so before the charge was due to explode, I stopped and looked back with the telescope. The nearest *Torn-ga* had reached the parcel and were standing round it, more coming up every second. Those on the flanks had also stopped, and they all seemed to be waiting for one of their number, as they were looking back. Even as I took this scene in, a *Torn-ga*, fully a head taller than the rest, burst through the knot standing irresolutely about, and gesticulated violently in our direction. As he did so the charge exploded.

When the snow and smoke cleared, I counted six bodies prone on the snow, and saw several more limping away or sitting down, evidently badly hurt. I turned and raced after the sled.

When I told In-noya what I had seen, she pressed her lips grimly together, saying, "It pays a little of the debt for Kyak-jua and Akko-molee." I inquired if she had looked at Panne-lou lately. I had not thought about him for some time, and it occurred to me that, if he were dead, we would cut the lashings and leave him. She nodded, saying, "He sleeps," then went to urging the dogs forward. I noticed the revolver was now taken out of its case and ready for instant action. We pushed steadily on for some time, improving our pace, as the dogs began to smell the land, and when next I looked back I saw about twenty of the *Torn-ga* five hundred yards or so in advance of the rest.

The dynamite had answered its purpose, and if it came to a fight close in on the land, I at first hoped we could handle these, for I knew I could depend on In-noya. But they drew up on us so steadily I saw this hope was vain, and, with a sinking feeling at my heart, thought of the savage determination the day before of only one of them—and he badly wounded.

Something must be done, however, and thinking it rapidly over, I decided to let the sled go on, and make a stand at a suitable hummock, with my magazine-rifle and the revolver, when they were about three hundred yards away. It sounds self-sacrificing, and all that sort of nonsense, but as a matter of fact it was only plain common-sense; it would be absurd to lose the advantage the firearms gave me by letting them get to close quarters before turning at bay. I should not have mentioned it, however, but for the part In-noya played. I told her my intention, whereon she said, "Yes, *kabloona*, but we will take all the rifles, and I will stay and reload for you. The dogs see the land now, and will not stop." I refused to allow this; but she was quietly obstinate, pointing out that she could do some shooting on her own account, and then reload my rifle while I used the others.

She took the revolver up and put the cord over her head, saying calmly, 'It is settled. Do not speak any more about it. I will take two rifles off the sled when you say the word; do you take the others and the cartridge-bag.' Suddenly she cried quickly, "Where is the thing which smokes [the fuse]? It will delay them a little." Fool! I had not thought of it. In half-a-minute I had wrapped the rest of the coil in deer-skin, lighted it at both ends to make more smoke—there was plenty of it—and laid it on the snow. It was quite harmless, but the bluff might go.

The nearest *Torn-ga* were about four hundred yards away from us, and when they saw the smoking parcel they halted a few seconds, and then made a wide detour on either side of it, allowing us to increase our lead considerably. About this time another of our dogs staggered and fell, but In-noya had been watching him, and whipping a knife from the sled, severed his trace without stopping the others.

Then Now-yea, who was about one hundred yards ahead, called out something, and In-noya said, "He says he can see the snow in the bay has been flooded—by the late spring-tide, of course—and it is all smooth ice." She cast a glance back. "We shall make the land, *kabloona*," she said quietly. "*Koya-nimik*" ("I am glad"). Glad! Blown as I was, I shouted for joy. "Hurrah! Hurrah, In-noya!" I said; but she only smiled back, and plied her skilful whip, and cheered on the weary dogs. We were running on either side of our sleds now, even lame Sal-pinna holding on to a lashing and limping gamely along.

I looked back, and could plainly see in the frosty air the smoking breath of the nearest *Torn-ga*, and got a glimpse of his savage face. He was obviously tired, and, I noticed, ran 'flat-footedly' and ungracefully, but with long jumping strides, which took him over the ground at a great pace. Some of his companions were lame.

When Now-yea reached the smooth ice he ran ahead of his dogs to encourage them—for a moment I thought he was deserting his sled—and they, knowing the land meant rest for them, broke into a tired gallop. Sal-pinna was able to ride on the sled.

Just before we reached the ice I took a snapshot at the crowd, and by a fluke hit one in the leg, and he sprawled over. The others did not stop or take the slightest notice of him, but came doggedly on. In-noya called on the team with voice and whip, and once on the smooth, almost 'glare' ice—save for a few frost-crystals which gave the dogs footing—they wearily galloped, and we could sit on the sled without slowing it down, so easily did it run.

We looked at each other; the hoods and breasts of our *kouletangs* were white with our frosted breath, and the perspiration was streaming off us. I was pretty well 'all in,' for I had not ridden on the sled since starting; In-noya, whom during the whole journey I saw on the sled only for a moment occasionally when looking at Panne-lou, seemed active and tireless yet.

She woke Panne-lou, and told him we should win the land, and the poor fellow's thin face lit up as he said, "That is good." I did not know till later how fully he realised our race from death—and what a death for him!

For the last mile over the smooth ice, which was also slippery going for our pursuers, we almost held our own, though at the ground-ice the nearest *Torn-ga* was not more than two hundred yards away. *Those behind him had stopped and were looking at us!* A wave of thankfulness swept over me, for I realised now the truth of the Eskimo's assertion: They would not come on the land.

We were too busy steadying and guiding the sled through the ground-ice to bother about the nearest *Torn-ga* then, but at the shore, as he still urged doggedly on, I took my rifle and turned. He was only fifty or sixty yards away, and I couldn't miss him. He pitched forward on his face—the same sort of savage, snarling face I had seen at the floe-edge—and lay still. As I live, his waiting companions turned, and trotted leisurely back the way we had come!

As soon as the panting, worn-out dogs had been urged over the shore and a few hundred yards up the rising ground, I stopped and looked back. Every *Torn-ga* in sight was lying prone. Those on the snow beyond the smooth ice were eating mouthfuls of it, as a dog does when thirsty in winter. A little cloud of steam rose in the air from their bodies. I called out, and both sleds stopped, the dogs flinging themselves down in utter exhaustion.

One more amazing incident occurred before we saw the last of the *Torn-ga*. As we started across the bay, a large bear came ambling round the southern point and headed for the opposite one. Instantly every *Torn-ga* was lying motionless, except that they raised their heads occasionally, and looked about as a seal does when out on the ice in spring for sleep. I could not have told the nearest of them from a seal without a telescope. A light land-breeze was quartering from the bear to the *Torn-ga*, and when he saw the—to him—welcome and, so early in the year, unusual sight, he evidently thought the supposed seals would soon wind him, so charged down at the nearest group, hoping to flurry one and catch him before he slipped down his hole through the ice.

Ten paces away from the bear the nearest *Torn-ga* sprang to his feet, and the next instant a dozen of them were at him, hurling their short ivory lances at his side, and leaping back with amazing activity. Each lance brought forth a roar of pain and anger. One of the *Torn-ga*, who slipped as he sprang away, came within reach of the bear's mighty paws, and was instantly killed by a blow which tore his head half off.

This did not check the others in the least, and in three minutes it was all over. One of them ripped the bear up from throat to tail with a knife, whether of flint, ivory, or steel I could not see, but the next second they were tearing the smoking flesh with their teeth and drinking the blood. I could plainly see with the telescope their fierce blood-stained faces, like a pack of human wolves; it was a sickening sight.

I might have made some long-range practice on them with the rifle, but, to tell the truth, I had had enough of them; I only wanted to get away. They did not take the least interest in our movements now, though they had chased us relentlessly for forty miles or so. I can offer no conjecture why, but they dared not come on the land. Repulsive travesties of human beings though they were, they possessed courage of a very high order; some mysterious law of their being ordained they must live and murder only on the salt sea.

Turning my attention to the sleds, I found In-noya giving Panne-lou some weak brandy-and-water we had placed in a flask in his blankets. She was self-possessed enough, but a few tears stole down her cheeks as she replaced the revolver in its case and fastened the strap. That she would have turned it on herself at the last, when all chance was gone, I have not the slightest doubt. Lion-hearted In-noya, may you get a mate more worthy of you, and some day be the mother of many children filled with your own heroic courage, and cool, resourceful mind; it will be a great thing for your tribe and race.

We pushed on up the rise of the tableland, travelled over it for an hour, built an igloo, and turned in. We were foodless, exhausted, and our eyes bloodshot and red-lidded for want of sleep—but we were safe.

My narrative has already extended in length far beyond my anticipation, and to detail our return is unnecessary. We found deer plentiful, nursed Panne-lou back to life, and reached Leopold Island on 15th April. I might have gone on to the depot, short as we were of dogs, but Sal-pinna's foot required constant dressing, for the stitches had all burst, and neither she nor, of course, Panne-lou could walk. My arm, too, had become badly swollen, and gave me some trouble, the slight wounds I received in the fight at the floe-edge festering and causing me a lot of pain. It was fortunate I had attended to them promptly, as they were undoubtedly very poisonous.

I therefore decided to wait at Leopold Island for my ship. The kayak—In-noya's suggestion, by-the-bye—was most useful, and we were not short of food during our nearly four months' detention there. Personally, I felt I had had enough of the floe-edge, and hunted deer on the mainland; but the natives were unafraid, asserting positively that nothing was ever seen of the *Torn-ga* east of North Somerset.

It was almost impossible to get the natives to talk about them at all, but during my stay at Leopold Island I dragged a little information out of Panne-lou.

The *Torn-ga* have been seen lying on the rocks off-shore, but never on the land. He said they bred on Spirit Island, which was 'their land,' but was very vague about it, and stated that no natives had ever come from there who had seen them ashore.

"Have any ever gone there?" I asked.

"*Ar-my*" ("I don't know"), he replied evasively, adding that they (the *Torn-ga*) were "all the same as seals, and lived in the water."

"Why don't they come here, or to Ponds Bay, if they live in the water?" I asked.

"I don't know," he replied. "No one knows about them but the Spirits of the Dead, and it is not good to talk about them at all, lest evil befall you."

This was all I could get out of him, and I found it just as unsatisfactory an explanation of the mystery as, no doubt, the reader will; but it is all I have to offer from the natives.

On 2nd August my ship hove in sight, and I heard that the Great War had been raging for a year. A few days later we were back at the depot. It was sad news I brought for the Eskimos gathered to welcome their friends home. I do not know if Panne-lou told them the true story. I mentioned it to no one, white man or Eskimo.

I have tried to write this narrative as plainly and as straight-forwardly as I could, always remembering it will be read by people most of whom are unfamiliar with Arctic conditions, and the mode of life and travel there. This must be my excuse for often being prolix. I might have added some more pages of details of my journey, but these had nothing to do with the main object—namely, making public the existence of a hitherto unheard and undreamt of animal in the Far North.

A scientific friend of mine returned me the MS. of this narrative with the following pithy comment: "Liven it up a bit; it's dull enough to be true." Had I the gift of imagination, and some literary skill, I have no doubt I could improve the story and 'liven it up a bit' with some touches of thrilling incidents to make it far more sensational and exciting—and far less truthful.

Later the same friend commenced to demonstrate to me the absurdity of the idea that the human organism could exist in the water as its habitat. I do not claim the *Torn-ga* are human, and I know nothing of their organism. Eons ago, before life existed on the land of this planet, it was, we now know, in full swing in its waters, and the lineal descendants of the animals of those unknown ages are the seals, walruses, and whales, which in countless numbers make their home in the icy waters of the Arctic Seas.

I once read in some magazine an account of a fossil skeleton found in Java which was neither ape nor man. Pithecanthropus, they called him. Why may not the seas, where life first began, have some yet undiscovered secrets of primeval life hidden in these lonely Arctic waters, teeming as they are with warm-blooded life? Why! ... Pah! what's the use? I am no scientist. I cannot prove my assertion with long words; but I know what I have seen, and fought, and killed. I know what gave me the five odd-looking little scars I carry on my left arm, and where I got the small ivory lance of narwhal horn which hangs on my wall. These are enough for me. And I know, too, what the terror of the hunted animal is when Death is following swiftly on its trail.

Let some naturalist winter where I have been, and bring home his specimens—dead or alive. But he will not get an Eskimo from

Hudson Bay to Lancaster Sound to stay there with him; and for me—well I there is not enough money in America and Europe to-gether to tempt me to visit Spirit Island again.

THE HORROR-HORN

E. F. Benson

The past ten days Alhubel had basked in the radiant midwinter weather proper to its eminence of over 6,000 feet. From rising to setting the sun (so surprising to those who have hitherto associated it with a pale, tepid plate indistinctly shining through the murky air of England) had blazed its way across the sparkling blue, and every night the serene and windless frost had made the stars sparkle like illuminated diamond dust. Sufficient snow had fallen before Christmas to content the skiers, and the big rink, sprinkled every evening, had given the skaters each morning a fresh surface on which to perform their slippery antics. Bridge and dancing served to while away the greater part of the night, and to me, now for the first time tasting the joys of a winter in the Engadine, it seemed that a new heaven and a new earth had been lighted, warmed, and refrigerated for the special benefit of those who like myself had been wise enough to save up their days of holiday for the winter.

But a break came in these ideal conditions: one afternoon the sun grew vapour-veiled and up the valley from the north-west a wind frozen with miles of travel over ice-bound hill-sides began scouting through the calm halls of the heavens. Soon it grew dusted with snow, first in small flakes driven almost horizontally before its congealing breath and then in larger tufts as of swans-down. And though all day for a fortnight before the fate of nations and life and death had seemed to me of far less importance than to get certain tracings of the skate-blades on the ice of proper shape and size, it now seemed that the one paramount consideration was to hurry back to the hotel for shelter: it was wiser to leave rocking-turns alone than to be frozen in their quest.

I had come out here with my cousin, Professor Ingram, the celebrated physiologist and Alpine climber. During the serenity of the last fortnight he had made a couple of notable winter ascents, but this morning his weather-wisdom had mistrusted the signs of the heavens, and instead of attempting the ascent of the Piz Passug he had waited to see whether his misgivings justified themselves. So there he sat now in the hall of the admirable hotel with his feet on the hot-water pipes and the latest delivery of the English post in his hands. This contained a pamphlet concerning the result of the Mount Everest expedition, of which he had just finished the perusal when I entered.

"A very interesting report," he said, passing it to me, "and they certainly deserve to succeed next year. But who can tell, what that final six thousand feet may entail? Six thousand feet more when you have already accomplished twenty-three thousand does not seem much, but at present no one knows whether the human frame can stand exertion at such a height. It may affect not the lungs and heart only, but possibly the brain. Delirious hallucinations may occur. In fact, if I did not know better, I should have said that one such hallucination had occurred to the climbers already."

"And what was that?" I asked.

"You will find that they thought they came across the tracks of some naked human foot at a great altitude. That looks at first sight like an hallucination. What more natural than that a brain excited and exhilarated by the extreme height should have interpreted certain marks in the snow as the footprints of a human being? Every bodily organ at these altitudes is exerting itself to the utmost to do its work, and the brain seizes on those marks in the snow and says 'Yes, I'm all right, I'm doing my job, and I perceive marks in the snow which I affirm are human footprints.' You know, even at this altitude, how restless and eager the brain is, how vividly, as you told me, you dream at night. Multiply that stimulus and that consequent eagerness and restlessness by three, and how natural that the brain should harbour illusions! What after all is the delirium which often accompanies high fever but the effort of the brain to do its work under the pressure of feverish conditions? It is so eager to continue perceiving that it perceives things which have no existence!"

"And yet you don't think that these naked human footprints were illusions," said I. "You told me you would have thought so, if you had not known better."

He shifted in his chair and looked out of the window a moment. The air was thick now with the density of the big snow-flakes that were driven along by the squealing north-west gale.

"Quite so," he said. "In all probability the human footprints were real human footprints. I expect that they were the footprints, anyhow, of a being more nearly a man than anything else. My reason for saying so is that I know such beings exist. I have even seen quite near at hand—and I assure you I did not wish to be nearer in spite of my intense curiosity—the creature, shall we say, which would make such footprints. And if the snow was not so dense, I could show you the place where I saw him."

He pointed straight out of the window, where across the valley lies the huge tower of the Ungeheuerhorn with the carved pinnacle of rock at the top like some gigantic rhinoceros-horn. On one side only, as I knew, was the mountain practicable, and that for none but the finest climbers; on the other three a succession of ledges and precipices rendered it unscalable. Two thousand feet of sheer rock form the tower; below are five hundred feet of fallen boulders, up to the edge of which grow dense woods of larch and pine.

"Upon the Ungeheuerhorn?" I asked.

"Yes. Up till twenty years ago it had never been ascended, and I, like several others, spent a lot of time in trying to find a route up it. My guide and I sometimes spent three nights together at the hut beside the Blumen glacier, prowling round it, and it was by luck really that we found the route, for the mountain looks even more impracticable from the far side than it does from this. But one day we found a long, transverse fissure in the side which led to a negotiable ledge; then there came a slanting ice couloir which you could not see till you got to the foot of it. However, I need not go into that."

The big room where we sat was filling up with cheerful groups driven indoors by this sudden gale and snowfall, and the cackle of merry tongues grew loud. The band, too, that invariable appanage of tea-time at Swiss resorts, had begun to tune up for the usual potpourri from the works of Puccini. Next moment the sugary, sentimental melodies began.

"Strange contrast!" said Ingram. "Here are we sitting warm and cosy, our ears pleasantly tickled with these little baby tunes and outside is the great storm growing more violent every moment, and swirling round the austere cliffs of the Ungeheuerhorn: the Horror-Horn, as indeed it was to me."

"I want to hear all about it," I said. "Every detail: make a short story long, if it's short. I want to know why it's *your* Horror-Horn?"

"Well, Chanton and I (he was my guide) used to spend days prowling about the cliffs, making a little progress on one side and then being stopped, and gaining perhaps five hundred feet on another side and then being confronted by some insuperable obstacle, till the day when by luck we found the route. Chanton never liked the job, for some reason that I could not fathom. It was not because of the difficulty or danger of the climbing, for he was he most fearless man I have ever met when dealing with rocks and ice, but he was always insistent that we should get off the mountain and back to the Blumen hut before sunset. He was scarcely easy even when we had got back to shelter and locked and barred the door, and I well remember one night when, as we ate our supper, we heard some animal, a wolf probably, howling somewhere out in the night. A positive panic seized him, and I don't think he closed his eyes till morning. It struck me then that there might be some grisly legend about the mountain, connected possibly with its name, and next day I asked him why the peak was called the Horror Horn. He put the question off at first, and said that, like the Schreckhorn, its name was due to its precipices and falling stones; but when I pressed him further he acknowledged that there was a legend about it, which his father had told him. There were creatures, so it was

supposed, that lived in its caves, things human in shape, and covered, except for the face and hands, with long black hair. They were
dwarfs in size, four feet high or thereabouts, but of prodigious
strength and agility, remnants of some wild primeval race. It
seemed that they were still in an upward stage of evolution, or so I
guessed, for the story ran that sometimes girls had been carried
off by them, not as prey, and not for any such fate as for those
captured by cannibals, but to be bred from. Young men also had
been raped by them, to be mated with the females of their tribe.
All this looked as if the creatures, as I said, were tending towards
humanity. But naturally I did not believe a word of it, as applied
to the conditions of the present day. Centuries ago, conceivably,
there may have been such beings, and, with the extraordinary tenacity of tradition, the news of this had been handed down and was
still current round the hearths of the peasants. As for their numbers, Chanton told me that three had been once seen together by a
man who owing to his swiftness on skis had escaped to tell the tale.
This man, he averred, was no other than his grand-father, who had
been benighted one winter evening as he passed through the dense
woods below the Ungeheuerhorn, and Chanton supposed that they
had been driven down to these lower altitudes in search of food
during severe winter weather, for otherwise the recorded sights of
them had always taken place among the rocks of the peak itself.
They had pursued his grandfather, then a young man, at an extraordinarily swift canter, running sometimes upright as men run, sometimes on all-fours in the manner of beasts, and their howls were
just such as that we had heard that night in the Blumen hut. Such
at any rate was the story Chanton told me, and, I like you, I regarded it as the very moonshine of superstition. But the very next
day I had reason to reconsider my judgment about it.

"It was on that day that after a week of exploration we hit on
the only route at present known to the top of our peak. We started
as soon as there was light enough to climb by, for, as you may guess,
on very difficult rocks it is impossible to climb by lantern or moonlight. We hit on the long fissure I have spoken of, we explored the
ledge which from below seemed to end in nothingness, and with

an hour's step-cutting ascended the couloir which led upwards from it. From there onwards it was a rock-climb, certainly of considerable difficulty, but with no heart-breaking discoveries ahead, and it was about nine in the morning that we stood on the top. We did not wait there long, for that side of the mountain is raked by falling stones loosened, when the sun grows hot, from the ice that holds them, and we made haste to pass the ledge where the falls are most frequent. After that there was the long fissure to descend, a matter of no great difficulty, and we were at the end of our work by midday, both of us, as you may imagine, in the state of the highest elation.

"A long and tiresome scramble among the huge boulders at the foot of the cliff then lay before us. Here the hill-side is very porous and great caves extend far into the mountain. We had unroped at the base of the fissure, and were picking our way as seemed good to either of us among these fallen rocks, many of them bigger than an ordinary house, when, on coming round the corner of one of these, I saw that which made it clear that the stories Chanton had told me were no figment of traditional superstition.

"Not twenty yards in front of me lay one of the beings of which he had spoken. There it sprawled naked and basking on its back with face turned up to the sun, which its narrow eyes regarded unwinking. In form it was completely human, but the growth of hair that covered limbs and trunk alike almost completely hid the sun-tanned skin beneath. But its face, save for the down on its cheeks and chin, was hairless, and I looked on a countenance the sensual and malevolent bestiality of which froze me with horror. Had the creature been an animal, one would have felt scarcely a shudder at the gross animalism of it; the horror lay in the fact that it was a man. There lay by it a couple of gnawed bones, and, its meal finished, it was lazily licking its protuberant lips, from which came a purring murmur of content. With one hand it scratched the thick hair on its belly, in the other it held one of these bones, which presently split in half beneath the pressure of its finger and thumb. But my horror was not based on the information of what happened to those men whom these creatures caught, it was due only to my proximity to a thing so human and so infernal. The peak, of which the ascent had a moment ago filled us with such elated satisfaction, because to me to me an Ungeheuerhorn indeed, for it was the home of beings more awful than the delirium of nightmare could ever have conceived.

"Chanton was a dozen paces behind me, and with a backward wave of my hand I caused him to halt. Then withdrawing myself with infinite precaution, so as not to attract the gaze of that basking creature, I slipped back round the rock, whispered to him what I had seen, and with blanched faces we made a long detour, peering round every corner, and crouching low, not knowing that at any step we might not come upon another of these beings, or that from the mouth of one of these caves in the mountain-side there might not appear another of those hairless and dreadful faces, with perhaps this time the breasts and insignia of womanhood. That would have been the worst of all.

"Luck favoured us, for we made our way among the boulders and shifting stones, the rattle of which might at any moment have betrayed us, without a repetition of my experience, and once among the trees we ran as if the Furies themselves were in pursuit. Well now did I understand, though I dare say I cannot convey, the qualms of Chanton's mind when he spoke to me of these creatures. Their very humanity was what made them so terrible, the fact that they were of the same race as ourselves, but of a type so abysmally degraded that the most brutal and inhuman of men would have seemed angelic in comparison."

The music of the small band was over before he had finished the narrative, and the chattering groups round the tea-table had dispersed. He paused a moment.

"There was a horror of the spirit," he said, "which I experienced then, from which, I verily believe, I have never entirely recovered. I saw then how terrible a living thing could be, and how terrible, in consequence, was life itself. In us all I suppose lurks some inherited germ of that ineffable bestiality, and who knows whether, sterile as it has apparently become in the course of centuries, it might no fructify again. When I saw that creature sun itself, I looked into the abyss out of which we have crawled. And these creatures are trying to crawl out of it now, if they exist any longer. Certainly for the last twenty years there has been no record of their being seen, until we come to this story of the footprint seen by the climbers on Everest. If that is authentic, if the party did no mistake the footprint of some bear, or what not, for a human tread, it seems as if still this bestranded remnant of mankind is in existence."

Now, Ingram, had told his story well; but sitting in this warm and civilised room, the horror which he had clearly felt had not communicated itself to me in any very vivid manner. Intellectually, I agreed, I could appreciate his horror, but certainly my spirit felt no shudder of interior comprehension.

"But it is odd," I said, "that your keen interest in physiology did not disperse your qualms. You were looking, so I take it, at some form of man more remote probably than the earliest human remains. Did not something inside you say 'This is of absorbing significance'?"

He shook his head.

"No: I only wanted to get away," said he. "It was not, as I have told you, the terror of what according to Chanton's story, might await us if we were captured; it was sheer horror at the creature itself. I quaked at it."

The snowstorm and the gale increased in violence that night, and I slept uneasily, plucked again and again from slumber by the fierce battling of the wind that shook my windows as if with an imperious demand for admittance. It came in billowy gusts, with strange noises intermingled with it as for a moment it abated, with flutings and moanings that rose to shrieks as the fury of it returned. These noises, no doubt, mingled themselves with my drowsed and sleepy consciousness, and once I tore myself out of nightmare, imagining that the creatures of the Horror-horn had gained footing on my balcony and were rattling at the window-bolts. But before morning the gale had died away, and I awoke to see the snow falling dense and fast in a windless air. For three days it continued, without intermission, and with its cessation there came a frost such as I have never felt before. Fifty degrees were registered one night, and more the next, and what the cold must have been on the cliffs of the Ungeheuerhorn I cannot imagine. Sufficient, so I thought, to have made an end altogether of its secret inhabitants: my cousin, on that day twenty years ago, had missed an opportunity for study which would probably never fall again either to him or another.

I received one morning a letter from a friend saying that he had arrived at the neighbouring winter resort of St. Luigi, and proposing that I should come over for a morning's skating and lunch afterwards. The place was not more than a couple of miles off, if one took the path over the low, pine-clad foot-hills above which lay the steep woods below the first rocky slopes of the Ungeheuerhorn; and accordingly, with a knapsack containing skates on my back, I went on skis over the wooded slopes and down by an easy descent again on to St. Luigi. The day was overcast, clouds entirely obscured the higher peaks though the sun was visible, pale and unluminous, through the mists. But as the morning went on, it gained the upper hand, and I slid down into St. Luigi beneath a sparkling firmament. We skated and lunched, and then, since it looked as if thick weather was coming up again, I set out early about three o'clock for my return journey.

Hardly had I got into the woods when the clouds gathered thick above, and streamers and skeins of them began to descend among the pines through which my path threaded its way. In ten minutes more their opacity had so increased that I could hardly see a couple of yards in front of me. Very soon I became aware that I must have got off the path, for snow-cowled shrubs lay directly in my way, and, casting back to find it again, I got altogether confused as to direction. But, though progress was difficult, I knew I had only to keep on the ascent, and presently I should come to the brow of these low foot-hills, and descend into the open valley where Alhubel stood. So on I went, stumbling and sliding over obstacles, and unable, owing to the thickness of the snow, to take off my skis, for I should have sunk over the knees at each step. Still the ascent continued, and looking at my watch I saw that I had already been near an hour on my way from St. Luigi, a period more than sufficient to complete my whole journey. But still I stuck to my idea that though

I had certainly strayed far from my proper route a few minutes more must surely see me over the top of the upward way, and I should find the ground declining into the next valley. About now, too, I noticed that the mists were growing suffused with rose-colour, and, though the inference was that it must be dose on sunset, there was consolation in the fact that they were there and might lift at any moment and disclose to me my whereabouts. But the fact that night would soon be on me made it needful to bar my mind against that despair of loneliness which so eats out the heart of a man who is lost in woods or on mountain-side, that, though still there is plenty of vigour in his limbs, his nervous force is sapped, and he can do no more than lie down and abandon himself to whatever fate may await him... And then I heard that which made the thought of loneliness seem bliss indeed, for there was a worse fate than loneliness. What I heard resembled the howl of a wolf, and it came from not far in front of me where the ridge—was it a ridge?—still rose higher in vestment of pines.

From behind me came a sudden puff of wind, which shook the frozen snow from the drooping pine-branches, and swept away the mists as a broom sweeps the dust from the floor. Radiant above me were the unclouded skies, already charged with the red of the sunset, and in front I saw that I had come to the very edge of the wood through which I had wandered so long. But it was no valley into which I had penetrated, for there right ahead of me rose the steep slope of boulders and rocks soaring upwards to the foot of the Ungeheuerhorn. What, then, was that cry of a wolf which had made my heart stand still? I saw.

Not twenty yards from me was a fallen tree, and leaning against the trunk of it was one of the denizens of the Horror-Horn, and it was a woman. She was enveloped in a thick growth of hair grey and tufted, and from her head it streamed down over her shoulders and her bosom, from which hung withered and pendulous breasts. And looking on her face I comprehended not with my mind alone, but with a shudder of my spirit, what Ingram had felt. Never had nightmare fashioned so terrible a countenance; the beauty of sun and stars and of the beasts of the field and the kindly race of men could not atone for so hellish an incarnation of the spirit of life. A fathomless bestiality modelled the slavering mouth and the narrow eyes; I looked into the abyss itself and knew that out of that abyss on the edge of which I leaned the generations of men had climbed. What if that ledge crumbled in front of me and pitched me headlong into its nethermost depths? ...

In one hand she held by the horns a chamois that kicked and struggled. A blow from its hindleg caught her withered thigh, and with a grunt of anger she seized the leg in her other hand, and, as a man may pull from its sheath a stem of meadow-grass, she plucked it off the body, leaving the torn skin hanging round the gaping wound. Then putting the red, bleeding member to her mouth she sucked at it as a child sucks a stick of sweetmeat. Through flesh and gristle her short, brown teeth penetrated, and she licked her lips with a sound of purring. Then dropping the leg by her side, she looked again at the body of the prey now quivering in its death-convulsion, and with finger and thumb gouged out one of its eyes. She snapped her teeth on it, and it cracked like a soft-shelled nut.

It must have been but a few seconds that I stood watching her, in some indescribable catalepsy of terror, while through my brain there pealed the panic-command of my mind to my stricken limbs "Begone, begone, while there is time." Then, recovering the power of my joints and muscles, I tried to slip behind a tree and hide myself from this apparition. But the woman—shall I say?—must have caught my stir of movement, for she raised her eyes from her living feast and saw me. She craned forward her neck, she dropped her prey, and half rising began to move towards me. As she did this, she opened her mouth, and gave forth a howl such as I had heard a moment before. It was answered by another, but faintly and distantly.

Sliding and slipping, with the toes of my skis tripping in the obstacles below the snow, I plunged forward down the hill between the pine-trunks. The low sun already sinking behind some rampart of mountain in the west reddened the snow and the pines with its ultimate rays. My knapsack with the skates in it swung to and fro on my back, one ski-stick had already been twitched out of my hand by a fallen branch of pine, but not a second's pause could I allow myself to recover it. I gave no glance behind, and I knew not at what pace my pursuer was on my track, or indeed whether any pursued at all, for my whole mind and energy, now working at full power again under the stress of my panic, was devoted to getting away down the hill and out of the wood as swiftly as my limbs could bear me. For a little while I heard nothing but the hissing snow of my headlong passage, and the rustle of the covered undergrowth beneath my feet, and then, from dose at hand behind me, once more the wolf-howl sounded and I heard the plunging of footsteps other than my own.

The strap of my knapsack had shifted, and as my skates swung to and fro on my back it chafed and pressed on my throat, hindering free passage of air, of which, God knew, my labouring lungs were in dire need, and without pausing I slipped it free from my neck, and held it in the hand from which my ski-stick had been jerked. I seemed to go a little more easily for this adjustment, and now, not so far distant, I could see below me the path from which I had strayed. If only I could reach that, the smoother going would surely enable me to outdistance my pursuer, who even on the rougher ground was but slowly overhauling me, and at the sight of that riband stretching unimpeded downhill, a ray of hope pierced the black panic of my soul. With that came the desire, keen and insistent, to see who or what it was that was on my tracks, and I spared a backward glance. It was she, the hag whom I had seen at her gruesome meal; her long grey hair flew out behind her, her mouth chattered and gibbered, her fingers made grabbing movements, as if already they closed on me.

But the path was now at hand, and the nearness of it I suppose made me incautious. A hump of snow-covered bush lay in my path, and, thinking I could jump over it, I tripped and fell, smothering myself in snow. I heard a maniac noise, half scream, half laugh, from close behind, and before I could recover myself the grabbing fingers were at my neck, as if a steel vice had closed there. But my right hand in which I held my knapsack of skates was free, and with a blind back-handed movement I whirled it behind me at the full length of its strap, and knew that my desperate blow had found its billet somewhere. Even before I could look round I felt the grip on my neck relax, and something subsided into the very bush which had entangled me. I recovered my feet and turned.

There she lay, twitching and quivering. The heel of one of my skates piercing the thin alpaca of the knapsack had hit her full on the temple, from which the blood was pouring, but a hundred yards away I could see another such figure coming downwards on my tracks, leaping and bounding. At that panic rose again within me, and I sped off down the white smooth path that led to the lights of the village already beckoning. Never once did I pause in my head-long going: there was no safety until I was back among the haunts of men. I flung myself against the door of the hotel, and screamed for admittance, though I had but to turn the handle and enter; and once more as when Ingram had told his tale, there was the sound of the band, and the chatter of voices, and there, too, was he him-self, who looked up and then rose swiftly to his feet as I made my clattering entrance.

"I have seen them too," I cried. "Look at my knapsack. Is there not blood on it? It is the blood of one of them, a woman, a hag, who tore off the leg of a chamois as I looked, and pursued me through the accursed wood. I—"

Whether it was I who spun round, or the room which seemed to spin round me, I knew not, but I heard myself falling, collapsed on the floor, and the next time that I was conscious at all I was in bed. There was Ingram there, who told me that I was quite safe, and another man, a stranger, who pricked my arm with the nozzle of a syringe, and reassured me...

A day or two later I gave a coherent account of my adventure, and three or four men, armed with guns, went over my traces. They found the bush in which I had stumbled, with a pool of blood which had soaked into the snow, and, still following my ski-tracks, they came on the body of a chamois, from which had been torn one of its hindlegs and one eye-socket was empty. That is all the corroboration of my story that I can give the reader, and for myself I imagine that the creature which pursued me was either not killed by my blow or that her fellows removed her body... Anyhow, it is open to the incredulous to prowl about the caves of the Ungeheuerhorn, and see if anything occurs that may convince them.

The Tale of the Abu Laheeb

Lord Dunsany

When I met my friend Murcote in London he talked much of his Club. I had seldom heard of it, and the name of the street in which Murcote told me it stood was quite unknown to me, though I think I had driven through it in a taxi, and remembered the houses as being mean and small. And Murcote admitted that it was not very large, and had no billiard-table and very few rooms; and yet there seemed something about the place that entirely filled his mind and made that trivial street for him the center of London. And when he wanted me to come and see it, I suggested the following day; but he put me off, and again when I suggested the next one. There was evidently nothing much to see, no pictures, no particular wines, nothing that other Clubs boast of; but one heard tales there, he said; very odd ones sometimes; and if I cared to come and see the Club, it would be a good thing to come some evening when old Jorkens was there. I asked who Jorkens was; and he said he had seen a lot of the world. And then we parted, and I forgot about Jorkens, and saw nothing more of Murcote for some days. And then one day Murcote rang me up, and asked me if I'd come to the Club that evening.

I had agreed to come; but before I left my house Murcote surprised me by coming round to see me. There was something he wanted to tell me about Jorkens. He sat and talked to me for some time about Jorkens before we started, though all he said of him might be expressed by one word. Jorkens was a good-hearted fellow, he said, and would always tell a story in the evening to anyone

347

who offered him a small drink; whisky and soda was what he pre-
ferred; and he really had seen a good deal of the world, and the
Club relied on stories in the evening; it was quite a feature of it;
and the Club wouldn't be the Club without them, and it helped the
evening to pass, anyway; but one thing he must warn me, and that
was never to believe a word he said. It wasn't Jorkens' fault; he
didn't mean to be inaccurate; he merely wished to interest his fel-
low-members and to make the evening pass pleasantly; he had
nothing to gain by any inaccuracies, and had no intention to deceive; he just did his best to entertain the Club, and all the members were grateful to him. But once more Murcote warned me never
to believe one of his tales nor any part of them, not even the smallest detail of local color.

"I see," I said, "a bit of a liar."

"Oh, poor old Jorkens," said Murcote, "that's rather hard. But
still, I've warned you, haven't I?"

And, with that quite clearly understood, we went down and
hailed a taxi.

It was after dinner that we arrived at the Club; and we went
straight up into a small room, in which a group of members was
sitting about near the fire, and I was introduced to Jorkens, who
was sitting gazing into the glow, with a small table at his right hand.
And then he turned to Murcote to pour out what he had probably
already said to all the other members.

"A most unpleasant episode occurred here last evening," he
said, "a thing I have never known before, and shouldn't have
thought possible in any decent club, shouldn't have thought possible."

"Oh, really," said Murcote. "What happened?"

"A young fellow came in yesterday," said Jorkens. "They tell
me he's called Carter. He came in here after dinner, and I happened to be speaking about a curious experience I had once had in
Africa, over the watershed of the Congo, somewhere about lati-
tude six, a long time ago. Well, never mind the experience, but I
had no sooner finished speaking about it when the young fellow,
Carter or whatever he is, said simply he didn't believe me, simply

and unmistakably that he disbelieved my story; claimed to know
something of geography or zoology which did not tally in his impudent mind with the actual experience that I had had on the Congo
side of the watershed. Now, what are you to do when a young fellow has the effrontery, the brazen-faced audacity..."

"Oh, but we must have him turned out," said Murcote. "A case
like that should come before the Committee at once. Don't you
think so?"

And his eye turned to the other members, roving till it fell on a
weary and weak individual who was evidently one of the Committee.

"Oh, er, yes," said he unconvincingly.

"Well, Mr. Jorkens," said Murcote, "we'll get that done at once."

And one or two more members muttered Yes, and Jorkens' indignation sank now to minor mutterings, and to occasional ejacula-
tions that shot out petulantly, but in an undertone. The waters of
his imagination were troubled still, though the storm was partly
abated.

"It seems to me outrageous," I said, but hardly liked to say any
more, being a guest in the Club.

"Outrageous!" the old man replied, and we seemed no nearer
to getting any story.

"I wonder if I might ask for a whisky and soda?" I said to
Murcote, for a silence had fallen; and at the same time I nodded
sideways towards Jorkens to suggest the destination of the whisky.
I had waited for Murcote to do this without being asked, and now
he ordered three whiskies and sodas listlessly, as though he thought
there weren't much good in it. And when the whisky drew near the
lonely table that waited desolate at Jorkens' right hand, Jorkens
said, "Not for me."

I thought I saw surprise for a moment pass like a ghost through
that room, although no one said anything.

"No," said old Jorkens, "I never drink whisky. Now and then I
use it in order to stimulate my memory. It has a wonderful effect
on the memory. But as a drink I never touch it. I dislike the taste
of it."

So his whisky went away. We seemed no nearer that story.

I took my glass with very little soda, sitting in a chair near Jorkens. I had nowhere to put it down.

"Might I put my glass on your table?" I said to Jorkens.

"Certainly," he said, with the utmost indifference in his voice, but not entirely in his eye, which caught the deep yellow flavor as I put it close to his elbow.

We sat for a long time in silence; everyone wanted to hear him talk. And at last his right hand opened wide enough to take a glass, and then closed again. And a while later it opened once more, and moved a little along the table and then drew back, as though for a moment he had thought the drink was his and then had realized his mistake. It was a mere movement of the hand, and yet it showed that here was a man who would not consciously take another man's drink. And, that being clearly established, a dreamy look came over his face as though he thought of far-off things, and his hand moved very absently. It reached the glass unguided by his eye and brought it to his lips, and he drained it, thinking of far other things.

"Dear me," he said suddenly, "I hope I haven't drunk your whisky."

"Not at all," I said.

"I was thinking of a very curious thing," he said, "and hardly noticed what I was doing."

"Might I ask what it was you were thinking of?" I said.

"I really hardly like to tell you," he said, "to tell anyone, after the most unpleasant incident that occurred yesterday."

As I looked at Murcote he seemed to divine my thoughts, and ordered three more whiskies.

It was wonderful how the whisky did brighten old Jorkens' memory, for he spoke with a vividness of little details that could only have been memory; imagination could not have done it. I leave out the details and give the main points of his story for its zoological interest; for it touches upon a gap in zoology which I believe is probably there, and if the story is true it bridges it.

Here then is the story: "One that you won't often hear in London," said Jorkens, "but in towns at the Empire's edge it's told of often. There's probably not a mess out there in which it's not been discussed, scarcely a bungalow where it's not been talked of, and always with derision. In places like Malakal there's not a white man that hasn't heard of it, and not one that believes it. But the last white man that you meet on lonely journeys, the last white man that there is before the swamps begin and you see nothing for weeks but papyrus, he believes in it.

"I have noticed that more than once. Where a lot of men get together, all knowing equally little, and this subject comes up, one will laugh, and they will all laugh at it, and none will trust his imagination to study the rumor; and it remains a rumor, no more. But when a man gets all alone by himself, somewhere on the fringe of that country out of which the rumor arises, and there's no silly laughter to scare his imagination—why, then he can study the thing and develop it, and get much nearer to facts than mere incredulity will ever get him. I find a touch of fever helps in working out problems like that.

"Well, the problem is a very simple one; it is simply the question whether man with his wisdom and curiosity has discovered all the animals that there are in the world, or whether there's one, and a very curious one too, hidden amongst the papyrus, that white men have never seen. And that's not quite what I mean, for there are white men that have seen things that not every young whippersnapper will believe. I should rather have said an animal that our civilization has not yet taken cognizance of. At Kosti, more than twenty years ago, I first heard two men definitely speak of it, the *abu laheeb* they called it, and I think they both believed in it too; but Khartoum was only a hundred and fifty miles off, and they had evening clothes with them, and used to wear them at dinner, and they had china plates and silver forks, and ornaments on their mantelpiece, and one thing and another; and all these things seemed to appall their imagination, and they wouldn't honestly let themselves believe it. 'Had three or four fires round his tent,' said one of them, telling of someone, 'and says that the *abu laheeb* came down about two A.M., and he saw it clear in the firelight.' 'Did it get what it wanted?' said the other. 'Yes, went away hugging it.'

"And one of them said in a rather wandering tone: 'The only animal that uses....' He was lowering his voice, and looking round, and he saw me, and said no more. They turned it all away at once with a laugh or two, as Columbus might have turned away from the long low line of land and refused to believe a new continent. I questioned them, but got no information that could be of any use; they seemed to like laughter more than imagination, so I got jokes instead of truth.

"It was weeks later and far southwards that I found a man who was ready to approach this most interesting point of zoology in the proper spirit of a scientist, a white man all alone in a hut that he had near the mouth of the Bahr el Zeraf. There are things in Africa that you couldn't believe, and the Bahr el Zeraf is one of them. It rises out of the marshes of the White Nile, and flows forty or fifty miles, and into the White Nile again. And one can't easily believe in a white man living all alone in such a place as that, but somebody has to be the last white man you see as you go through the final fringes of civilization, and it was him. He had had full opportunities of studying the whole question of the *abu laheeb*, he had had years of leisure to compare all the stories the natives brought him, which they shyly told when he had won their confidence, though what he won it with he never told. He had sifted the evidence and knew all that was told about it; and in long malarial nights, with no one and nothing to care for him but quinine, he had pictured the beast so clearly that he could make me a very good drawing of it. I have that drawing to this very day, a beast on his hind legs something like a South American sloth that I once saw, stuffed, in a museum; built rather on the lines of a kangaroo, but much stouter and bigger, and with nothing pointed about his face; it was square and blunt, with great teeth. He had hand-like paws on shortish arms or forelegs.

"I must tell you that I was in a small *dahabeeyah* going up those great rivers, any great rivers I might meet, leaving civilization because I was tired of it, and looking for wonders in Africa. And I came to this lonely man, Lindon his name was, full of curiosity aroused by those words that I had heard in Malakal. And talking to Lindon like two old friends that have spent all their schooldays together, as white men will who meet in that part of Africa, I soon came to the *abu laheeb*, thinking he would know more of it than they knew in Malakal. And I found a man grown sensitive, as you only can grow in loneliness: he feared I would disbelieve him, and would scarcely say a word. Yes, the natives believed in some such animal, but his own opinion he would not expose to the possibility of my ridicule. The more questions I asked, the shorter the answers became. And then I drew him by saying, 'Well, there's one thing he uses that no other animal ever did,' the one mysterious thing about this beast that had haunted my mind for weeks, though I did not know what on earth the mystery was. And that got him talking. He saw that I was committed to belief in the beast, and was no longer shy of his own. He told me that the upper reaches of the Bahr el Zeraf were a god-forsaken place: 'And if God forsook the Zeraf,' he said, 'He certainly didn't go to the Jebel,' for the Bahr el Jebel was worse. And somewhere between those two rivers in the desolation of papyrus the *abu laheeb* certainly lived. He very reasonably said that there were beasts in the plains, beasts in the forests, and beasts in the sea; why not in the huge area of the papyrus into which no man had ever penetrated? If I chose to go to these god-forsaken places I could see the *abu laheeb*, he said. 'But, of course,' he added, 'you must never go up wind on him.' 'Down wind?' I said.

"'No, nor down wind either,' he answered. 'He can smell as well as a rhino. That's the difficulty; you have to go just between up wind and down wind; and you always find the north wind blowing there.'

"It was some while before I discovered why one can't go up wind on him. I didn't like to over-question Lindon, for questions are akin to criticism, and you cannot apply criticism and cross-examination to the patient work of imagination upon rumor; it is liable to destroy the whole fabric, and one loses valuable scientific data. Nor was Lindon in the mood for the superior belief of a traveler only just come from civilization; he had had malaria too recently to put up with that sort of thing. It was as he was giving me various clear proofs of the existence of some such animal that I suddenly realized what it all meant. He was telling me how more than once he had seen fires in the reeds, not only earlier in the year than the Dinkas light their fires, but in marshes where no Dinka would ever come, nor a Shillook either, or any kind of man, marshes utterly desolate and forever shut to humanity. It was then that the truth flashed on me; truth, sir, that I have since verified with my own eyes: that the *abu laheeb* plays with fire.

"Well, I needn't tell you how the idea flared up in my mind to be the first white man that had even seen the *abu laheeb*, and to shoot him and bring his huge skin home, and have something to show for all that lonely wandering. It was a fascinating idea. I asked Lindon if he thought my rifle was big enough, I only had a .350, and whether to use soft-nosed or solid bullets. 'Soft,' he said. I sat up late and asked him many questions. And he warned me about those marshes. I needn't tell you of all the things he warned me against, because you see me alive before you; but they were there all right, they were there. And I went down the little path he'd made from his house to the bank of the river, and went on board my sailing boat under huge white bands of stars, and lay down on board and looked up at them from under my blankets until I fell asleep, while the Arabs cast off and the north wind held good. And when the sun blazed on me at dawn I woke to the Bahr el Zeraf. Scarlet trees with green foliage at first; we were not yet come to those marshes.

"Well, for days we went up the Zeraf, past the white fish-eagles, haughty and silent and watchful on queer trees, with birds sailing over us that I daren't describe to you for fear you should think I exaggerate the brilliancy of their colors. And so we came to those marshes where anything might hide, and be utterly hidden by those miles of rushes, and be well enough protected from explorers by a region of monotony more dismal than any other desolate land I've seen. And all the while the sailors were talking a language I did not know, till my imagination, brooding in that monotony, seemed to hear clear English phrases now and then starting suddenly out of their talk, commonest phrases of our daily affairs, on the other side of the earth. I would swear that I heard one of them say one evening, 'Stop the bus a moment.' But it couldn't have been, for they were talking Dinka talk, and not one of them knew a single word of English; I used to talk Arabic of a sort to the reis.

"Well, at last we came on fires in the reeds, burning at different points. Who lit them I couldn't say, there were no men there, black, white, or gray (the Dinkas are gray, you know). But I wanted absolute proof; and then one day I found his tracks in the rushes. He bounds through the rushes, you know, often breaking several of them where he takes off, and sometimes scattering mud on the tips of them as he springs through; then alighting and taking off again, leaving another huge mark.

"I examined the rushes carefully, till I was sure that I had his tracks. And then I followed them, always watching the wind. It was a dreadful walk. I went alone so as to make less noise. I wanted to get quite close and make sure of my shot. I had a haversack tied close round my neck, and my cartridges were in that. Even then it got wet sometimes. The water was always up to my waist, and often it came higher. I had to hold up my rifle in one hand all the time. The reeds were far over my head.

"Sometimes one came to open spaces of water, with huge blue water-lilies floating on them. And it was always deeper there. Sometimes one walked upon the roots of the rushes, and all the rushes trembled round one for yards, and sometimes one found a bottom of good hard clay and knew one could sink no further. And all the while I was tracking the *abu laheeb*.

"The north wind blew as usual. I was too old a shikari to be walking down wind, but I was not always able to act strictly on Lindon's advice about never going up wind on the *abu laheeb*, because his tracks sometimes led that way. At any rate, that was better than the other direction, for he would have been off at once. You wouldn't believe how tired one can be of blue water-lilies. At any rate the water was not cold, but the weariness of lifting each foot was terrible. Each foot, as one lifted it for every step, one would rather have left just where it was forever. I don't know how many hours I tracked the beast, I don't know what time was doing while I walked in those marshes. But in all that weariness of spirit and utter fatigue of limb I suddenly saw a scrap of quite fresh mud on the tip of one of the reeds, and knew that I was getting near him at last. I put the safety catch of my rifle over, and suddenly saw in my mind what I was so nearly doing for Science. Of all the steps Science had taken from out of the early darkness toward that distant point of which we cannot guess, which shall be full of revelations to man, one of her footsteps would be due to me. I could, as it were, write my name on that one footprint, and no one would question my right to.

"I got nearer and nearer, I was no longer weary now; and suddenly, closer than I had dared to hope, was a little puff of smoke above the rushes. I stopped for one moment to steady my breath, and got my rifle ready. In that moment I named him; yes, I called him *Prometheus Jorkensi.* There was a patch of dry land ahead, and the rushes still protected me. I moved with ten-inch paces so as to make no ripple, but I couldn't keep the rushes quiet; perhaps the north wind blew stronger than I thought, for he never seemed to hear me. And then, oh so close that it couldn't have been ten yards, I saw the little fire on a patch of earth; and the rushes still hid me completely. I saw a patch of brown fur and a huge body crouching. I could only guess what part of the body I saw, but a vital part I thought, and I raised my rifle. Still it had no idea I was anywhere near it. And then I saw its hands stretched out to the fire, warming themselves by the edge of those bleak marshes. I don't cut much ice, you know; I didn't then; no one had ever heard my name, or, if they had, it meant nothing; and here was I on the verge of this discovery, with the proof of it ten yards away just waiting for a rifle bullet. I'd shoot a monkey, I'd shoot an ape, I'd shoot a poor old hippo; I wouldn't mind shooting a horse if it had to be killed, though lots of men can't bear that; but those black hands stretched out over the fire were the one thing I couldn't destroy. The idea that flashed on me standing amongst those reeds I have been turning over in my mind for years, and it always seemed sound to me, and it does even now. You see, of all the links in the world that there are between us, and of all the barriers against those that are not as us, it seems to me that there is one link, one barrier, more outstanding than any other you could possibly name. We talk of our human reason, that may or may not be superior to the dream of the dog or the elephant: we say it is; that is all. We say that we alone have belief in an after-life, and that the lion has not: we say so; that's all. Some of them are stronger, some live longer than us, many may be more cunning. But there is one thing, gentlemen, one thing they haven't got, and that is the knowledge of fire. That seems to me the great link, the great bond between all who have it and the barrier against all who have not. Look what we've done with it: look at those fire-irons, that fender, the bricks of which this house is made, and the steel structure of it; look at this whole city. That's our one great possession, knowledge of fire. And, when I saw those dark hands stretched out to that fire on the edge of the marshes, that is what I thought of all at once, not at such length as I have told you of course; it flashed all through my mind in a moment; but during that moment I hesitated, and the *abu laheeb* saw the sun on the tip of my rifle or heard me breathing there, for he suddenly craned his great neck over the rushes, then stooped again and scattered the fire with his forepaws with one swift jerk into the reeds all round me. They were alight at once, and through the flame and smoke I only dimly caught sight of him leaping away, but, above the crackle of the burning reeds and the thump of his hind legs leaping, I heard him uttering gusts of human-like laughter."

He paused a moment. We were all quite silent, thinking what he had lost. He had lost a famous name. He shook his head, and seemed full of the same thoughts as the rest of us.

"I never went after him again," he said. "I had seen him, but who'll believe that? I have never quite been able to bring myself any more to try to shoot a creature that shared that great secret with us."

There was silence again; we were wondering, I think, whether his scruples should have prevented him from doing so much for Science. I suppose that the too-sensitive and over-scrupulous seldom make famous names. A man leaning forward, and smoking a pipe, took his pipe out of his mouth and broke the silence at last.

"Mightn't you have photographed him?" he said.

"Photographed him!" said Mr. Jorkens, straightening himself up in his chair. "Photographed him! Aren't half the photographs fakes? Here, look at the *Evening Picture*; look at that, now. There's a child handing a bouquet to someone with its left hand, so that both of them may expose as much of their surface as possible to the camera. And here's a man welcoming his brother from abroad. Welcoming indeed! They are both of them being photographed, and that's obviously all that they're doing."

We looked at the paper and it was so; they were almost turning their backs on one another in order to be photographed.

"No," he said, and he looked me straight in the eyes, and flashed that glance of his from face to face. "If Truth cannot stand alone, she scorns the cheap aid of photography."

So dominant was his voice as he said these words, so flashed his eyes in the dim light of the room, that none of us spoke any more. I think we felt that our voices would shock the silence. And we all went quietly away.